CAPE GREED

CAPE GREED

Sam Cole

MINOTAUR BOOKS

A Thomas Dunne Book
New York

This is a work of fiction. All of the characters, organizations, and events portrayed in this novel are either products of the author's imagination or are used fictitiously.

A THOMAS DUNNE BOOK FOR MINOTAUR BOOKS.
An imprint of St. Martin's Publishing Group.

CAPE GREED. Copyright © 2006 by Mike Nicol and Joanne Hichens. All rights reserved. Printed in the United States of America. For information, address St. Martin's Press, 175 Fifth Avenue, New York, N.Y. 10010.

Acknowledgment is made for lines quoted from "Murdergram," words and music by Jay-Z © 1998, Roc.a.Fella Records, New York, USA.

www.thomasdunnebooks.com
www.minotaurbooks.com

Library of Congress Cataloging-in-Publication Data

Cole, Sam (Joint pseudonym)
    Cape greed / Sam Cole. — 1st U.S. ed.
        p. cm.
    ISBN 978-0-312-37340-5
    1. Private investigators—South Africa—Fiction.
2. Commercial crimes—Investigation—Fiction. 3. Cape Town (South Africa)—Fiction. I. Title.
PR9369.4.C65C37 2009
823'.92—dc22

                                                            2009028469

First published in South Africa as Out to Score by Umuzi, an imprint of Random House (Pty) Ltd.

First U.S. Edition: November 2009

10 9 8 7 6 5 4 3 2 1

CAPE GREED

I

The first meal Mullet made for the new bird in his life, Rae-Anne, was fried abalone steaks.

Almost didn't happen. Not a shellfish in the city. The dozen fish and seafood merchants he stopped at, from Island Deli to Patel's Bait Shop, hadn't seen stock in a month. Enough to give up and buy in Chinese.

"You read of the tons being smuggled out, you'd think we'd have some," he complained to old man Patel.

The old man shrugged. "Who can pay at any rate?"

"For a special I'd put down the bucks."

Patel looked up at him, right in the eyes. "Try your friends why don't you?"

Mullet snapped his fingers. "There's an idea." This Rae-Anne worth a call to his mate Vince at the Anti-Poaching Unit.

"Free from the sea," said Vincent. "Made a bust this morning. Could swing you half a dozen. Who's gonna know?"

Within the hour Mullet was staring at a big red cooler box on Vincent's desk. State's evidence. Vincent shut his office door, grinned.

"What's the deal, you aiming to impress someone? Some ladyfriend? Try out the Cape aphrodisiac?"

"Yeah, yeah," Mullet said.

"Hey, you're blushing. Guy gets to your age, aphrodisiac is a serious consideration."

"At forty!"

"Ask around." Vincent flipped the lid of the cooler box, releasing a smell of salt and seaweed. "Erectile dysfunction. It happens." He gestured at the contents. "Help yourself."

Mullet did, digging six large shells out of the ice and slipping them into a plastic bag.

"Nice size."

"For you, only the best. Street value in Shanghai, Hong Kong, Taipei about twenty US apiece. What you're looking at here is more'n my annual salary. You wonder guys are killing for the stuff? Never mind. Enjoy."

Mullet pointed at the blood-soaked bandage on Vincent's arm. "That doesn't look good."

"Bastard attacked me. Poacher we've been trying to nail."

"That right?"

"Some guys gotta show their muscle." Vincent grimaced. He closed the lid of the cooler box. "Things didn't work out so well for them today." He looked at Mullet. "Want to go for a beer? The Kimberley? Stag's Head?"

"Nah." Mullet hefted the bag of abalone. "Like you guessed, I've got a date." He headed out the office door. "You should see a doctor, Vince. Get that treated."

Vincent laughed. "When I've had a beer."

Or six, Mullet thought.

At home he took a wooden mallet to the shellfish. A whack on the 'mouth' made cutting them from the shell easier. The shells he stacked for washing in the outside sink: mother-of-pearl ashtrays you couldn't have enough of. He decided two steaks would be fine. Hesitated: maybe three. Cold leftovers being good dipped in mayo.

With the scissors from his fishing pack he trimmed the skirt off the meat and cut out the battered mouths. Getting rid of the black slime took a hard brush and five minutes' scrubbing. He rinsed the steaks, put the three extra in the freezer, sliced the others thinly and tenderised with the mallet. He lined up breadcrumbs and beaten eggs for the coating.

The recipe said a three-to-four-minute fry in olive oil and butter until crisp and golden. A feast with chips and a salad. He'd bought the salad at the local Spar, the chips from a takeout on the main road. You were gonna do this sort of thing, you did it properly.

Mullet set the kitchen table: mismatched cutlery, mismatched crockery, different wine glasses. What the heck, the food was five-star. He did have cotton serviettes. A present from his mother of family stuff that had belonged to her mother. White with yellow edging and embroidered flower motifs in the corners. He stood back to admire the effect.

"Candles, boykie," he said out loud. "You've gotta have candles."

He found a long white one at the back of a drawer, snapped it in half, melted wax on two saucers and stuck the candles upright. Switched off the lights, fired up the wicks. Into the boombox went Neil Young's *Harvest*.

On the nose of seven-thirty Rae-Anne ding-dong'd his bell. Mullet finished his beer in a gulp and headed for the front door.

2

Abalone *n.* an edible rock-clinging mollusc of warm seas, with a shallow ear-shaped shell lined with mother-of-pearl. [Genus *Haliotis*] In the East a delicacy, regarded as restoring virility. **Ormer** – a telescoping of the French *oreille de mer* or 'sea ear', abalone, a shellfish delicacy found off Brittany, California and Cape coastline of South Africa. **Perlemoen** *n.* an abalone. [*Haliotis midae*] Origin from obsolete Afrikaans *perlemoer*, from Middle Dutch *perlenmoeder* 'mother-of-pearl', because of the pearlised lining inside the shell.

3

Tommy Fortune cut the outboard engine and let the rubber duck drift over the reef. He could see its shadow four, five metres below. Sometimes it was clear enough to make out the rocks but today the water was still settling after the last south-east blow. The reef was a gift, more perlemoen in one cluster than he'd seen in six months. What was amazing was how no one had found it before. What was also amazing was how few boats were out, most of them positioned along the kelp line. A good day like this he'd have expected major shit, everybody fighting for the pearlies. Sometimes the guys had firefights out here. AK'ing one another. Like it was a forking war zone.

"You gonna anchor us anytime soon, bro?" Tommy said to the guy nestled in the bows putting sunscreen on his face.

Adonis pouted, dropped a bag of half-bricks over the side, not bothering to play out the rope.

Tommy shook his head. "How many times I've told you, slow-ly. Check how the rope's burning the rubber!"

Adonis shook the bottle of blockout and ran a line of cream up his right leg. A smooth leg that he razored hairless.

"You like a girl," said Tommy.

"You want to rub it in?" Adonis shot back, gave him a grin.

Tommy ignored him. He pulled on a wetsuit and zipped it. "Not what you'd call a forking crowd on the sea today." He shrugged the tank onto his back. "That gives me the whistling shits. What you say?"

Adonis shrugged. "Bee-yooo-ti-ful day, Adonis, bee-yooo-ti-ful day. That's what you said."

Tommy spat in his mask and smeared the spit over the glass. Went back at what was nagging him. "What gives me the dog, is no other guys diving. All this perlemoen lying down there like money, 'n nobody's interested. Calm sea, good viz. Only a few stupids pulling shells, gotta mean something." He leant over the side, scooped water into the mask and rinsed it.

For three months Tommy and Adonis had been working perlemoen off the reefs for a guy called Jim Woo. In three months they'd seen more money than they'd scored in three years pushing dagga and Mandrax tabs. Pearlies was hot stuff.

"Where I come from," Woo told Tommy, "guys get a rod just thinking of this meat. Know what I'm saying? They eat abalone, they believe it goes straight to their dicks."

He'd also said, "Whatever you can get I'll buy. Top rate."

He'd also said, "You get bust by the cops, you take it by yourself. You mention my name you're dead."

Tommy and Adonis took turns at the diving. They'd heard stories of guys who'd left their boats unattended and came up from a poach with a bag of sweet meat to find they were bobbing alone in the ocean a long swim offshore.

"You ever gonna get on with it today," said Adonis, lying back, making himself comfortable.

Tommy glanced at him: the guy had stripped down to a Speedo so tight it moulded his goolies.

"Whatya looking at?"

Tommy sucked at the mouthpiece of the oxygen tank. He spat it out again and grinned toothless at Adonis. "Don't you love it, darlin," then he grabbed a screwdriver and a hessian sack and toppled backwards into the water.

Tommy let the lead weights strapped round his waist take him down, like he was parachuting, hardly moving his fins. The visibility cleared the closer he got to the bottom. He had oxygen for an hour, enough time to fill the bag. On this reef with the shellfish packed so tight all he had to do was work one rock at a time to get everything he needed. No hunting around like in the kelp beds. He bumped gently against the rocks and steadied himself with his free hand. With the other he slid the screwdriver under a shell and levered up before the sucker had time to limpet itself to the rock face. When they did that a crowbar wouldn't get them loose. The perlemoen came free and Tommy flipped the shell to look at the fleshy side, the mouth. Hey, man, all that meat would give some Chink a mighty hard-on. He bagged it. When Woo'd told him the sex angle he'd fried some perlemoen steaks. His verdict: McDonald's burgers were as good a turn-on. Less jaw exercise too.

By the time the bag was full, Tommy had been down forty-five minutes. He'd chosen big ones the size of his hand because with Woo weight counted. Heavy equalled top dollar. He headed for the surface, holding the sack against his body. Halfway up he heard the noise. Serious engines. Not the whine of a boat, it had to be a chopper. So forking loud they had to be right above the rubber duck, chances were they could even see him. Forking cops. That was why there were so few boats out. He should've realised. The main brothers had been tipped off so the stupids could take the fall.

Tommy sank back to the reef. If the cops had a chopper, they'd also have guys in rubber ducks. They caught anyone with pearlies they'd throw away the key.

He found a rock overhang on the edge of the reef and pushed the bag of perlemoen under it. Ten minutes later and they'd have been bust. Big time. Tough shit on the cops. He and Adonis would walk, no problems.

When Tommy hauled himself back onto the boat the chopper was overhead, a cop with a loudhailer booming at them, "Head for the shore. Head for the shore." Adonis waved. There were two inflatables with cops herding the guys who had been in the kelp forests.

Adonis started the engine. "You got a story?"

"What's with a story? No rules against diving last time I heard." Tommy reached for a pack of smokes and shook one loose. "No meat, no sheet."

Those in the bust squad were Coastal Management and cops from the Anti-Poaching Unit. They pulled fifteen guys off the water and lined them up on the beach next to their boats. Sonny Furniss, from Coastal, read the riot act. Anyone over the abalone quota limit would be arrested. Tommy and Adonis were the last in the line, the only clean boat.

Furniss squinted at Tommy.

"What's your name?"

"You know," said Tommy.

A cop came up to Tommy, jabbed him in the ribs with a stiff finger.

"Your name, Chommy-boy."

Tommy hated the Chommy tag. The last guy called him Tommy Chommy he broke his nose. He knew the cop, Vincent Saldana. Slitty-eyed forker on a crusade.

The cop poked again at his ribs.

"Spit it out," said Furniss.

Tommy hawked up sputum and unloaded it next to the cop's boots. "Tommy Fortune."

"A real smart," said the cop. He brought his knee hard into Tommy's balls. Tommy retched and doubled, howling the pain.

"Where'a the shells, Tommy?"

"Where's it, Fortune? Tell us, shitface."

Vincent Saldana karate-chopped Tommy's neck which took him down face first into the sand.

"You gonna tell me, Fortune?"

Tommy gritted his teeth, crunching sand. "Go fork yourself."

Vincent lost it. Stomped on Tommy's fingers. Shouted: "What about Manuel? What about Petersen? Daniels? Good cops, Chommy. All dead because of you poachers." He stopped. "You're dogturd, Fortune. When I get you, you're gonna go down big time. You hearing me?"

Tommy spat blood where he'd bitten his lip, his eyes watering.

"Get up."

He got to his feet slowly, Adonis helping him up.

"And who're you, pretty boy?" The cop again, hooking his finger into Adonis's T-shirt.

Adonis pursed his lips. "Adonis," he said. "You want my phone number?"

Before Vincent could react Furniss fastened a hand round Tommy's forearm. "Come on, let's go. Let's go take a joyride, find your bag of goodies."

Tommy didn't move. Vincent Saldana got into his face again.

"You reckon you're the main man, Fortune. Don't you, hey! BMW. Snappy threads. The main guy. Hey, you reckon this?" He came up to Tommy's right ear. "So listen, you listening?"

Tommy nodded, wiping blood off his lip.

"Hey, there's a little sweetie." Vincent pinched his cheek. "Here's the scheme, Fortune, what I'm gonna do is wreck you. You with me?"

Tommy could smell Vincent Saldana's breath: beer and brandy.

"All you gotta do is nod."

Tommy obliged.

"OK," said Vincent. "Now listen arsehole, what we're gonna do is get your abalone. Know what I'm saying?" He paused, twisted his grip on Tommy's cheek. "Know what I'm saying?"

Tommy nodded, his face burning.

"Tell me?" Vincent clamped his hand over Tommy's mouth, his fingers squeezing. "What I'm saying, Fortune, is we're going out there to get your bag. Get me?" He let go of Tommy's face.

Tommy stepped away. "Fork you! We haven't got a bag."

Vincent Saldana grinned. "You and the bumbandit."

"Come on," said Sonny Furniss, dragging the rubber duck into the shallows. "Let's get it done."

Vincent pushed Tommy ahead of him. "And you, pretty boy," he said, shoving at Adonis too. "Next you're gonna tell me you were sixty-nine all morning with Tommy-Chommy."

When Sonny Furniss glanced up, Vincent Saldana had his arm raised as a shield. Tommy Fortune was slashing at him with a screwdriver.

The magistrate put Tommy Fortune away for two years. Resisting arrest. Assault with intent to do grievous bodily harm. Adonis got a year for aiding and abetting.

On his way to the jail transport Tommy Fortune said to Sonny Furniss and Vincent Saldana, "I'm gonna fork yous. Fork yous both."

Sonny Furniss laughed.

Vincent Saldana said, "I'm trembling."

Eighteen Months Later

4

Mullet sat, feet on his desk, clicking down the thumb catch on the Astra Police. Each release the six-shot cylinder swung out. A full load. He flicked his wrist and the cylinder relocked.

"Pow," he said, aiming the revolver at Vincent's empty chair.

"Pow" – swivelling at the kettle on the bar fridge in the corner.

"Pow, pow, pow" – tracking along the camp bed behind Vincent's desk, the mess of clothing, the takeaway cartons.

"Pow" – feeling it would be no loss to take out the telephone.

Except that it started ringing, when it hadn't rung all morning. He swung his feet down, shifted the gun to his left hand and reached for the phone.

A woman said, "Is that Saldana & Mendes?"

"Nope," said Mullet. "Other way round."

The woman said, "Am I speaking to Vincent Saldana?"

Good voice, strong. Upper Cape Town.

"Nope," said Mullet. "Vincent's not in right now." Mightn't even be sober for all he knew.

"You are Jeffrey Mendes then?"

"Yup." Mullet raised his eyebrows. Someone had done their homework.

"Good." A beat. "Look, I got your name . . . the name of your agency . . .

from our insurance company. They said Vincent Saldana was an ex-cop, used to work the abalone rackets. They recommended him."

"Sure." Mullet put down his revolver and changed the phone to his left hand, drawing out an envelope from the pile of unopened mail on his desk in case he needed to take notes.

"Is there some way I can get hold of him? A cellphone number, perhaps?"

"He's outta town and outta range," said Mullet, thinking in a manner of speaking this wasn't far from the truth. Vince off his face somewhere being about the same thing.

The woman said, "When will he be back?"

"Later today. Saturday for certain sure." Mullet drew a skull on the envelope. "Anything I can do for you?"

"If you can ask him to call me, that would be good." She gave him her phone number. "My name is Marina Welsh."

The line went dead before Mullet could say goodbye. He dropped the phone into its cradle thinking, in four months no one had ever asked for Vincent Saldana. And then to have his own services turned down! It quite pissed him off. Like wasn't he the one keeping things together, then this bird phones and actually wants Vincent. Jesus, did she know what she was after! He rolled his chair backwards, jolting against the wall. The phone rang again.

"Yeah," he answered. "Mendes & Saldana."

"Are you the private investigators?" a woman asked.

Mullet changed his tone, coming on helpful. "That's what it says in the *Yellow Pages*."

"I wouldn't know. You were recommended."

"Word of mouth's always better than an advert." He could hear a dog barking fiercely in the background. "Would you like me to come round? Explain the set-up" – wasn't any way he could have a client in this dump.

"I suppose so," said the woman. "I suppose I have no alternative."

She introduced herself as Judith Oxford. A blonde with short spiky hair, fortyish, sharp-featured, too sharp for Mullet. Fine nose, thin lips, high cheekbones, blue eyes that didn't look away but went at your eyes like lasers. An attractive woman in tight jeans and T-shirt. Posh accent that was probably English English. He made her for a Brit.

She sat on a scatter-cushioned couch noticing every twitch you made. Mullet sat opposite in a deep green chair, too low for his long legs. His knees were higher than the seat. She went straight in, no preliminaries.

"I have reason to believe my husband is using prostitutes, Mr Mendes." A pause. "It might be worse than that."

Out a window behind her, Mullet saw a gardener heading across the lawn towards the flowerbeds. A Doberman trotted at his heels.

"You think so? What d'you mean?"

"Not only women. Rent boys as well."

Mullet fished a notebook out of his jacket pocket. Judith Oxford had her hands folded in her lap, watching him. She didn't look agitated, as a woman might who thought her husband was cruising.

"I want to know if this is true. I want to know where he goes. I want to know what he gets them to do."

"Like everything?"

"I want documentary proof. Explicit photographs."

Mullet shrugged. "It's your call."

"Precisely." The way she said it, the only emotion in the word was bitterness. She laid out five thousand bucks in one-grand heaps saying, "Four nights' work, Mr Mendes. Plus the report. Plus the pictures." She stood up.

"Whoa," said Mullet, holding up his hands, "you've gotta tell me something about him, Mrs Oxford." He flipped open the notebook.

"Such as?" She sat down, sliding an arm along the back of the couch.

"For starters, why you think he's picking up prostitutes?"

"Rent boys." She said it harshly, putting a crack on each word, and stared at him until Mullet had to flick his eyes down, scribbling on the notebook to get his pen working.

"One of my husband's clients saw him solicit a boy in Long Street. He saw the boy get into my husband's car. The client considered I had a right to know."

"You believe the client?"

"Absolutely." She let him off the ice-eyed stare and smiled. A half smile of no amusement. "The client in question has most of his investments managed by my dear husband. He would not want to see his name associated with anything distasteful."

Mullet leaned forward, resting his elbows on his knees. "I gotta ask you some personal questions, Mrs Oxford." The woman shifted her gaze back to him.

"Within reason, I'll answer."

"Right then. Can I ask how long you've been married?"

"Five years. Six in July."

"First time?"

"For me. Not for Roger. His first wife committed suicide."

Mullet whistled. "Heavy stuff."

"Very, Mr Mendes. The night she heard of our affair."

"This was where?"

"Taipei. Roger's first wife was Chinese. He was well connected there, for a foreigner."

"So why'd you come here?"

"At the request of a client."

"The one you mentioned gave you the tip-off."

"Very astute, Mr Mendes. Precisely him."

Mullet ignored the patronising, wondering could he go in a bit closer? Decided, why not?

"How's stuff between you?" he asked. "Your relationship?"

Judith Oxford folded her arms. "I beg your pardon."

"You know. How you're getting on?"

"Do you mean are we having sex?"

"That too." Mullet sat back, tapping the pen against his teeth.

"I don't think I'm going to answer your question."

Mullet shrugged. "What I need is his phone numbers, office address, maybe a pic."

She fetched a photograph from a bureau drawer and handed it to him: two men in slacks and untucked shirts walking in a garden, the vegetation dense and green behind them. "That was taken last year. In Taipei. The Chinese gentleman with him is one of his oldest contacts. He has the quaint name of Dragon Fire. An extremely charming man."

Mullet clicked his pen, was about to close his notebook. "Oh ja, what's his car?"

"A Pajero 4x4." She pushed the stacks of hundred-buck notes across the coffee table towards him. "What some would call a good ride."

Mullet wrote down the make, closed his notebook. He folded the money bundle by bundle into his pockets. "You gonna divorce him if it's true?"

Judith Oxford smiled. Not enough to show her teeth, just stretching her lips. Didn't say anything. He tried more questions about her husband's business. She told him just enough with some acid in her replies.

Mullet pocketed his notebook and pen, stood tall and bulky over her. "Right then. I'll see what's what."

"Nice jacket," she said, looking up at him. "Burnt orange suits you."

"Thanks." Mullet gave a quick smile, pleased that she noticed. It was a jacket he wore to impress, a warm colour gave people confidence in you. A jacket and gear he felt good in: white golf shirt, charcoal chinos, grey loafers without socks. You checked the adverts you saw without socks was hip.

Mullet followed Judith Oxford out of the sitting room, thinking good denim arse.

Her handshake at the door firm and cool, his hand afterwards smelling faintly of the kind of cologne airlines used on the warm towels they gave you in business class. The one time he'd flown business class. To Czechoslovakia. Before it became the Czech Republic.

"I look forward to hearing from you," she said.

Mullet drove down the driveway with the Doberman bounding beside him, the dog's head turned, eyeing him, its lips peeled away from a jagged row of canines. Where the hell had it come from? Before him the gates opened, the Doberman stopped, seeing Mullet off the property. Mullet drove out, watching the gates close behind him. The way it looked the dog was grinning. Had to be Judith Oxford's dog.

One chilly woman. An expat expensive Constantia lady. All the same, what they did in the leafy suburbs was what they did in the slums. Different weapons, different strategies, but if stuff went too far you ended up the same kind of dead.

5

Sea Street, 7.30 p.m., late summer with twilight fading. Mullet nosed the Subaru against the kerb, killed the engine. His was the only car in the street. You found yourself in a Sea Street this time of evening you had to be outta your skull. Like this street was empty, no one about, no chance of anyone being about. Office blocks all around. One battered Subaru parked right under a no-parking sign the only oddity. You came out of your parking garage this time of evening you might wonder what that Subaru was doing there. Something Mullet had considered. Decided, nah, if Judith Oxford was right about hubby Roger he'd have other matters on his mind when he left the parking garage. Wasn't going to notice anything in Sea Street.

Mullet dug a mint chew out of the bag on the passenger seat. Sea Street. Had to be about a kilometre to the sea now. High-rises, hotels, the conference centre, the motorway in-between before you even hit docklands and the Waterfront.

Maybe once you could've gone down here to the sea, eighty, ninety years ago. When Cape Town had the sea at the end of the street. Fishing boats pulled up on the beach, fishermen coiling ropes, mending their nets, lobster traps, oars, nets hanging to dry, whaling cottages either side the street. Kids playing. Sailors wandering around searching out booze and a screw.

Mullet had toked a head of dagga before he left his office, wondered if this wasn't a reefer dream, especially as to look at Sea Street now there wasn't even a rat muzzling the gutters.

Few hours back he hadn't heard of Sea Street. Not until Judith Oxford in her chichi lounge said, "My dear Roger's got offices on Long. Back of that's Sea Street. That's where the entrance is to the office parking garage. All you have to do is wait until he leaves. Follow him."

Mullet popped another mint chew. Thumbed through his notebook to the number of the private line she'd given him and dialled Roger Oxford, just checking he was still in the office.

"Oxford."

"Yo, is that you Donnie?" said Mullet.

A hesitation, the voice coming back irritated: "You've got the wrong number."

"Hey, sorry, man," said Mullet. "You have a good one."

The director of Blue Sky Investments hanging up without another word. Mullet settled back in the Subaru and slid Meat Loaf's *Bat Out of*

Hell into the CD player, thinking, the guy's in his office so it's only a matter of time till he comes down. Also this being Friday evening even the chairman's not going to be working late. Sooner rather than later he's going to hit the town, according to his wife.

Meat Loaf segued from the title track into 'Hot Summer Night'. Mullet wanting to sing along, pressed the volume way up. Heck man the street was empty, why not give it a blast? Which he did until his Nokia rang six tracks later, Mullet's ears zinging so badly he couldn't hear the ringing. If the cell hadn't vibrated off the dashboard he would've missed the call. "Prof Summers" showing on the display.

Mullet cleared his throat. "Yeah, prof."

"Mullet."

Mullet pressed the volume down on the CD.

"Yeah, prof."

"You into Meat Loaf, Mullet?"

"Every single disc."

"Christ, Mullet. Where's your taste?"

"You complaining about the little packets, prof?"

"Touchy, boy."

"So, are you?"

"Have I ever?"

"How much?" asked Mullet, the professor one of the clients he least liked.

"Two-fifty."

What the professor did in a week. The last of the big-time smokers. What he was professor of Mullet had never asked. This little jerk in stained suits, his house reeking of cat piss and cigarettes.

"Right then," said Mullet.

"When?"

"Sunday," Mullet came back knowing a wait would freak him.

"Can't you do it tonight?"

"I'm on a job."

"Someone's hired you! I'm impressed. What about when you're finished?"

"Could be early morning."

"Wake me."

The professor disconnected. Mullet looked at his phone in disgust. What he reckoned he was going to do one day was sell the little professor some pre-rolled roaches laced with white buttons to give him a serious trip. So what if he lost the damn account. Plenty more where Professor Summers came from who didn't want to risk their arses on the street.

Supplying the uni-guys, the medics, the legal eagles was a rare business Mullet had picked up from a dealer as part of an unofficial plea bargain. The dealer was a politician's son busted by Mullet in his last months as a cop. Mullet had let him walk in exchange for the client list of professionals with a soft spot for marijuana, figuring in the long term this was probably worth more than his severance package.

A wise decision, the package didn't exactly say thank you for twenty-two years on the Force. But he was outta there, couldn't stand cop work anymore. Seeing guys you knew taking a bullet every week, some of them eating their own guns, whacking their wives, girlfriends, kids, whatever, it wasn't worth it. The firepower out there greater than any firepower you've got. Also the law was on the wrong side. You caught a guy in the old days for assault, rape, murder, you told him run. The incident went down in the book as shot resisting arrest. Now the bad guys had human rights. You wanted to save the justice system any cost, you had to be damn sure what you did had no comebacks. Because your own friends were going to investigate what you said happened.

Other hand, if the perp ever got done for murder the most he was gonna get was life. And life wasn't life, it was fifteen years. No more death penalty. Stuff it! Mullet reckoned he wasn't putting his life on the line anymore. Took the package. Then four months back opened Mendes & Saldana with Vincent Saldana, a guy even more strung out by the cop situation, the hits they were taking.

His cell rang again. After eight, people were down a drink or two and their thoughts turned to getting stoned.

"Elizabeth" on his phone's screen. One nice lady.

"Elizabeth."

"Hi Jeffrey."

No Mullet. She couldn't bring herself to call him Mullet. "That's my nickname. That's what everybody calls me," he'd said. "After the haircut." But no, she insisted on his real name, Jeffrey. He'd had a mullet since his teenage years in the late 1970s. Short sides, long in the back, Mullet couldn't imagine it any other way. It suited his face. Guy had a big face like his you had to set it off. You were a big guy, fast on your feet, a mullet made you faster. Also, what a disguise. You could be a motor mac. The last thing anyone thought you were was a plain-clothes cop. That was then, this was now. Now a mullet made you for an investigator. So what?

"You in a rush?" asked Mullet, hoping she'd say no, not wanting to disappoint her.

"Not at all," she replied. "Tomorrow. Sunday'd be fine."

"Sunday's good," said Mullet. "I'm taking the boat out tomorrow. Coupla guys're coming fishing."

"What's running?"

Actually interested. Goddamned doctor of classical whatever interested in what fish's running.

"Long-fin. Yellowtail."

"You catch any extra, I'll buy one," she said.

"Deal," replied Mullet.

"Till Sunday."

She disconnected. Had to be fifty-five years old. She told him once she'd been at Woodstock. The real one. The original. She had bootleg Neil Young tapes he drooled over. And then the next time he dropped off her supply she had made copies for him.

Mullet switched the music to Young's *Harvest*. Not loud, his mood gone contemplative, his thoughts on Rae-Anne, her talk of maybe they should get together. Sell her flat and his house and buy a place on the coast, somewhere with a slipway he could launch the boat. A lovely idea that scared the shit out of him. It was long years since he'd lived with anyone. After his marriage bust-up that was it, any woman started talking about moving in, he fled. Except Rae-Anne had been around for eighteen months and never put the pressure on. She had liked the separate homes arrangement and while he was a cop could see no reason to change things. As they said, that was then, this was now. Now was different. Mendes & Saldana not being exactly a hot-shot agency.

Her talk of getting together was practical, based on money. Mullet knew it. Two could live as cheaply as one. What she said made perfect sense. She was good that way, at considering all the options, weighing up the pros and cons, putting out what she thought would be the best solution.

"Not just for me, doll," she told him. "For you, too."

He'd smiled weakly, seeing her point, knowing he couldn't argue against it but for the panic in his chest.

"Think about it," she'd said.

For a week he'd been doing just that every moment the future came calling, which was way too often when you had not much on your hands. They did this thing, what was he to lose? He wasn't going to give up the grass nor stop fishing. What he was throwing away was time alone. The nights he went through to dawn smoking dope, listening to music, staring at nothing. The nights he couldn't sleep. In eighteen months she didn't know about the nights he couldn't sleep. Not even the grass did it for him anymore. It had stopped him dreaming, thankfully, but it couldn't put him to sleep, only daylight could do that.

Thinking about Rae-Anne's point made Mullet edgy. He took the flask of coffee, got out of the car and poured himself a cup: instant with a shot of brandy. Heaps of sugar, lots of milk, none of this fancy cappuccino, espresso, latte nonsense. All his life there'd been instant and there was no reason to change, not even with Rae-Anne kidding him, "Drinking instant's like so nowhere," thrusting some bitter muck at him that she'd brewed from an Italian contraption. Black. No milk, no sugar. "Real coffee, mister. It's a blend of French Roast and Colombian." More like sludge with a taste of bile. He took a long swallow of his blend. Smooth with a kick.

Mullet hoisted himself onto the car's bonnet and gazed up at the mountain: a straight line of black against the stars. No cloud, meant the wind had dropped on False Bay. Tomorrow the sea would be warm, glassy, bringing in the yellowtail. Guys who made a living out of fishing had a life. No hanging about in empty streets, waiting for some prick to go get his rocks off so you could take the photies home to his old lady. Sleaze work. Enough to make you puke. Only thing to be said for it was you weren't going to see someone bleeding to death, raped and buggered, or beaten raw. Mullet poured a quarter of coffee, took it in a swallow.

For the next few hours he wandered about the street, amazed that a street in the city could be this empty. Hadn't seen a living soul since he'd set up the stake-out. You considered the hordes of street kids, the vagrants sleeping rough, you'd have thought Sea Street was a haven. A street this quiet you'd have reckoned somebody would be curled in a doorway. But no. Dead boring street. Kitchen-tile boutiques. Couple of lighting emporiums. Couple of tyre dealers. Two corner cafés, Big Jack pies, slices of processed cheese, polony in the coolers. A string of places you couldn't tell what they were about: nondescript nameplates on the doors, vertical blinds at the windows, didn't bother to leave security lights on. Of all the places you could end up waiting, how about this? Not even a drunk for distraction.

Somewhat close to eleven Mullet thought the problem with the stake-out was the foyer entrance to the building in Long. Supposing the guy had called for a taxi, waltzed out the foyer door? He could have done that four hours ago, right after he'd taken Mullet's phoney call.

Mullet wondered if he should risk another call. Maybe not even answer but ring off as soon as the guy picked up. If he failed on this one Judith Oxford would have the dog eat him. The name Mendes & Saldana wouldn't even rate with people wanting to track down old schoolfriends.

Maybe he should've got Vince to sit in the other street. Like this was possible the way Vince had been at six o'clock, hard up against the bar at the Kimberley, shooting brandy chasers between his Black Labels! Vince's attitude: weekends begin on Friday afternoon. Weekends are for one long drunk. Sometimes during the week Vince was also out of it, but less recently than before. Before had been seriously bad news. Mullet's feeling was he needed time and maybe some professional help eventually, when he hit the bottom. Till then, hell, Vince on a drunk when there was no work wasn't a huge problem. Besides, Judith Oxford needed to pay a lot more to have them both on the job.

Mullet dug a standby cellphone out of the glove box, just in case the guy had caller ID on his private line. The same cell number showing up twice would be careless. He pressed in the numbers with his thumb, spastic, hitting a wrong digit. He redialled. On the third ring Oxford answered.

"Yes."

Mullet kept the line open, his finger over the mic hole.

"Hello." A pause. "Who is this?" Another beat. "Now listen here . . ." The sound of Oxford moving in his chair then the phone went dead. Mullet thumbed the off button.

Now listen here . . . The tone of a man trying to sound in control and unafraid.

"What's it your husband does, exactly?" Mullet had asked Judith Oxford.

She'd given him a slight smile, revealing a glint of white teeth beneath her upper lip. "I told you, finance. He's what you'd call a smoke and mirrors man. Now you see it. Now you don't."

Mullet had shrugged. "Meaning?"

"International broker."

"Like an investment adviser?"

"You could say something like that." She'd crossed her legs, leant towards him. "Something like that. But not quite. You see Roger knows how to move money around, Mr Mendes. Even here with all the restrictions and currency controls, Roger's never found it to be . . ." – she searched for a word, decided on – "limiting. Do you know what I mean?" She'd stared at him, that half smile on her lips. Cynical. Worldly. "He has a most amazing list of clients, Mr Mendes. You would be intrigued to see them. But first things first."

Would he be intrigued to see the list? Mullet doubted it, that wasn't his province, although lists always had a financial value.

What did intrigue him was the underlying fear in Roger Oxford's voice. Then again a smoke and mirrors man couldn't be any stranger to fear. It must go with the territory. Now listen here . . .

Both Mullet's phones rang simultaneously, enough of a surprise to make his stomach muscles contract. Oxford's private number was on the standby, an unknown on his Nokia. He let Oxford go to voicemail and took the other.

It was the woman who'd wanted Vincent: Marina Welsh.

"I'm still waiting for your Mr Saldana to call," she said.

Mullet said, "Ah really!"

She laughed. "Maybe he's not back in cellphone range!"

Her laugh as rich as her voice. Mullet caught a sound of crooner music in the background, some sound-alike Sinatra.

"Do you have a moment?"

"I'm not doing anything," he said, gazing at the empty street.

"I'm an attorney," she said. "But this is not about me, it's about a business I'm invested in."

"Yes," said Mullet, wondering what the career tag was supposed to signify: status or don't mess with me, I'm wise to your type? Could be either. "Right then, tell me about it."

A faint clink of a glass against her teeth. Whisky? Wine? Mineral water? Mullet opted for whisky. Blend or single malt? This time of night had to be single malt, Mullet reckoned. Good smoky rich taste. That's what Marina Welsh sounded like: money.

She said, "The business cultivates abalone up the coast."

"Uh huh," Mullet thumbed through to voicemail on the other cellphone.

"What has happened," she said, "is that we have a problem of stock shrinkage."

"Shrinkage?"

"Theft. Actually the word heist would be more accurate."

"Figures." Mullet heard her take another swallow.

"Do you know anything about abalone cultivation?"

Mullet said nope, not much. The voicemail on the other phone told him he had one new message, except the caller had not left a message.

"As I expected," she said. The way she said it he could smell her whisky breath. "This is a way of cashing in on the market without plundering the natural resources. You know what sort of profits are yielded whether it's legit or poached?"

Who didn't? Smuggling abalone was a better deal than smuggling diamonds, given the going rates in the East. A damn sight more dangerous, too. The poachers tied into syndicates, the syndicates not averse to the odd strategic liquidation. Places like Dutch Bay along the coast had gun battles in the streets when the gangs got too cocky. The cops blundering about in the mess, sometimes making busts which upped the ante for everyone.

He said, "You've reported this to the police?"

"Of course."

"So?" Mullet thought, where's this going? The trouble was some people didn't know the difference between the cops and private investigators.

"So, Mr Mendes, I want Vincent Saldana to find the thieves."

Mullet whistled. "We're a two-man agency. We track guys who're cheating on their wives. Or wives screwing their neighbours. Short-term insurance fraud. That's the extent of our bag. You go up against the abalone gangs you need a platoon. You see where I'm going? Anyhow you've got the cops on this. Leave it to them. That's the game: cops 'n robbers."

"They can't. They tried but got nowhere."

"At which point your insurance company recommended Vincent Saldana?"

"Quite." A pause. "Look, Mr Mendes, our business has been hit once and as long as there are abalone in the tanks, it is going to be hit again. The cops can't hang about there indefinitely. Last time the insurance paid out, reluctantly. The word is that we're going to be hit in the next few days. If that happens the insurers will tell us, sorry, read the small print."

"Two things," said Mullet. "I'm not security. And who tipped you off?"

Marina gave a sarcastic laugh. "Come on, Mr Mendes. You were a cop. You know the abalone business is tied up in syndicates. Someone's discovered our operation. They won't stop until it's cleaned out. End of story."

"Mmmm," said Mullet, juggling the standby cell in his left hand.

Ms Whisky Voice said, "I heard Mr Saldana was a pretty good cop. I was told he has particular experience of these people."

"Sure he has. Major pearlie buster in his day. You give him a chance he'll jump at a game like this."

"I'm giving him a chance. All we want is names and addresses." A tinkle of ice.

"What then?"

"Then the law can take its course."

Like bloody hell, thought Mullet.

Marina Welsh said, "There's one other thing."

"Being?"

"Money. We'll pay your normal rate plus twenty per cent and expenses."

Mullet chewed that over, wondering who the we was? What was there to lose? You went out there, checked the place, asked a few questions in the right quarters. The normal plus twenty for some names and addresses. What a pleasure! He was about to say yes, when he saw car lights coming out of the parking garage. The car was a Pajero 4x4, the driver had to be Roger Oxford. Mullet went down on the passenger seat, face first into the mint chews, Marina Welsh going in his ear, "Are you there? Are you there? Talk to me."

"I'll get my partner to call you tomorrow," said Mullet, coming up, glimpsing the Pajero turn right at the first intersection. He fired the Subaru, lights off, taking the first left to catch Oxford in the next street, Buitengracht.

"Excellent," she said.

Oxford was headed towards the Green Point mile, taking his time. Mullet popped his headlights and joined a bunch of cars at a traffic light, the Pajero two ahead.

"I look forward to hearing from him."

"You will," said Mullet, shifting the cell into the hands-free bracket. "He'll call you. I'm outta town tomorrow, Ms Welsh," going for the Ms because that's what Marina Welsh sounded like. The light went green, Mullet rode the clutch. "I'll give Vince your number. He'll call you. You've got my word on it."

"Is there no way I can reach him now?"

"Hey! I said he'd call." Thinking: probably two to one against.

"Of course." Mullet caught the sarcasm.

The Pajero stopped a block past Giovanni's. A woman in a skimpy red dress came out of the shadows, got into the open passenger door. Not exactly a rent boy. But hey, Mrs Oxford, good news, Mr Oxford's your regular john. Except it probably wouldn't make her feel any better.

"Look, Ms Welsh, I've gotta go. Business is hotting up."

"Who is cheating on whom?"

"Client confidentiality," said Mullet, hearing her laugh before she disconnected.

6

In the mirror in the restaurant's loo, Judith Oxford reapplied her lipstick and patted her lips with a tissue to tone down the shine. The fluorescent light turned her face a luminous white, made her lips a thin bloody gash.

She gave a quick smile and dropped the tissue in a wastebin, ran a hand through her spiky-blonde hair. "Right, Mr Woo," she said to herself. "Let's hear what more you have to say." A breath of harbour air came through the window: fish, Jik, diesel. She sighed. Sometimes authentic got too authentic. The Waterfront was about as much harbour as she wanted. Somewhere without these container ships and derricks and the grind of trucks in low gear. When Woo had said Panama Jack's, she'd almost said anywhere but, then remembered his thing about seafood.

"Panama Jack's," she'd confirmed. "I'll meet you there."

"I could send a driver."

"It's fine. Just be there on time."

Judith got back to the table as Jim Woo was ordering the wine.

"You want a drink first?" he asked.

"No," she shook her head, "the wine will do."

"More than do," he said. "It's my neighbour's: Hartenberg sauvignon blanc."

She nodded. Sat down and stared across the candle at Woo. "So. Give me the grim."

Woo caught her eyes then glanced down at his menu. "Perhaps we should order first." He scanned the entrées. "They do good mussels here. And, of course, abalone as a main course. The best in the city."

"I'll have the fish of the day," Judith said, without glancing at the menu. "Whatever it is. Grilled. Nothing to start."

"Alright." He said it without looking at her and took some time hesitating between the abalone and the lobster. "I'll do the abalone" – snapping the menu closed. "Food for the dragon."

Judith did not smile at his quip, she'd heard it too often before. "Tell me again about Roger, James." She never used the informality of his preferred Jim.

He leaned back and swirled the wine in the glass, nosed it. "Perfect." He tasted. "Wonderful." He indicated for the waiter to fill their glasses. "This is difficult, Judith. Usually what people do, I say is their business. Adult to adult. But here we've got a perversion. You'll excuse the straight talk." When the waiter had jammed the bottle into the ice bucket and left, Woo raised his glass. "A toast." He paused while she reached for her wine. "To sorting out our mutual concerns."

Judith said nothing. Clinked her glass gently against his and sipped at the cold wine.

"I told you on the phone, about a week ago I'm in town one evening. I come out of Kennedy's Cigar Bar, nine, nine-thirty, it's dark but the street's lit and humming. Across the road I see Roger talking to this kid. Next thing they get into Roger's 4x4 and off he goes. I think, Christ, not Roger Oxford." He swallowed wine, dabbed at his lips. "For a few days I sit on it. What should I do? Leave it? Speak to Roger? Speak to you? I decide you've got a right to know."

Judith sipped again at the wine, put the glass down. "I'm not going to thank you."

"You don't have to. I'm not expecting it." He shifted on his chair, getting comfortable. "You phone the private detective I suggested?"

"We met this morning."

"And?"

"He seems fine."

"You've got him on the job yet?"

"Even as we speak."

Woo nodded encouragement. "It was the right thing to do. Only thing." He stopped, pursed his lips. Judith looked at him: the slicked-down black hair, the white open-necked shirt, the collar splayed over the suit jacket. Mr Cool. Mr Completely Untrustworthy.

"I'll be honest, Judith. This is not good timing for me. I need Roger to have his mind on my affairs, not little boys or little girls or wherever he gets his kicks. This is not a good business environment for me any longer. Also, I'm shifting my market. Taipei's out, Shanghai's in."

"Following the money."

"That's the idea. Taipei was a good margin, Shanghai is five times better. So I'm under a little pressure to change markets. As my financial adviser, this affects Roger too. I need him to be ahead of the game. I do not need him distracted."

"You expect me to do something?"

"Only when the investigator comes up with hard evidence."

"Assuming he does."

"Assuming."

"Then?" Judith reached for her glass.

"Next week I'm away," said Woo. "This trip will clarify certain issues for me. When I return I'll have more focus."

"Taipei's out. Shanghai's in."

The waiter arrived with their food. When he'd gone, Woo laughed. "You're one sharp woman, Judith." He picked up his knife and fork. "What I'd appreciate, Judith, is if you did not confront Roger till after I'm back."

"For your sake?"

Woo laid down his fork and stretched across the table to take her hand. "I'm asking a favour."

She shook her head, withdrawing her hand from his tightening squeeze. "That's one enormous favour. I'm expected to play the good wife while my husband's getting his rocks off around town with whores and rent boys?"

Woo took a roll from the bread basket. Judith knew he disliked her. Could see it in the set of his mouth, his lips thin and clamped. To him, she was impertinent. Nosey. Controlling. He'd once told her to stop dominating her husband. Probably it made sense for him, this story of Roger trawling the streets to compensate for living with a first-class bitch.

His cellphone rang in his jacket pocket. Within two rings it went to voicemail.

Judith watched him reach into his jacket and produce the phone. Without so much as an excuse me he connected to get the message.

Rude bastard, she thought. A cocky rude bastard. Vicious too. If Roger was going to pull off this one he would have to be sharp. Very sharp.

"I think," he'd said to her when she told him about Woo's allegations, "that we need to play along. Contact the private investigator, meet with him, hire him. Come over the betrayed wife. Have supper with Woo, hear what he's got to say."

Woo listened to the message. Tommy Fortune oozing I'm the man, look at me. He folded the phone, slipped it into his pocket. "Do you believe in making plans, Judith?" He picked up his knife and fork.

"Mostly, yes," said Judith. "Occasionally it's best to go with the flow, as they say."

"I prefer plans." Woo cut at the remainder of his abalone steak. "That way you can consider all the options. Connect all the dots. That's what I enjoy especially. Making the connections. Putting people in touch with one another."

"Playing games."

"Ha!" Woo laughed, even as he took a mouthful. "You make me sound malicious when what I'm doing is helping people realise their dreams." He chewed and before he spoke again Judith glimpsed masticated food on his tongue. "We all play games. Everything we do is a game."

7

That afternoon Tommy Fortune had taken the N2 out of the city. Up Eastern Boulevard, round Hospital Bend, through the death curves onto the crazy straight, working the lanes for gaps in the Friday traffic. Radio Five on the Becker system: the DJ doing Eminem back to back. 'Sing for the Moment.' 'Cleaning out my Closet.' Tommy was on a roll, everything going his way what with Mister Forking Woo paying up major bucks.

At the cooling towers Tommy ran the needle to one-fifty. The Beemer a dream in a tailgate situation. He flashed, he hooted, the suits heading for the airport slid out of his way chop-chop. Everyone got the message, the fast lane was his. Tommy sailed it, unfazed, the steering wheel light in his left hand, his right out the window drumming the rap.

One hour down the afternoon he turned into Dutch Bay, a scattering of fisher houses among the dunes, a small harbour. If a storm came in and a boat wasn't high and dry that boat was matchwood. Dutch Bay: dirt-poor picturesque, loved by film companies shooting ads. Nowadays, mostly, the mood among the fisher folk was like a sweet-wine hangover, everyone pissed at government's new regulations about perlemoen quotas. Everyone was a perlemoen poacher, telling these fishermen they had a quota was like telling them not to breathe.

This afternoon Dutch Bay was in ugly mood. To Tommy it looked like every fisherman along the coast and his mommy's auntie had come to demonstrate.

Tommy turned down a side street, planning to get the BM well out of the way in case the masses took a mind to razing the whole village.

People got this stoked, the mood could swing quicker than a bitch's tongue. It might be their village but that didn't stop them wrecking it.

He found a place under gum trees, beyond were scrub and dunegrass. An old man sat there tarring his boat. Tommy switched off the engine, angled the rear-view mirror to reflect his image: blue-lens Ray-Bans, pencil moustache. He grinned: false front teeth inlaid with emeralds courtesy of Mr Woo. Puckered his lips in a kiss. Don't you love it, darlin? He got out of the car. The old man in the shade eyed him.

Tommy jerked his head in greeting. "You know what's going on down there?"

The fisherman nodded, went back to his caulking. Tommy pressed the locking remote and the car squealed twice.

"You should be shouting down there, daddy. Tell the government you got your rights." He headed down the street, the fisherman watching him every step of the way.

Tommy took a sand path between the cottages, kids staring at him from the dark insides. He came out to the side of the harbour, on a slope above the mob: a grandstand position to see the job get done. Below was full-on carnival: guys blowing kelp trumpets, people wearing chains, people tied up with ropes, every single one of them waving a placard.

PERLEMOEN IS FOOD

HANDS OFF OUR BIRTHRIGHT

QUOTA SUCKS

Tommy tore the silver off a pack of Marlboro, tapped a stick loose, rolling it about his lips unlit. There was Sonny Furniss on the jetty, a brave man with a loudhailer, alone facing a crowd of craziness. Tommy flicked a Zippo, bringing the flame to his cigarette. Sonny the righteous. Put your hand in the hand of the man who stilled the water. What was amazing was that after all the killings there'd been, cops shooting perlemoen poachers, perlemoen poachers shooting cops, Inspector Furniss still came out alone. Like receiving a petition was not a big-deal situation.

Tommy scanned the mob, not a sign of Adonis.

Furniss climbed onto an up-turned boat, raised his arms for quiet, a clipboard in his right hand. The people quietened. Furniss the preacher.

The guy in tight grey trousers and white shirt with the sleeves rolled onto his biceps, holding forth.

"We must respect the sea. If you're going to take perlemoen like you're doing, you're going to kill it." The words rising to Tommy. "You've got quotas." The dread word getting the crowd vocal again. Furniss held out his arms like his saviour on the cross. Shouted: "Those quotas earn you a living. You don't have to poach as well."

The crowd laughed. A placard came sailing over the heads and Furniss ducked.

"We can protect your quotas."

The crowd booed. Tommy opened his mouth, letting smoke cloud over his emeralds. Sonny Furniss didn't have a Jesus hope of convincing them, and he knew it. The locals knew it. If they didn't poach, the likes of Tommy were going to do it anyhow. The rule was simple: take your quota during the day, at night outpoach the poachers.

"Catch the poachers and we'll put them in jail," Furniss shouted. "The law's on your side."

The mob came back at him with more anger. Tommy noticed Adonis then, noticed he was right up there in front, behind some wide-bummed fisherwoman pumping the air with her fist, moving forward. Tommy shook his head. What was with the guy? He comes to a job as Mr Street Fashion. Baseball cap, peak to the back. Faded jeans ripped at the knee, pale blue jacket with fur on the cuffs and collar. In this weather. Thirty degrees C in the shade, Adonis is more concerned about the cuddly look than being anonymous. He'd probably got on the laceless green Reeboks.

The crowd was solid, chanting. Furniss bellowed back: "It's the law. The law. We've gotta have law."

Which was when someone raised a placard, whacking the clipboard out of Furniss' hand. Furniss staggered back a pace, balancing on the spine of the boat, his arms out tightrope walking. He was shouting, "People, people, people, listen to me." Except nobody was. What was running through the mob was, the TV's here.

Tommy saw two lighties no more than ten years old, breaking out of the crowd to hurl bomb-bags at Sonny Furniss. One caught him on the chest and burst; the other bounced off his crotch and broke at his feet soaking his cheapo imitation leather shoes. Sonny went speechless, the crowd pulled back. The kids were gone. The cameraman closed in on Sonny, elbowing through the mob, shouting to clear his path.

Tommy wondered, Jesus, what's this? – too far back to see clearly what was happening. The forest of placards, waving. The mob surging again. Adonis disappeared. The cameraman popped out of the mass, panning from the faces up to Furniss. Freeze frame.

Someone tossed a flame at Furniss. Tommy saw it in slow motion: this little streak of fire arcing over the heads.

Whoosh.

Furniss was a furnace.

Tommy took a deep draw on what was left of his cigarette. The kids had thrown petrol at him! There was the news guy with a story like he'd never had before: a man in the lens dancing in fire. The guy kept the camera focused. Furniss beat at his clothes, stomped his feet but the fire exploded up him, this flame coming out of his chest, catching in his hair.

He fell off the boat then, sliding onto the sand. Nobody reached for him. Those closest watched Sonny Furniss raise himself to his knees, kneel there in the fire. Those at the back chanted and shook their placards.

Tommy ground the butt and looked for Adonis. There he was behind the mob, heading off with that skippy walk of his.

Tommy made to move, thinking to catch up with Adonis on the road out of the village. He gave a last glance at the burning Furniss still kneeling, saw him sag forward a bit, his head bowed. The inspector toppled over. A guy rushed up to beat out the flames using what looked like a wet towel, lashing again and again at Furniss's body which gave the cameraman some extra footage for the final cut: Sonny Furniss curled smouldering, shrouded by a singed towel. The emblem on the towel, a palm tree.

He found Adonis behind the cottages, Adonis revving the guts out of a battered Siesta.

"You didn't think I'd do it?" asked Adonis when Tommy leered in at the open window.

Tommy shook his head.

Adonis gave him the safe-my-mate sign, waving his right hand with the index and small fingers out like horns, the others tucked.

"Special for you."

Tommy ignored this. Said, "What's with the jacket? Looks like a girl's."

Adonis stroked the fur at the collar, pouted. "Sexy" – and blew him a kiss. "My arse or yours?"

Tommy stared at him. The guy was enough to give you a hard-on just looking at him. Those eyes. Those lips.

Adonis ran his tongue over his lips. "You got the brown sugar, sugar?"

"What you think?"

"We gonna party?"

"All night long."

8

Mullet followed the Pajero through the Sea Point nightclub strip down a side street to La Perla on the promenade, a place Jewish machers took their bimbos, a restaurant you'd find tables of Taiwanese eating mussel soup.

Roger Oxford took a parking outside the restaurant, Mullet found a space farther along and sat watching them in the rear-view mirror. The prozzie didn't look much like a prozzie. If he hadn't seen the pickup, he would have reckoned she was dressed for a good time: short red sequined dress, the cut showing boob, and the spiked heels stylish. She was going to be right at home with the chicks inside. A strange thing was she took Oxford's arm as they went up the steps, the style of a sugar daddy and his bit o' fluff.

Mullet shrugged into his jacket, smoothed his hair, getting quite revved at the thought of calamari and chips. Everything went well he could snap a photie of the amorous couple for Judith Oxford and make her feel he was earning his fee. Get her charged simultaneously.

La Perla wasn't doing badly for the end of Friday night. The lights down: some coochie tables, a main party of eight Taiwanese in the window, two loners, with Mullet that made three. He took a table up a level from Oxford and the prozzie and ordered a half portion of fried calamari rings, a glass of house red. The music was Frank Sinatra, too loud to overhear anything being said below him. From what he could see a lot was being said, the body language more animated than hot talk.

Mullet let it drift. Ate his squid, the best in town, drank his wine, skipped on the coffee. What he had in the car was better than any Irish La Perla could put together. His thoughts went to the Marina Welsh phone call. A nice job. The sort of stuff could give them a reputation. Couldn't be too difficult if Vince pulled his snout out of the trough for long enough. He knew the calls to make. Bingo, bango, here you go ma'am. Two jobs in one day. Maybe the start of a bull market. Mullet couldn't stop a grin spreading ear to ear. Anyone was watching they'd think he was nuts, grinning at his own thoughts. He signalled the waiter for the bill.

When he got up to leave, Mullet stumbled against the railing, snapping a surreptitious picture of the couple in the chaos. Neither of them gave him a moment's notice.

In the car clocked up another forty-five minutes at Judith Oxford's expense, his eyes beginning to ache, Neil Young playing softly to keep him focused. The way things were working out he'd get maybe four hours' kip. He'd promised the guys, seven o'clock the boat was afloat. Mullet started nodding, his head rolling. In one of these orbits he missed Oxford and the woman leave the restaurant. If it hadn't been for the Pajero's passing roar he would have been left stupid. He got after them: action time.

Except it wasn't. Oxford dropped the woman where he'd picked her up, drove on home. Mullet thought, guy takes a woman off a street corner, buys her dinner, drops her back on the street corner has to be running something strange. Question was, what? Mullet reckoned it wasn't his brief. He sat five minutes in a nearby driveway in case Oxford reappeared, then headed home via Prof. Summers. He had to wake the bastard.

"What time do you call this?" the little professor demanded, standing there in striped pyjama bottoms. His chest was concave, a bunch of black hair in the centre.

"You said to wake you," said Mullet.

"Not at one-thirty."

Mullet held out his hand for the money.

"This better be worth it." Summers gave the money with his right hand, took the packet with his left.

"You ever tried Ecstasy, prof?" asked Mullet.

The man shook his head.

"Maybe it's time you graduated."

36

"What's that supposed to mean?"

"Like you're missing something," said Mullet, and winked.

9

Jim Woo had his own keys to the Victorian house. He let himself in quietly, left his shoes at the door and padded barefoot into the sitting room. The curtains weren't drawn and there was enough light to help him find his way between the sofas. He breathed in the lingering scent. She did to Chanel No.5 what no other woman managed: turned an expensive perfume into the stench of lust and fired a deep instinct. In a crowd he believed he could smell her out.

Woo undressed in the living room, draped his jacket over the back of a chair, folded his trousers to keep the crease. He slipped his shirt over his head without unbuttoning and hung it on the chair back. His socks and jocks went onto the seat of the chair. The act of undressing gave him a hard-on.

The truth of it was the dinner with Judith had kicked it off. Maybe he didn't like the woman but her body spoke of sex. That spunky hairstyle, the gloss of her lips, the sort of woman you had to taste. Or it was the abalone pumping up his juices. Either way, when he kissed Judith's hand at the end of the evening and saw the distaste cross her face it stirred him. From nowhere he caught the scent of Chanel No.5.

He went upstairs, treading off-centre to prevent the boards creaking. The bedroom door was ajar. He could see the outline of the woman's body under the sheet. Her back was to him. Slowly he approached until he stood at her head and breathed in the muskiness. His hand went into her hair, gave a tug. She turned onto her back, her hand rising to meet his then drifting to his thigh and into his crotch.

Her voice was heavy with sleep. "Hey." The sound drawn out. She pulled him towards her. "Nice surprise."

"Everything playing?" he said.

"Like a dream."

Marina opened her body as he ran his tongue from her chin down the length of her.

10

Mullet got three hours' sleep. Not enough, but the thought of being on the ocean had him awake the moment the radio clock exploded into pop music. Britney nasal-twang Spears. He pressed the snooze button on his way out of bed. He'd slept in his clothes to save time.

In the kitchen he boiled up a thermos of instant, laced it, pulled a rack of sandwiches Rae-Anne had prepared from the freezer. Ate a two-day-old raisin bun with a smear of butter, softened with milk.

While he ate, Mullet glanced round the kitchen: unwashed dishes in the sink, half a loaf of white going stale on the breadboard. Two roaches crushed in the perlemoen-shell ashtray, the butts from a good few days back. This was what Rae-Anne would come to in the afternoon, depending on who got in first. Mullet shrugged. She knew him.

He put the thermos and sandwiches in his canvas haversack, killed the lights and opened the kitchen door. At five-thirty it was still dark, Mullet stepping out blind. The boy was sitting on the stoep bed.

Mullet sensed him. "Bom-Bom?" As his eyes grew accustomed to the dark he saw the boy. "Heck, Bom-Bom, can't you knock on the door, let me know you're here?"

The boy looked at him, not smiling. He was about twelve years old, a street kid who'd taken to sleeping on Mullet's back stoep some three months previously. Mullet had put out a bed and a sleeping bag as the boy was not interested in coming inside. If Mullet gave him food he ate it, if Mullet didn't he wouldn't beg. The boy never said a word. He might have been deaf 'n dumb for all Mullet knew. His street territory seemed to take in the CBD, the industrial zone off the motorway, even some of the beach resorts in the southern Peninsula. The boy made Rae-Anne edgy but Mullet reckoned the kid was harmless, wanting only a safe sleeping place from time to time.

"He's creepy," said Rae-Anne. "It's creepy having him sleep on the stoep."

"One day he'll stop pitching up," Mullet said.

A time Rae-Anne felt couldn't come soon enough.

Mullet had taken to calling the boy Bom-Bom after a graffito that read: "Bom boys." Maybe bom being Afrikaans for bomb, referring to some years back when pipe bombs, car bombs, bombs in bars, clubs, restaurants had been part of the city scene. Mullet's choice of the name was a generic for street kids that ran in packs.

"Want to come fishing?" Mullet pointed into the yard at the boat.

The boy shook his head.

"Right then." Mullet went back indoors to fetch bread and milk and put them on the stoep table. "Help yourself."

The boy didn't move.

"Where've you been anyhow? It's been what, about two weeks since last time?" He wasn't expecting a response. He talked to the boy the way he'd talked to his cat before it died.

Mullet headed for his Isuzu, slinging the fishing bag onto the bench seat. The boat was hitched to the bakkie, ready to roll. Truth be told the boat was never unhitched. Any chance of some hours' fishing, Mullet didn't want to waste time getting ready. He started the engine. Over the knock of the diesel, he called again to the boy, "You sure?"

The boy was hidden in the dark. Not that seeing his face helped as Mullet couldn't read his expressions. And Mullet had been good at reading faces during interrogations.

He pushed in the gear, let out the clutch and waved to the invisible figure.

Mullet had the *Maryjane* in the Miller's Point slip-way at seven-twenty, not early enough for his friends Ted and André.

Ted stood there tapping his watch, "Hey, what sorta time's this?"

André joining in the joshing, "African time. That's what happens to guys that don't work."

"After all those years on the Force."

Mullet grinned, floating the boat off the trailer. "Not the Force anymore. The Service. Got to think about your clients. Keep up the customer service."

"Ah, bug off," said Ted. He handed in rods, bait, fishing bags, a cooler box of beers and Cokes. "Can we get going?"

"A minute," said Mullet, taking out his cellphone.

"And now?" Ted turned to André. "The private eye's got to make a phone call first. What's so important?"

39

"A job." Mullet thumbed to the office number. Chances were Vincent wouldn't have it on answerphone. Chances were if the phone rang long enough it would get through Vincent's sozzled brain. Vincent having moved into the office. What that amounted to was the litter of a suitcase, a foam mattress and a sleeping bag. Vincent's life pared down to only slightly more than Bom-Bom's.

Mullet counted the rings. Twenty-seven.

The ringing stopped, there was a pause. Vincent answered slurry.

"Hey Vince! Listen to me, Vince. Listen to me. You listening to me?"

He gave Vincent a chance to mumble.

"Right then. I got this call last night from a woman, Marina Welsh. She's got a job for us. I said you'd call her, Vince." He read out the phone number. "This morning."

Vincent came back at him, he said, "I'm fishing, Vince. Like we agreed, hey. Anyhow she wants you. Specifically said Saldana." He listened, Vincent indistinct. "That's what I said. Good rates. Phone her Vince. About nine-thirty, ten. This morning? You gottit."

A pause.

"Vince? You've gotta do it. Her name's Marina Welsh."

He stopped to give Vincent a chance to respond.

"You got that? Marina Welsh."

The phone went dead. Mullet thumbed off the connection with a sigh. "Hey, yay yay."

Ted said, "Some guys don't get through it."

"He'll get through it." Mullet pressed the starter, the engine spluttered and came to life.

"You need him?"

"He's good."

"What about AA?" André had been through the programme and still sponsored a couple of younger cops.

"The old story," said Mullet.

"Ja," said André slowly, remembering aloud the day he came to with his head in a toilet bowl, the bowl filled with his own vomit. That was the day he went to his first meeting, his mouth tasting of sick and his hair smelling of it.

Mullet pushed the engine a fraction beyond idling to nose the boat out of the inlet. Beyond the groyne he swung along the kelp edge, giving the engine more juice. They went parallel to the rocks that made Miller's bad news when the weather got up, and beyond them swung again towards Cape Point.

Mullet opened the motor, squinting at the horizon. This was what he wanted: standing at the helm with the wind bringing tears to his eyes, the engine whine, the boat thumping across a glassy sea.

He cut the engine when they came in line with Cape Point, about two kilometres off. Mullet dropped a drag anchor. For a moment the three of them sat, not doing anything, the sudden silence blotting out their thoughts.

It didn't last: André peeled the cellophane from a pack of menthols and offered the pack to Ted.

Ted shook his head vigorously. "Jesus, André. Quitting's better." He took a Gunston from a packet in his shirt pocket and bent into the flare of André's lighter.

The two men smoked, Ted letting the exhale stream from his nostrils, André blowing it from the corner of his mouth. Mullet caught the tang of the smoke ghosting past him. He thought a joint would be a good idea except André and Ted had standard notions about dagga.

"You ever think about smoking again?" said André.

"Comes and goes," said Mullet.

"I stopped the booze, I can't stop this." André flicked a nose of ash overboard.

"I can't see a reason to stop either one," said Ted. "Hit them both until they hit you. Then go down fighting. They put me in ICU I'll have the nicotine in an IV thank you very much."

Mullet took a Coke from the cooler box and pulled the tab. The trouble with Ted and André was that they didn't like silence. Great fishermen but they didn't get the mood of the sea.

Sometimes when Mullet was out alone he could hear voices in the silence. Voices talking in strange languages. Voices, he reckoned, of sailors who'd been rounding the Cape for centuries. He couldn't make out what they said, just caught sudden snatches of human sound. He'd glance around expecting to see a yacht had come up on him unawares. There'd be only emptiness. He'd smoke a short stop hoping to entice back the ghosts. Zilch. Nothing but the slap of the sea against the hull.

Ted was going on about his sister-in-law on an IV. How where they'd hooked it in, her arm had gone septic. "She goes to hospital because her lungs are being gobbled by the big C, but what's she die of? Septicaemia. There's more bacteria crawling round your average hospital than on a rubbish dump."

"That's not bacteria on a rubbish dump, that's people," said André.

Ted snorted. "Or corpses." He flicked his cigarette butt into the sea. "Hey, Mullet, if you were going to kill somebody where'd you ditch the body?"

Mullet shrugged. "Probably out here. Tied to an anchor."

"Good. So where does this guy put his bodies? On the municipal dump site. Not exactly your out of the way spot. The profiler reckons that's how he views his victims, as garbage. Also that he wants the buckos to be found. Big deal. For that insight we pay her a special salary. Hasn't brought us any closer to the bastard. Four down in four weeks. All teenagers. You don't want to know what he did to them."

Ted popped another cigarette, extracted a lighter from his back pocket. "You want to guess how many possible serials we've got running at the moment?"

Mullet took a swallow of the Coke. "Hey, come on. What's this?"

"No, take a guess," said André.

"Then we'll talk about love," said Ted, letting two smoke rings circle over Mullet's head like halos.

"I dunno," said Mullet. It was the last thing he wanted to be guessing.

"How about three, at one station," said André.

"Bloody three, would you believe," said Ted. "A record. Last Wednesday the body of a boy in the dunes. Minus head. The fourth stiff in a series. We got one in a sewer. One beside a highway. One . . ."

"Come on, guys, enough." Mullet crushed the empty tin in his hand.

"You don't want to know the details? Capital W for weird."

"That's right, I don't wanna know."

André squinted at Mullet. "You worked the Station Strangler, not so?"

"Ja." Mullet sighed. "And a couple of others."

Ted waited, drumming his fingers on the gunwale, said, "So what're you working on now?"

"Extramarital."

"Jesus!" Ted exploded. "What a waste! What an absolute bloody waste." He reached forward, put a hand on Mullet's knee. "We need you back. Badly."

Mullet shook his head. "No ways. No ways in hell. I'm out of it."

"No one's out of it," said Ted, bouncing his fist on Mullet's knee. "There has to be a reason for three serials. It has to be society fucking up. Has to be the K factor I would say."

"That's hate speech." André grinned as he spoke. "Human rights guys will pull your nails out for that sort of stuff. You say K it's as bad as saying kaffir."

"So I'm a racist. Big bloody deal." Ted manoeuvred himself to the bows, unzipped and stood there, not so much as a dribble. Zipped, turning back to them. "Only time I can piss now is when I've sunk a six-pack." He looked up at the sky. "Thank you, Jesus."

Mullet was thinking maybe it would've been a better idea to have come out alone. On a perfect morning like this, the last thing he needed was this sort of bullshit.

Ted went for a Black Label in the cooler box. "Anyone?"

André said a Coke. Mullet said later.

"Cheers." Ted pulled the tab, took a long swallow, burping out the gas. "The Deputy Commissioner showed me this joke he got off the internet the other day. Chief Naidoo's got no candles for the darkies." He glanced from André to Mullet, sizing up his audience. Ted, the cop with more solveds in his file than anyone on Serious Crime. Ted the man. He took another slurp at the can.

"So it's about this rich Constantia guy who throws a party and invites all his buddies and neighbours. Living two mansions down is Philemon, affirmative action chief executive, he comes along too.

"The rich guy has the party around his pool, one of those black-bottom jobs that flows over the edge. So everyone's having a good time drinking, dancing, eating shrimps, oysters, lobster, cocktail abalone.

"When things are jumping the rich guy says, 'I've got a two-metre man-eating crocodile in my pool. Anyone with the balls to jump in I'll give a million bucks.'

"The words are hardly spoken when splash, Philemon's in the pool.

There's Philemon wrestling the croc, going kaffir: chokeholds, headbutts, thumb-jabs to the eyes, flipping it about like some kind of Japanese judo instructor. The water's churning and splashing everywhere. Philemon's raising hell.

"Finally Philemon strangles the croc, the croc floating there belly up.

"Slowly Philemon climbs out of the pool with everybody staring at him in disbelief.

"The rich guy says, 'Wow, Philemon, I reckon I owe you a million bucks.' 'No, that's alright. I don't want it,' says Philemon.

"The rich guy says, 'Hey, I have to give you something. You won the bet. How about half a million bucks then?' Philemon shakes his head, no.

"The host says, 'Come on, I insist on giving you something. That was amazing. How about a new Porsche, a Rolex, some stock options?' The brother still says no.

"The rich guy's confused. The Ks he knows, you offer them stock options they want the company. 'OK, Philemon,' he says, 'what do you want?' Philemon answers, 'Just give me the name of the bastard who pushed me in the pool!'"

Ted laughed. André and Mullet joining him.

"Billy Naidoo, hey. He thought it was a scream."

After the laughter they were silent. Ted leaned over the side, holding the beer can beneath the surface while a lace of bubbles streamed from it. When they stopped he let go. Mullet watched the can sinking, the sun flashing on it, a red semaphore.

To break the silence Ted said, "So where're these yellowtail of yours, Mr Mendes?"

Mullet put his hand in the water. "It's warm enough."

"Warm as piss," said Ted.

If you could piss, thought Mullet.

I I

Jim Woo and his assistant, Arno Loots, met the hunters at Cape Town International Airport and drove them out along the N2 to his estate in the winelands, Helderrand.

The approach was along a dirt road through the vineyards with Woo telling the men that the grapes were mostly cabernet sauvignon and merlot with some shiraz because the terroir was good for plumy full-bodied wines.

"This is a true connoisseur speaking," said one of the hunters, an Argentinian.

"You start dealing with wines, you start tasting heaven," Woo replied. "What do you say, Arno?"

Arno, at the wheel of the Syncro minibus, was thinking of a cold beer. "Each to his own. Mine's beer." He laughed. Heh, heh, heh, heh – as if someone had told him about laughter but he'd never actually heard it.

The men in the back laughed at the sound, unsure of this thin wiry guy. By the looks of him – ginger-haired with blond eyebrows, small eyes, blue lips, a freckled skin – sort of man was contrary for the hell of trouble. Had a handshake like a clutch of bones.

The road came to an avenue of oak trees, the Cape Dutch manor house a startling white at the end, maybe half a kilometre away. A sight as pretty as any Woo knew and got to his heart every time he saw it. The greatest loss would be giving up the estate.

"Some Dutchmen started making wine here in the late seventeenth century," he said, unable to resist a history lesson. "Called the estate Helderrand which Arno tells me means something like on the edge of paradise. Myself I think it is paradise."

They got to the house where four women dressed in jeans and halter tops waited on the stoep.

"Jesus, Jim," said the American, "where d'you find them?"

"Stunning, would you say?"

"Ev-e-ry-one."

"You will excuse me if I select the black lady first," said the German.

Arno went heh, heh, heh, heh.

"She's especially for you, my friend," said Woo. "Let them treat you. Enjoy."

Woo had converted the old slave quarters into luxury suites each with a Jacuzzi for guests to relax in after the long-haul flight.

"The day is yours," he told his guests. "If you wish to play golf, Arno will make the necessary arrangements. If you wish to spend the time here on the estate, make yourselves at home. We will have dinner at nine. I have arranged the hunt for after midnight."

12

Vincent Saldana dreamed that she was lying right there next to him. He leaned over and touched her, stroked the coolness of her back. He edged closer. She moved onto her side, shifting her buttocks into him, then reached back, her hand softly sliding down his stomach. He slipped a hand under her arm to grip her breasts and cupped one, resisting the urge to squeeze.

Vincent woke coughing. He had parrot-cage mouth with a taste of sick at the back of his throat.

He groaned. Jesus, Jesus, Jesus. Always he could get so close. Have her back for a moment. Have her again.

Amber. Five months dead and he couldn't bury her.

He got up, busting for a pee. His head beating, pounding like only another drink would still it. He stumbled down the corridor to the toilet and stood pissing into the bowl without closing the door. Nobody likely to be around this time of a Saturday morning. The only other office on the floor was rented by a photographer who never said anything that wasn't pure Neanderthal.

Vincent put one hand against the wall to steady himself, used the other to keep the flow going where it should. He had a vague idea maybe he'd hurled in the loo earlier. If so he must've pulled the chain. Pulled the chain! Jesus, one of the few toilets left in the world with a chain.

The phone started ringing before he'd finished: the tring-tring, tring-tring, tring-tring bouncing round his skull enough to make him squint. The phone going on and on and on. 7.30 a.m. Jesus, didn't they get the message this was a Saturday? He took a breath, stopped his water. Saying, "OK, OK. Give it a break."

He got back to the office and found the phone on the desk under a pizza box.

"Vincent Saldana," slurring the 's', dragging the second-last 'a'. Knowing he sounded pissed.

The voice came back: "Hey Vince!"

Bloody Mullet.

"Listen to me, Vince. Listen to me."

Vincent thought, I've got an option? Mullet going on and on about ring this chickaboo, Marina Welsh.

Jesus' sake, Vincent thinking. Mullet was so keen why didn't he bloody do it himself. "What about you?"

That got a peeved answer.

Fishing! The guy gets a prospective client he goes fishing. Leave it to Vince.

More yadda yadda yadda.

"Ja. I'll do it." Coming on stronger than he meant. More irked than he had reason to be. Mullet not listening to him, patronising him for a drunk. "I'll do it. Yeah, yeah, let it go." Slamming the receiver into its cradle before Mullet could say another word. Before he told him, Jesus, this is my time, I can do what I want in my time.

Let's form an agency, Mullet had said. Mendes & Saldana. It'll fly. Believe me. Mullet ever the optimist, dragging him out of the bar at the Kimberley after he'd taken the severance package. After he'd been drunk for five days straight. Six weeks after Amber's death. And not twenty-four consecutive hours in the intervening months he'd been sober.

Vincent sat down on the mattress, put his head in his hands. He wanted a beer but there was no beer in the fridge.

"This's an office, Vince. We're not keeping beer in the fridge," Mullet had said. Meaning not while you're sleeping here.

Four months he'd been sleeping there. Showering at his mother's or doing a splash wash in the basin down the corridor. His clothes were on hangers behind the door. Mullet never said a thing. Never looked like he was going to say a thing. Certainly not about the sleeping arrangements. About the booze yes, but not about where he slept.

Vincent pulled out a small Jack Daniel's he'd bought at the pub last night as an emergency. Now was an emergency. He uncapped it, took a good swallow, the liquor burning into his gut. Heaven would have been a beer to chase it, and simultaneously get rid of his thirst. The whiskey did nothing to ease the pain in his head, though it eased the pain in his heart and allowed him to lie down and forget about her.

For two hours he lay there, awake, staring at the ceiling, staring at the black behind his eyelids. Whiskey-numb.

When the phone rang he heard it distantly, at first unable to work out if it was in his head or for real. He sat up, reached for the cord, pulling the phone off the desk into his lap. While he fumbled to get the handset he could hear a woman's voice going, "Vincent Saldana? Is that Vincent Saldana?"

"Yes," he said, the word a dry rasp in his throat. He considered doing a quick oiling with a gulp of the Jack.

The voice said, "Have I got Mendes & Saldana?"

Vincent said, "I'm Saldana."

"Good," said the woman. "I spoke to your Mr Mendes last night. He said you'd phone me."

"Yeah," said Vincent, "that's right."

"I was next on the list?" said Marina Welsh.

Vincent picked up the bottle. "What's that?"

"You were going to phone me next?" said the woman, Vincent failing to hear the humour in her voice.

"I was gonna phone you," he said, taking a sip at the Jack.

"Of course," she said. "Am I disturbing your breakfast?"

Vincent put down the bottle and wiped his mouth. "Nah. It's fine."

"Look, I was referred to you and Mendes. I heard you were a major abalone buster in the Anti-Poaching Unit."

Vincent snorted.

"That's what I was told."

"Sure," said Vincent, wondering if he could take another swallow without her hearing.

"This is about abalone, Mr Saldana. I need to talk to you." Her voice was soft but firm. "How about I come round to your office? I could be there in fifteen, twenty minutes."

The suggestion brought him to his feet. Vincent gazed about the office: his mattress and sleeping bag, the stained pillow without a slip, the hangers of clothes, old newspapers, polystyrene cups, greasy takeaway packaging, fluff balls, dust, the stale smell of sweat, booze, grief.

"Aah," he said drawing out the sound, "aah, this is that urgent?"

"You could say."

"It wouldn't keep till this afternoon?"

Vincent heard her sigh. "I tell you what: do you know the Oyster Shack?"

He had to think about that. "At the Waterfront?"

"The very one. Say six o'clock?"

"Six is good," said Vincent, thinking how to stay sober till six. "How'll I know you?"

"You'll know me," she said. "I'm the one with black hair."

"No kidding." Black hair. Eyes had to be green. Uma Thurman in *Pulp Fiction*.

"Till then, Mr Saldana."

"Sure," said Vincent.

He put the phone down to take a swallow of the Jack. This would need fresh clothes and a shower. That voice. A helluva voice. The sort of voice it'd be a pleasure to wake up to. Vincent kicked a shoe across the room. Jesus. Picked up the phone, speed-dialled the corner shop for a double espresso and croissant. He took two more slugs at the Jack Daniel's and started pacing the office.

In came Mullet: Vince, maybe this is enough, guy. Know what I'm saying. Enough already.

To hell with you, Mendes. You know what I'm feeling? You know what it feels like? Hey? Do you? When your wife dies? You know about the ache? No. Then take a hike.

Vincent held up the bottle to check the level. It was down to a quarter.

Shit! He threw the bottle against the wall, whiskey and shards going everywhere. Up yours, Mendes.

The intercom buzzed. He pressed the button. "Yeah."

A voice said, "Double and cheese croissant, Mr Vincent."

"About bloody time." He pressed the lock release, heard the guy enter and went to wait for the delivery at the top of the stairs. The teenager came huffing up, winded after the three-floor climb.

"What took you so long?"

"It's Saturday, Mr Vince. A lotta custom today. Lotsa tourists."

The waiter looked at him, smelling the booze.

"Thanks," said Vincent, taking the mug and the croissant wrapped in a serviette. "Put it on my tab."

What he was grateful for was that he slept after the coffee. Four hours straight to wake in a sweat with the sun full on the mattress. Rolling out of the heat he caught the sourness of his BO. So much for the myth you couldn't smell yourself. Jesus, he stank worse than a goat. He had to shower. He still wanted a beer. If he was going to make the six o'clock meeting he had to move.

Vincent brushed his teeth at the basin as a concession to personal hygiene. It would make the beer taste awful but his teeth tasted worse. And they were furry. He glimpsed his face in the mirror: bulging eyes, too much stubble. He felt like shit, he looked like shit. His mother would be pleased to see him.

"Vlinclent, you stlink like a vlaglant" – he said at the mirror, taking the piss with her accent that hadn't changed in the forty years she'd lived in Cape Town. The thought of her grimacing, pulling away from his embrace, made him smile.

"It's a new deodorant, Ma. Macho for men."

To which she'd respond in her Mandarin dialect. A string of sound with maybe every fifth word intelligible to him. But he loved the lilting pitch of the language.

He went back to the office and the mess: Mendes & Saldana, what a joke! When he couldn't smell himself, all he could smell was whiskey. Mullet would love it.

"Hell, Vince, you gotta make the place honk like an alkie's den?"

Alkie. Mullet had called him that once. He'd got right into Mullet's face: "I am not an alcoholic."

"A guy who drinks at ten a.m. I call an alcoholic," Mullet had said.

"Bugger you, Mendes." Then he'd gone off on a serious bender and it was three days before Mullet found him.

Vincent shook his head to dislodge the memory, took his black leather bomber jacket, heading out the door. He bought a bottle of beer from the liquor store and drank it walking up Long Street.

The street was happening. Music blasting from cafés. The pavement tables full of backpacker crowds, girls showing belly and labelled knicker elastic, boys with wispy beards. They didn't even see him. The only people who noticed him were tourists, dawdling. He pushed past a couple and the guy shouted after him, "Take a bath, mate." Vincent half turned:

there was a short fella in pressed shorts to below his knees, ankle socks and sandals, paunch under a Big Five T-shirt, his dumpy wife in much the same without the socks. Both of them glaring at him. Vincent smiled and waved, crossed the intersection into Kloof Street.

After his father's fishing boat was lost at sea, his mother had opened a small Chinese restaurant, the Hot Wok, higher up Kloof. A five-table place that'd been a five-table place and takeaway most of his life. Widow and son moved into the flat upstairs. In those days against the law to be living in a white area, but no one complained.

His mother was the last person he wanted to see right now, but he needed the shower and a change of clothes.

He came through the restaurant stinking worse than earlier, shining with new sweat from the walk up the hill. His mother said, "Vlinclent, you stlink like a vlaglant."

He grinned at her. "It's a new deodorant, Ma. Macho for men."

"Go shower. Go shower," she said. "There are people eating."

The people eating were a couple his mother played mah-jong with, Chris and Hulan. They'd played mah-jong together for at least two decades. The couple greeted him. Chris saying, "How's the private dick business?"

"A wank," said Vincent.

"Vlinclent," shouted his mother, "your mouth" – but he was out the back door, crossing the tiny courtyard to the stairs that went to the flat above.

13

Later the three men fished a reef for musselcracker. They caught two and closer to the Point Mullet pulled a ten-kilo red stumpnose.

In the early afternoon Ted said, "That's it. No sense to this at all."

Mullet wasn't ready yet to be off the sea. "How about an arc back to Miller's?" It would take an hour more than a run along the coast.

"Forget the yellowtail."

"One last try."

"Yeah, yeah," said Ted. "You're the captain."

Four kilometres out Mullet saw the disturbance coming straight for them, a huge school powering close to the surface, beating up a maelstrom. Ted and André gazing at the mountains to leeward didn't notice until Mullet throttled back and they glanced round at him quizzically.

"You might wanna do some real fishing," said Mullet, gesturing ahead.

André shaded his eyes. "Christ!"

Ted whistled. "Will you look at that! We're gonna foul-hook them just casting into that lot."

Both men scrabbled for the rods knotted up with spinners.

Mullet clicked the engine to idle. They could hear the noise of the fish now: the sheeesch building to a drumming like rain on a corrugated-iron roof. André shouting "Whaaaa!" as the school engulfed them, spray getting in their eyes, the men casting blind.

Mullet felt the spinner smack into water and started reeling in. A fish took it the moment the line tightened. He struck, the hooks going into flesh, he knew it. He screamed with exhilaration, slipped the brake on the reel to stop the line shrieking and braced the play of the yellowtail on his forearms.

The fish kept coming past them, huge silvers on the hunt, whatever they were feeding on was in and among them. Mullet concentrated on the point where his line went into the sea. He could feel the boat turning, being dragged by the fish.

For three or four minutes they were in the chaos, each man held to his fish as his fish was to him. Then the school was past, the sound fading.

Ted laughed. "They're bloody pulling us."

The men grinned at one another, crowded in the bows, hyped on the action.

"What d'you say?" yelled Mullet.

"Amazing kind of wonderful," André yelled back.

"Hey-ya," howled Ted. "Mullet the nugget."

They played the fish for fifteen minutes, then brought them in one at a time, forty to fifty kilos each. Soon the yellowtail thumped in the bottom of the boat, giving them the hard eye. Mullet and Ted cracked beers in celebration, André took a Coke.

Ted clapped Mullet on the shoulder. "Well, aren't we the happy punters."

14

Was a Vincent renewed who appeared at the Oyster Shack at five to six. Clean jeans, a white golf shirt, no socks, loafers, black leather bag over his shoulder. All it contained was a notebook and ballpoint.

To look at him there wasn't a trace of last night's drunk in his face. No beard, skin as smooth as. A lithe guy easy on his feet. Since the beer he had walking to his ma's, no alcohol had washed his gullet as much as he'd fancied another ale and perhaps a chaser. He stood at the entrance glancing around for a black-haired woman. There were no black-haired women. The only single woman there had auburn hair. She sat at a table to the side facing the door, one hand keeping down the pages of a hard-cover, the other gently holding the stem of a wine glass. She didn't look up, the message Do Not Disturb writ large. He sat at the bar, ordered a sparkling mineral water. When he'd been served, he turned round to survey the patrons.

"Vincent Saldana?"

He hesitated, about to take a sip. "You haven't got black hair." He took in the strappy sundress, freckles on her shoulders, strong shoulder blades, the hint of her boobs under the softness of the dress.

"I lied."

"Why?"

She did something with her lips that brought a dimple to the corner of her mouth. "In case I decided I didn't like the look of you."

"You in the habit of doing that?"

"Not always."

"Only when you're wary?"

"Something like that."

"And why were you wary?"

"You can never tell. You might have been a sleazeball."

"You reckon I'm not?"

She nodded. "You look like a nice guy. Personable."

Vincent took the mouthful of water that had been interrupted, lots of bubbles fizzing around his teeth. It would have been better if they'd been bursts of wine. The waiter was looking at them. So was a couple in the corner.

"Are we going to discuss this thing across the restaurant or should I join you?" He didn't wait for her invitation, getting off the stool before he'd finished talking.

"Seems like you've taken it as read," she said as he sat down.

He held out his hand. "I'm Vincent Saldana. Mendes & Saldana."

She took his hand, both their hands cool and firm. They squeezed. "Do you want a proper drink?" she said.

"Nah," he said. "It's not a good idea. I've been drinking too much." Coming out with it just like that: smack, the honesty. It surprised him but what the hell.

She gave him the dimple. "Goes with the territory, doesn't it?"

"Yeah. I guess. Doesn't mean you don't have to watch it." He could hardly believe what he was saying, talking like Mullet sermonising on the booze devil.

She had closed the book and was looking at him, amusement on her lips. She had green eyes, he'd got that right.

Marina said, "You obviously know about abalone, Mr Saldana?"

"Vincent," he said.

"Why did you leave the cops, Vincent?" she said, not waiting for his answer to the first question.

Vincent swirled the lemon in his mineral water. "The same reason most guys leave, I guess. It gets to you. The violence. Dealing with it day after day." He flicked his eyes to her face; she was fastened on him. "Then there's the Service. It's in a mess. There's not much in the way of opportunity."

"No?" She sipped at the wine, her lips taking on a gloss.

"Too affirmative. If you're previously disadvantaged, you're smoking. I wasn't previously disadvantaged enough." He noticed a faint purplish imprint of her lower lip on the rim of the glass.

"Doing divorces and insurance frauds is better?"

Vincent shrugged. "For the time being."

"Meaning?"

"It's a start."

She smiled, just enough to show the edge of her teeth, white against the dark lipstick. A gap between the two front teeth that you could slide a knife blade through. "So here's something different."

Vincent rode back on the chair, lifting the front legs. "Let's hear it."

Marina paused a moment, running a finger around the rim of the wine glass, said, "Do you have a pen?"

Vincent fished his ballpoint out of the leather bag. She took it, drew a map of the southern Cape coastline on a serviette, hatching in a small area. "You know abalone are only found naturally off one section of the south-eastern coast?" She pointed at the marked region, not waiting for his response. "Well, we are cultivating abalone over here." She put an X on the West Coast, high up, some three hundred kilometres away from where the poaching took place. "Recently we had a robbery. The first time it's ever happened. Tanks and tanks cleared out."

Vincent nodded.

"We – my brother's the farmer – notified the police but they've been unable to track down the thieves. Our insurers paid out. However, they have instituted a huge excess should we be so unfortunate again." She glanced at Vincent. "My brother . . . how shall I put this . . . Let me say my brother is a peculiar individual. His approach is somewhat unorthodox. He believes he can control the situation. Personally, I think it's merely a matter of time before we're hit again."

"Who all's in the we?"

Marina took some wine.

"Me, a partner and my brother."

Vincent said, "A heist of cultivated abalone has to be organised by a syndicate. This wouldn't be small-time."

"I don't see how that would change things."

"Ms Welsh," he said, "people die in this business. You've heard of the abalone wars."

"Of course."

Vincent came forward, bracing his hands against the table. "What if we find your thieves? What then?"

Marina inclined her head. "You get paid."

"That's not what I mean."

"I know. However, what happens after you give us the information is for the cops to work out. We want to know who they are and the cops can't do that for us. They can't hang around waiting." She paused, gave him the full eyeball. "Look, there's been a guy snooping around. He pitched up and asked my brother for a job. My brother runs a tight ship employment-wise, he doesn't take on just anybody. He told the guy, no vacancies. But the guy lingers, he won't leave. He keeps pestering: can't he sweep the floors, do some painting, any odd jobs. David almost loses his temper trying to get rid of him. Then, hours later, five o'clock in the afternoon, David leaves the premises and there's the guy sitting on the side of the road. When David stops to find out why he's loitering, the guy runs into the veld." Marina clicked the pen's nib in and out. "Understandably, David feels the factory is being watched prior to another robbery." She put down the pen. "Also, my contacts say there's a job being organised. Maybe for early next week."

"Your contacts?"

"People I know."

She gave a smile that sent a jolt through Vincent. Jesus, he could kiss those lips.

To cover his thoughts he said, "We're not security."

"I know. I was thinking more along the lines of entrapment."

"Meaning?"

"We let the heist happen. You follow them. They take you to their leader."

"As simple as that?" Vincent glanced at the title of her book: *Dead Before Dying.* "If you've got it all worked out why do you need us?"

"Because stake-outs are your speciality."

"And all you want is the information."

"That's all."

They both looked down at the table as if the future were written there. Vincent was the first to speak. "The place's called?"

"Sea Farm."

He hadn't heard of it. "How long've you been cultivating?"

Marina counted back on the fingers of her left hand. "Five years."

He nodded.

"Mr Saldana. Vincent," she said. "I'd like you to come out and see the farm. Talk to my brother, meet Jim Woo, the other partner. We don't intend doing anything illegal. We simply want the evidence, the information. You're a cop. Ex-cop. You can read the situation. Is it small-timers, a once-off? Is it a racket moving in? As soon as we have that the cops can take over." She picked up the ballpoint and drew a dollar sign on the serviette. "I told your partner, Mr Mendes, we'll pay over the top."

Mullet had said, "Good rates." "You gotta do it."

Mullet was the bottom line. Vincent had no option. "Alright," he said.

Marina said, "Good." Nothing more. No relief, no thank you, just good. Then: "How about driving up tomorrow?"

"Sunday?"

"Sure. Do you mind working on a Sunday?"

"Sunday's fine," said Vincent, hearing the words, thinking, Jesus, he'd have to stay off the sauce. Saturday night was yawning wide.

"Good."

Marina got a cellphone from a backpack at her feet, keyed in a number. Vincent watched the flutter of her fingers. Maybe a day with a client as attractive as her wouldn't be a day wasted.

She spoke: "David, we're coming up tomorrow."

Listened.

"That's right. The sooner the better."

Listened.

"Early afternoon. I'll tell Woo?"

Listened.

"This's the way we're doing it."

She disconnected. "That's settled then." She finished her wine. "Tomorrow, Vincent. Let's say half nine outside the Castle."

He took her hand and her mouth did the dimple.

"I'll be there."

She dropped his hand, picked up the book. "Good."

As she left Vincent slid his eyes to her legs, the sundress swirling about her knees. She had shapely calves, her thighs would be strong.

The waiter brought him the bill.

15

Rae-Anne had done a make-over by the time Mullet got home.

"The reason you don't need a cleaning girl is because you've got one," she said as he came in the kitchen door holding forty-five kilos of fish by its yellow tail. Rae-Anne was at the sink drying the last of his plates and pots.

"Is that how you greet a fisherman?" he said.

Rae-Anne shook her head, laughing. "Pig-face. Maybe living together wouldn't be a good idea."

Mullet bounced the fish on the kitchen table. "Gimme a hug." Advancing on her.

"Oh no, you don't," said Rae-Anne, backing off, hobbling a little, the delicate way she moved that got to Mullet every time. "Firstly you stink. And secondly get that out of this clean kitchen." She pointed at the fish, then held out her hand to keep him away. "Out."

Mullet grabbed her wrist and pulled her to him, almost roughly, almost causing her to lose her balance as she locked against him. They went into a hard kiss, her tongue teasing him. Mullet thought, what if she were around all the time, would he get used to her? Take her for granted? It'd been four days since they'd last been together. The gaps were like having a lover not a wife.

Rae-Anne broke the kiss, tilting her head back to stare up at him, the laughter in her eyes. "You still stink."

Mullet let her go, turned to his fish. "So what d'you think? Not bad! And if it'd been Ted's way this beauty would be swimming free. All these years and he's still no feeling for the sea." He gripped the tail and gestured with his chin at the back stoep. "Bom-Bom here when you arrived?"

Rae-Anne nodded, keeping her thoughts to herself about being alone in the house with Bom-Bom skulking on the stoep.

"He pitched up before I went."

Rae-Anne ran a finger over the fish. The scales were coming loose. "You could've SMSed."

"He's harmless."

"So you keep saying."

Mullet caught the tone. "Come'n, doll, he's a street kid. With all the work you do with kids, why's he freak you?"

She shrugged, smiling at him. "Dunno." The difference was those kids were in schools, jails, reformatories, church halls. They weren't on the back stoep, staring at you, wordless, sealed into some scary world of their own. "I can't get to him, Mull."

"Makes two of us," said Mullet, going out to scale the fish.

Bom-Bom was curled on his bed facing the wall.

Mullet took the yellowtail to a makeshift sink and work surface and sharpened his knife against the whetstone. He rasped the blade over the fish, a silver shower spraying from the stroke.

The boy sat up, watching Mullet. Mullet glanced over. "You want to do this?" He held out the knife. The boy made no move either way.

"You stick around, you can have this grilled tomorrow," he said, wondering if the guy was deaf, what it was like not to hear a word people were saying at you. In some situations probably a bonus. Then again, you could never hear Neil Young. 'Horses in a Rainstorm.' The refrain starting in Mullet's head. "Have you ever . . ."

He worked steadily to the song: scaled, tailed, chopped off the head with two mallet blows to a broad-blade knife. For a moment felt a sadness that there was no cat rubbing against his legs, anticipating the head. He filleted the flesh off the bone in two long cuts, sliced off a kilo steak for his weed-client Elizabeth. Back indoors the smell was Rae-Anne's chicken breyani. Mullet was suddenly ravenous.

"Go wash," said Rae-Anne, as he dipped a spoon into the marinade. "And keep out of my food. By the time you're ready, it'll be." Mullet's ablutions being lengthy affairs that involved his fishing magazines, a Discman, sometimes a short pull of Durban poison.

They ate by candlelight at Rae-Anne's insistence that there had to be romance or what was it all about? Two people gobbling their food glued to the box was not her idea of the meaning of love. Meals were ritual. "When you've been through as many needle suppers as me, you'll understand this point," she'd said the first time she made a meal for him. Macaroni cheese. Second on his list of favourite foods after curry.

Mullet heaped on the sambals, going mostly for banana and the red chilli sauce. Rae-Anne as ever amazed at the heat he could take, watching him spooning out the relishes with gusto. He was not a bad-looking man. And it was good to watch him eat.

"With your hair blow-dried, in this light you look like Rod Stewart." She giggled.

"Because you can't see the acne scars," Mullet came back, sucking at a chicken bone. "Rod still rocks."

Rae-Anne laughed. "For a cop you've got a strange sense of humour."

"Ex-cop."

"Ex-cop. Still there aren't many cops ex or otherwise who take the piss out of themselves." Then again it had to be a guy with a strange sense of humour to fall for an ex-junkie with a peg leg.

Mullet cut some chicken, dipped it in the dhal, adding chilli. "Ted thinks I'm wasted."

"What? Not being a cop?"

"Uh huh."

"You did your time."

"For some guys it's for life."

"But not for Mullet Mendes!"

"No."

"So what is it for Mullet Mendes?"

Mullet glanced at her. She wasn't eating, was gazing at him intently. "What d'you mean?"

"Come on, Mull. You know."

He paused. "I've been thinking about it."

"And?"

"And what?"

"Exactly. And what?"

Mullet chewed, swallowed, his mouth burning. "I dunno yet."

Rae-Anne went back to her food, forking up rice with tomato and onion salad. Eventually she said, "Sometimes, you know, you've just gotta have faith. Believe that it'll work out." She toyed with another helping of rice. "It's like leaving the Force. That took faith. That you could make it."

Later, in bed, she sat astride him, keeping her balance centred on her good leg, his left hand clamped on her thigh above the amputation to steady her. She moved slowly, pausing occasionally for long moments of stillness.

They'd shared a joint, his eyes were closed, his mind nowhere. After a period of stillness her movements made his breath rasp.

Rae-Anne couldn't take her eyes from Mullet's face. She'd brought the candles through to the bedroom, put them either side the headboard. In their light he looked like he'd died and gone to heaven. Except a muscle twitched in his cheek in response to her pressure. He raised a hand and stroked her face, sliding his palm down her neck to the tip of her breast. She leaned forward, which was all it took to make him groan.

16

The dinner at Helderrand was lavish. The men in tuxedos, the women in black spaghetti-strap numbers. Woo was up and invincible after a line of grade-A charlie, solicitous as a moth, circling among his guests. He had drinks served on the stoep to get the best of a soft night.

At nine-thirty a bell tinkled for dinner. A starter of mussels in white wine followed by medallions of abalone on a rice bed with roasted peppers. A chocolate and whisky mousse to sweeten the palate. Bottles of plumy Fat Bastard shiraz to take it down. He brought out cigars, a Paul Cluver noble late harvest. When they were finished, Woo gave the nod. The way the women exited was pure Swiss finishing school.

The banter died.

Woo stood, leaning on the back of his chair and cut straight to the chase. "The deal's this," he said. "You are here for the ultimate hunt." He glanced round: the men nodding at him, rolling ash off their cigars, reaching for the wine. Woo lifted his hands from the back of the chair, held them up in the attitude of a preacher. "The terms are these: the trophy's worth twenty thousand US. The hunt's worth ten thousand each. You draw lots for who shoots first. If that guy misses, number two goes. If number two scores that is the end of the hunt. If he misses, number three goes. You get the picture." Woo glanced at the faces, none of the men were looking at him. "There is one trophy. Maybe you will see trophies scattering wildly, I'm telling you there is only one. That's the deal."

The men grunted acceptance.

"What about the trophy?" asked the Argentinian.

Woo took a swallow of wine. "I'll get it to you. Special courier service." He raised his glass in a toast. "To the hunt."

The men rose: "To the hunt."

"To the hunt!" Woo shouted.

"To the hunt!" they yelled back.

He had them now, the men knocking glasses, some breaking, wine spraying about.

"Where's it to be, Jim?" the American bellowed above the noise.

"In the dark streets of Cape Town city," said Woo.

17

Jim Woo sat at his desk in the winery tapping his pencil against the blotter. The hunt had gone off well enough, thanks to Arno. As so often when it came to the moment and the van doors slid open, the men went to pieces, bolts zinging every which way. Hadn't been for Arno's coup de grâce, number three would've lost his trophy. The bloody German. Woo smiled to himself. It was a pity really – it could have been such a good scheme.

But as with the rest of the businesses it was time to get out before the Brotherhood got too jumpy. This was the only smudge on his horizon: the brothers were wising up, why else had they summoned him? Probably they weren't going to kill him, merely threaten. Certainly it was worth taking the risk to find out how much time he had: weeks, days? A couple of weeks, he believed. The Brotherhood took their time getting to a decision, it was once they'd made a decision that things happened fast. But he was prepared. Sea Farm belonged to the bank. Helderrand belonged to the bank. The safari lodge belonged to the bank. The Brotherhood's venture capital had been washed clean and, thanks to Roger Oxford, awaited him on the Cayman Islands. All that remained was to sort out the pompous Roger Oxford. If only bitch Judith knew what was on the cards for her husband. The thought almost made Woo laugh out loud. As did his plans for Tommy Fortune. Put him back in touch with his old friend, Vincent Saldana.

Upstairs in the sitting room the huge grandfather bonged out the hour, the reverberation even loud in the cellar. Automatically Woo looked at his watch. He had told Tommy nine sharp, but the guy still had to push his button and make a statement: I'm Tommy, the main man, don't mess with me.

All the same Jim Woo wasn't irked. He liked it here in the cool depths of the cellar with its racks of wine, the barrels, the reed ceiling. He breathed in the smell of fermentation. The winery's door to the courtyard opened, Arno stuck his head in. "The goffel's just pulled up."

Woo stretched, rocked back in his leather chair. "About time."

Arno hesitated. "In case you wanna know, it's done."

Woo caught the set of his henchman's face. "Except?"

"Except the cops've been there."

"So?"

"So nothing. I'm telling you, that's all."

"This is not a big deal. In the scheme of things."

"Cops're cops."

Woo smiled. "You should know."

Arno shrugged.

"You still did as agreed?"

"Sure. Fits the profile."

Arno went heh, heh, heh, heh, and disappeared. Woo heard him say to Tommy Fortune, "You'd better get your arse in there."

Tommy Fortune said, "Fork you."

Arno's reply was indistinct but it made Tommy hiss. Woo watched him come into the cellar, standing there back-lit, peering into the gloom. "Mornings, mornings. Hello, Boss Jim."

In your face, up your nose, Tommy Fortune.

"In here." Woo switched on a desk light.

"I didn't see you," said Tommy, heading across the flagstones towards the little office. "Nice place, Boss Jim. Nice place, hey." He stopped in the doorway.

Woo indicated a chair. Tommy sat.

"This all your wine? I never been down here before."

Jim Woo steepled his fingers, rested his chin on their tips and examined Tommy Fortune sitting there in branded threads. Clothes he'd bought him. The Animal pants, the Cockfighter T-shirt, Gravis flip-flops. Even the Ray-Bans he stuck in his hair. Bought because it amused Woo to see Tommy and his pal Adonis strutting about, figuring themselves for the hippest gangsters on the streets.

Under the gaze Tommy jiggled himself lower in the chair.

"Tommy," said Woo, "sit up properly."

Tommy glanced at Woo, then pulled himself upright. He reached into his back pocket, brought out a crumpled pack of Marlboro.

Woo wagged a finger at him. "No smoking."

Tommy made a point of sniffing at the air. Air tinged with smoke.

"Cigars," Woo told him. "Cigars only."

Tommy slid his cigarettes back into his pocket.

Woo noticed Tommy's sulk and smiled. "Great gear, Tommy."

Tommy gave him a flash of emeralds. They sat in silence for a moment, Tommy fidgeting, shifting his eyes about. Woo's gaze never leaving his face.

Eventually Woo said, "I want you to do me favour."

For a moment Tommy paused. "Favour?"

"Another little robbery at Sea Farm."

Tommy frowned. "You want us to steal your perlemoen again?"

"Um hm. On Tuesday." Woo tapped his pen.

"The same as last time? That crazy big bastard won't be there?"

"The same as last time. On Tuesday Mr Welsh won't be there. Only this time you need a freeze truck and somewhere to hide it for a day or two, until I'm back."

Tommy clicked his fingers. "I can do that."

"Good. Shall we say twenty thousand?"

"Twenty thousand bucks!" Tommy spluttered. He'd been thinking he would try and push Woo to seven, maybe seven and a half. Twenty thou was major league. A sign Woo was taking him seriously. About bloody time.

"That's what it's worth to me," said Woo. "Just don't screw up."

"Nah. Never. No chance," said Tommy, leaning forward to reassure Woo.

Woo smiled. "So you're pleased with yourself, Tommy. You've got a big job. He ran his chair back, crossed his legs. "I see on the TV you got rid of the inspector. One down, one to go."

"I sorted the other one a long time back."

"You sorted his wife."

"Same thing."

"Not quite." Woo reached into a drawer and brought out a breath freshener. He squirted two short bursts into his mouth. "In my culture when we" – he paused – "settle a score, we kill our enemies face to face using blades. Not to stab but to slice." He put the freshener back into the drawer, slid it gently closed. "We razor through the skin, through the muscle while the betrayer runs screaming round our circle. Everywhere he turns someone stands with a blade to open him until he has to hold his guts in with his hands. It takes a long time to die this way. Sometimes so long the blades start slicing at his organs." Woo blew onto his palm and smelt the peppermint blowback. "What is the point of revenge if the dying man doesn't know why he is dying?"

Tommy said, "Same in my culture."

"I'm sure." Woo looked at his watch: half past nine. He stood up. "Our meeting is over, the day is yours." He walked Tommy to the door and went out with him into the courtyard. "Don't forget. Tuesday. Not tomorrow. Not Wednesday. Tuesday."

Tommy went two paces, half turned back. "When you gonna pay us, Mr Woo?"

"When you've done the job, Tommy. You got a problem with that?"

Up yours, Tommy muttered getting into his Beemer. Fork you Boss Woo. He swung the engine. Twenty thousand! Twenty thousand bucks! He laughed out loud even though Woo was watching him.

Woo waited until Tommy had driven off before turning back into the winery. The loose ends were being tied up. After the Taipei trip it would be Mr Jim Woo the multimillionaire of Grand Cayman, lounging on the beach, snorkelling along the reefs. The only work he would have to do was to keep his money cooking. What a pleasure!

Upstairs he joined the hunters on the stoep, all drinking champagne and orange juice from long-stem flutes, with the girls in attendance. The men hailed him their good mornings.

"Guys," Woo said, gesticulating at the sky. "You come in sunshine, you leave in sunshine. What a great country!" He took a flute from the breakfast table. "Hey, Arno," he called, "what about some movies?"

The men were easy today, chatty, pleased to be going home, even acting as Arno worked the video camera over them. They had got away with it. Thanks to Jim Woo who dared do things others dreamed about.

During brunch the American rose and tinkled a knife against an empty wine glass. The voices quietened. He glanced round the table, cleared his throat.

"Unaccustomed as I am . . ." piped in the German.

"Yeah, sure," said the American, breaking a smile, hesitating.

The German clucked his tongue. "You must write down the speech first, Gary, that way it is not embarrassing."

"What I'm gonna say," said the American, ignoring the interjection, "I'm gonna make short."

"This is good."

"What I'm gonna say is, hell, Jim, you're the ultimate, man. This's been one helluva safari." He raised his glass, toasted. "Jim."

The two other men stood, no one joking now. The girls sat, eyes on Woo. Arno got to his feet.

The American said, "Everyone have a full glass?"

The bottle of bubbly went round, those who needed, topping up.

"Jim."

They drank, no one putting his glass down until it was empty.

"OK," said Woo, getting up as the men sat. "I need to say this: there are not many men who have the take for what we did. That makes us different."

Another bottle of champagne was opened, the glasses filled.

Woo held up his hand. "Gentlemen, you've got three hours left, then Arno will take you to the airport. Enjoy."

"Salut to the girls," said the Argentinian. "They have been magnificent, no?"

Woo waited for the raucousness to fade. The pity of it was that he had not been able to develop the concept. After four safaris word had yet to get out. Eventually, he would have had hunters queuing up for the ultimate hunt. Forget the big five. This would have drawn them out of their clubs and lodges. He could have twinned it with a big-game safari operation and made a killing. Ha, ha!

"You are not able to see us off?" asked the German.

Woo shook his head. "Business up the coast. You don't want to know." Everyone laughed. "But like I said, enjoy!"

"You gotta learn to take time out," the American quipped, clasping his hands behind his head, tilting back in his chair: the picture of the executive unstressed.

"There you go," said Woo. "What can I say?" He hushed the table with a patting motion of his left hand. When they were still said, "To the hunt." Paused, raising his glass, glancing at each one of the men, each one of them meeting his eyes. "To the hunters."

18

Marina Welsh was there before him, leaning against a cannon – shades pushed into her hair, T-shirt not quite reaching her hipster jeans, her feet in thongs. Looking lovely. The Castle behind her, huge blue sky, the red Z parked to the side, top down. It could have been a set-up for a car shoot. Get the mountain, get the gulls, get the empty parade ground, the city white and quiet. Get the babe. The babe pushing mid-thirties but no other word for her.

Jesus! Vincent thought, pulling his rust-bucket Corolla behind the roadster. The broad and the Beemer.

"Maybe we should leave that somewhere," Marina said, coming up to stand at his side window. "Maybe we should take one car." She did the thing with her mouth that was so alluring.

Vincent grinned. Was this for real?

"Sure," he said.

She indicated the parade ground. "It'll be safe enough. No one's going to want it." Said with a smile.

Vincent wasn't about to take offence anyhow. What he really wanted to do was lick her belly button, this piece of anatomy being right at eye level. Probably no more than forty centimetres from his tongue.

He parked his car beneath some trees and hoped it would still be there when he got back. What he was glad about was that he'd spent the night watching TV with his mother. Enforced sobriety. All the tablets he'd swallowed had taken the shake out of his hands, relieved his headache.

The car was cute. Marina cute at the wheel, wearing a white peak cap.

"Are you rich?" he asked getting in.

"An inheritance," he was told. "From my husband."

She drove off, the engine a subdued growl. Vincent interpreted her remark as acrimonious divorce.

"Your hubby a hairdresser?" he asked, the Z3 having that sort of reputation, not expecting Marina to nod, 'Yup' – a trace of tension about her mouth.

"A whole chain of stores across the country. You know Snip? They were his."

"He sold out?"

"Taken out last November. Hijacked and shot in our driveway. With the insurance I paid off the car. He'd have liked that."

"Jesus," Vincent said. "Christ." The way she told it, no niceties.

"Here we go," she shouted, taking the on-ramp to Eastern Boulevard, accelerating. Vincent thankful to have the drive noise end the conversation.

Five months ago, Vincent worked out. The same month Amber was killed. As they went round Hospital Bend nearly said, this is where my wife died, but he didn't. There was something bittersweet about Amber ghosting in his head and this warm presence of another woman alongside him.

For two hours they powered up the coast road, the wind in their hair. On the rises the sea was visible off to the left, sparkling. The drive ended sooner than Vincent wanted.

The gate at the entrance to Sea Farm was open.

Vincent said, "Your brother's not the worrying kind."

She laughed. "My brother's world is not quite the same as ours. Great abalone farmer, no sense of security."

They drove along a gravel road for a kilometre to a huddle of buildings on a rocky promontory. From the look of it, an old farmhouse and some sheds, surrounded by a fence that hadn't been erected with much expertise. Dogs came bounding at them: a Rottie, a Great Dane, two frantic Jack Russells.

A big man appeared on the stoep. Jesus beard, sandy hair. Huge arms. Weathered suntanned skin. Dressed in tatty shorts and an old collared shirt, the sleeves rolled. He came up and hugged his sister.

"David Welsh," he said, crushing Vincent's hand.

"That creep going to be here?" he asked Marina.

She said, "I guess so, this afternoon." To Vincent she explained, "He's referring to our partner, Jim Woo. Major slimeball. On the other hand, without him, we'd be nowhere. We've got to remember where the bucks came from." Marina grimaced. "So what have you got us for brunch, Dave? Wholewheat bread? Mussels? Oysters? Crumbed abalone steaks? A cold chardonnay? We're starved."

David snorted. "Hey, you know me . . ."

"David," said Marina. "It's amazing you're the size you are. What do you eat?" She popped the boot on the Z3 and hauled out a cooler box. "At least you've got the abalone?"

"By the ton." David turned to Vincent. "Want to down a beer while we're waiting?"

Vincent hesitated.

"Do something useful like show him the sheds," said Marina, hefting the cooler box. "While I do the girl thing."

The size of the main sheds surprised Vincent. From the approach the place looked Mickey Mouse. Even nearing the outbuildings the sheds weren't visible. Whoever had pulled the heist knew a thing or two.

Sheds was a misnomer, warehouses was a more accurate description.

Vincent whistled.

"Cunning, hey," said David. "A slight depression hides them completely from the house. If you didn't know they were here, you wouldn't know they were here."

They went down to the first one, the dogs following. David slid open the door along its track and stood back for Vincent to enter first. Vincent walked into rows of blue tanks, about twenty of them, with pumps bubbling air through the water. He did a quick scope: sloping corrugated-iron roof with skylights of pale plastic. Some sort of corrugated-iron sheeting used for the walls, painted with wave patterns. Like why would you bother with decoration? Only the one door.

"Five hundred square metres," said David. "What we've got here is the nursery."

"Does the door lock?" asked Vincent.

"Oh yeah," said David. "Last time I tried."

He led Vincent to a tank.

"Fellas you're looking at in there are your juveniles. We grow them until they're about the size of a thumbnail. Then plop them into holding tanks. Lots of air, lots of kelp to feed on, six months later out into the sea they go. As you know abalone's not a great wanderer, fastens onto a rock that's where he's going to spend his life, more or less. Seven years down the line we scoop them out, fly them off to feed the dragon."

"How much was stolen?"

David pulled a hand over his beard. "Sixteen thousand cocktails."

"Someone knew what he was doing."

"Dead right. The tenderest little numbers. A major delicacy in the East." David trailed his hand through the water in a tank, testing the temperature. "You're going to steal them, you better have airfreight lined up. You want them straight into ice, and max twenty-four, thirty-six hours onto the tables." He flipped his hand to dry it. "That's the schedule we work to, but we're geared. Twice a month we fly to Taipei. Next consignment's in ten days."

"You gonna make it?"

"Just. The following one's going to be down. That's when the bitching'll start. These guys place an order, they want it met."

Vincent stared into the tank. Crowds of cocktails. All the same, getting sixteen thousand must've taken a few hours.

"You heard nothing? The dogs didn't bark?"

"I wasn't here at all that night."

Vincent reckoned it had to be nooky. "This happen often? You're away?"

"Every Tuesday. Every Friday. Sometimes in-between."

"But Tuesday and Friday are set dates?"

David nodded. "My time off."

Vincent didn't respond but tried to imagine where this guy would be off to in the middle of nowhere.

David said, "I know what you're thinking. Someone's been watching. Gives me the shits. There was this guy round here last week I reckoned was checking us out."

"Marina said."

"I told him I caught him anywhere near here I'd bring out the whip."

He would too, Vincent thought. Said, "Or it's staff?"

"Two guys. Local guys. That's all the staff I've got."

"Even so?"

"Nah. I can't see it."

"Anyone else in on this?"

"A marine biologist. Comes by once a month to check out the babies."

"Brings us back to the guy last week," said Vincent. "Nothing subtle about him."

They went outside. "You want to see the rest of the stuff?"

"Whatever there is."

He got shown the packing sheds, the cleaning tanks for the cocktail abalone, the conditioning room, settlement shed, larvae room, weaning station. Also the workshop and garages, the generator. A big operation. An operation this size needed security, given the abalone wars. What Vincent couldn't understand was why they didn't have any?

David shrugged. "I look the paranoid type? The whole country's walled, fenced, spiked. Live like that? No way."

Marina had laid the table on the stoep. Even put some snips of honeysuckle in a jar as decoration. A spread of seed bread, pâtés, olives, salad, seafood, including half a dozen fried cocktail abalone.

"Awesome," said David, sitting down to it. "Not brunch anymore. More like lunch."

"Don't wait for the guest," said Marina as her brother hit the olives, fingered a cherry tomato from the bowl of salad. To Vincent: "Forgive him. He was brought up with manners. Something happened along the way." She indicated the bottle in a plastic bucket filled with ice. "Glass of wine?"

Vincent caught himself about to say yes. Wine would ease the pain starting behind his eyes. Wine would have steadied the world. One glass wouldn't be a catastrophe. Instead he said, "Mineral water'd be good." She handed him a bottle.

"There's beer," said David through a mouthful of abalone, "if you'd rather." He got up. "I'd rather."

Vincent shook his head, no thanks.

"Impressed with what you saw?" Marina poured herself some chardonnay.

Vincent made a fist, popped an olive pit into the curl of his forefinger and thumb. "With the farming, yeah." He flicked the pit into the sand and dunegrass that was the garden.

"But you're wondering why there's no security?"

"Yes."

"Strange you should say that."

She waited until her brother returned.

"So how d'you think they got in, the robbers?" She said it so deadpan Vincent had to glance at her.

"Marina," said David, "we don't have to go there again."

"No," she came back, "then soon as this is done you're going to lock the doors. Put up a security fence. Employ guards. Get a radio hook-up to the cops or a security company or even a goddamned neighbour."

She took a swallow of the wine. The men concentrated on their food. For a while they ate in silence.

Vincent inventoried the stoep: the Jack Russells on a couch, the Great Dane and the Rottweiler sprawled asleep. Sea debris used as decor: trawl floats and anchors, driftwood, whale bones, shells hanging as mobiles. And beyond: the sheen of heat in the dunegrass, kelp heaps along the tideline, the sea hardly breathing. You could see why David wasn't getting the message. The message was about the end of his paradise. Vincent felt her glare.

"They will come back. When they do, your job begins."

He kept his eyes down. "Why don't you put in security? It would be the simplest."

"I told you," she said. "We want these guys first. Then we get security. Despite David."

Her brother stayed with his food, barely nodding.

"Another thing," said Vincent chewing hard at the cocktail abalone, unsure why this went down big in the East. "How much've you got out there in the sea?"

David lifted his head. "Maybe sixty thousand. Thirty thousand harvestable or as near as. The rest juveniles across the age spectrum."

Vincent cleared abalone from his mouth with a swig of water, wishing it were booze. "That size stock sitting out there, what's to stop the poachers? Or fishermen?"

Marina laughed. "Good question."

David said, "The law."

"Of course," said Marina, "like it's working on the east coast. If you had television, David, you'd have seen an inspector burned to death by a mob. Ordinary fisherfolk doused him with petrol and set him alight. So much for the law."

"It's too far for the poachers."

"Wasn't too far for someone."

"OK, OK." David pushed back his chair. "I said go ahead didn't I?" He finished his beer. "I've gotta check the tanks."

Marina and Vincent watched him walk across to the outbuildings, the dogs following.

She sighed. "What do I do about him? You can't imagine what it took to get him to see you. To him it's a small robbery. No big deal. Some guys chancing their luck. He wasn't even going to tell our partner. What for? That's not the attitude, David, I told him. Not the attitude at all, especially with my money tied up. Now his ego's smarting." She rose. "Would you like tea, coffee?"

"Tea thanks," said Vincent, eyes on her backside as she headed for the kitchen. She had a really sweet arse. But that aside, the set-up was crazy. That he should sit out here for a couple of days waiting for something that might not happen? And that they would pay him for it. This was strange.

When Marina came back with a pot of tea, Vincent said, "Tell me about Jim Woo."

She gave the tea five stirs clockwise, five anti-clockwise. Said, "He came out of the blue. Shortly after David started the farm, a magazine ran a piece on him. It was a crazy idea then. This wild-looking man who used to be a diamond diver living by himself on the wild West Coast, growing abalone. It made a good story and the pictures took the mickey a bit."

She poured tea into mugs.

"Sugar? Milk?"

He shook his head. She shook out a Canderel.

"Anyhow, about a month after the article was published Jim Woo appeared. He'd tracked David down via the magazine and came out here to see the operation. A few days later he phoned back to say he was interested in investing. He talked about increasing production, erecting more sheds, adding tanks, bringing in pumps and filters, you name it. David heard him out but this wasn't his idea of Sea Farm at all. Not that Woo was pushy. He left matters for a week and then got in touch with David again. David said, thanks for the offer but no thanks. Woo asked why and David gave him the I don't need the big time, because that means labour and labour means people and people have problems. They get drunk, they beat their wives, abuse their kids, no thank you. To which Woo says, the trick about abalone farming is to mechanise. The only time you need labour is for harvesting from the tanks and the sea. A few well-trained staff would do it."

Marina sipped at her tea.

"He was astute enough to realise David's priorities. Money doesn't talk to my brother, what speaks to him is a way of life. The rest, as they say, is history."

Vincent put his feet up on the stoep railing.

"And your investment?"

"My investment?" She toyed with the teaspoon in the sugar bowl. "David arranged for me to meet Jim Woo. I didn't like him, but so what. In order to prevent Woo getting a complete hold financially I took out a second bond on my house and sank the money into Sea Farm. That's how I became a partner."

"You and your husband?"

"At the time I wasn't married."

Vincent let the pause ride, waiting for her to continue. Into the silence he said, "Obviously things worked out?"

"Like a dream. Woo put in the promised capital, opened markets in the East, set up the logistics, the prices sky-rocketed, the money came pouring in."

"Didn't change your idea of him though?"

She shook her head, the sun catching in the auburn of her hair. "Not one little bit."

"Why?"

She pointed at dust swirling up from the dirt road. "When you meet him you'll see why."

19

Rae-Anne had on a red one-piece cozzie that did it for Mullet. Showed off her body like it was encased in latex, almost better than seeing her naked. He kept glancing at her, the way he would a pretty chick on the beach. Furtive. Covert.

Come'n, guy, he said to himself, she's your bird. You can look. Still was too embarrassed to do it blatantly.

She lay on a white plastic lounger under an umbrella, a *Sunday Times* spread about her. He stood at the Weber, fillets of yellowtail sizzling over the coals.

All Mullet wore was a khaki broad-brim hat and surfer's baggies, his stomach bulging slightly over the drawstring knot. The late-afternoon sun came down warm on his back.

"Mull," she said, without raising her eyes from the paper, "you're looking guilty."

"Me?" Mullet's voice hit a squeak.

"See what I mean." She moved her shades down her nose, stared over them at him.

Mullet gave his attention to the fish, flipped the fillets to reveal the browning underside seared with parallel black lines by the grill, basted them with a garlic and chilli sauce.

"You want me to take my costume off?"

"Heck no." Mullet kept his back to her, applied more sauce to the fish with a brush. "Why d'you say that?"

"On account of what I can see," she teased, shifting her stump leg, the prosthesis on the ground beside her. She laughed, her light tinkle laughter. "You're embarrassed. Mullet Mendes you're actually embarrassed. Hey, Mull, turn round. Go on!"

Mullet didn't.

She gave the tinkle laugh again. "You're a love. Eighteen months on. The guy's hit forty, he's still bulging the fabric at the sight of his bird. Wow!"

Mullet had to grin, but kept that from her too.

Rae-Anne pushed the shades back up her nose. "Just don't get too close to the fire, doll, you'll singe your baggies."

Mullet heard the newspaper crack as she folded pages.

"We moved in together you wouldn't have these problems cooking fish."

That was just it, thought Mullet. You saw each other every day where'd be the lust? The magic. Tonight she'd go home, what he'd be left with was her absence. A longing. How much sweeter could it be?

When the fish was done he served it with a salad, taking a plateful over to Bom-Bom on the stoep. The boy seemed asleep, lying on his bed facing the wall. Mullet touched him on the shoulder but he didn't respond. Nor to the plate being wafted under his nose.

"You want it, it's on the floor. I was you I'd eat it before the ants do." Useless to say it except Mullet felt he had to say something. The guy might not be a talker, he still had to know you talked to him. You stopped doing that it was like saying he didn't exist.

"He give you the vaguest of thank-yous?" Rae-Anne wanted to know when Mullet sat down beside her on the lounger.

"You know him," said Mullet, cutting into his fish, the flesh succulent brown, the outside crisp, charred a shade off black the way he liked it. He tasted a forkful. Chewed, swallowed. Reached for his glass of stein to chase it. "What a chef!"

"You've got it," said Rae-Anne leaning forward to clink glasses. Even under her tan Mullet could see the needle scars marching up the inside of her arm.

They ate hungrily.

Rae-Anne said, "You've got to do something about him, Mull."

"You think?" Mullet smeared juice across his chin.

"Stop him from coming here. Stop letting him sleep on the stoep."

"He's a kid."

"His body's small, I'll give you. The part he showed me belongs to a thirteen-, fourteen-year-old."

Mullet shot her a glance. "He flashed you?"

"Earlier. I went in to get sunscreen, on my way out he gives me Mr One Eye. Pulls the blanket down so I can see his boner."

Mullet groaned. "Aah shit." He ate a mouthful but the taste had gone. "Why didn't you say something?"

"I did. I stopped and shook my finger at him."

"He covered up?"

"Slowly. The look on his face wasn't good, though."

Mullet put his plate aside, stood. "He goes right now."

"No." Rae-Anne reached for his hand. "No, you do it when I'm not here."

He sat down again, picked up his plate, moved food about.

"Why'd he have to choose today? This day of all days. How many days are there like this, he has to pick it? Jesus! You do something good, the kid turns round and bites your hand."

"With some kids that's the way it is," said Rae-Anne. "There's nothing you can do for them."

Mullet downed his wine in a single swallow, refilled both their glasses.

"You can see it in their faces. I see it in his."

"What?"

"Evil, Mull. Evil."

Mullet's cellphone rang, vibrating in the pocket of his baggies. For five rings he ignored it, then hauled it out. Judith Oxford. He sighed. "This is all I need." Thumbed her on. "Mendes."

"I'm sorry to disturb your Sunday, Mr Mendes . . . Mullet . . . but my husband is about to go out, ostensibly to his office. At least that's where he says he's going."

"Aah, we agreed . . ." Mullet tried to put in.

"Yes, yes, I know," she said, not letting him finish. "No weekend work."

"No weekend work," Mullet echoed her.

She paused.

"I've changed my mind. I'll double your rates."

Mullet grimaced at Rae-Anne. She got the drift, raised her eyebrows: no chance now of what had been on offer earlier. If they lived together it wouldn't be an issue. Another reason to say yes. Mullet sensed what was going through her mind. On the other hand a couple or three grand would be handy.

"Mr Mendes?"

"Right then," said Mullet, keeping his gaze on Rae-Anne. She had her eyes down.

"He's in the shower," said Judith Oxford. "He'll probably leave in twenty minutes."

"I'll revert," said Mullet, thumbed her off. He pocketed the phone. "What you're gonna tell me is if we're shacked up this wouldn't matter."

"I was," she said. "But we aren't, so it does."

20

Vincent realised right away what irked Marina, Woo was smooth. Sat there twirling his sunglasses, listening, poker-faced. His car keys and cellphone on the table, some sort of statement of ownership. No way to read the guy. When Vincent finished his Mendes & Saldana spiel Woo said, "Impressive, Mr Saldana." He turned to Marina. "A good choice."

Vincent saw Marina's fist tighten. This was how Woo worked her up, going for the patronising.

"You understand what we want?"

"Surveillance. Investigation."

Woo stopped his sunglasses mid-twirl and pointed them at him. "Surveillance. That's all, Mr Saldana. No matter how long it takes." Woo looked at David. "You've a spare room for him?"

David nodded.

"Excellent." Woo put his sunglasses on so he could examine the half-caste. In a Mandarin dialect he asked Vincent where his mother had come from.

Vincent said, "What's that?"

Woo said, "I asked where your mother was from?"

"China," said Vincent. "Yours?"

Woo smiled, supercilious behind the shades.

"Yang Ming Shan. Taipei. Taiwan. The rightful government of China."

"That so?"

Woo cut the smile, lifted his cellphone and car keys from the table. "Business calls. I must go." He stood. "This is a highly profitable venture for me, Mr Saldana. For us. We don't want small-time gangsters fucking it up. Know what I'm saying?"

"Sure," said Vincent.

"What I'm saying is, we wouldn't want it to happen a third time." Woo glanced at Marina. She kept her gaze on the horizon. David hoisted himself slowly out of his chair. "I'm pleased we met, Mr Saldana. I should add that your reputation preceded you. From your stint in the Anti-Poaching Unit."

Vincent frowned, wondering what he'd heard.

"A tough nut, they call you."

Woo stepped off the stoep, turned back to them: "I'm out of town for a few days. Let's hope by the time I'm back this is sorted out."

"The word is it's going to be soon," said Marina.

Woo headed for his car. He opened the door, paused before he got in. "You should learn the language, Mr Saldana. It's part of your heritage."

21

What was different about Sea Street was there'd been a sea change: street kids in many of the doorways. Filth in the gutters. Fast-food boxes, chip packets, bottles, glue dispensers littered about. Still no other cars parked at the curb, but this sense of being watched.

Mullet cruised the length of the street, came back, did it again. Decided to pull onto the pavement a block down from the entrance to Oxford's parking garage. In a street this quiet you didn't get anything more obvious than a lone car. If Oxford was the paranoid type he might've factored in that his wife had him tailed.

Problem was, was Oxford up there or still to come? Or had he gone some place else? Mullet toyed with this. Maybe the best was to get confirmation via Judith. Get her to ring him. The man was her hubby after all.

He killed the Subaru's engine. Counted one, two, three, four, five. At six the shadow of a doorway released two kids. Images of Bom-Bom. They approached quickly, mouthing at him. The one leant against the bonnet, the other knocked on the side window.

Mullet pressed the window button. Let the window go all the way down.

The kid said, "Money for bread?"

The kid on the bonnet had a bicycle spoke, sharpened both ends. He tapped this against the bodywork.

Mullet said, "Tell your friend, stop that or I put it through his ear."

The kid did. The other kid grinned, held the spoke up for Mullet to understand the points.

Mullet said, "You see a car go into that garage?" – he indicated up the street.

The kid nodded.

"What sort?"

"Pajero 4x4."

Street kids knew their cars. You wanted eyes on a street you paid a street kid. Mullet peeled a brown twenty from a roll he stored in the pouch of the door, held it between his fingers. "For you and your pal." The kid made a grab for it. Mullet gripped his arm. "You see the gun?" The Astra was in the tray behind the gear shift. The kid nodded. "Then scram." The kid took the money and belted, Spokes hot after him.

Mullet settled in his seat, got Neil Young into the CD player. *Harvest.* Good stake-out tunes.

Come the second track he considered phoning Rae-Anne. Been a less than perfect end to their Sunday, the girl saying to him as she left, "You've gotta get your life sorted, Mull. Really."

Really? Maybe.

He tapped his cellphone against the steering wheel, the same rhythm Spokes had played. Thought, right then.

Before he could dial there was Roger Oxford in his Pajero 4x4 rolling into Sea Street, heading up a block, going right to Buitengracht. Same as before.

Oxford got a parking space outside the News Café. As he approached a car pulled out and he reversed in.

Three cars back in the traffic Mullet cursed. He came up parallel as Oxford remote-locked his vehicle. Passed him. In the rear-view saw his subject heading for the café. Jaunty. Not a care in the world.

Great one, Mullet. Sunday rates to watch a guy drink coffee in the twilight hours. You took a single table there too the question was: would he think, hey, you're the guy followed me into La Perla Friday night? Answer: odds on unlikely.

Mullet found a parking space in a back street five hundred metres on. This sort of hour, this sort of day, hot and still, the beautiful people were out being beautiful. Being seen. Trawling the street in their top-down coupés, calling to their friends at the pavement cafés. Marimba bands keeping the jive. He pushed through the knots of people lingering on the corners. There was Roger Oxford and Friday's young bird at an outside table. Blatant in-your-face chutzpah. The girl dressed like she'd stepped out of karate class. Miss Kill Bill herself.

Mullet went up the steps fast, straight into the café. From what he could tell the guy didn't even bother with a casual glance as he passed. Not in the least distracted from his adoration of the bint.

Inside was hot, pungent with coffee. He took a table at the window where he could look right at them through the blinds. Perfect. What wasn't so perfect was the waiter wanted a coffee order.

Mullet wavered, went for American, the least offensive choice. He could whiten it, pile in sugar cubes.

When he got his attention back to Roger Oxford, he saw the girl circle an arm round the guy's shoulders and hug him. A short squeeze, then they separated, the girl talking a streak.

Because of her get-up definitely not a whore, Mullet decided. Had to be an affair. Yeah, the sugar daddy type of thing. Which was going to make it a whole lot more difficult for wifey Judith to accept. The chick was young enough to be Roger the Dodger's daughter. Except she was chinkified à la Vincent. Some slit to the eye, really fetching. The shape of her face, delicate. The whole of her fine-boned like a bird. Small boobies probably loose in the killer outfit. You had to give it to Roger, he could pull the girls, Judith being no slag in the beauty stakes herself.

Mullet's coffee arrived, he doctored it. Considered again whether he should phone Rae-Anne. Outside neither party seemed in any hurry. They'd ordered another round of drinks, a side order of chocolate cake. Roger had a mouthful, the babe feeding it into his face. But that was all, she took the rest without hesitation. A chick after his own heart, Mullet thought. Food as foreplay. Which brought him back to Rae-Anne.

He reached for his cell as it started ringing. Vincent.

"Hey, Vince."

Vincent said, "Listen, Mullet, listen to sweetness." What Mullet heard was wind howl. "You hear that?"

"The wind?"

"The engine growl."

"What engine growl?"

"Z3, my man. Beemer Z3."

Mullet thought, Vincent on a drunk. The pitch of his voice, he was well out of it.

Mullet said, "You changing careers?"

"What d'you mean?"

"Hairdresser car, Vince. Cutesy."

Vincent snorted back something Mullet didn't catch.

"Where are you any rate?"

"Driving this babe, one hundred and sixty on the clock as we speak."

Mullet could hardly make him out above the wind noise. What he did hear was a woman's laughter. He clicked on a scenario: Vincent had picked up a woman in a bar, they were off their faces, fooling in a car somewhere.

"You're kidding me?"

"It's our client. Marina Welsh."

Another scenario: Vincent had gone out to assess the client's problem. He was drunk. The client was drunk. They were fooling in a car somewhere.

This was a worse scenario than the first one.

Mullet said slowly, "Vince, what's happening?"

He heard laughter. Vincent's and the woman's.

"Vince, where are you?"

More laughter but the wind howl was lessening.

"Hang in there, I'm stopping," Vincent said.

The ambient quietened, Mullet could hear the car's engine.

Vincent said, "You want to speak to our new client?"

Before he could respond Marina said, "Mr Mendes, your partner exudes confidence. I like him. We have a deal."

"Right then," said Mullet, pleased to hear she sounded sober.

"We'll meet tomorrow."

Vincent came on again. "The Hun's won, the Jap's crap," he said, disconnecting.

Brilliant line, thought Mullet, if you knew what it meant.

Two pluses: a new job and Vincent wasn't drunk.

Outside his subjects were two thirds down on their drinks, the chocolate cake a memory in crumbs. What he needed was photies. Judith Oxford's "documentary proof", "explicit photographs". This was not the sort of opportunity you could miss.

Mullet paid for his coffee, asked the waiter if he minded taking a happy snap of him outside. The waiter said no problem.

"I'm on holiday," said Mullet. "I need a bit of atmosphere, you know, to show people at home. Glitzy Cape Town."

The waiter said no problem.

"A long shot maybe down the patio taking in the patrons," said Mullet. "Me to one side."

No problem, said the waiter.

Mullet handed him an Instamatic, the waiter obliged. Then Mullet insisted he take one of the waiter. Roger and his piece were nicely framed, amused by the tourist's antics.

Mullet nodded thanks all round, told the waiter no problem, he'd send him a print.

Another half an hour Mullet had to wait before Oxford made a move. He kissed the girl goodbye: air kisses left cheek, right cheek, left cheek. For a moment he held her hand, standing, looking at her. Then he was down the steps zapping the remote lock on his drive. She stayed at the table watching. As he pulled into the traffic he raised a hand, she waved back, smiling.

Some affair! Takes her to dinner on Friday, buys her two toots on Sunday. Not exactly your major sex scandal.

Mullet followed Oxford out of town and into the winelands. He popped a mint chew. He couldn't see his client getting all fired up by the photographs. What sort of leverage would that get her? Really. In the real world. Rich guys screwed around all the time. Not that Oxford had done this yet with the Chinese chick.

Up ahead Oxford in his Pajero took an off-ramp. At the intersection went right, the road narrowing between vineyards.

Mullet followed, musing on Judith, fantasising. How would she ride his case? He couldn't imagine her doing subtle. Not with the sort of photies she wanted. But he could see her suggesting the pictures might get a wider viewing. Like among the guy's clientele. He shook his head. Not the sort of woman you wanted to cross.

Oxford took another right through a gate onto a dirt road, he was three hundred metres down the track when Mullet passed the farm entrance. He eased to the hard shoulder. A board said the estate was called Helderrand. A phone number beneath the name.

Mullet waited until Oxford's 4x4 disappeared into the trees around the manor, then dialled. A male voice said, "Helderrand."

"Could I speak to . . ." Mullet paused as if reading the name from a document.

The voice said, "What's this about? You want to leave a message for Mr Woo?"

"A survey," replied Mullet. "For television."

"No thanks," said the voice. The line went dead.

Woo? thought Mullet, but the name meant nothing. He settled back to the *Greatest Hits* of Blood, Sweat and Tears.

Half an hour later Oxford's Pajero reappeared. Mullet tracked him all the way back to the suburbs, watched the driveway gates close behind Roger Oxford before it was fully dark. End of tail. What Judith Oxford was going to make of it was anybody's guess.

On his way home Mullet made a drop. One hundred grams of the finest weed for which he was paid, a fillet of yellowtail wrapped in tinfoil for which he refused payment.

"Jeffrey," said Elizabeth the doctor of classical whatever, "please. I can't just take it."

"It's a present," said Mullet, feeling the prickle of a blush. "Free from the sea."

She laughed. "Hardly. You had to take your boat out. That costs."

He shrugged. "It's what I do."

"Still."

He indicated the fish parcel. "You planning to pan-fry it?"

"If that's what you recommend."

"Very hot in butter and Tabasco sauce. Some garlic."

She stood in the doorway, packet of grass in one hand, fish in the other, wearing a pink housecoat. The checked sort madams gave to their maids. Weird.

"Thank you," she said. "I'll do that."

He backed away onto the garden path.

"Give me a call when you're getting short."

"I will. And Jeffrey, thanks again."

Mullet smiled all the way home at the thought of Elizabeth in the nylon housecoat. Academics were Martians.

Bom-Bom was still on the stoep, curled asleep beneath a blanket. His empty plate swarming with ants. Mullet decided no drama now, he'd talk to him tomorrow.

Instead he rolled a spliff, slotted CSNY's *So Far* into the CD, put his feet up and grooved. By the time he crushed the roach he wasn't going to phone Rae-Anne.

22

Roger Oxford settled into his chair and swung round to look over the Waterfront. From fifteen floors up he had one of the grandest views in the city.

"Make mine Earl Grey," he said swivelling back to face his receptionist. "Settle Mr Kuzwayo in the conference room. Tell him I'll be ten minutes."

He phoned his wife. "Thought you'd like to know I have a Revenue Services man waiting in the conference room as we speak."

"They don't waste time," said Judith. "How efficient."

"Indeed. You're now an official whistle-blower. Doing your citizen's duty in reporting tax dodgers."

Judith laughed. "Anonymous whistle-blower I hope."

Oxford hung up and flipped at his diary. Lunch with Investment Bank. Dentist at three. A consultation pencilled for five. At the bottom of the page he noticed a phone number, bracketed by question marks. He remembered: the silent call he'd had on Friday evening, the private investigator Judith had hired. Out of curiosity he dialled it from his cellphone. The person who answered said his name was Mendes. Roger Oxford disconnected without speaking. He turned back to the Waterfront, beyond it the bay with cargo ships waiting in the roadstead. The first tourist shuttle churning a white wake towards Robben Island. "Well, Mullet Mendes," he said aloud, "I'm sure you're used to being taken for a ride."

Oxford sipped at his milky tea. Having Revenue at his service was an excellent start to a Monday morning. When he'd finished the cup he went through to the conference room.

The man from Revenue Services was gazing at the view.

"Quite a vista you have," he said. He introduced himself and they shook hands, Oxford indicating that they should sit at a round table.

Winston Kuzwayo put his palms flat on the table. "I believe a Mr Jim Woo is a client of yours. A foreign national. You are his tax consultant?"

Oxford inclined his head.

Kuzwayo drew a copy of Woo's last tax return from a document case.

"Is Mr Woo under investigation?"

Kuzwayo folded his arms.

"Yes."

"Then, if I or my client were approached formally in writing, I would be happy to respond."

"We like to make the first visit informal," said Kuzwayo. "It can sometimes pre-empt what would otherwise take a considerable amount of time. Our time, and yours, and your client's."

"I see," said Oxford.

Kuzwayo smiled. "What would help," he said, "was if you could tell me if you act for Mr Woo in matters other than tax advice. Investment, for instance. And in which jurisdictions if you do."

Kuzwayo drew an A4 jotter pad from his document case, clicked a silver ballpoint. "The point is really that this would assist us in determining the extent of your services in regard of Mr Woo."

"There is such a thing as client confidentiality."

"Absolutely."

Oxford pursed his lips. "May I ask you something?"

"Of course."

"Why are you investigating Mr Woo?"

"His name came up as part of our policy of random checks. This is simply routine."

86

Kuzwayo spent another twenty minutes with Oxford asking rudimentary questions about Woo's accounting procedures and business ventures, and where his investments were located. Nothing that breached client confidentiality. Everything Oxford said was noted in a small neat script on the jotter pad.

When Kuzwayo had gone, with the assurance that the next occasion would be formally arranged, Oxford put through a call to a man in Taipei called Ge Fei, Dragon Fire to those in the Brotherhood. Oxford greeted him in stilted Mandarin, then said, "I think there are matters about Jim Woo you need to reconsider."

There was a delay on the line, some feedback. Oxford caught the echo of his words. He waited.

"Tell me how is your beautiful wife?"

"As beautiful as ever," said Oxford, beaming, anticipating the next question.

"And my warrior?"

"Settling down."

"Good, good. I shall be in touch with her shortly."

Oxford waited, the hiss on the line growing louder.

"Now tell me about our brother."

"He is about to come under investigation by the Revenue Services."

"Aah. This is unfortunate. Is there some reason?"

"I am told it is a random check."

"But you do not believe that."

"No."

"Continue."

"Random checks are department policy and it could be coincidence. On the other hand perhaps this is a result of Jim Woo's business interests in the abalone industry."

"Perhaps."

International line crackle interfered.

Oxford said, "Could you repeat please."

Dragon Fire did. "Perhaps he has been, as the Americans say, snitched."

"This is entirely possible. The industry is volatile."

"Meanwhile you have everything under control?"

"As much as I know of."

"You believe he has kept interests from you?"

"Yes."

"I see."

Oxford swore he heard the man sigh.

"We will talk to him when we meet." In English Dragon Fire said, "Goodbye."

"Goodbye," said Oxford, and heard his words come back at him. He hung up.

Would they kill Woo?

He wasn't a betting man. On the balance of probabilities, however, Roger Oxford rather thought they might.

How, was really the question. Slice off his ears. Disembowel him. Let him get a sight of his own spilled guts. Then behead him. Dismember his corpse, dispose of it in a river.

End of Jim Woo. Oxford wouldn't mourn. Few would.

The next phone call Roger Oxford made was to Jim Woo. He got an answering machine at Helderrand and voicemail on Woo's cell. On both Oxford said, "Nothing urgent. I'll call you in Taipei."

He phoned his wife and reached her on her cell. It rang ten times before she answered.

"All done?"

"An extremely pleasant young man. Where are you?"

"At bridge. Where else on a Monday morning?" She was pacing on her host's porch. Through the dining-room window could see the women waiting for her. "Have you been in touch with Woo?"

"Only to leave a message."

Oxford started to say something then stopped.

"Roger, what is it?"

Oxford caught the concern in her voice. "Nothing alarming. I think our Mr Woo might not come back from Taipei."

"That would be no loss." He imagined she was smiling.

"Indeed. All the same, it's best not to relax our guard."

"I haven't the slightest intention of doing so," she said.

23

"No," said Mullet. "No, no, no. Out of the question. Not a possibility. Don't even ask."

"But . . ." said Vincent.

"No."

"Be reasonable."

"I said no. N. O. No."

Mullet heard his back-up cellphone ringing. He hauled it from the bottom of his shoulder bag.

"It's essential."

"Forget it."

Without looking at the screen, Mullet answered, "Mendes." A beat then the caller disconnected.

"We'll need water accessibility."

"Vince, what am I saying? Read my lips. No." He looked at the number on the screen. "Shit!"

"A week max. That's all."

"Look . . ." He scrabbled through the notes he'd taken at the Judith Oxford interview. There it was: Roger Oxford's office number, Roger Oxford's private line, Roger Oxford's cellphone number. The number on the screen of his cell. "Bugger it!"

"What?"

"Zapped. That's what. Bloody zapped. Like some punk appie."

"That right?"

"The phone rings, I don't check it. The guy ringing is the guy I'm staking. I bloody tell him my name."

"The guy . . ." Vincent gestured at the tall buildings downtown.

"Ja."

"So? It happens."

"It's careless, Vince. It's the sorta carelessness loses jobs."

Vincent waited, Mullet gone furrow-browed. "About the boat . . ."

Mullet ignored him, started stalking the office. Stopped at the crunch of glass beneath his shoes. The stench of whiskey.

"Heck, Vince. What the hell's this?" Bending to pick up a large piece of a Jack Daniel's bottle.

Vincent went sheepish. "Saturday morning. The scene of my last drink."

Mullet tossed the shard into the wastebin. Held up his hands, palms out to Vincent. "Right then. Let's start this again. She's coming when?"

Vincent checked his watch. "Fifteen minutes."

"Christ! Place looks like a squat." What it was, Mullet thought, was Vincent's sorrow heaped everywhere.

He and Vincent whirlwinded the office. Swept up the glass. Binned take-away boxes. Stowed the mattress and bedding. Sprayed air-freshener.

"You gonna get this laundry seen to?" Mullet indicated a heap of jeans, jocks, T-shirts on a chair.

Vincent produced a black bin-liner, started stuffing in his clothing. "I'm moving out," he said. "To my mother's."

"Yeah." Mullet had heard it before.

"New leaf."

"We've been there."

"No, seriously."

Mullet collected empty mugs from window sills, desks, top of the fil-ing cabinet.

"What's happened?"

"Nothing's happened. I've just made a decision."

Mullet ran water into the basin, squirted in wash-up liquid.

"That was your last drink, Saturday morning?"

"Sure."

He handed Vincent mugs to dry.

"You're gonna stick to it?"

"I told you."

"You told me before, you didn't then."

"This is different."

Sounded it too from what Mullet could hear in Vincent's voice. For the first time some genuine conviction.

"You don't have to move out."

"I do. That scene's over."

"Just like that?"

"Just like that."

Mullet dried his hands on his jeans. Had to be something else going on here with Vincent. Obsessive types went from one fix to another. "You up for this Sea Farm lark?"

"Hell yes."

"From what you tell it's not our bag."

"What d'you mean?"

"It's firing-line stuff, Vince. Guns 'n roses. Why I left the SAPS was to get outta that. Too many roses on too many coffins. Come to that, why you left the SAPS."

Vincent beat a fist into his palm. "I can't believe I'm hearing this. You told me take the job. We're investigators. That's what it says in the telephone book."

"Investigators of marital infidelity. Insurance scams. Maybe at an outer limit business espionage. The no-gun stuff."

"We need the bucks, Mullet. It's what you're always on about. We're running on empty, you say. Get your arse on the street Vince we need the bucks. These are good bucks."

Mullet had no argument here. Too right they needed the bucks. Maybe if this was going to pull Vincent out of the self-pity it was good for that too.

He sat down at his desk. "Lay it on me again. The shed doors were unlocked. They walked in, helped themselves."

"The part-owner, this bushwhacker David, goes out Tuesday and Friday nights to poke some dame he's got."

"Like where, for heck's sake? It's the middle of nowhere. What's he got? A farmer's wife?"

Vincent grinned. "A meid."

"Some coloured chick in the backlands?"

"Strue's."

Mullet laughed. "How about that!"

"You gotta imagine this huge guy, wild beard, going down on some rinky dinky."

Mullet clicked on the image. No kidding, the world was weird and wonderful.

When the laughing stopped he said, "You reckon these were pros?"

Vincent didn't get a chance to confirm. To the minute, bang on half ten the intercom buzzed.

Vincent made a rush for it, "Hi."

"It's Marina."

He pushed the lock release. "Come on up. Third floor. You've gotta walk."

Mullet frowned at him. Maybe this was the something else. "You got a pash going here, Vince?"

"No, man. What d'you mean?"

"The tone of your voice."

"Jesus. We just met. She's a client."

"With a Z3."

"Her ride, her suggestion. Saved us a petrol expense."

Mullet rocked back on his chair. "Yeah, yeah."

There was a knock at the door, Vincent opened. Enter Marina Welsh, one stunning number. Mullet didn't need a second glance to see what was rushing through Vincent. Marina Welsh was Amber. Same body shape, same eyes, different nose, same hair colour, even the same height. Maybe fuller boobs. More confidence though, walking in, shaking hands.

Vincent said, "How about something to drink?"

Marina took the client's chair. The only chair. "What're you offering?"

Vincent punched numbers into the phone. "Espresso. Cappuccino. Latte. Filter. We call down for it."

"Or instant," said Mullet, reaching for the tin on the bar fridge. "You go ahead. I'll make mine."

"It's empty," said Vincent.

Mullet lobbed the tin into a wastebin. "Bloody wonderful."

"Hey," said Vincent, placing an order for two cappuccinos and a filter. "We got a new client we can afford real coffee." He winked at Marina.

Mullet thought, hmm. Said, "Vincent's given me the breakdown, seems the way to go here is surveillance first."

Marina said, "Yes. That's what we want."

"Not exactly our normal line of business," Mullet said. "But why not, we're flexible." What he didn't add was, especially as the landlord was after him for two months' rent. "If I've got this right you reckon the guys'll be back soon and the trick's to let them do another heist and follow them home. End of story."

"Absolutely."

"And then what?"

"That's our business, Mr Mendes."

"You'll take it to the cops?"

"Of course."

"Fair enough," Mullet said. "Vincent also figures on some water capability. How's your brother's boat?"

"A shredded rubber duck."

"Don't believe me," said Vincent.

"Right then," said Mullet. A hollow opening in his stomach at the realisation he might have to lend Vincent the *Maryjane*.

"A new one is being delivered next week."

"No big deal," said Vincent. "We've got a boat."

"Sure." Mullet coughed. "Sure. We've got a boat."

The intercom crackled, a voice said, two caps and a filter. Vincent buzzed him up. Looked straight at Mullet: "It can be towed there this afternoon."

Mullet's stomach turned to fire.

"What service," said Marina. "Real professionals. I'll come along with you."

"Ah, no," said Mullet, "there's no need. Best to let Vincent handle it alone. For safety's sake."

"You don't understand," said Marina, latching her green eyes onto his, "I'm going to be there."

"We can't allow it."

"End of story."

Mullet heard Vincent splutter and cough, the blood heating his cheeks. Had the coffee not arrived he might have pushed his point. Instead he sat back, letting the situation ease, stirring in three sachets of sugar. "Maybe you don't need the boat right off. These guys come back they're gonna come back to finish what they started. They're not gonna take to the water. Chances are you'll get them first time out, Vince."

"Chances are," Vincent admitted. "Thing is, what if they come back for a night dive? It's like poaching in paradise. They know that. No one to say don't. That sort of situation all I can do is stand on the shore calling them names."

"He's got a point," said Marina.

Right through my heart, thought Mullet. Vincent having some fun here, watching him squirm.

"It's my boat," said Mullet. "For fishing."

Marina caught the intonation, glanced across at Mullet Mendes. Such a calm, laid-back-seeming guy. Vincent taking the boat pressed a sore button deep in his cool. A thing here between the two men.

She came in. "I hear what you're saying. You've got insurance?"

"Theft 'n accident. Doesn't cover bullet holes."

She stirred her coffee. "Here's a thought. If something happens to the boat, the Z3 is yours." Marina caught Mullet's eye, he looked away. "Would you like that in writing?"

Mullet shook his head. He could see what'd got Vincent revved. The chick was hot. Still the fires burned in his gut. They sat there, no one making eye contact.

Mullet said, "Alright. Just be goddamned careful."

Vincent wasn't sure if maybe he didn't float out of the office.

Marina saw the downer in Mullet's face. "You could come and do some fishing."

Like it was a holiday. The two of them tripping out the light fantastic.

Mullet closed the door on them, pressed his forehead against it. Heck of it, guy. You've lent Vince the pirate your boat. The coffee churned in his gut. He heard Cohen singing 'So Long Marianne'. Except it wasn't Marianne, it was the pretty *Maryjane*.

24

Jim Woo clipped his fingernails on the stoep of the manor. Awesome, this sweep across the vineyards to the distant mountains. Not a trace of anxiety in the day. Yet he was ratcheted tighter than a crossbow.

He checked his watch. Heard Arno behind him.

"Seems there's shit happening here, Arno," he said without turning round.

Arno came up, slurping his first beer of the morning. "Like?"

"Friend Roger."

"That so?"

Woo gestured over the estate. "Would you look at that? Isn't that amazing." He turned to the freckled man beside him. Saw the look of indifference in Arno's eyes. No one understood what this place meant to him. He slammed his fist on the table, a milk jug toppled.

Arno gave his heh, heh, heh laugh.

"What's the cunt up to? We get this thing flying. All the ducks lined up and he cracks. Puts Revenue up my pipe. You get this, Arno? Do you understand where this arsehole's coming from?"

Arno righted the milk jug. "Why'd he want to go to Revenue? Makes no sense."

Woo spun from the view. "No? You think it's coincidence? You think Revenue flipped through the files and said, hey, let's rattle Jim Woo today?" He came up to Arno. "It doesn't work like that. They get tipped off. Mostly they get tipped off by guys hanging out their clients."

"You're talking shakedown?"

"The name of the game."

"Oxford?"

"That's right."

"Nah. Not a chance."

"You don't think so? Suppose this: suppose Revenue's onto him. Suppose he does a plea bargain. Gets them round the table whingeing, listen chaps, I'm small fry. But how about my client Jim Woo? He comes flying in here with investment capital. Buys game farms, builds this premium lodge, shifts finance into abalone farming, acquires plant, warehouses, vehicles. Then whoosh, changes his money for bank loans and takes it all offshore again. In my book that would be laundering, chaps. And chaps, you got this from a little birdy, he owns a wine estate, too. Cash payment in full."

Arno went thoughtful. Oxford was a prick. A desk man. Desk men could pull invisible strings. "You wanted a Brit."

"Mistake." Woo helped himself to a slim-shake. "Another thing."

Arno waited.

"While I'm gone track him."

"Him and Tommy?"

Woo slit his mouth in a smile. "What's the big deal for a pro? Roger tonight. Tommy tomorrow. Only make sure the rogering Roger gets the message. And yeah, why not courier Judith that photograph of her husband. Wind her up a little more. People start tiptoeing, they dance better."

25

"Not a good move, Mull," said Ted, squashing a cigarette into a saucer. The two of them taking a quick break with the seagulls and the tourists in the Gardens Tearoom. "Saldana's not the sort of guy you trust with equipment. You heard what he did to the unit's rubber duck?"

"I heard," said Mullet.

"Totalled it. Put the bloody thing on the rocks." Ted fired up another Gunston. "No one could believe how he'd done it."

"That right?" said Mullet.

"They'd've given him a hauling, his wife hadn't died in that accident." Ted glanced at the burning tip of his cigarette. "Then he resigned anyway."

Mullet took a pull at the two straws in his Coke. "I was over a barrel."

"You still had a choice." Ted streamed smoke upwards. "You coulda said no."

Could of, thought Mullet. Didn't though. And that was the point, he should have taken a stand.

Ted's cellphone rang. He said "Yup", and listened, and "Gimme half an hour", before he disconnected. Then took the remains of his cream soda in a single swallow. "Wanna come with me? Take your mind off your problems."

"Where?" said Mullet.

"For a walk in the dunes. We've got another body."

"Oh, bloody wonderful."

Ted shrugged. "Suit yourself." He called for the bill.

Mullet thought, what was he going to do? Go back to the office sit and brood about his boat? Feel bad that Rae-Anne had gone sulky? When he could be staring at a dead body. On a fair day like this, too, endless sunshine dancing on the bay. What choices? "Right then," he said. "Let's go."

Ted scooped up his pack of cigarettes and cellphone – "Car's in Queen Victoria Street," he said, heading towards the gate.

They reached the turn-off into the Atlantis dunes halfway through a radio talk show on the abalone inspector that was fried at Dutch Bay. A caller was saying, "God gave us the perlemoen. It's all we got to feed our families."

"What's it you do, Tommy?" says the jock.

"I'm a fisherman."

"From Dutch Bay?"

"No, I fish all over."

"Do you poach?"

"Nay, never. Not me."

"Like bloody hell," said Ted, pulling off the road alongside a 4x4 double-cab cop van. "Isn't an abalone fisherman that doesn't poach."

The jock said, "You think what the mob did was right?"

"They tell us what to do all the time, stopping us fishing," said caller Tommy.

"But to burn a man to death?"

"People's justice."

Ted switched off. "Wasn't that Sonny Firness, Saldana's mate?"

"Far as I know," said Mullet.

"He cut up about it?"

"Hasn't said anything."

They got into the 4x4. The uniform at the wheel headed the van along a track that threaded the base of the sand dunes. Ted said, "You want to know the gist of this?"

Mullet said, "Can't wait."

Ted glanced at him. "I don't need the sarky bits."

Mullet didn't respond.

"Last Wednesday two young guys come out here sandboarding," Ted began. "One guy takes a piss in some dunegrass, he sees this candle sticking out of the sand. He calls his mate, they scratch around, then puke up all over the show. The body's about a week old. Probably a street kid. Body's buried head down, arse up, sort of vertical foetal position. Except there's no head. And the candle's stuck up the guy's bum. Had been lit too."

"Thanks for this," said Mullet.

Ted shrugged. "D'you think he sat there after he lit the candle?"

Mullet considered the height of the dunes. Must have been quite a ride for the sandboarders. "Probably," he said. "And this new one?"

"Exactly the same."

The uniform engaged the diff lock, said, "Sand's loose from here on." He kept the 4x4 at a steady fifteen Ks.

Ted said, "Because the first one was the same modus as some others we'd found, we thought had to be a serial. From time to time we'd check out the site. André visits this morning, finds another candle in the wind. This one's maybe Friday, Saturday night's doings. The perp comes back here, sees the first body's gone, but this's what he wants, right?"

"I'm smarter than you."

"So he replays."

They came round a dune, Mullet could see another 4x4 ahead, cops standing about. The uniform stopped behind the other vehicle.

"One thing," Ted said, giving Mullet the no-bullshit gaze, "the Deputy Commissioner's on his way. He tells you to piss off, then piss off. I'll get someone to drive you back. No winding him up, hey!"

"Great," said Mullet. "Why didn't you mention this at the café?"

"Cos you needed to take a break," said Ted.

André came up and ground his menthol into the sand. Behind him Mullet heard Ted flicking his lighter.

André said, "You come to see what we got?"

"Can't wait." Mullet nodded at a couple of cops he recognised. Technicians. Forensics.

The corpse was still in the grave, bum up, the candle well secured. Sand had been scooped away down the back, Mullet could see there was no head. One case he'd worked on the killer had stuffed twigs and leaves in the first victim's vagina. Number two he'd pushed up a bottle. Put stones in a third. A dead lizard in the fourth. They'd nailed him before there was a fifth. Guy'd lived with his mother. A sometime john. Had worked in clothing shops throughout the town as a job.

"Decapitation was done somewhere else," said André. "Same with the others. An electric saw, most probably."

The kid looked like a street boy. Thin, scrawny body. Ribs showing.

"No clothes?"

André shook his head. "Nor last time."

"You identify the first kid?"

"No chance."

"How'd they die?"

Mullet smelt Ted's smoke exhale drift over him.

"Cupid-style. Arrow through the heart."

Mullet glanced from Ted to André. "Arrow?"

"Or a bolt."

"You're kidding."

Ted sucked at his cigarette, blank-eyed.

André said, "Not at all."

"And this one?"

"Probably the same, from what we can tell. This one's got another hit, in the stomach. Looking at it, it's the same sort of wound."

Mullet stepped away from the grave. There were insects starting on the body he didn't want to see.

"No other body parts missing," said Ted. "It's not ritual."

"A deviant," said André. "What d'you say?"

Mullet didn't say anything.

From back down the dunes he could hear the grind of a vehicle approaching. Had to be Deputy Commissioner Naidoo. Bloody wonderful. Ted went off to meet him.

André said, "This's unfortunate. The timing."

Very, thought Mullet.

"Ja, Mendes," said the Deputy Commissioner, "what's your business here?"

"He came along for the ride," said Ted.

The Deputy Commissioner ignored this. "You angling to get back in the cops, Mendes?"

"No sir," said Mullet.

"Then get your nose the fuck out of cop work." The Deputy Commissioner turned to the men standing around the corpse.

André put a hand on Mullet's shoulder, he shrugged him off. Ted gestured towards the 4x4, and Mullet went meekly. What had always riled Naidoo, in those days Brigadier Naidoo, was that Mullet came up with the goods. Hard work had got him to the vagina violator way ahead of the Brigadier. Which seriously rattled Naidoo's police procedure manual.

Before Mullet reached the vehicle, the Deputy Commissioner shouted at him: "So who did it, Mendes? Let's have the benefit of your wisdom, while you're here."

"It's not a typical serial killer," said Mullet, getting into the double-cab before the Deputy Commissioner could respond. He saw Naidoo look at him, shake his head, turn away. "You're sad, Mendes. Very sad."

"What you mean it's not a serial killer?" said Ted as he drove Mullet back to town. "Serial is more than two bodies, same modus, same deviancy."

Mullet wished he could pop a mint chew. His mouth tasted foul. "A feeling. I don't know. The way they were killed. The way they're buried. Doesn't read like serial killer."

"That's your take?"

"It is."

Ted shook his head. "The perp's a fudgepacker paedophile. No doubt does a handjob at the candle vigil."

"Maybe," said Mullet. Then again, maybe not.

26

Tommy picked up Adonis from a separate entrance the guy lived at in the Muslim quarter. Might be above the town but whyfor he had to live among the clothheads Tommy couldn't figure. Like he didn't have the bucks for a Sea Point flat?

The first thing Adonis wanted was a hit.

"Fork," said Tommy, "this time of morning." He brought out a packet of snow and a couple of buttons. "It's all I got."

Adonis shrugged. "Better'n nothing."

They did a line each in the car, laying them down on the dashboard with Tommy's flick knife.

"That's sweet," said Adonis, swallowing two buttons. "We gonna live."

Tommy pinched his nostrils, snorting whatever powder hadn't gone up the first time. "You a drug addict." He folded the bag into the leg pocket of his cargoes. "We can go now 'n pick up Delmont?"

Adonis grinned back at him. "What's stopping you?"

They drove to the slums of Lavender Hill, a hyper Adonis mouthing off about some mama in a shimmering dress with a halo over her head. Come back from upstairs to help her family.

Tommy said, "A Slams?"

Adonis sniggered. "Not a Slams, a angel. Her people going through a hard time, she tells them what to do."

"She's got a halo?"

"Like a ghost. You can see it. On TV. *Bold and the Beautiful.*"

Tommy burst out laughing. "A soapie? The way you talking it sounds like she right there inna main house. Soapies're shit. American shit."

"Switch on, tune in." Adonis hit the theme tune to *Isidingo*, beat the rhythm on his thighs. "Subscribe, catch the vibe."

Tommy took a corner with the tyres squealing. "American shit."

"Is home brew." Adonis put his feet on the dashboard, in the movement knocking the steering wheel.

Tommy almost bounced the Beemer off the curb. "Hey, man, hey. Mind your feet. This's a car we in."

"German shit," smirked Adonis, smacked the dashboard. "Everywhere you look it's not our shit. So what? Everything on you come from somewhere else."

Tommy swatted at his legs. "Sit straight. You want the cops to stop us? Buckle up."

Adonis curled sideways in the seat to face him. "What you gotta think about is the world you missing. The entertainment."

"Fork, man. Put the forking belt on."

Adonis did as he was told. "That better, bay-bee?" – launched into how he was going to get a leather thong round his neck, like Chad in *Passions*. One with shells on it.

Tommy thought, what's it with bumbandits?

They hit Prince George's Drive he turned left at the traffic lights into the tenements. There was Delmont on the corner playing cool cat in catalogue threads, leaning against an electricity pole, smoking. Above his head disconnected wires clanging in the breeze.

As he came to the car, Tommy opened his side window, whistled. "Lookit the dude."

Delmont grinned, got in stinking of cologne.

"Oh, shit, no," went Tommy. "That is cat pee."

Adonis took a deep breath. Rattled off: "Kouros, Hugo, Calvin, DKNY?"

"Hugo," said Delmont. "Dark Blue."

Adonis winked at Tommy, corkscrewed in his seat to face Delmont. "You lovely, babe."

Delmont ground out his Winston in the side-door ashtray. Guys always taking the piss.

"Where we going, Del?" said Tommy. "You the man with the man."

"You betta stop at your mommy's first," said Delmont. "She's not good."

Tommy banged the steering wheel with the palm of his left hand. "I come riding here to buy guns, I come riding here to buy guns. 'N not to have my mommy crying at me." He had a mommy like the Yiddish in flat 33 that would be different. There was a cool old broad selling on his pearlies to her mates. Very cheeky.

"You got to," said Delmont.

Tommy laid rubber through two gear changes, stopped three hundred metres down in a short skid. "She better be dying," he said to Delmont.

She wasn't. She was in a green housecoat vacuum-cleaning. Tommy came banging in she switched off. Stared wearily at him.

"Turn to Jesus, Tommy," she said. "The Holy Threesome's not listening to my prayers anymore."

"Mommy, I thought you was sick? I come to visit."

She switched on the vacuum cleaner. "Jesus will save you, Tommy. Jesus saves. Praise the Lord."

Tommy backed out, noticed she'd taken his photo off the wall: the one he was getting a prize in primary school. He stopped, pointed at the hook where it'd hung. "Where's my picture?"

His mother heard him shouting over the vacuum's whine. "In the drawer. You not that little boy, Tommy."

Tommy slammed shut the door. Forking Delmont. Forking type of joke he thought this was!

Delmont and Adonis killing themselves in the car. Wasn't his Beemer he'd put a brick through the window. "Blerry funny, Del," he said, getting in the driver's seat. "Like I need this, china."

It got quiet in the car. They drove a block down, two blocks along into

Dirty Boys territory. Old men watched them. Brothers stared. Women hanging washing paused. Cruising Beemers with tinted windows could mean a drive-by. Only the kids didn't stop playing.

Tommy liked it. This reek of fear.

Delmont told him stop, switch off. To the left was a tenement with two gang soljas at the street door. The soljas pulled guns. Delmont jumped out. "Yo!" The soljas jerked their heads in greeting. "Come to see Mista September." The one patted him down.

Tommy shouted, "Remember to get bullets, Del."

Delmont gave him the finger.

Tommy surveyed the scene. The dead-end people. The filth. A dog dying in the gutter, jerking. "You wanna live back in this shit? Lavender Hell."

Adonis was playing Space Impact on his phone, drifting through the asteroids. "No way, José."

"So why does Delmont?"

"Dunno."

"I'll tell you," said Tommy. "He's got no self-respect."

Adonis lost concentration, the asteroids pinging his space capsule. "He told me as soon as this job's over, he's out."

"Like fork. He's got a fiancée. That's expense. Big time payout."

Adonis ran through the menu, selected a new game.

Tommy heard schoolgirl giggles, saw two pretties coming up in the rear-view mirror. A major reason to stay here, you got to pop cherry anytime you wanted. He pressed the window button as the chicks came alongside, said, "Hello, sweethearts."

The one chick stuck out her tongue. The other mimicked his words.

Tommy loved it. Attitude. Long legs. School tunics. He gave them a wet grin. "Wanna ride?"

They blew raspberries. Took off giggling, tunics hitching up their running legs to show a flash of red panties.

Tommy said, "You wanna play schoolteacher, bro?"

Adonis kept at his game. "They's daddy's girls."

The girls darted into a doorway. The one turned, lifted her tunic to tease him. Tommy licked his lips. Don't you love it, darlin! "Your problem, bro, is you too what they call focused."

Adonis got through the asteroids, gave a shout of triumph. Tommy glanced at him. Behind he saw Delmont step out of the tenement, twirling a pistol round his finger. He plopped into the back seat.

"You got bullets?" Tommy wanted to know.

Delmont shot the clip. "See!"

Tommy saw fully-loaded. "Just checking, Del. Just checking."

"He says when we finished with this he'll take it back."

"For a discount."

Delmont shrugged.

One of the soljas knocked at Tommy's window, motioned him to move off.

"We outta here, china," Tommy said, firing the engine. "Live a little, bro." But the solja didn't hear him.

Tommy dropped Delmont back at the busted electricity pole. "Tomorrow, hey. Two-thirty." He tapped the accelerator twice. Vroom. Vroom.

27

Come 3 p.m. Mullet collected the photographs from Quickprint, drove over to Judith Oxford, thinking, not much for her money.

Judith Oxford's initial response: "She's Chinese!"

Her second: "She's young enough to be his daughter."

Mullet shifted uncomfortably. He hated this bit where the spouse saw her competition for the first time. Judith wasn't the tears type, but her hand was trembling.

She said, "I need a drink." Her movement from the couch to the sideboard stirred the potpourri fragrance. Mullet thought, not a bad idea.

From a decanter she poured a stiff two fingers. One block of ice tonged out of a silver bucket.

"Can I offer you something?"

"I'll do the same," said Mullet.

She brought it to him. They both drank, no salut. Mullet sipped, she took half in one go.

"Christ! What am I supposed to do with this? What?" She stabbed at the picture of Oxford and the girl at the News Café. The two of them clear enough in the background, amused by the antics of the tourist. "Tell me again what happened."

Mullet did.

"You're telling me they're not screwing? Come on. Look at his face. That's a lecher."

Mullet didn't comment.

"His mouth's all wet and grinning."

This was pushing it but what could he say? Judith pulled again at the whisky. Mullet matched her. Single malt it had to be: smooth and round.

"What's her name?"

"You want her name?"

"It's what I'm paying you for, isn't it?"

"Not exactly," said Mullet. "You're paying for me to check out what your hubby does."

"Well, now I want her name. And I want pictures of them fucking."

Mullet tried saying something about maybe they weren't having an affair, maybe something else was happening here. She shut him up.

"Forget it. Don't even go there."

Mullet thought, what's with the broad? She could pull a lover fifteen, twenty years younger. Walk into any chic scene at 2 a.m., Rhodes House, Mano's, Buddhabar, she's going to have the wolves baying at her feet. Take her pick. What they'd see would be: funky, sexy, money. Their tongues drooling.

She was saying, "I want you to stay on it until they fuck. I don't care about costs. I want him nailed."

"Why?" said Mullet.

"You want to know why? I'll tell you. I'm divorcing him. And I want as much as I can lay my hands on." She barked a forced laugh of bitterness and got up from the couch to leave the room. "I'll show you something."

Mullet saw he was being watched by the Doberman other side the sliding-glass doors. The dog snarled. "Nice doggie," he said, raising his whisky in a toast.

Judith came back, handed him an envelope. "Here. Reality check." Inside, a jeweller's invoice for an expensive watch, dated the day before she'd hired him. He handed the slip back to the spiky-haired blonde.

"You see the watch on the woman's arm?" She tapped the photograph. "That's it."

Judith Oxford finished her drink.

"So you provide the pictures. Then I can have a meaningful conversation with my husband."

Mullet glimpsed the moves she was making: revenge. She smiled, held her hand out for his empty glass. You didn't get many smiles, Mullet reckoned, that you could call dazzling. Hers was.

28

Vincent worked out a possible way the heist would go. It'd be night. The guys would come in, drive past the house, go down the track to the sheds. Reverse their van so there were no problems getting out. Shed two had what was left of the cocktail abalone. He reckoned five guys max. They'd be maybe three hours cleaning out the tanks, depending on their numbers. The van parked next to the shed door to make loading easy. One guy standing point.

Question: would they wander around?

Question: would they put in a recce?

Answers: probably and probably.

Vincent took a walk into the sand hills on the land side of the Sea Farm sheds. What he could do was hide the Isuzu behind the rise right near shed two and when the guys took off he'd follow them. Chances were they did any wandering around it would be in the other sheds and the house. He could sit in the bakkie ten metres from them and they wouldn't know he was there. Especially not in the pitch black West Coast dark. Someone swinging by to check the scene in the afternoon wouldn't see the bakkie parked there either.

The problem remained, the *Maryjane*. Where to hide her?

Say they didn't come for the cocktails. Say they came to poach. In that situation he'd need to follow them in the boat.

He walked back to the house, the two Jack Russells buzzing moleheaps along the path. On the stoep Vincent spread a map. Chances were if they came in off the sea they'd launched from one of three bays.

Two possibles to the south, one to the north. On a crow-flying trajectory the outer bays maybe fifteen Ks away. Vincent stabbed at the outer south. If he was going to do it, he'd do it from there. More roads, more options for the getaway.

The flyscreen door squeaked and Marina backed onto the stoep carrying a tray of crisps, dips, peanuts, celery sticks, a jug of iced tea with mint leaves floating on top. Vincent jumped to hold the door.

"What manners," Marina said, putting the tray on the table, covering the map.

"Well brought up," said Vincent.

She tucked a wisp of hair behind her ears, pulled out a chair. "Help yourself."

Vincent took a fistful of peanuts. "Isn't David gonna join us?"

She poured two glasses. "Don't worry about him. He sorts himself out."

They went quiet.

Vincent spoke first. "You ever think about moving up here?"

Marina shook her head. "No. The city's my place." She glanced at him digging crisps into the mayo dip. "I like the nightlife. Even after Harry was killed I couldn't see a reason to leave." Toyed with her iced tea but didn't drink. "Harry was fun."

Vincent let the quiet lengthen while she stared at the sea, getting lost. "How'd you meet?"

She snapped back to the here and now. "I needed a make-over. I walked into his salon on a whim and said, do your thing."

"Just like that?"

"He was wonderful. Sat me down, looked me in the eyes and told me he was doing red that week. I said, fine by me. When he was finished he asked me to dinner. What could I say? My hair was stunning." She put down the glass. Vincent saw water in her eyes. She dabbed at her face with a clean serviette. "I'm sorry." She took a breath. "Sometimes it feels over. Sometimes it feels as if it won't end." Vincent knew what she meant. She crunched up the serviette.

"Let's walk," he said.

They took the track beside the sheds to the end where the dunegrass started, the Jack Russells in their element, the Rottweiler joining them from nowhere.

As they turned the corner at the last shed she said, "I'm sorry I got so emotional. I don't usually talk about the details."

Vincent said, "Nothing to be sorry about."

They stood at the top of a dune, the beach spread below them. Miles of it, low-tide wide, curving away to the right like a scimitar blade. Endless sea rising into the horizon. The dogs raced ahead. Vincent paused taking in the prospects. To the left a headland. Over the headland was the bay where David released abalone. Anyone poaching there wouldn't know what was going on here.

"I reckon my wife was murdered," he said. The words rushing from the back of his mind. Bats coming out of the night.

Marina sat down and Vincent crouched next to her.

"It was a crash," he said. "That killed her."

Marina kept silent.

"Looked like she'd lost control. Spun. Flipped. Totalled on Hospital Bend. She was on her cell to a friend. She heard her scream."

"There was nobody else involved?"

"No." Vincent shook his head. "But something wasn't right."

"What do you think happened?"

"She was run off the road."

"Deliberately?"

"That's how I see it."

Vincent jumped up, agitated. He pointed. "Is that a slipway? Alongside the headland?"

Marina followed his finger. "It's where David launches when the weather's rough." She held out a hand. "Help me up."

Vincent reached for her hand, warm, gritty with sand yet he could feel the softness underneath.

"I want to take a look," he said.

They slid down the sand slope, not talking, until Marina said, "Why do you think it was deliberate?"

Vincent rolled his head, easing the muscles in his neck. "There was this abalone poacher I'd nailed. We'd had a few run-ins. Then one day we bust him and he tried to stab me. For that he got two years. As he went down he said to me, I'll get you, cop. I laughed at him."

They saw the dogs worrying at a seal carcass and angled towards it.

"Just another hard-faced, wall-eyed thug. A no-hope big-mouth young-ster. But he sends me these notes from prison. Stuff cut out of maga-zines. Pictures of bomb-blast victims. Burnt bodies. Severed limbs. Whatever he can find. No words, only the pictures."

"How many?"

"Five."

"And you knew they were from him."

"He signed his name."

They stood over the dead seal, washed up on the high tide. The skin eaten away from the snout, exposing bone. Its flippers caught in netting.

The dogs had lost interest. Vincent and Marina followed them towards the slipway.

Marina picked up an abalone shell the size of an old man's ear and rubbed at the mother-of-pearl to make it shine.

"But why do you think there's a connection?"

"I got an SMS later that night. She'd been dead a few hours. It said, I'm after you. I found out the guy was on parole."

She flicked away the shell. "Bit circumstantial."

Vincent made a sucking noise. "You're right. No hard evidence. Noth-ing but a feeling. Nothing to connect it."

"The SMS?"

"From a stolen cellphone."

"And your suspect?"

"Disappeared."

"So why d'you think he's tied in?"

Vincent expelled a whistle of breath. Marina glanced at him.

"Because he's gone. Because I was this close" – he held up his left hand to show the gap between his thumb and index finger, about two centi-metres. His fingers rigid as claws. "I was that far from breaking a major syndicate. A scheme that was passing out poached abalone under legiti-mate exports. What we wanted was the big names. There was a guy in Coastal Management, Sonny Furniss, working the case too. He'd tipped us in the first place."

"The man they burnt at Dutch Bay?"

"The same." Vincent coughed back the acid in his throat.

29

At 5 p.m. Mullet was in Sea Street again. What made him nervous was the number of people about. People going home, hurrying for buses, taxis, trains. Too many people gave Mullet the worries. He poured coffee from his flask and added a slug of brandy. It didn't settle his nerves. He had flashbacks. Cop days.

There was Hennie smoking, talking absolute crap, the two of them laughing. Windows down. Relaxed. Sitting bum-numb in the stake-out for three hours of the afternoon. Lots of people about. Shoppers. Shopkeepers. Schoolkids. Delivery guys. Imams. Major Friday busy-street activity. Their problem was they weren't taking it seriously enough. Two guys sitting in a car for three hours were wrong after twenty minutes. Next thing Hennie's brain exploded. Significant bits caught Mullet in the face. Through the gore he saw the gun come on him. A misfire. The whole thing took his breath away.

He sat agitated now in Sea Street. Ten minutes in one place. Drove round the block, five in another. Restless, a packet of Lays chips unopened; chaining the mint chews. What he craved was some Joan Baez and a huge spliff.

Come six a white Golf cruised the street twice and parked close to the access to Roger Oxford's parking garage, a block up from Mullet. A thin guy at the wheel. Brush-cut ginger hair gave him a skinhead look. His eyes invisible behind shades.

Mullet wondered if he didn't know him from somewhere.

The street was quiet now. Street kids in the doorways but the workers all gone home. A scattering of commuter cars against the curb. In half an hour they'd be gone. The guy in the Golf sat tight. Soon there wasn't a car left between Mullet and the Golf.

Mullet thought, he's gonna make me. Has to. One glance in the rearview mirror he sees a guy in a car sitting and sitting and sitting he's gonna think, hello.

Mullet switched the ignition, went unhassled out of Sea Street. He reckoned if Oxford stuck to his routine he could pick him up at the Buitengracht intersection. For forty-odd minutes he sat pondering who is the guy in the Golf? What's his agenda?

The second question was answered in part when Oxford came through the intersection and took the route home. Right behind him was the white Golf. Mullet joined the caravan. All the way to the suburbs the guy in the white Golf tailed the Pajero. Mullet kept discreet. Intrigued. When they reached Oxford's place the guy kept on down the street.

Mullet thought, to heck with it, he'd get another early night. On the way home he dropped off weed for a lawyer, two dentists, the professor.

The professor gave him lip.

"You promised some E."

Mullet couldn't remember.

"You're supposed to be Mr Sugarman. Keep the customer satisfied."

Mullet grinned. "Rodriguez. Simon and Garfunkel."

"What?"

Mullet tutted. "Your references."

"What?" The professor shook his head. "Your problem is you smoke too much."

He gave Mullet two hundreds and a fifty. His nails were rimmed with black dirt. His breath smelt like tinned cat food. The stench of cat wafting out the house.

"You really want E?"

Some screechy violins rose in the background.

"Just do it."

Mullet said, "Impossible is nothing."

The professor frowned. "You're an alien, Mullet. A goddamned alien."

At his kitchen table Mullet rolled a short stop with Baez on the boombox. He played out scenarios about the guy in the white Golf. Either Oxford had spooked when he heard the name Mendes and arranged protection muscle which was the reason the guy stayed obvious. Or, Judith had hired a heavy to stoke her husband's pulse rate. To what end Mullet couldn't see. Or, the guy was an outside agency. Unrelated business dovetailing in. Throwing a scare tactic.

The heck of it was, when he stubbed the roach, Mullet couldn't care. Not the best state in the world to sort out his problems but at least he was going to stay calm.

He opened the back door, called, "Bom-Bom, we've gotta have words."

Not that he was sure Bom-Bom could hear. Not that Bom-Bom was there to hear. He switched on the stoep light: a mess of sleeping bag on the mattress. The kid had been there last night. The kid had been there this morning. He'd be back. Meantime Mullet was grateful. How d'you tell a street kid to piss off anyhow?

Inside, he phoned Rae-Anne.

She said, "You didn't call me last night."

"No."

"Why not, Mull? That's what people do after a fight. They call to make up."

"We didn't fight."

"Fighting's not only shouting, Mullet. It's also an atmosphere. We had an atmosphere."

Silence.

"Why don't you say something?"

Mullet couldn't think of anything to say.

"You've gotta talk, Mullet. You can't just shut up."

More silence.

Mullet said, "I dunno what to say."

Rae-Anne screamed. "Aaaaaaaaaah!"

Mullet held the phone away from his ear. Nonetheless heard: "Your trouble Mullet Mendes is you won't let anybody into your heart. You're a selfish bastard. You don't know what love is."

Mullet caught the riff: I wanna know what love is. Foreigner. I want you to show me. From the album *Agent Provocateur*.

The heartache and pain of this lonely life.

"Doll," he said. He didn't get to say come over, on account of Rae-Anne had hung up.

30

The driver parked the truck at the delivery entrance, reversing into the loading bay. From the cab he stared across at the empty parking lot, lit by high mast lights. The only movement at this dark time of morning was the flailing palm trees, wind tearing through their top knots.

"Bloody wind," he swore in Xhosa, leaned across to jab the security guard in the ribs. "Hey! We're here."

The guard yawned and cracked his eyes a slit. "It's still night."He put a hand over the Beretta lying on the seat between them and pushed himself upright. "Now we've gotta wait."

The driver said, "When I drive I drive." From his shirt pocket he took two loose Lucky Strikes, offering one to the guard and pressing in the dashboard lighter. When it popped, the driver put the glowing coil to his cigarette before passing it to the guard.

The guard sucked, but the coil had lost its heat. "Shit, man, it's out." He spoke in English, looking at the lighter, stabbing it back into the socket.

The guard was twenty-two with a corn-row hairstyle, a dinky cellphone dangling on a lanyard round his neck, and bangles of beads on his wrists. Before this job he'd been a nightwatchman for a cement company but yard patrols in the rain and freezing cold were not his idea of a promising career.

The driver was in his mid-fifties. He'd driven long-haul furniture trucks, construction site tippers and ten-tonners on asbestos mines which had left him with a racking cough, a pain in the chest, sometimes blood in the phlegm he hawked up. Driving sea products in small refrigerated trucks was lighter work and the pay was a major plus. This was the first time in a lifetime he'd earned decent bucks. What he didn't like was having a guard along.

The cigarette lighter jumped in the socket and the guard reached for it, put the coil to his cigarette, inhaled, let the smoke drift down his nostrils. The side window exploded. A man stood grinning at him, showing him the business end of a pistol. Bam, the window shattered on the driver's side. A voice said, "China, leave the gun, hey!" The grinning guy said, "Come'n, darkies, out."

The driver remembered his manager saying: "Abalone, Moses, are worth a fortune. You've got to have a guard."

He'd looked at the crates of abalone, this shellfish, a slab of meat the size of his palm. "What's it taste like?" he'd asked the manager. "Rubber," he'd been told. "But the Japs 'n the Chinks go mad for it. The larney rich too. They sit down to an abalone meal, Moses, they're gonna spend more than your pay. Here in town, at the best restaurants."

Right now they were outside the service door of one of those best restaurants waiting to unload the shellfish. Except two coloured guys had got him and the guard legs spread, arms high against the truck.

"Take it," said Moses.

"What's that, tata?" came back the guy with green gems in his front teeth.

"You can take the lorry."

"Hey, thanks. You hear that Adonis, they giving us the truck."

Adonis giggled. Put his face up against the guard's and kissed his ear. The guard pulled away, slapping at his ear as if he'd been stung. Adonis chopped him with the pistol, two blows to the neck.

"Yo, bro," he said. "Don't move. I know you like it."

"OK, my darkies," said Tommy. "What you gonna do is move what's not abalone out of your truck. Cos, see, we got no use for your delivery. So Mista Driver, now's the time you open the fridge."

"We don't want trouble," said Moses, a catch in his voice like he was swallowing too much air. "I've got a family."

"No shit," said Tommy. "You a family man." Taking a step closer to the driver. "How many kids, darkie? Eight? Ten?"

"Leave him," said the security guard.

Tommy took the nine mil Adonis handed him and pressed it hard into the guard's balls. The guard sucked in sharply.

"Young darkie like you, has to have one, two picannins already," said Tommy. "To prove you a man. Different mamas I imagine. Like you don't know about AIDS. Like you 'n the presi-dent think there's no such thing. All these people dying from not eating enough. Even the president's aides." Tommy laughed. "You get that? Aides. AIDS." He got no response. "Jeez, darkies!"

"Come on, Tommy," called a third voice. "Let's go. Let's go."

"Shut up, Delmont," said Tommy. "Stay cool." Delmont was running the engine to rival a Kyalami start.

Adonis came round the back of the truck brandishing the machine pistol with a shoulder stock fitted to the butt. "Nice piece." Holding it on the driver and the guard. "Better'n the shit Delmont got us."

Tommy racked the pistol, stepping from the two men. "Time to get kaalgat. Let's do it, chinas. Let's do it. Outta the threads."

They did, the two men standing there naked in the van's headlights, hands over their privates.

Delmont in the cab pressed the hooter, the sound was the opening bars to Beethoven's fifth. Da, da, da, daaah.

Tommy wheeled. "Fork, Delmont. Whyn't you just go out 'n call the cops?"

"Come on," shouted Delmont. "What you doing?"

Tommy gave him the finger and snagged the barrel of his pistol into the driver's pot belly.

"OK, tata, let's get the load shifted."

When the driver and the guard were done hefting polystyrene containers of wet fish, mussels and prawns out of the fridge truck, stacking them at the restaurant's trade entrance, Tommy had them sit against the building.

"Are you going to shoot us?" the guard wanted to know.

Tommy smiled at him. One cool character. "Nah." He held up the gun. "We kindly types." Still, he sighted at the guy, right between the eyes. It would be so easy.

Delmont in the cab was shouting, "We got the truck, let's go. Let's get outta here. You don't want to corpse them, Tommy."

"Hear the guy," said Tommy, lowering the gun. "What he say's right. No corpsing. Nice clean job." He looked from one to the other. The guard was ultra-calm; the driver not doing too well, suddenly squirting his water, most of it over Tommy's trainers. "Fork," said Tommy, dancing away, "what's with you, bro?"

He waited for the guy to stop pissing.

"Here's the plan," he said. "We gonna drive away." He grinned at them. "Been a pleasure working with yous."

The guard said, "What about our clothes?"

Tommy and Adonis sniggered.

The guard swore and bunched his fists. He went into a crouch. Tommy put the gun on him, straight at his heart.

"Don't," he said. The guard eased back. "There's a guy," said Tommy and gave him a flash of his emeralds. "You ready?" he said to Adonis.

Adonis wiggled his hips. "Always."

Delmont did another run of Beethoven to cover the shooting.

31

Bao Dao to early Chinese settlers: the Treasure Island. Formosa during Portuguese rule: the Beautiful Island. Taiwan: the Emerald Island to the Japanese invaders. Even when they got out in 1949 it stuck. Jim Woo liked the name. That's what it looked like, flying in, the bright green coast against the dark of the sea.

He drummed his fingers on the armrest, impatient. Agitated.

The air hostess asked him please to fasten his seat belt.

He made no move to comply. "We on schedule?"

"Yes, sir," she said. "We'll land in ten minutes." She waited until she heard his buckle lock closed.

Woo glanced down at the Emerald Island. He hated coming back. The constant reminder that he couldn't escape.

When the plane lurched as the wheels hit the runway, Woo's stomach tightened. Any situation anywhere else he could handle it. Being here was bad news. High tension. Hidden agendas. One thing being said, another meant.

Woo unbuckled and hustled with the tourists and the businessmen to get his baggage from the overhead locker.

To know the dragon you had to go into the lair. To pacify the dragon you had to feed it.

The brothers want to know about your operations. The words of Dragon Fire.

The brothers want to know . . . You must ease their minds.

The brothers couldn't know zip. Couldn't suspect anything about his dealings. Woo reasoned what they wanted to do was keep him on the edge. Keep him uneasy. In that case, he'd feed them. Facts. Figures. Projections. Everything they wanted to hear.

The billboard in the arrivals lounge said: Welcome to the Republic of China on Taiwan.

Woo wanted to spit a bad taste from his mouth.

He passed through passport control and customs, then stepped into the antechamber of the lair: the arrivals hall, Chiang Kai-shek International Airport.

The Grand Hotel was where Woo always stayed. It had some class, a sense of grandeur. A palace in the imperial style of old China up on the ridge overlooking Taipei, high above the cesspit.

A porter in a red jacket and gold buttons carried his luggage to suite 503. Supposed to be a lucky number if you believed in that shit. Normally Woo didn't, here he did.

The porter opened the curtains on the view: skyscrapers at every angle, sun-reflected glass. Green distant hills hazing in the humidity.

He showed Woo a TV in a cupboard, a bar fridge, a basket of fruit.

"Yeah, thanks," said Woo in English, palming him a local dollar note.

The porter bowed out.

Woo unpacked. Shirts, underwear, socks on separate shelves. A suit, a pair of slacks onto hangers.

He sat on the edge of the bed while he used the gilt phone to call an agency he favoured when he hit the city. A girl for luck, the younger the better. He could expect her in thirty minutes. He made another call, this time using his cellphone.

"Mr Woo, you are in Shanghai?" the man asked.

"Not yet," said Woo. "Tomorrow."

"You will come to have a meal? See our establishments?"

"Of course," said Woo. "But please tell me you are satisfied with the first consignment?"

"Good fish," said the man. "First-class cocktail abalone."

"Excellent. You should have another supply shortly."

"Haaa! Our customers are rejoicing."

Woo disconnected and threw the cell onto the bed. Stood at the window gazing at the distant city, couldn't help grinning at the move he'd pulled. As far as Dragon Fire was concerned, there'd been a heist at Sea Farm and this delayed his order. The guys in Shanghai were happy, and the insurance had paid out. Having heist number two watched by the private investigator would keep Dragon Fire off his back, and the Shanghai connection smiling. Might even convince the insurance to pay out a second time. Woo laughed. The sort of caper you couldn't pull three times running. The sort of caper you shouldn't even pull twice. Except it was too neat to let go.

Then again . . .

Oath Ten: *I shall never embezzle cash or property from my sworn brothers. If I break this oath I will be killed by a myriad of swords.*

They couldn't know.

The girl said her name was Lotus Flower. Weren't they all. She was delicate. A hint of rouge on her cheeks, eyeliner, cherry gloss on her lips.

"How old are you?" he asked.

She told him fifteen.

Sure, he thought. Fourteen. Fifteen. Eighteen. Whatever you want. Just not more than twenty.

He said she should undress. When she stood naked he ran his hands from her shoulders down her back to her ankles then up her thighs to her breasts. She fumbled with his belt. He smiled and pushed her onto the bed.

Oath Sixteen: *If I knowingly convert my sworn brother's cash or property to my own use I shall be killed by five thunderbolts.*

What reasons could they have for suspicion?

The girl was holding something up to him. A condom. He took it from her and frisbeed it across the room.

"I'll take the risk," he said. "So will you."

The girl named a higher price.

"Fine." What Woo wanted was that she should bring him luck. *I will be killed by a myriad of swords. I shall be killed by five thunderbolts.* He stepped out of his boxers and fell on her, hearing her stifle a cry at his force.

When the girl had gone, Woo phoned Marina. She caught the edge in his voice right off.

"You OK?" she asked.

"Sure," he said. "Sure. A bit strung out after the flight. Wired, you know . . ."

"Try and sleep. Take a bath, that'll wind you down. Relax, Jimbo, you're on home ground."

"That's the problem." Woo bent to look at the contents of the minibar. He took out a Jameson, clutched the miniature in his fist. "They won't know anything. How can they?"

"Dazzle them with figures. Tell them about the heist. The more details you throw at them the better. People want detail. The truth is in the detail." She gave a half laugh. "I'm sounding like Jim Woo."

He poured the whiskey into a tumbler. "You at Sea Farm?"

"Settling in," she said.

"With Saldana?"

"He's cute."

Woo snorted. "You going to sit out the watch?"

"Why not, should be fun. Especially if he realises who he's watching. He's got a raw wound when it comes to Tommy Fortune."

Her words ended and Woo didn't say anything.

"Jim? Jim, you still there?"

"I want you," he said. "You don't know how much."

"Get through this," she said.

"I want you."

"I know, baby," she said. "I know."

Woo dozed through the afternoon, dreaming of balance sheets: the brothers quizzing him about the wine estate; Revenue Services wanting to know if the capital from Sea Farm had been used to fund the purchase of the estate.

The phone woke him, his cellphone, with Roger Oxford's name on the screen.

Woo toyed: should he, shouldn't he? What was it that couldn't wait three days? He thumbed him on.

"Thought you might want to know this," Oxford said straight off, no niceties. "Two hours ago Mr Kuzwayo from Revenue Services delivered an official letter. Personally."

Woo caught a waft of stale sex as he moved. He pinched his nose closed. "Big deal."

"It is," said Oxford. "They want bank statements from all accounts. Chequebook stubs. Credit card statements. Going back five years. That's a big deal."

"Is this personal or business?"

"Personal."

"So? I'm a director of companies. Each month I take a draw. Pay a car rental, insurance, medical aid, buy food, go to restaurants, sometimes I splash out, buy new clothes like everyone else. Business trips go through the companies. Holidays I do twice a year for my own account. Income stream equals spend. Paper trails everywhere. It couldn't be simpler. That's what you do, Roger, make the paper trails simple. For me and for them. You understand what I'm saying?"

"Jim," said Oxford, the patience clear in his voice to Woo's amusement. "Jim, I don't believe it is that simple. As I told you they could move from you to the companies."

While Oxford talked Woo padded naked through to the bathroom. He flipped up the toilet lid.

"Where are you?" said Oxford.

"In my hotel suite," said Woo. "Can't you hear?"

"All too well." Oxford's irritation was undisguised.

Woo laughed. "Sort it out," he said. "They bite my arse, they'll bite yours, Rog. Believe it." In mock-posh English, added, "What do you say, old man!"

"I say that I don't think it's as easy as you would like to believe."

Woo flushed the toilet, holding the phone to the water gush.

"Another thing," said Oxford, "call off your dog" – cutting the connection before Woo could.

Woo stared at the swirl of blue water in the bowl. Call off your dog! He gave an imitation of Arno's heh, heh, heh, heh laugh.

32

On the way to the office Mullet made some drops.

To the Rev having his first Red Bull at a pavement cafe. "Praise the Lord, bro." The man looked so relieved.

To the Doc taking a smoke break in the courtyard between patients. "Cheers, Mullet. Just what the doctor ordered."

He said that every time. Mullet grimaced.

To the account exec of a top agency waiting in her car outside the Archives as always.

Mullet gave her the parcel, pointed at the portcullis. "You know this was once a jail?"

She put her nose deep into the packet and inhaled. "Times change."

"They hanged people here."

"Pity they still don't," she came back.

Mullet grinned. "Tell me about it."

She paid him, squealed her A-class Merc into the traffic. Nice lady. He bunched her notes into his pocket. If he was younger he'd have tried the schmooze. Couldn't help but sigh at that.

Mullet headed downtown, circled for a street parking outside the office building and got a lucky break. He paid the car guard for an hour: one thing he wasn't intending was putting in desk work.

Upstairs he plugged in the kettle for an instant coffee and made his first call while waiting for the boil.

"Judith Oxford."

"This is Mullet."

"Yes," she said, not giving him the politeness of a hello.

Mullet cleared his throat. "Ah, you wouldn't know anything about a guy with a brush cut?"

He could imagine Judith Oxford in jeans and a knit top, the shape of her pleasing, standing with her mobile on the patio. The Doberman a statue at her side.

"Like what?"

"Like why he'd be following your husband."

Mullet could hear the gurgle of the swimming pool.

"No."

Judith paused. Mullet let the silence go.

"What guy with a brush cut?"

"A man who made no bones he was on your hubby's tail."

Bird chatter in the background of Judith's phone.

"You don't think . . .?"

"What?"

Judith laughed. "Good God, you think I've hired some thug."

"Well?"

"You've got to be kidding."

Mullet switched off the kettle. "Just checking." Poured water on two spoons of instant.

"So what's going on, Mullet?"

"You've got me." The sugar packet had less than a spoonful in it. Mullet up-ended it over the mug, shaking out every crystal. He balled the packet and tossed it into a wastebin. "The guy waited for him, then followed him home. That's all I know." He heard her doorbell ring, the Dobie going ballistic.

"I've got to go," she said. "Nothing on the . . .?"

Mullet couldn't hear her for the barking. "The what?"

"The girl."

"He hasn't seen her since Sunday."

"You'll find her though . . ."

"Sure."

Judith snapped at the dog. The racket became a growl. Rolling and ominous.

"I've got to go," she said.

Mullet hung up. He tasted the coffee. It needed at least another two spoons of sugar.

He punched in Rae-Anne's cell number. The ubiquitous voice that answered all switched-off cellphones said he could leave a message.

"It's me," he said.

"About last night . . ." he said. "Ah . . . How about I'll make you dinner? Sort of maybe eightish."

He pushed the hash button as the voice instructed him. "Your message has been sent," said the voice.

"You have a good day now," he muttered, disconnecting.

There was nothing for it but to go look for the girl. Take a walk along Main Road, check out the cafés, squeeze whatever from the prozzies pulling day trade. Not that he thought she was of their ranks but, hey, you needed to tell the client something. He took another pull at the coffee and decided it had to be hit with brandy. Against his rules this early, then again unsweetened coffee demanded drastic measures. The half-jack he kept in his bottom drawer wasn't there.

He groaned. "Ah, to heck with it" – yanked the drawer out further, disbelieving, stared at the emptiness. "Jesus, Vincent." Slammed it back. You gave the guy a place to stay, he drank your emergencies. Didn't even leave an IOU. Nice one, Vince.

The desk phone rang. Mullet slurped at the coffee, swallowed without tasting. Caller ID told him Ted Halliday. He snatched up the receiver.

"Can you tell me what's worse than someone stealing your booze?"

"Someone screwing your wife."

"I haven't got a wife."

"You know what I mean."

"It's . . . the bloody pits!"

"Vincent?"

"Bloody Vincent."

"You wanna keep an alkie in your office what d'you expect?"

"There's no sugar in the place. He drains every last drop. Heck man!"

"Mullet?"

"What?"

"Give me a break, will you! I've got a guy sticking candles in boys' arses, chopping off their heads, I don't wanna know about your grocery problems."

Mullet tried another mouthful of coffee. You might as well drink extract of seaweed. "What do you wanna know about?"

"What d'you think?"

"I already told you. The way it looks to me it's not serial or muti. This is not some guy wanting body parts to keep the ancestors pacified."

Mullet heard Ted sigh. "You're not helping."

"I don't have to. I went along for the ride."

"All the same."

"You've gotta hear me. What I'm saying is something else's going on."

"Like what?"

"How'd I know? The bodies are too staged, Ted."

"That's what serials do."

"This is different."

"How, Mullet? For Christ's sake, how?"

"If I knew I'd tell you. It's a feeling."

Ted snorted. "You're a big help."

"You're getting it free," said Mullet.

"Have a great day," said Ted, hanging up before Mullet could answer.

"You too," Mullet said, dropping the receiver onto its cradle. He drummed his fingers on the instrument. Sometimes people didn't appreciate what others had to say.

33

"Fork it!" Tommy hit the door so hard with his fist the hardboard broke. "Jesus," he said, "how's this cheap shit." Kicked at the door putting his Cats right through the panelling. "Don't people have any self-respect putting in doors like this?"

"The doors at your fancy flat are the same." Delmont sat on the floor, back against the wall, flicking his lighter. He opened the gas to see how tall a flame he could raise.

"My flat?"

"Sure. New doors is just hardboard nailed to a frame. That's standard renovating."

"You a builder now, Del?"

"I've done some of that."

"So my doors is just cheap shit?"

Delmont cut the flamethrower. "From what I've seen. Yeah."

"Four thousand bucks a month for cheap-shit doors?"

"You got a sea view."

Tommy squatted on the floor next to Delmont. The room was empty except for five freezer chests, three filled with cocktail perlemoen, the other two waiting for the night's haul. Apart from the freezers the house was empty, not even a chair to ease his weight. A house Tommy was borrowing for a few days, the owner happy with a thousand-buck rental. Grim little house in a grim little neighbourhood, still, it suited him. Nobody poking their nose into what was going on.

"Fork it," Tommy shouted again, his voice bouncing round the rooms. "You tell Adonis one thing, he does something else. You tell him two-thirty, what time does he pitch? Not two-thirty. Not three. Not three forking thirty. He knows we gotta check the place out."

"He'll pitch."

"He forking does it to piss me off. Tryin to play the main man."

"Phone him again."

"It's switched off, Delmont. Been switched off for all afternoon."

Tommy reached into his cargo pants for his cell. "Adonis schemes cos he charred Furniss he's now the larney."

Delmont shook his head. "You got it wrong."

"No, china. Adonis is a bitch. Schemes like a bitch. I know." Tommy tapped an SMS: Wer u poes? Pressed send.

Delmont lit two cigarettes, passed one to Tommy. Tommy sucked at it, wafting smoke circles towards the light bulbs. Delmont broke the silence.

"That big guy's not gonna be there?"

Tommy flicked ash off the tip. "Nah." He took a drag.

"Why's he want us to do it again?"

"The fork should I know, Del?"

"Jesus, bro." Delmont stood, jiggered at his crotch. "This's bad. We being staged."

"Sit down, Del," said Tommy, patting the cement beside him. "Relax."

Delmont did as he was told.

"It's cool. We just gotta play the hand, Del."

Tommy crushed his butt, jumped up. "Where's forking Adonis? We gotta check the place out."

Delmont squinted at him. "You said."

"What, china?"

"It'd be clean."

"Right. Except Woo's a Chink. Chink-a-ling cunning. So" – Tommy crouched before Delmont, finger tapping the guy's nose – "so, we hit any problems, thank Adonis. The big rambo's there, thank Adonis. You don't get to marry your fiancée in a big white wedding. Thank Adonis."

"I'm outta this then," said Delmont. "When we married, her and me."

"Forget it, bro." Tommy laughed. "You gonna do cheap-shit renovations instead?"

"Maybe."

"Whaaah," Tommy snorted. His cellphone vibrated with the *Star Wars* tune. An SMS from Adonis: Open the door chommy.

34

Woo showered. Dressed sober: navy suit, white shirt, dark tie. In a buffed leather satchel was all the documentation the Brotherhood could want.

He took a limousine downtown. At five o'clock the day was no cooler, the heat damp, the sweat starting in his armpits, then drying in the air-conditioned car, leaving him sticky. Yet another irritation in an irritating city of traffic congestion, too many people, too much going on.

The limo slowed behind a military truck on Tun Hua Drive. Motorbikes, mopeds, bicycles weaved through the vehicle build-up, the riders wearing surgical masks against the fumes. The masks painted with mouths, hibiscus flowers, cartoon characters, brand names.

Crazy to live here. Woo sat tense and upright on the back seat, his hands palms down on his legs, and watched a laden scooter: father and mother, a kid on the handlebars, a kid on the gas tank, a kid on the fender, the father zapping past the truck towards an oncoming bus, zipping in, the bus blaring. Even the limo driver exclaimed.

"Sometimes it is not your fate," he said to Woo.

Woo grunted an American yeah. The driver glanced at his passenger in the rear-view mirror. Woo let him look.

"You like opera?" the driver asked, pointing at the car's music deck. "I have CDs."

"Sure," said Woo in Mandarin. "Whatever."

The driver slotted in a disk. Odd Mandarin whispers and melodies filtered to the back. Woo didn't recognise anything.

He leaned forward and tapped the driver's shoulder. "Not that one," he said. "Something happier."

The driver shrugged as he stabbed off the CD. A radio station came on playing Western pop.

"That's good," said Woo.

The driver flashed him a brief glance in the rear-view. This time Woo met his eyes.

Off the hill the limo entered the dragon's den. Taipei city: tower blocks, neon, traffic, crowds.

Steel and glass. Octagonal pat kwa mirrors outside windows to deflect evil spirits, protecting office workers from inexplicable bad joss.

The limo went past the markets of fish, meat, poultry, spices, vegetables that by night would become markets of clothing and cheap goods before reverting to sell produce with the dawn.

Woo told the driver to stop at a barbershop. He was early, he could spare the time to freshen up.

A quartet of barbermaids bowed around him in white smocks, their hair in twists and braids. He was shown to a recliner. For a moment Woo thought maybe he would take the full service. He had the time, the girls were pretty. The girls were girls. They bobbed before him in expectation.

He shook his head and told them only a grooming. A short rest, a hsion-his.

Warm water soothed his feet and hands. Scented towels wrapped him. Hands as light as butterflies manicured his nails, trimmed his hair. Afterwards, he lay supine beneath their massaging. They brought him jasmine tea before he left.

The emporium was on four floors, a thousand tables.

At a table on the third floor the brothers were seated, waiting for him. Although he was early they were waiting. Woo paused, felt the muscles tighten in his neck. They could know nothing. They could suspect nothing. This was a public place, a restaurant for families. There would be no trouble.

Dragon Fire rose to greet him. "Welcome, Jim."

"Dragon Fire," said Woo in response.

They bowed to one another. The three other men rose. One, the old man, bowed. Woo knew him: White Paper Fan. The others were strangers, they shook his hand.

"Please," said Dragon Fire indicating a place for Woo at the table, as the guest of honour directly opposite White Paper Fan. His back was to the door but Woo let this go.

Rice wine and starters were already on the table.

"I have ordered the meal," said Dragon Fire, "but perhaps there is some speciality you would like. Abalone, maybe?"

The men laughed. Woo smiled.

"Here it is very good," said Dragon Fire. "You can taste the ocean. You can relish the sea in your mouth when you chew. You will leave here a stronger man for having savoured the abalone."

One of the men filled Woo's glass with rice wine. He knew Dragon Fire was riding him. What he couldn't tell was how. In threat? Or in brotherhood?

"The best in the world," he said.

"This is true," said Dragon Fire. "Let us hope it continues."

"No reason why not," said Woo. "When there is nothing left in the sea, there will always be the product of Sea Farm."

Dragon Fire laughed. "So. No abalone for the abalone man. Something else perhaps?"

Woo wiped crumbs from his setting with a red serviette. White Paper Fan handed him a menu edged in red and gold, gold binding cord, tassels hanging out the bottom. The symbols on it meant long life, happiness, dragons. He glanced at the lists of delicacies, rice staples, the Szechuan and Hunan specials. Selected shark-fin stew.

"A good choice," said Dragon Fire.

"Not as good as monkey brain," said White Paper Fan.

"Or bear's paw," said one of the henchmen.

"Or turtle," said Dragon Fire.

"Or live mice." Woo smiled. They were playing with him. He had to join the game.

"Mice very good for ulcers," said White Paper Fan.

"If these dishes were not illegal."

"There are places," said Dragon Fire.

"There are always places," said Woo.

The men made eye contact, held it, until Dragon Fire's booming voice called above the din for a waiter.

Woo watched a man come scrambling to appease. Dragon Fire gave him the additional order, the waiter retreating backwards, face low.

"You like that, Jim? They take care of us here." He reached out and gripped Woo's forearm. "When you taste the food you will know how we are honoured."

On cue came medallions of suckling pig stuffed with dates, wrapped in hemp and mint, deep-fried frog legs in batter and crushed almonds, duck, fish, shark-fin, meat, steamed vegetables, rice and noodles.

"No gweilo compromises, Jim." Dragon Fire leaned back in his chair. The corners of his mouth were liquid with saliva. "No sweet-and-sour pork. No fortune cookies. No tourists."

Which meant what? That he had become a foreigner? A tourist? Woo let the jibe pass. There were knives beneath the banter, but no blood yet. If the dragon smelt blood he would strike.

In a hand so old it was transparent, White Paper Fan raised his glass to Jim Woo, supporting it at the bottom with the fingers of his other hand. The men did the same.

"Ganbei, Jim."

Woo drained his glass, felt the sake slide into his empty stomach, burning. "To you, White Paper Fan, a man with the capacity of the ocean."

White Paper Fan nodded. "When drinking among intimate friends, even a thousand rounds are not enough."

Woo lifted his glass again. The whispery voice of White Paper Fan could lure you deep into the lair. You might even think you were among brothers.

The men began their meal. Dragon Fire picked a small lobster from the pot, held it up for inspection. The creature's legs clawing at air.

"A good one, would you say?" A question asked of nobody in particular.

He put the lobster onto his plate, broke off a leg to suck out the flesh. The lobster crawled across the porcelain.

"What do you think, Jim?" Dragon Fire raised a sharp knife. "A fighter. From the Australian suppliers." He slit the carapace, cracking open the tail to draw out the glutinous mass. This he put in a bowl. "Try it." He passed the bowl to Woo.

Woo dipped his chopsticks into the flesh, lifted out a morsel. It was fresh, salty. He handed the bowl to White Paper Fan.

"You want a leg?" Dragon Fire snapped off the slowly-moving limbs, sucked out the meat. The shells he threw onto the tablecloth. "Take one. Doesn't come better than this, Jim. Delicious. Juicy." He lifted another lobster from the pot. "Relax. Eat. Enjoy. In honour of you we are eating the produce of other seas. So you can test the competition."

Woo nodded, concentrated on his food. He was aware of the men at the table. Of how the henchmen ate ravenously, as did Dragon Fire, while White Paper Fan picked like a bird at choice bits. They ate without talking.

Throughout Woo worked at the hidden message. They liked the abalone he supplied. They wanted him to appreciate the competition. The henchmen were muscle. White Paper Fan was tradition. Dragon Fire was the dragon. The message was: if you fail us, we will miss you but you will be replaced. If you fail us, we will kill you as we have always done to those who betray us. Listen to us. Understand what we say.

Except no message was complete until after the meal. More was to come. The more troubled Woo.

A dish of steamed angelfish was placed before them. White Paper Fan helped himself first.

"Please," said Dragon Fire to Woo. "You are our guest."

Woo took a piece of fish, let the flesh infused with ginger and spring onions melt in his mouth. They ate without talking further until the meal was at an end. Then the old man held his bowl at his chin, scraping the last of the rice into his mouth. Woo did likewise. They drank a clear light broth. The men burped and settled back with toothpicks to clean their teeth, while the debris was cleared from the stained tablecloth.

Woo tensed, whatever they had to say would be said now. Whatever game they had been playing now would be revealed.

White Paper Fan spoke first. "A man in my position has many worries, Jim."

Woo nodded. The old man was looking at him, although his eyes were focused on objects more distant.

"For years we have been degenerating. We do not maintain the spirit of fraternity. Devotion. Filial piety. We show no respect. No honour. Some have become no better than bands of robbers."

"It is not like that with us," said Woo.

"No. It is not." White Paper Fan sipped at his tea. "We try to be true to the spirit. We honour the oaths. We keep the promises. But." He replaced his cup delicately in its saucer. "These days it is easier to be tempted by self-interest."

"By greed." Dragon Fire cut in, impatient with the older man's long-winded protocol.

"I have not finished my tea," said White Paper Fan.

Dragon Fire snapped his toothpick. "We have business to discuss."

But the old man ignored him. "You know the oaths, Jim. The ritual of cleansing. Remember the West Gate. It's easier to cut off your head. Only one swipe of a single blade."

"I know the oaths," said Woo, as irritated by the old man's posturing as Dragon Fire. Softly softly catchee monkey not a strategy he cherished.

"Of course." White Paper Fan went silent.

Dragon Fire let the silence drag. It was Woo who broke it.

"There is no reason, revered brother, why I would breach your trust."

"For no reason, or maybe for many reasons. It is not you we are concerned about, but we fear the cunning and mischievous nature of the Monkey. The tempter. We have known you as a boy and as a young man. We have let you prosper." The old man finished his tea.

Woo opened his satchel and handed a set of documents to Dragon Fire, a duplicate to White Paper Fan.

"Here," he said, "is everything you want to know. Balance sheets. Reconciliations. Profit and loss. Projections."

White Paper Fan pushed the papers aside. "This is not what I am talking about," he said.

"It is," said Dragon Fire, scanning the sheets. "It is exactly what we are talking about." He glanced at Woo. "This is very reassuring. Very professional, I would say."

"These figures are not yet audited," said Woo. "But that is a mere formality."

Dragon Fire stacked the sheets. "I'm sure. I'm sure." But.

The but unspoken yet it clanged in Woo's skull.

As did Oath Ten: *I shall never embezzle cash or property from my sworn brothers.*

"It has been five years," said Dragon Fire, "since your ventures began." He filled Woo's glass with sake, then his own. "When you asked for finance we gave it. Start-up capital. Expansion budgets. Whatever you presented we approved. We did this partly because we are brothers, partly because we are businessmen. We can see good opportunities as easily as Chase Manhattan. The difference is Chase Manhattan wants interest upfront. We can wait."

Until now, thought Woo, lifting his glass of rice wine.

"But five years is five years."

"And you want to know when you're going to get some return?" Woo put down his glass without drinking. He indicated the documents. "Look at the page headed projections. It's all there."

"Of course it is. In two years we see income on investment. In four years the capital is all paid back. I appreciate this, Jim."

"Exactly," said Woo. "That's the intention." This time he raised his glass, drank some wine. No one commented on his breach of etiquette.

Dragon Fire came in obliquely. "You tasted the lobster."

"Yes."

"What did you think?"

"It was good. Like you said: juicy." Woo groping here, Dragon Fire two or three moves ahead.

"We're thinking of it as a new venture."

Woo saw a gap. "You want me to explore the lobster market?"

Dragon Fire shook his head. "No. We're diversifying. Different product, different source. Isn't this what they taught you at the Harvard Business School?"

"It makes sense."

Dragon Fire tapped the documents lying on the table. "What I see here are successful ventures. Good product. Strong turnover. Conservative projections. Which is good."

"You got it," said Woo in English.

White Paper Fan glanced at him, not understanding the foreign words.

Dragon Fire smiled. "You don't want to confuse the old man." He too used English.

"You have nothing to worry about," said Woo, switching back to their dialect.

"I never thought we did. Our trust is implicit."

Dragon Fire swirled the wine in his glass. Still Woo could not relax. Still Woo felt something was unsaid. They could not know about the off-shore investments. They could not know what he had done.

Oath Sixteen: *If I knowingly convert my sworn brother's cash or property to my own use . . .*

"Our new venture," said Dragon Fire, "requires capital. I look at what you have done and I think, here is a business that needs conventional backing. Bank loans. Bank overdrafts. I look at what you have done and I think our capital could be replaced by bank finance. What bank would turn down balance sheets as strong as these?"

Woo suddenly realised where this was going.

"I see," he said.

"What's that you see?" asked Dragon Fire.

"You want me to recapitalise."

"You anticipate a problem?"

The two men held a stare, eye-wrestling.

"No. Except."

"Except?"

"It might take some time. Banks do not move fast."

Dragon Fire held up his hands, fanned his fingers.

"Persuade them. We can wait ten days."

35

When his phone rang, Roger Oxford was engrossed in watching a container ship being piloted out of the harbour. He swivelled back to his desk.

"Mr Fire on line one," said the receptionist.

Oxford said, "Is he now?" – punched button one. It was what time there? After 11 p.m.

"Dragon Fire."

"My brother," came the deep tones of Dragon Fire in slow English, "our mutual friend will be on his way back soon."

"Aah," said Oxford. What a pity.

"It is my belief he will do a runner, as the Americans call it. Do you agree?"

"Yes." Oxford doodled dollar signs on his diary. That could mean mayhem.

"He does not suspect your involvement. Of this I am certain."

Oxford cleared his throat and said in Mandarin, "What do you want me to do?"

"Let us know his intentions," said Dragon Fire, switching to his native tongue. "If he is going to run please inform me as a matter of urgency." Oxford heard a match strike and Dragon Fire inhaling. "We are fair, Roger. We are allowing him to make amends. Do you agree?"

Oxford turned back to the view. The container ship was beyond the breakwater, diesel exhaust clouding from its stacks. "He won't."

"No?"

"No. You know that."

"You have no faith in human nature, Roger."

Nor do you, thought Oxford. You would rather kill him here than there. Probably the hitman would be on the same plane as Woo.

"Either way," said Dragon Fire, "I look forward to your call."

Oxford waited to hear the disconnection click before he put down the receiver.

He would rather have heard that Woo was not returning.

36

Five on the nose Mullet cruised Sea Street before taking a parking space that was more or less his usual. No sign of Brush Cut. Heck of it was that staking Roger Oxford had to be the most boring five grand he'd earned. Ever.

All afternoon he'd tramped up and down Main buzzing the prozzies.

"You know a little Chink chick, black hair, slitty eyes, has a patch near News Café?"

The answers he got:

"You gotta buy local, bootiful."

"All Chinks got slitty eyes, darl."

"Sweetie, hows about my black hair?" Followed by an uproarious screeching.

And a lot worse.

He moved on to traipse the back streets in the hopes of a lucky break. Like there she'd be coming out of a block of flats to turn a coupla tricks before sundowners. Nada. He spent an hour in the News Café nursing rock shandies in case she put in there. Nada again. It'd been a long shot anyhow. Sucking on the last of the ice cubes from his shandy he drove to Sea Street.

About six Mullet phoned Vincent, more out of boredom than out of interest.

"So what you doing?"

"Sitting on the stoep drinking beer," he was told. "Looking at the sea."

"Nice work. The client still hanging in?"

"She's determined."

"And you're not gonna chase her away."

Vincent laughed. "Client's rights."

"I've heard tell." Mullet switched tack. "You had anyone come calling this afternoon? Checking the place out."

"Not a one."

"Maybe they won't do it."

"Always a possibility." He heard Vincent slurp at his beer. "But we're gonna wait for them anyhow."

"Thought you weren't drinking?"

"A beer's not drinking."

"Tell that to AA."

"Jesus, Mullet. Let it go."

Mullet let it go, considering whether to mention the half-jack missing from his bottom drawer.

Vincent said, "Look, it's no problem. I'm up to this."

"Didn't think you weren't," Mullet came back, putting aside the bone of contention for another day. "How's my boat?"

"Safer than in your backyard."

"I'd like to think so," said Mullet. "But I don't."

"Yeah, well, believe so, pal. Where're you anyhow?"

"Waiting on Mr Oxford."

"Your life can be so exciting," said Vincent, hardly keeping down the snigger in his tone.

"You betta believe it."

They disconnected, Mullet feeling the ways of the universe were working against him. He went over to the corner café, bought their last copy of the evening paper, the front page stained with food grease and torn. Back in the car he skim-read. Bottom of page three was a small story about the bodies in the dunes.

GRUESOME FINDS

The headless corpses of two boys have been found buried in the sand dunes up the west coast, according to a police spokesperson.

This brings to four the number

of headless corpses found in the last two months.

The bodies have not been identified but police suspect they were street children. The boys were between nine and twelve years old.

The bodies were decapitated. The heads have not been found.

It is not known whether they were sexually abused.

The police spokesperson would not comment on the prospect of a serial killer stalking street children who earn money as rent boys.

Why nothing about the candles? Why nothing about the witchdoctor muti theory?

"You want to flush him out, Ted, you've gotta do better than that," Mullet said aloud.

Or was this Naidoo being tight-arsed with the press? Most likely. Give them as little as possible they'll always be hungry. Grateful for titbits. He could hear him now. Whatever you say they'll print. Give them the works all you get is lurid headlines. A Naidoo press strategy that made detectives leak details anonymously to move their cases. As Mullet had done plenty of times.

He turned the page, was about to start in on a story about the Vice-President's million-buck sweeteners in the arms deal when Rae-Anne phoned.

"Hi, babe, we still set for tonight?"

All perky. Wonder of wonders.

"Can't see why not."

"What're you cooking?"

"A surprise." Mostly because he hadn't a clue.

"I'll bring the wine. And maybe a slab of Belgian."

From you-give-me-the-fig to coochy-coo overnight!

"That'd be good." Mullet wary here, sensing a move being played.

"Mullet?"

"Yeah."

A catch of breath.

"What's it?"

"No. Nothing that can't wait." A pause. "Still eightish?"

"Depends. Roger the Dodger stays off the nooky seven-thirty should be do-able."

"What're the chances?"

"Law of averages. Very good."

"Till then, then."

"Yup."

Mullet cut the connection. Wondered why he had that Crosby 'Déjà Vu' feeling.

And in the wondering nearly missed the Pajero heading out of the garage. To his relief Oxford put in no detours, made no love calls. Went straight home.

"There's a good boy," said Mullet, watching the Oxfords' driveway gates close. He went round the block and headed back for town, supper on his mind, Blood, Sweat and Tears playing. You make me so very happy. Was how he felt driving the De Waal curves above the shadowed city, the mountain's cloak thrown over the houses and the buildings and onto the bay.

Chinese, Mullet decided, there was nothing to beat a good Chinese takeout. The only place for that was the Hot Wok.

"Where you been, fishelman?" Mrs Saldana cried out when she saw him walk in. "I never see you anymore."

"Catching the two-timers," Mullet said.

"You like Vlinclent." She wiped her hands on a cloth, took up a pad and pencil. "He comes here rushing in last Saturday, goes rushing out Sunday. Where's he now I don't know." She licked at the pencil. "How's my boy?"

"He's doing better, Mrs S."

"I tell him he's got to get over the glief. Five months is enough."

"He's doing that."

She squinted at him. "You sure?"

Mullet nodded. The woman kept focused on him for any sign he might be holding out.

She relaxed, smiled. "What you want?"

"Dinner for two," he said, picking his choice off the menu: spring rolls, sweet-and-sour pork, veg chow mein, prawn rice: a feast.

When Mrs Saldana had the order boxed, she sorted out a bag of fortune cookies and bow-ties.

"My gilft," she said.

Mullet didn't argue.

"Sometimes you should eat here," she said as he leaned over the counter to peck her cheek, thanks. "You and your ladyfliend."

"Next time, Mrs S."

"Next time, Mrs S. Always next time, Mrs S."

He waved without turning round as he went out the door.

Mullet got to his house before Rae-Anne, for which he was thankful. Time to warm the oven, heat up the supper, clear dirty coffee mugs, crushed roaches, a pizza box, make the bed, create an atmosphere: candles, incense, Van the Man's *Moondance* on the Sony. Time to check the back stoep for Bom-Bom but not a sign that the boy had been around. Between visits he could be gone for two, three weeks at a time. One thing was certain, he would be back. Later rather than sooner, Mullet hoped.

On the kitchen table he set Chinese bowls, new chopsticks he couldn't remember when he'd acquired. Cracked a beer at the end to admire his handiwork.

Bang on seven-thirty there was Rae-Anne's key in the front door, the pock-pock of her leg on the wooden boards as she came down the passage. Some days, when she was tired, the leg seemed to get in her way. Like it was new and she wasn't used to it.

She had this spiel going into a school on an anti-drugs mission where she started by taking off her leg. "You want to scare the kids, you show them a peg leg." That got their focus. "You shoot up enough times, sooner or later you're gonna get gangrene," she'd say, waving the peg about. "A man comes with a saw to sort that out." Next show them the needle stick marks between her toes, scars of a true addict. Then toss her peg leg into their midst. Watch them back off like it was serious voodoo. Getting someone to pick it up and hand it back always took some persuading. Rae-Anne loved their boggle eyes.

Pock, pock.

"Hi, babe," she called out. "What's with the incense?"

Mullet waited, hands in the sink washing up the debris he'd collected from around the house.

She stopped in the kitchen doorway.

"Hey, so domestic. You're gonna make someone a good wife."

He turned to blow a raspberry at her. She was holding up a six-pack of beers and a large bar of Belgian dark.

"Judging by the setting just as well I didn't buy wine."

"How'd you guess?"

"Intuition, babe. A female thing." She went to him. From behind slid her hands under his T-shirt, pulled him against her. Smelt his day. Comforting if you weren't too fussy.

He turned round, soapsud hands warm and wet on her blouse. She looked up at him, smiled and waited for his lips to lock hers in a full French.

She let it linger, pleased he was in no rush. About three minutes down she broke it.

"Nice table," she said. "Candles even" – moving past him to open the back door onto the empty stoep.

"You mean that much to me," said Mullet.

"Bon Jovi?"

Mullet was about to correct her.

Rae-Anne said, "No Bom-Bom?" Glanced back at him.

"Not since yesterday." Mullet dried his hands. "Want a beer?"

"Thought you'd never ask."

He put the six-pack in the fridge, took out a frosty from his stock. While he popped it, Rae-Anne switched on the spotlights to flood the backyard. No boat visible.

"You harbouring the *Maryjane* elsewhere?"

"Vincent's got her."

She took the bottle of beer Mullet held out.

"Is that wise?"

"No."

"Necessity?"

"Something like that."

She sipped off the head.

"I'll say a prayer."

They knocked bottles and drank.

"You wanna finish one or go straight in?" said Mullet.

Rae-Anne sat down at the table where she always did, facing the window. "Let's chow. I'm famished." She watched Mullet take the cartons out of the oven. "Mrs S's?"

"Where else?"

She was onto a spring roll before he'd finished putting down the spread.

When they slowed up after the first rush of appetite, Rae-Anne said, "You get a look at the newspaper?"

"The gruesome finds story?"

"Yeah. Sounds like medicine killings."

"Uh huh. That's Ted's theory."

"You heard the price heads're going for? Twenty thousand apiece and rising."

"He told me."

She forked more noodles into her bowl.

"But you're not convinced?"

"They had candles stuck in their bums," he said. "Witchdoctors pulling muti killings don't do that. This's some guy working off a weird page."

"You're not kidding." Rae-Anne stomped to the fridge for another beer. "You want one?"

Mullet, mouth full, nodded yes.

She uncapped the bottles, plunked his on the table and sat down. "How's your other client?" Tingeing the other – as in only other – with sarcasm.

Mullet caught the dig but let it go. "If her hubby's having an affair it's not dick-driven."

"Meaning?"

"Since I've been watching he hasn't laid the bird once."

Rae-Anne took a mouthful of beer.

"'N I don't think she's a prozzie."

"Maybe they get off on hiring a PI. He grooves on the unknown stalker. She thrills on telling you stories." Rae-Anne giggled.

"Dunno. It's too strange." He raised his bowl, scraping the last of the rice into his mouth.

"Stranger than the decapitator? I don't think so."

Van the Man had ended, Mullet got up to change the disk. "What d'you fancy?"

"Something schmaltzy."

"I don't do schmaltzy."

Rae-Anne dug into her bag, fished out a CD. "Here. This." Eva Cassidy: *Songbird*.

Mullet shrugged. It could be worse. Could be Streisand. Could even be bloody Sinatra. Or the brat warbler Michael Bublé. The way Mullet evaluated Rae-Anne's taste, Eva Cassidy was the high end. He obliged. The girl had a voice you might get used to.

When he got back to the kitchen table, Rae-Anne was lining a Rizla with grass. He sat down. She glanced across at him, and said straight out, "We've gotta stop ducking this one, Mull. We've gotta make a decision."

Mullet knew what she meant. Thought, Eva, Nora, Barbara, Frank, Michael, Nat and Natalie. That was who'd be moving in too.

"At the moment I'm like, why isn't the guy saying let's do it? Why the hesitation? Or's he telling me something else? Like, actually, I don't think we should move into one pad cos I think we should split." She rolled the spliff, licked the edge. "Is that it, Mullet? Is that what you're saying?"

He shook his head. She kept her eyes on him.

"Listen, what you gotta do is talk to me. Understand? Instinct I'm strong on. Mind-reading I don't do. I wanna hear you say something."

"It's just . . ." Mullet left it there. Eva sang into their silence.

"Just what?"

The heck was, Mullet thought, he didn't want to fight with her. He just wanted things not to change. Her flat, his house. Times together, times apart. What was wrong with that?

"D'you want to split? That maybe we stop seeing each other for a while?"

"No." The word came out raspy.

"What then?" She paused, hoping he'd take the opportunity. He didn't look at her, swirled the dregs of his beer round and round the bottle. "Jesus, Mullet," Rae-Anne exploded, "tell me!" Her hand trembling, she lifted the spliff to her lips. "Say something."

Mullet leaned over with a Zippo. Fired it. "Right, then," he said. "We'll try it." Thinking even as he spoke, what're you saying?

Rae-Anne forced a laugh. "Hell, babe." She inhaled a lungful. Held it, went into his eyes for the truth. The truth was, she saw, he was doing it for her. Right, that was good enough for now. For now she could handle that. The rest would come. Or it wouldn't. She exhaled, gave him the stop. When she'd got her breath back, said, "Know it, babe, you're a hard case."

37

Woo sat alone at the table and poured the last of the sake into his glass.

There was nothing the Brotherhood could not find out. Everywhere they had spies. Which was why he had placed his accounts with Roger Oxford. A British national was unlikely to have Eastern links. He believed what he saw. He accepted the explanations he was told. His world was not one of devious plots and plans. Yet the moment Revenue Services rears its head, the brothers want their bucks. Coincidence? It had to be. The brothers could not know that he had already recapitalised. They could not know that the money was dispersed over a myriad Cayman accounts. They could not know that he was under tax investigation. The timing was an accident, it held no hidden meaning.

Nevertheless.

Woo drained off the sake, the wine bitter in his mouth.

Ten days. Ten days was too short. He would have to move fast. Take the next flight back. Put into place his contingency plans. Plans he had not expected to use for another few weeks. A pity. But what use was regret? Regret could ruin everything. He had to be flexible. Decisive. Bold.

In the lair of the dragon only the quick survived.

To hell with them. Woo left the restaurant.

Outside he turned along Huashi Street towards Snake Alley, strolling. Past department stores, piano bars, discos. He stopped to light a cigarillo, cupping his hand around the lighter, half turning. In that moment he caught sight of one of the henchmen, a way back along the street, gazing into a shop window. Woo exhaled. Another coincidence? Or a message? He grimaced at the wail of a karaoke singer doing 'Danny Boy', crossed the street to a snake vendor.

Woo indicated a fat reptile coiled around a branch at the back of the cage. The vendor nodded, opened the cage, gripped the snake behind the head with pincers. A tug and the snake came free. He held it up.

"Good," said Woo.

"Best-seller," said the vendor in English.

In one movement the man secured the snake on a wire, fastened its tail. Took a knife, slit open the stomach. The blood and bile drained into a polystyrene cup, the vendor squeezing the snake for the last drops.

To the snake's blood he added herbs, a few drops of venom. In the gesture of a man proposing a toast he offered the cup to Woo. Woo took it in a swallow, gave the vendor back his cup. He noticed the henchman had moved off.

While Woo dug in his pockets for a wad of notes, the vendor hung the snake up to dry. In the morning he'd sell the meat to a restaurant. He handed Woo a piece of paper. On it was written: You will be strong, bigger, stiffer.

Woo crumpled the note, flipped it into the street. In Mandarin added, "You stand straight?"

The vendor grinned. "Best-seller."

Woo moved off, glimpsing the henchman outside the karaoke bar, making no effort to conceal himself. Not a coincidence, a message: we're watching. Dragon Fire made him for a tourist, he'd bloody act like one. Give the henchman something to report.

Woo headed on, ignored the herbalists, the rhino horn, the bear's paw, the caged monkey, the birds, the dog carcasses. He stopped in front of a girl, maybe eleven, twelve, sleeping in a cot lined with cardboard. A man approached him.

"How much?" Woo asked.

The man wanted to know what he wanted.

"You her father?"

The man said he was.

Woo considered the sleeping child. She wasn't pretty. Her cheek reddened by a birthmark. He turned away; the henchman was standing behind him, grinning. Woo pushed past.

There is always the West Gate. At the West Gate your head will be cut off in the single pass of a blade. To appease the Brotherhood.

See the young brother, Jim. He stole. He lied. For this we took out his tongue, chopped off his hands, beheaded him.

These are the rules of the Brotherhood.

Woo walked away fast. On Huashi Street again he flagged a taxi, told him the Grand. At the hotel entrance it was the other henchman who opened the taxi door for Woo. Bland-faced. Not a hint of recognition.

Woo checked over his room. If it had been tossed there was no telling. Except the condom the girl had offered, that he'd flipped away, was in his toiletry bag.

Dragon Fire.

Your head. In the single pass of a blade. At the West Gate.

The hotel staff would've binned it.

I will be killed by a myriad of swords. I shall be killed by five thunderbolts.

Woo hit the minibar for the whiskies: two Scotch, two bourbons. He poured a Scotch first. Plopped in ice cubes.

What to do? Propped on the bed, he considered his housekeeping: there was much to do. Only a few days to do it.

Next, put through a call to the airline: cancelled the Shanghai leg and changed his booking for a seat on that night's flight out. With that settled, he took a Jack Daniel's with ice to sweeten his palate while he packed.

38

"You've gotta leave," Vincent said to David Welsh, the huge guy standing on the stoep like a spare part, stroking his beard. "Everything's gotta look normal."

"You think they're watching us?"

"No. But I figure if they're gonna do it on your night out they're somewhere down the road, waiting for you to drive past."

David kept his eyes fastened to the darkening horizon. "Strictly no interference."

"That's the deal."

He looked no happier with Vincent's reassurance.

"You've got a gun?"

Vincent shook his head.

"What if there's trouble?"

"There's not gonna be. They're not even gonna know we're here."

Marina came out of the house carrying a thermos flask of coffee in one hand, a plastic container of sandwiches in the other.

"Time you left, David," she said. "It's going to be dark soon."

For a moment Vincent thought, Jesus, the guy's digging in. He saw an anger working David's face. Even under the bush he could see jaw muscles moving.

"I'll be alright."

David nodded. "Suit yourself." Picked his keys from the table. "Another time."

Vincent noticed something happen in his eyes: a dullness spread across the pupils, resignation slackened his squint lines.

"That's what this is about," said Marina, rubbing her brother's back.

David stepped onto the sand. "We'll talk in the morning." To Vincent he said, "Why doesn't a guy like you have a gun anyhow?"

Vincent shrugged. "No call."

David slammed his bakkie door and shouted through the open window. "There's always a call."

"Complex guy," said Marina, as they stood on the stoep watching him drive off. "More ingredients than minestrone."

She and Vincent locked the dogs inside, then headed for the Isuzu hidden in the sand dunes. They carried thick jackets, the sandwiches and coffee. Vincent had night binoculars dangling round his neck.

For the first hour they sat in the Isuzu, the twilight leaching away to night. Marina wanted to talk but Vincent had gone distant, his senses alert to picking up a car approaching before he heard it.

"I thought cops talked a lot on stake-outs," she said.

Vincent bit into a sandwich. "Only in movies."

"Mostly you just sit in silence?"

"Uh huh."

"Great fun."

"Umm," he said through a mouthful of cheese-and-tomato, wondering maybe it wasn't a good idea having the client along, even a sassy client. He finished the sandwich.

"Tell me one thing," said Marina, "why haven't you got a gun?"

Vincent sipped at a coffee. "As I said, there's been no need. The type of work we do, people cheating on insurance claims, hubbies cheating on wives, wives cheating on hubbies, guys stealing petty cash, you don't need a gun."

"People stealing abalone you do."

"Might do. If you're planning to interfere."

"One thing I don't understand," she said then paused. "Can I ask you a straight question?"

Vincent nodded, felt the seat rock as she shifted sideways to face him, not that she could see him in the darkness. "I don't have to answer."

"You don't."

"Ask anyhow."

"You told me your wife was murdered. Why would they kill her instead of you?"

Vincent shut his eyes. He hadn't stopped thinking about this sober, drunk, hung over, always the two questions: Why her? Why not me?

"Assuming it's the guy you bust."

Vincent's flesh burned. He let a silence settle between them. Eventually he answered. "I don't know."

"It doesn't make sense," she said.

"Except it worked. It may as well've been me." His voice kept even. "I cracked. Left the cops. Went on the booze big time. They scored a luck. Hit the weak link."

"You might have gone crazy for revenge."

"That's why he disappeared. Playing safe." Vincent drummed his palm on the steering wheel. "You want to scare cops, you hit their families. Then always there's this thing in the back of their minds, when're they gonna get my kids, my wife, my mother, my sister. Better to mess up their minds than shoot them." He gripped the steering wheel with both hands. "Worked with me."

Suddenly the cab was too small, too airless, too enclosing. He had to move or explode with agitation.

"I'm gonna take a pee," he said, cracking the door open, almost falling out in his rush. He disappeared into the dark before Marina's "Are you alright?" had even been spoken.

The grass was damp, the wind off the sea cutting chill through his T-shirt. He headed up a dune his legs pumping at the soft sand. Tears started at the corners of his eyes.

Jesus, why now? When he wasn't thinking about Amber. Hadn't thought about her for two days. Was so of the moment he was enjoying himself. Then: pow! Why'd they kill her and not you? Factor the guilt in that you're the one left living. Your life was spared. You can live but she's gotta die for you. Jesus, Jesus, Jesus.

"Aaaaaah," he screamed at the sky.

The echo came back, "Vinceeent." Marina shouting to him. "Vinceeent."

It wasn't Marina that made him look round but headlights at the entrance to the property and the diesel throb of a truck. The lights started to move forward.

Jesus!

"Vinceeent."

Vincent went stride-running down the dune and caught Marina struggling up. They went down in a heap behind a patch of clumpgrass, his hand covering her mouth.

"They're coming," he said. "We're gonna have to stay here."

Here in the damp and the cold breeze with neither of them dressed for it. One consolation, the line of sight on the shed door was good. He let her go.

"Vincent," she said, panting from the exertion, "I'm sorry. I didn't mean . . ."

"It's fine. Leave it." He blew sand from the lenses of the binoculars. "We've got this now."

Propped on his elbows in the sand he focused on the truck. Three guys in the cab from what he could make out. Had to be complete in-your-face dickheads to think they could pull the caper twice running.

They drove slowly, by-passing the house, coming along the track to the sheds. At the first door, the shed with the tanks of cocktail abalone, the driver cut the engine.

A guy got out the passenger side and tried the shed door.

"Forking door's locked."

To Vincent and Marina his words were as clear as if he were talking to them.

"You gonna get us in here, Del, or'm I s'posed to shoot out the lock?"
The guy had a serious-looking shooter. Beretta, Vincent reckoned.

The driver's door opened, a guy slid out and fiddled at the shed door.

Mr Shooter banged on the cab roof with his gun.

"Get out, Adonis. Work time, girlie."

Number three emerged on the driver's side. Any other time Vincent would've sworn the guy was a girl. Down to wearing a fur-collared jacket. Except the way he minced had queen writ large. A bloody queer!

The guy Del clicked the lock, swung the door open.

"Forking right, Del," said Mr Shooter. "Mista Raffles personally himself."

The one Del and the queen Adonis took buckets from the back of the truck, carried them inside, Mr Shooter following.

Marina breathed out. "Bloody hell."

Vincent could feel her trembling.

"What are we going to do?"

"Nothing," he said. "Wait. Probably won't be too long." An hour max, he thought. By that time they'd be hypothermic. "You're gonna last?"

"Is there an alternative?" she said.

"No."

"Not even to get our jackets while they're busy?"

Like this was some sport they were watching and you could just dash back to the car for warmer gear.

"Too risky." Vincent lifted the binoculars. "Mr Shooter's got a big gun." Mr Shooter turned at the door.

Marina ducked involuntarily. "Oh shit."

You're right, oh shit, thought Vincent. What he wished was for more light to see clearly.

The guy lit a cigarette, the flare too brief for Vincent's wish, the match flicked into the grass. He leaned against the shed, gazing up at the stars, taking in the outline of the dunes against the night, and stared right at them for a moment. At least that was what it seemed, enough to quicken Vincent's pulse.

"Can you see his face?" whispered Marina.

Vincent adjusted the binoculars: the figure came sharp, his face still dark, then turned away, calling back into the shed.

"Come on. You filled those yet?"

He got some lip back that made him snort.

"Big deal, darlin. You wanna take your finger out, get your ring round something hot?"

More lip. Another snort. Mr Shooter stubbed the butt on the truck, pocketed the dead end.

"You better be finished," he said, going into the shed.

Vincent was impressed. A professional type. A guy with a record, wised-up enough not to leave finger-printed butts lying around.

They heard shouting, banging. Mr Shooter whacking the tanks with his gun, a likely scenario. Then the two other guys came out carrying the buckets and emptied the cocktails into the back of the truck.

For the next half-hour that was how they worked: each bucket probably a hundred cocktails in Vincent's estimation. Five buckets each at a dollar fifty US a piece, times the exchange rate equalled easy bucks. Shit-hot easy bucks. Except that didn't seem to be the opinion on the ground.

They heard Mr Shooter getting loud.

"Fork you, Adonis. What you here for is to forking work."

Vincent watched the fairy clank the bucket against Mr Shooter's chest.

Heard him scream, "Jou ma se poes."

Saw Mr Shooter hit the homo guy across the head with the gun. A one-blow pistol-whip. Mr Shooter gone mad-dog now, the stream of invective unstoppable. The homo guy reeling around dazed, heading for the gap that would take him behind the dunes to the Isuzu.

"Shit." Vincent lost him from his line of sight.

Marina got antsy beside him. "Chrissake, Vincent, where's he gone?"

"Dunno," said Vincent, focused on Mr Shooter.

Mr Shooter standing there, a bucket at his feet, the gun pointed at where the other guy had disappeared. In the door the third guy with a bucket of cocktails.

Mr Shooter shouting, "Get your arse here, darlin. Now."

He pulled a shot. Marina jerked at the report. Vincent felt the adrenaline kick in his stomach.

The homo guy screamed. Not from hurt, from anger. He came rushing into Vincent's line of sight, heading for Mr Shooter. The two going into a clasp, the homo guy pummelling at Mr Shooter's chest with both fists.

Mr Shooter laughing. "Don't you love it, darlin."

"Jesus," said Vincent. "Jesus! That's Tommy Fortune."

39

Tommy manoeuvred Adonis into the shed, picking up the bucket on the way in.

"I'm pissed off with you, girlfriend," he said, shoving him against a tank. "From this afternoon I been pissed off with you."

Adonis spat in his face.

Tommy went quiet, put the gun barrel to Adonis's forehead.

"Tommy, man, don't . . ." Delmont started, angling round the tank towards Tommy.

"Forking shut up, Del. Don't move, Del," said Tommy, eyes never leaving Adonis. He grinned. "Know what, darlin, now you gonna clean your spit off my cheek." He thrust his face forward. "Come'n."

Adonis leaned towards him, and used the sleeve of his jacket to wipe Tommy's cheek. "You satisfied?"

Tommy and Adonis standing close together, Tommy with the gun against Adonis's head.

Behind them Delmont said, "We gonna get this finished?"

Adonis smirked. Tommy pushed him away, the anger over. "So what you waiting for, Del. Start collecting, china." He put the gun down on a table.

Adonis said, "I'm not doing anymore."

"You the queen mother now," said Tommy taking the bucket. But he was laughing. "What you say, Del? Queenie doesn't wanna ruin her nail varnish."

Tommy and Delmont cleared two tanks while Adonis sat in the cab, smoking. Another five buckets and Tommy was done, shivering from scooping through the cold water.

"You think we got enough here, Del?"

"Suppose," said Delmont, unsure what answer Tommy wanted.

"Better than boat work. Just not better than heisting the truck." Tommy put a finger to his nostril, shot a glob of mucus into a tank. "Cold as a witch's tit." He jerked a thumb at the door.

40

"Who?"

Vincent kept the binoculars trained on Mr Shooter. He had to grip them hard to keep his hands from shaking. Marina squirmed closer.

"The man who killed your wife?"

He exhaled a quiet, "Sssh."

"Vincent, is it?"

"Yes." He was wound so tight he had to force himself to breathe slowly. Marina fastened her hand on his arm. His stomach muscles were a knot, a blackness moved across his vision and he blinked to clear his sight.

"What are you going to do?"

Vincent relaxed his fingers, lowering the binoculars. Sometimes it was best not to have a gun. "Wait," he said. He had waited so many months for this moment. A few more hours, even another day, would make no difference. Especially now that he had the drop on Tommy Chommy. He should have realised the instant he heard the guy talk.

They watched the fridge truck reverse away from the shed up the short rise. It did a two point outside the house, wheels spinning on the gravel.

"Let's go."

Vincent jumped up and started running. They slid fast down the dune.

"We're going to lose them," Marina shouted as they wrenched at the cab doors.

"No ways," said Vincent, turning the ignition, swearing, the engine dead under the key.

"For heaven's sake!" Marina was out the cab, making for the garage beside the house. "We'll take the Z3."

She tossed him the keys. "Let's go."

By the time they were down the sand track and onto the tar road, the fridge truck was gone. Vincent hesitated, chances were they'd be headed for a drop in the city. He jerked the wheel right, took off on maximum revs.

"We'll never catch them," said Marina.

Vincent didn't respond, working the gears through the numbers, the speedo up at one-ninety.

Ten minutes later they came up behind the heist van stopped at a traffic light in a small town. Vincent stayed well back in the dark between street lights.

"You embarrassed?" said Marina.

"I've known worse," Vincent replied, riding the clutch. The light went green, the fridge truck rolling smoothly off.

"Just keep us with them," she said, shifting forward to make him put his foot down. "Before the light catches us."

"It's cool." Vincent glanced at her. "They're headed for the city."

"You'd better be right."

The light turned orange, red, Vincent slowed to a stop.

"Jesus!" He felt the force of Marina's spittle.

"Stay cool. He won't get away."

"He'd better not."

Vincent slipped the gear into first. In the rear-view mirror saw a car come out of a side street and turn in behind them. A white Golf with city plates. Details he noted automatically without knowing he was doing it.

The light changed and they drove off, the Golf following. The truck was a little more than a kilometre ahead, cruising. Vincent stuck at ninety to let the Golf overtake. Eventually the guy did but was in no hurry, opening up a gap and then sitting there all the way into the city.

On the approaches Vincent closed the distance, the traffic was sparse enough but to get caught at a red light now would be a major problem. He came up behind the Golf, pleased to have a shield. When the truck took an off-ramp, the Golf kept straight on, and Vincent cursed softly.

"Not so easy now," said Marina.

They entered a main arterial that headed into the poor neighbourhoods. The only cars were kerb crawlers cruising the strip for prostitutes. Vincent held well back, skipping through traffic lights on the orange until the truck turned suddenly left into the suburb.

"God!" Marina swung on him. "Now you've lost them."

Vincent accelerated, squealing the tyres as they cornered. The street was empty.

Marina thumped at the dashboard. "Bloody dammit!"

They went through one intersection, two, on the third Vincent saw a flash of tail lights to his right, about a hundred metres down the street. He went round the block to approach from the other side. In the driveway of a face-brick and stucco house stood the fridge truck, its headlights on a guy unlocking the doors to a garage.

Vincent let out a sigh of relief.

Marina said, "You're a lucky man, Vincent Saldana." She wrote down the address as they went past.

The number on the wall seared itself into Vincent's brain.

41

As he turned onto the dirt road that led to Helderrand, Arno Loots caught the boy in the car's headlights. He was about fifty metres away, facing the car, ghosting, his face painted white. Arno thought, tribal initiate? What the fuck's the bastard doing on the estate? He floored the accelerator. The boy leapt into the vine rows and disappeared. Arno braked, skidding the car to face into the trellises. He grabbed the Maglite lying on the passenger-side floor and popped open the driver's door.

"Hey," he yelled. "Hey boy!" – flashing the torch over the tops of the vines.

Off to the right he picked out the spook-face, the dark holes of the eyes and the mouth making it a disembodied skull floating free. Arno started to run, bashing through the vines, the loam sucking at his boots.

"Boy!" he shouted. "Come here, boy."

Then he stopped, clicked off the torch and listened. He could hear the throb of the Golf's engine and the boy running far off to his left now, and behind him. Somehow their paths had crossed, the boy slipping past without his even sensing it. Then the car's engine died. Arno flashed his torch back towards the road: in the beam the white face gleamed briefly and was gone.

Arno killed the light and bent down, moving along the vine row fast and silent. There had to be two of them. From the dark of the vines he scoped his car: no sign of anyone, nor among the vines opposite. He approached the Golf. The door was open, the keys in the ignition. He didn't like being played with.

"Hey," he called, "come here fuckers. What's your game?" – sweeping the torch beam across a one-eighty-degree arc. At the furthest extremity he thought he glimpsed a flick of white but couldn't be sure.

"I'll get you fuckers. You don't want to mess here." He laughed his heh, heh, heh, heh, and got into the car. All the way through the vineyards and then along the oak avenue he drove slowly, waving the torch into the darkness as he would when hunting game.

Nothing. Not so much as a glint off furtive eyes.

The white faces disturbed him. The way the boys had played with him particularly.

Arno went in the manor's front door and straight to the bar. He poured three fingers of some ten-year-old vintage Woo was always on about and knocked down a mouthful that brought tears to his eyes. The shit he had to do for Woo was un-fucking-believable. Keep score on the cocksucking Tommy. Ride shotgun for Marina except she didn't know it. What for? In case the ex-cop lost it at the sight of his wife's killer? In case Marina had it off with the guy? Come on! The guy was an alkie. He wasn't going to do anything untanked. Woo's fucking games within games like this was some kind of amusement park. Disneyland for psychopaths. Arno finished the brandy, poured another.

The thing that worried him about the white-faced boys in the vineyard was that they were too young for initiates. Too small. This was some other shit going down here. Like the street kids had come to the country for a fucking holiday.

Heh, heh, heh, heh. Arno swirled the brandy, took two pulls in quick succession. Maybe he should hunt them? See what the difference was between a town and a country shoot. He went to the armoury and selected a crossbow. A walk-in safe set in the wall, but to Woo an armoury.

The boy stepped into the road. The car was well ahead, its tail lights dull red in the dust. He hitched a small backpack onto his shoulder and started walking towards the house. As he neared he could see the open front door, the entrance hall stark with light. He kept to the shadows, approaching slowly.

The man appeared in the doorway. He placed a crossbow and a box on a side table, then disappeared into a room the boy couldn't see. The boy eased the backpack from his shoulder, taking out the pistol. He edged along a low wall until he was opposite the door.

The man came out and sat on a bench beside the door. He took a drink from the glass he held. The boy watched him put down the glass and take a cigar out of his shirt pocket and clip the end. The man said something as he flicked at his lighter to raise a flame.

"Come on, damn you." Arno shook the lighter and flicked at it again. Woo and his goddamned Dunhills that never goddamned worked. A flame shot up. Arno stuck the cigar into it and sucked.

Some kind of wonderful. With a sigh let the smoke from his mouth.

Glass in one hand, cigar in the other he contemplated the darkness. Did he really have the juice to hunt the boys? Wouldn't it just be better to chill? Slot one of Woo's pornos into the DVD. Fuck the kids. If they were still hanging around in the morning, he'd sort them then.

He raised the glass and beyond its bulge saw a shadow detach itself from the night.

The boy slid over the werf wall. He crossed the grass towards the steps that led onto the stoep of the manor house. The man sat there smoking and drinking, unconcerned. The boy realised that when he reached the steps the man would see him. He took the pistol in both hands and racked in a load. This much he knew.

Arno reacted more to the slide of the pistol being cocked than the shadow. The shadow could have been imagination. No mistaking the sound of a gun being readied.

The boy stood one step down at the edge of the stoep. White-faced, expressionless. The gun not wavering.

"You're one lucky bastard I didn't catch you in the vineyard," said Arno, blowing smoke at the boy.

The boy said nothing, moved up the final step.

Arno stuck the cigar in his mouth and shifted the glass to his right hand.

"So, tottie? Where's your mate?"

The boy motioned with the gun from Arno to the floor.

"Huh?" Arno took the cigar from his mouth. "What's the deal? Use your tongue, tottie."

Again the boy moved the gun up and down.

Arno frowned. "What's it, hey? What's it?" Then he understood. Heh, heh, heh, heh. "You want me on my knees? Forget it, tottie. You're gonna shoot me, shoot me right here." Arno held out his arms, crucifixion-style.

The boy adjusted his aim towards the man's body.

"Bugger me," said Arno. "We're a wised-up little tottie, aren't we?"

Arno brought down his arms. What concerned him more than the boy with the gun was the other one somewhere in the dark, creeping around so silently. He took a toke on the cigar. In puffs from the corner of his mouth, exhaled the smoke. He and the boy held in an eye-lock. Wherever the other one was, he was deadly quiet. Arno shifted on the bench to give his right arm more swing.

"Right, tottie. Let's get down to it."

No response from the boy.

"What've you got that white shit on your face for anyway? You're not kidding me you're tribal initiates. Kid your size's got a wee willy winkie. Know what I mean." Heh, heh, heh, heh.

As he went into the laugh, Arno threw the glass. Saw it smash against the boy's head. The boy fired twice. The first bullet clipped Arno's shoulder as he rolled. The second thunked into the manor house door. When he made the entrance hall, Arno scrabbled for the crossbow, pulling the side table over.

The boy stood in the doorway and fired again. Arno felt the whistle of the bullet but no pain. The kid wasn't a fucking shooter. He heard the click of a misfire and lunged and caught the boy's ankle. They went down, the boy hammering at him but the boy had no strength against the man. Arno locked him in a hold, smashed his head against the wall until the boy went limp.

When the boy came round he was tied to a post. A spotlight trained on him. Blood had dried in streaks down his face.

From the darkness the man said to him, "You awake at last, tottie?"

The boy pissed himself.

"No longer Mista Tough Guy, heh!" The man laughed: heh, heh, heh, heh.

Arno put the first bolt into the post above the boy's head.

"That was on purpose, tottie."

The boy had his mouth open, screaming.

The second bolt tore a chunk out of the boy's thigh.

"No misfires with a crossbow," said Arno.

He lowered the bow, stepped into the grip, drew the string, raised the bow, put in the bolt.

"Coming ready or not, tottie."

Arno brought up the bow, sighted, squeezed the trigger, bracing against the crossbow's shudder. He saw the bolt go home. Smack through the heart.

42

"It was Tommy Fortune."

"You reckon?"

"I was there."

"It was dark. You were what, a hundred metres away?"

"I had night binoculars."

"Big deal."

"It was Tommy Fortune, I'm telling you."

Mullet sighed, gazed across his empty backyard, hoping to God the *Maryjane* was safe and secure. That the problem with the Isuzu was a dud battery. "Right then, it was Tommy Fortune. So what?"

"So lend me your gun."

"You're joking! What're you gonna do? Shoot him?"

"Probably." Vincent put down his coffee. What Mullet managed to do with instant was make the worst cup of coffee in the world. "Come on, Mullet. The guy's dangerous."

"So're you."

"It's for protection."

"That's what everybody says." Mullet added a shot of brandy to his coffee. "You want some of this?"

Vincent shook his head. "I want to borrow your gun."

"Maybe a better idea would be to get my boat back. To put the invoice in so we can be paid. Job's over. Where's the bucks, Vince?"

"I'm gonna phone her when I get to the office."

"So what're we waiting for?"

"You." Vincent stared at the brandy bottle on the stoep table: a tot would be great. A tot would be fatal. "For you to get the gun."

"I'm not gonna do that," said Mullet. "Because right now you don't need it. This Tommy Fortune didn't kill Amber. She died in a car crash, Vince. An accident. So he sent you funny notes. So he threatened to get you. So what? Big talk. That's what it was, Vince. Posturing. Dump the paranoia, guy. Kick the fixation, you're dealing with some yobbo-thug who looks like the yobbo-thug Tommy Fortune."

"Sorry I asked."

"Right then. You're gonna drop the idea?"

"I didn't say that."

"Leave it, Vince. Just leave it." Mullet watched a rat creeping along his yard fence. When the cat was around, the only rats you found were dead. He reached for the catapult he kept hanging from a nail on the stoep, took aim, zinged a metal ball bearing at the rodent. The bearing struck the fence and the rat jumped vertically, cartoon-like, before leaping into the pile of wood, bricks and junk piled against the fence. "Bastard."

Vincent forced a laugh. "You should use a gun."

"That's what I mean," said Mullet. "That's why I'm not lending it to you."

Vincent shrugged. "Suit yourself."

They went silent. Mullet considered if he shouldn't put out poison. Or get another cat. With Rae-Anne moving in he wouldn't feel guilty about not getting home on time to feed it. He turned to Vincent.

"You're gonna tune him?"

"Eventually. Probably. Right now I'm gonna follow him around a bit. Get to learn his scene."

"This's not work."

"There're jobs piling up at the office?"

"I've got things that need doing." Mullet put down the catapult. He wanted to take a shower, ease his way into the day. Getting hauled out of sleep before sparrows wasn't good. That Vincent stank of stale sweat and needed a shower more than he did wasn't helping. Mostly he couldn't see how he was going to hold out on the gun. In the end he knew he'd back down. It was part of trusting the guy. Trusting the guy wouldn't do anything stupid.

Eventually he said, "Right then." He stood up. "I'm doing this against my feelings, Vince, but I'm doing this because I think if I don't you're gonna get some shit shooter from someone. No doubt I'm gonna regret this either way." Mullet moved towards the kitchen. "I'm hitting the shower. So should you. How about we meet later at the office. Yeah?"

Vincent grinned. "Yeah. I'll see myself out." He sloshed the rest of his coffee onto the patchy grass when Mullet wasn't looking.

"Hey, something else that happened I meant to tell you." And he told Mullet about the white Golf. "Could have been pure coincidence. But if you want a gut reaction he was keeping tabs on them."

Mullet thought, white Golf? "You get the number?"

Vincent handed him a scrap of paper. Mullet glanced at it.

"This's the plate I gave Ted to check out. Interesting, hey? Two days ago a guy in a white Golf put in an appearance to follow my fella home."

"You're saying?"

"Dunno. More'n coincidence."

After he'd showered and dressed, Mullet went to get his spare gun. He kept it in the built-in wardrobe, in the drawer with his socks. Not exactly the wall-mounted safe the law required but as his house wasn't the sort of house a burglar was likely to hit, a good alternative. He rummaged, anticipating the solidity of the metal. Just socks. He scooped out bundles and singles, and dumped them on the bed. Nothing. No Tokarev keepsake. Mullet pulled out the drawer. Pulled out the one below it with his jocks, upended it over the bed. No gun there either. Nothing in the third drawer but an old tracksuit bottom and a pair of surfer's baggies.

He sat on the bed, doing a slow inventory of any place he could've put it. Not in the kitchen, not in the spare room. The pistol had no other home but his sock drawer. That's where he'd put it. Two weeks back, a Saturday afternoon, he'd taken Rae-Anne to the quarry for shooting practice. Afterwards she'd made macaroni cheese while he'd sat at the kitchen table cleaning the guns: his Astra and the Tokarev. Afterwards he'd stowed them. He leaned over, opened the door of his bedside table. The Astra was there on the upper shelf where he'd put it last night. Maybe Rae-Anne had taken the spare when she came in and found Bom-Bom on the stoep.

He dialled her cellphone.

"Doll?" she said. "What's happening?"

"Strange shit," he said. "D'you take the pistol maybe?"

"You can't find it?"

"Nowhere."

"You've looked?"

"I only keep it one place, Rae. If the gun's not there, then the gun's missing."

"I haven't got it."

"Heck of it," he said.

Mullet tossed his house. Nowhere the gun.

He left the place wrecked and headed for town. Maybe, just maybe, it was at the office. Given the ache in his stomach Mullet didn't believe so. But he had to hope. Otherwise suspect number one was Bom-Bom. And what an arse would that make him out? One scary thought that Bom-Bom had access any time he pleased.

43

Halfway to the office Mullet's cellphone rang: his one and only client, blonde spiky-haired Judith.

"Where are you?" she said.

"Eastern Boulevard. You want to see me?" Mullet angled for the Wood-stock turn-off before she answered.

"I've got something to show you. Something completely perverted. Disgusting."

"To do with your husband?"

"Who else, Mr Mendes? Who fucking else?"

Persuasive language, Mullet thought as he thumbed off the connection.

What she had was a photograph of a kid giving Roger a blow job. A big glossy print in black and white that had been delivered by courier before she'd had her first cup of tea. Its brown A4 envelope lay on the coffee table with the courier's tracking record in a plastic pocket glued beside the address.

Mullet put down the photograph, picked up the envelope.

"They must have got it from somewhere," he said. "Be easy enough to find out where."

"I'm not interested in where they got it," said Judith.

He glanced up at her standing at the window looking at the Doberman in the garden. Red Capri pants tight across her bum. Thin ankles, her feet in white takkies, what she probably called tennis shoes. Her blouse white too. A tumbler of orange juice on the coffee table. Apart from the language slip on the phone you wouldn't say she'd just received a photie of her husband coming on the paedophile.

"Can I have a glass of that?" asked Mullet.

Judith turned towards him. "I'm sorry. Of course. With gin?"

"If that's what you're having."

"It is."

Mullet pulled a wry face and took a closer look at the photograph as she headed for the kitchen. Roger was naked, the boy dressed but barefoot. The camera to the side and behind putting Roger almost in profile, but the print was too blurred to see his face or much of the boy's face for that matter. If you didn't imagine what was going on there was nothing explicit to tell you. The room could have been anywhere. Board floors and white wall. No furniture, nothing hanging on the wall. The boy had his hands by his sides bending into Roger's crotch. Roger was leaning, slightly on his toes, his heels barely touching the floor, one hand against the wall taking his weight, his right hand massaging the boy's scalp.

"It's horrible." Judith handed Mullet a tall orange juice. "That's my husband. For Chrissakes!" She shuddered her revulsion.

Mullet took a swallow of the drink, real squeezed oranges.

"There're some funny things going on here," he said.

"Bloody right there are."

"Like why's the boy dressed and Roger's naked? Shoulda been the other way round I'd of thought. The sort of place that has this stuff happening, the punters want to get an eyeful too. Run their hands over the goods."

"Oh God, must you?"

"So that's strange."

"Nauseating, you mean."

"Then you look at the shadows and they're kinda not quite right. And also you can't see his dick. From this angle you shoulda been able to see his dick."

Judith groaned. "It's in the child's mouth."

"Well, not all of it. Some of it should be visible." Mullet sipped at his gin and orange. "Have you got a magnifying glass, perhaps?"

"You're kidding?"

He tapped at the photograph. "You're sure this is your husband?"

"You know it's him."

"It's his face. Is it his body?"

Judith stared at him. "What?"

Mullet shrugged. "Is this his body?"

Judith went to a side table and pulled out a drawer. She rummaged inside, removing packs of playing cards, a box of dominoes, until she hauled out a pair of cheap reading glasses. She peered at the photograph.

"It's his body."

"Can you see his dick?"

"Look for yourself. It's him alright."

Mullet did. There was no way this would've made it to the porno sites. The boy seemed to be praying. He had his eyes closed and there was too much shadow to see his mouth. And Roger couldn't even have been at half mast. No action, no satisfaction.

"How d'you know?" Mullet asked.

"The scar on his backside."

Mullet shifted the glasses. He saw the scar. "Looks like a bullet wound."

"I've no idea," said Judith. "He brought it to our marriage. Apparently when he was a youngster he sat on a nail and it festered."

"So who d'you think sent you this?" Mullet put down the photograph and the specs and lifted his drink. The gin made the orange smell like dawn freshness. He caught some pieces of pulp against his teeth.

Judith sighed. "It could have been any one of a hundred people. I told you last time, Roger is not a nice man. There's confirmation lying in front of you. He behaves despicably. He has enemies. We've not made a secret of the fact that we don't get on. Maybe someone is doing me a favour."

Mullet leaned back on the couch. All the time he'd been there Judith hadn't sat down.

"What I don't understand," he said, "is why you wanted me to see this?"

Judith glanced at him sharply and away. She sat on the other couch.

"I would have thought it was obvious. A client tells me my husband is soliciting rent boys. You tell me he's having an affair with a woman young enough to be his daughter. The next thing I know he's getting a blow job from a child. I would have thought this is the sort of information you would need for your investigation?"

"I don't know," said Mullet. "So far he's done nothing but take this chick out to dinner 'n have a drink with her. The only thing strange that's happened is the guy followed him home one evening."

Judith drained off her glass, set it on the coffee table, flashed an eye contact at Mullet. Then got up and went to the window. The Doberman started barking.

Mullet stood, talking to her back. "You want me to start digging around, I can do that too."

Judith turned to face him. "OK. I still want the name of that girl. And if you see the man again I want to know." She took an envelope from the drawer where the specs had been. "If you need more money this will cover it."

Mullet judged by the thickness of the envelope about five thousand. He frowned.

"Take it."

"You're in the black still."

"Whatever. I want results, Mr Mendes. I want her name."

Mullet pocketed the envelope. He pointed at the photograph. "I'd like to have someone have a look at that. And the envelope."

"Not yet." She smiled. "After I've shown my lawyer."

When the driveway gates closed behind Mullet's car and the Doberman had padded back to her side, Judith dialled her husband on his cellphone.

"I've shown Mendes the pornographic photograph," she said.

She could imagine Roger swivelling in his chair to gaze at the harbour. "And he said?"

"That he couldn't see your prick. Although he used the word dick."

Oxford laughed.

"He thought maybe the picture was a fake."

"Smart man."

Judith shut the front door, leaving the dog outside.

"I think what I'd like to do is cut Jim Woo to ribbons."

"You and many others," said Oxford. "Including my friend Dragon Fire."

"He's a complete bastard."

"He plays a mean hand, Judith. But we've always known that. And so does the Brotherhood."

"I know." She said it faintly, walking back into the room where the photograph of her husband in flagrante lay on the coffee table. A Jim Woo masterpiece. She took the dregs of her gin and orange.

"It'll be organised," Oxford was saying. "The money will simply up and disappear."

Judith sat on the couch, sliding the photograph towards her. "I just hope we know what we're doing."

"We do, precious. Trust me."

They rang off, Judith wondering, what if the photograph wasn't a fake?

Mullet pulled over in a side street to count the money. Five thousand bucks. Enough to keep him on the job. He rummaged among the debris on the passenger seat for a mint chew. The gin had settled a warm hand on his neck that was lulling, made the day a more benign place. He had a feeling there was weird stuff happening in the background but did he care? Heck no. If Judith Oxford wanted to drink gin first thing in the morning he'd go with it. If Judith Oxford wanted the name of the girl, he'd get her the name of the girl. What he couldn't figure out was where the fake porno pic fitted in. But hey, God worked in mysterious ways.

Mullet fired the ignition. If the girl was to be found, now was as good a time as any.

44

Marina said, "Why don't we do it this way, Vincent? Why don't you and your partner come up over the weekend to collect the boat and the bakkie? He can do some fishing. Maybe we can dive some abalone?"

"Sounds good," said Vincent.

"You don't mind waiting a few days for your money?"

"It's no problem."

"If you want to spend the night, that would be fine."

Was it a come-on? He couldn't be sure. Like he'd been unable to read the signals the day of the heist. Was she, wasn't she? She flirted. At the first meeting, asking him to drive the roadster. Always a suggestive edge. Like now.

Her creamy voice: "And Vincent, thanks. You've been a great help."

Vincent felt the heat in his cheeks. He mumbled, sure.

"Despite the ignition problems."

"Coulda done without that hitch," he said.

She laughed. "Things happen. Anyhow, David's fixed it. Something to do with a battery terminal." He could hear a kettle boiling. "Only other thing, Vincent, could we have the report soonest. For the police and our insurers."

Vincent thought, Shit!, as he retraced the streets they'd driven through not ten hours before following the fridge truck to the drop house. Instead he said, "It'll be with you this afternoon. A fax good?"

"Appreciated. Till Saturday, Vincent."

They disconnected and Vincent stopped the car two houses down from the one where he'd seen Tommy Fortune take a piss. There were other cars in the street, an old guy walking a skinny dog on a lead, otherwise no one, it could have been a cemetery. The trouble with hanging out in this sort of street was that in most houses someone was home, nightshift workers, unemployed boilermakers, slackers on disability grants. The last thing he wanted was a chat with some bored guy in a tank vest. Vincent settled lower in the seat. There were two things he regretted not having: a gun and a hipflask of VO brandy.

Four hours later Vincent thought, gun or no gun he was going to take a look-see. Also he kept nodding off in the heat. If he didn't move he wasn't going to stay awake. He got out and stretched. Guy some houses down sitting on the stoep with a smoke and a Coke, watching him. He looked at the drop house: two rooms with curtains open. Maybe the boys were still asleep? The guy on the stoep went indoors. Vincent popped the boot and sorted through the tools, selecting the tyre iron, more with a weapon in mind than any idea of breaking and entering. He held it in his right hand, the shaft up against his forearm. Firepower would have been better, given the likes of Tommy Chommy.

He said out loud, "Here goes" – and dropped the boot lid.

Vincent hitched his jeans and walked down the street until he was opposite the house, then crossed over. The gate was latched and clicked open under his thumb, Vincent pausing at the noise, an eye on the windows. He pushed at the gate. It scraped back across the flagstone path. The garden was a mess. Dead plants, weeds, litter under the shrubs. The grass burnt brown. Dogshit giving off a sweet stench. He swatted at a fly buzzing his ear. Still no movement at the window. He walked up the path, mounted the two steps onto the stoep. Once the stoep floor would have been red, shiny, now the paint was flaking, patches of concrete showing through. The front door had full-length glass panels, the glass thick and ridged, impossible to see through. He pressed the buzzer. If it rang in the house he couldn't hear it. He pressed again, then rapped his knuckles on a glass panel. Next door a dog started barking. Vincent took a step back.

45

Mullet cruised Main Road. There were prozzies in the shade of the trees, but as yet no one actively touting for business. Too early for the lunch johns. They gave him the eye, one hoiked her miniskirt. Mullet waved. Oxford's little favourite not among them. In a break in the traffic he

U-turned towards the city, ramped the pavement and parked beneath the bluegums. A car guard whistled at him.

"Watch your car?"

"It's not going anywhere," said Mullet.

The guy didn't break his grin, angling over with a tatty piece of white card held out to seal the contract. Mullet took it. He hated car guards. All the same paid up.

"You want a nice girl?" the guy asked.

Heck of it, Mullet thought, a pimp too. Talk about multi-tasking. Probably could arrange a side order of Colombian snow if you wanted it. Given the advertising habitués of this strip no doubt a really neat arrangement.

"Not today," said Mullet.

"Desirée gives fine head." The guy's grin still hadn't stopped.

"I'm sure."

"For you fifty bucks."

Mullet whistled. "Desirée a man or a woman?"

The guy cracked up. "Whichever you want."

Mullet locked his car. The guy had a high-end cellphone out, a photo of Desirée on the screen. "How's forty bucks?"

"Tell you what . . ." Mullet glanced at the name on the card, Gabriel. "Tell you what, Gabriel, some other time, hey."

The car guard snapped closed his cellphone. "Any time," he said. "For you special price" – moved off, whistling at another customer driving in.

Mullet crossed the road, a flash of red on a poster catching his eye. There on the lamppost a picture of Oxford's squeeze in a sequined mini. Candy Liu. Her name in cursive black, spread across the poster, her hands cradling a mike, her mouth crooning. Behind her a pianist, a Latin-looking greasy guy, head down. No doubt that it was her. Mullet hauled out the photographs he'd snapped of her at the News Café. Exact match. The poster told him Candy Liu and Ricardo would be at the Blue Dolphin Wednesday to Sunday for six weeks. Starting tonight. Mullet tried to strip off the poster but the corner tore. He looked across the street at the car guard busy selling a blow job to a ponytail.

Mullet called, "Gabriel."

The guy stopped his spiel, turned round.

Mullet waved him over.

Gabriel shouted, "What you want?"

Mullet kept up the wave.

"You making me lose business," said Gabriel. He gestured at the cars driving onto his patch. "Three cars."

"How about this?" said Mullet. "For forty bucks you take a picture of this poster and send it to my phone." He held up his cellphone and four tens.

Gabriel gave him the are-you-mad frown. "You wanna do that, you need a phone like this" – he waggled the Nokia in Mullet's face.

"That right?"

"State of the art." Gabriel grinning at him a full set of white.

"How much?" said Mullet.

"Five hundred. With the picture of Desirée." He handed Mullet the phone.

"Deal. You wanna take out the sim card?"

Gabriel shook his head. "Nothing on it but Desirée."

"Then how about you snap a picture of the poster?"

Gabriel shrugged, taking Mullet through the motions.

From his jacket pocket Mullet extracted the envelope Judith had given him. Gabriel jigged from foot to foot like he was about to do the hundred metres.

"If you're thinking of snatching it, don't. I've got a very big gun." He let Gabriel glimpse the hardware stuck in his belt while he counted five blue ones onto the guy's hand a note at a time.

The money disappeared into Gabriel's jeans and he pulled out a chirping cellphone.

"Quite the connected man."

"I'm cool," said Gabriel turning away to answer the call in a language Mullet couldn't place, though he thought it might be some kind of French.

Twenty minutes later he stood at the Blue Dolphin's reception desk, a waitress hovering beside him asking if he had a booking. How many would there be for lunch? Smoking or non-smoking? On the desktop were flyers advertising Candy Liu and Ricardo. Mullet lifted one, said he didn't want to eat but could he see the manager? The waitress told him one moment sir and fetched a woman who could have run a second career as a TV announcer, her smile was that permanent.

"I'm trying to contact Candy Liu," said Mullet, "you don't have a number perhaps, or an address?"

"I'm afraid not," said the smiler.

"Her agency then?"

"She's not with an agency as far as I know."

There was none of the smile in the woman's eyes. Mullet could see she had him slotted as a debt collector.

"You mean she just walked in here one day and you hired her for a six-week stint?"

The smile stayed firm. "I heard her singing at another restaurant. When her gig finished there, she and Ricardo came here. They're very popular." The woman moved behind the desk. "May I ask why you want to contact her?"

"Sure," said Mullet. "I want an autograph."

The woman picked up a pen. "Then she's on tonight. Should I make a booking?"

Mullet unleashed a smile of equal charm. "Why not? For two for eight. In the name of Mendes."

His stomach growled at the thought of eating.

Mullet hit Quay Four, ordered calamari rings and chips and a large draught. The tables in the sun were filled with tourists but he found a place at the end of a bench of Germans. They ja-ja'd to let him know they didn't mind. Mullet got straight into the food he was that ravenous, enjoying the lulling flow of gutturals. When the Germans stood up to leave one of the men asked him where the ferries departed for Robben Island. Mullet pointed at the Mandela Gateway, his mouth crammed with chips.

"You have been there?" the man asked. "To Robben Island?" The whole group looking at him now.

Mullet nodded. He swallowed and wiped his mouth. "If Dachau's ten, this doesn't make it onto the scale," he said.

They all laughed, although Mullet couldn't understand why.

When he'd finished eating he tried calling Judith but there was voicemail on both the landline and the cellphone. He ordered another beer and sent an SMS. Not his favourite means of communication but heck it would show her he moved in the modern world. He held the phone in his left hand, poked at the buttons with the index finger of his right.

Her name candy liu a singr mor 2nite

He sent it and the photo of the poster.

Now more than before he thought Judith was wrong. Oxford wasn't having an affair unless he was merrily poking the crooner at lunchtimes. But a late-night supper and an afternoon drink didn't equal lust in the dust. As for the picture, sure he could buy Rog as a paedophile, then again the picture looked dicey. What nagged at Mullet was the drama. Judith's hype. Kiddie blow jobs. Yet Rog went home most nights like your average nine-to-fiver. What the heck? The lady was paying, he'd get what she wanted.

"Another beer?" The waiter wiped a cloth across the table and removed his empty plate.

"Great idea." Mullet glanced at the guy over his sunglasses. "And the bill."

Half an hour in the sun with a cold pint wouldn't alter the course of destiny. He watched a seal haul out on the slipway of the sea rescue services. It didn't go far, collapsing in the first patch of sun. There was something about the life of seals that was infinitely better than the life of humans. Mullet gave a half sigh. The waiter put down his beer. Except seals didn't have cold beer in frosted glasses. He toasted the flippered creature.

They didn't have missing guns. Or girlfriends moving in either. Complications life would be easier without. But he'd said OK to Rae-Anne and OK it would be until it wasn't OK any longer. That day Mullet reckoned was going to dawn as surely as any other. The only question was: when? He took a long pull at the beer to drown the thought. It helped too that his cellphone started squirming on the table top.

Vincent calling.

"You're gonna tell me you zapped out to collect the bucks?"

"What?"

"Nothing," said Mullet.

"I've sorted it. She said why don't we come on Saturday. Do some fishing. Dive some abalone. Have a braai. Rae-Anne too. I said fine."

"This's business? Or the chick?"

"We can wait a coupla days."

"That's not an answer. Driving her Z3's not making out, Vince. She's a client."

"Yeah, yeah. You've got the gun for me?"

Mullet grimaced at Vincent's change of subject.

"It's missing."

"What d'you mean missing?"

"Gone. Stolen. But I reckon I know who's got it?"

"Your street kid?"

"Sharp one, Sherlock."

"Jesus."

"You said it." Mullet watched the seal. Swim, bask, eat. If there weren't sharks in the sea, seal would be a good lifestyle. "So where're you Vince?"

"Going home to get some sleep. I checked out the drop house, there's nothing there. No fridge truck in the garage, no one home. Some dirty cups in the kitchen. TV and a coupla chairs in the lounge."

"You broke in?"

"I thought about it. But the house had these things called windows. You know, glass."

"Very funny." Mullet finished his beer. "It's not our scene, Vince. Let it go."

"It's weird. The whole thing's just really weird."

"Let it go, right? Forget Tommy. We'll do the fishing on Saturday, collect the boat, the Isuzu, the money, say thanks and cheers. They bought surveillance, they got surveillance. End of story."

"Still doesn't sit straight," said Vincent.

Damn right, thought Mullet. He put cash into the bill folder and signalled the waiter he was outta there.

At 5 p.m. Mullet was back in Sea Street. Not ten minutes later he caught Oxford's Pajero driving in. He'd buzzed Judith twice during the afternoon on both phones and got her voicemail. He tried her cell again. Same thing. Of course the lady had a life but surely she'd have had a chance to get back to him before now.

His phone rang. Professor Wanker Summers.

Mullet chewed on a mint as he answered, sharing with the professor the full suck and chomp.

"You shouldn't talk with your mouth full," said Summers.

Mullet went chomp, chomp. "You want to leave a message?"

"There's no need for you to talk, just listen. My usual and I'd like to try some candy, Mr Sugarman."

"I don't deal the hard stuff."

"Last time you said you'd get me Ecstasy."

"That's different."

"Drugs are drugs, Mullet."

"You wanna know what the kids in your class're doing I'll get you a coupla Es. You wanna do the celeb vacuum try the car guard opposite the News Café. Guy called Gabriel. Also he's got a contact who gives good head if you fancy a quickie."

The professor snorted. "Your world is sordid, Mendes."

"No more than yours, prof. Friday noon at the visitors' centre."

"Are you crazy? Not on campus."

"Special brown-bag delivery," said Mullet. "No one'll guess."

He rang off. And his phone buzzed immediately with an SMS from his cop mate, Ted. Mullet was impressed. It read: White golf avis car to james woo helderrand wine estate. A phone number followed. Mullet popped another mint chew.

Helderrand? Where Oxford had gone one evening. Woo: according to Vincent a partner in Sea Farm. Who puts his muscle onto tracking Oxford home which spooks Judith. Who the next night trails the heist truck most of the way to the drop house. Strange stuff, Mullet thought. No matter how you looked at it, there was a caper going down. This sort of situation, you stayed wide awake.

At six-fifteen Oxford's Pajero nosed into Sea Street and Mullet took a three-to-one bet that Oxford was heading home. He waited until the 4x4 right-turned towards Buitengracht before he fired the ignition and followed the money with no expectation other than he would be home in an hour. Into the CD he slotted Blood, Sweat and Tears, clicked through to 'Fire and Rain' and brought up the volume. James Taylor's best song. Such a mystery there. A mystery that had puzzled him from the first time he heard the song. What was it they'd done to Susan?

Going up Eastern Boulevard, stoked on the music, Mullet tucked in behind Oxford for the hell of it. The guy didn't move over but put foot powering round Hospital Bend down the hill and up towards the Mill way over the speed limit. Mullet kept with him until they slowed into the bumper-to-bumper along Newlands Forest. Stopped at the Rhodes Drive lights he caught Oxford watching him in the rear-view mirror. Their eyes fastened and the guy took a moment too long to break the connection in Mullet's reckoning. He may even have smiled. That was the impression. A snap of greeting.

Mullet dropped back after that. No doubt about it, Oxford was onto him. The little game of speed merchants, the knowing glance couldn't mean anything else. How the guy twigged was beyond imagining, but so much for his invisible presence. Rule one: don't play silly buggers. Heck of it, Mullet cursed.

He kept to the rules for the rest of the ride into the suburbs. Stayed well out of sight as the traffic thinned into the high-walled streets. Mullet pulled to the curb. The guy was heading home, following him farther wasn't worth the trouble. If Oxford intended making out with the singer later on, well, wouldn't that be convenient. If he went searching for little boys instead, tough, it might be what he'd been hired for, but for now, enough already.

When he got home Rae-Anne was standing on the back porch, Bom-Bom's bedding strewn about.

"I found this," she said, holding out a small metal arrow.

Mullet took it. "Crossbow bolt," he said, measuring the weight of it in his hand. "Where'd it come from?"

"Under the sleeping bag. In your search for the missing gun you tossed everything but his bedding."

"Major oversight."

"You said it."

Mullet tested the tip against the cushion of his thumb. "Lethal, hey. Wonder where he got it? Thing like this is not the sorta thing you play around with."

"Neither's a gun."

He winced at the bite in her voice.

"What're you gonna do about the gun?"

"Wait till he pitches up."

"And then?"

He tapped the bolt against the stoep table. "Get it back."

She laughed. "For a cop you've got some strange ideas about human nature."

"And find out where this came from."

"He doesn't talk, Mull. You gonna give him the bright light?"

"Depends."

Rae-Anne bent to bundle the street kid's sleeping bag into a bin-liner. His pillow too. "Yech." She shivered, revolted by the stickiness of the bedding and the musty smell it released. "I'm going to burn this."

Mullet kept quiet.

"When he comes back you can buy him new stuff. And take him to a proper shelter. The Mendes dosshouse is closed." She knotted the plastic bag. "New rules Mullet, if I'm staying here."

He nodded. He was thinking about the bodies in the dunes. Something Ted had said. A joke response about dying Cupid-style, an arrow through the heart. Maybe not an arrow but a bolt. He heard Rae-Anne say something.

"What's that?"

"You're not even listening," she said. "This's useless."

They stood staring at one another.

"Mullet, talk to me. Don't shut me out."

"I was thinking," he said. Then unleashed the smile that ripped her heart. "Hey, we're eating on the town. Forget this scene." He stepped towards her, arms going around her shoulders. "I've booked a table at the Blue Dolphin."

Rae-Anne went soft in the hug.

"Don't shut me out," she whispered at his chest. "You've got to tell me what's in your head. I can't guess. You've got to talk to me."

He squeezed her, not saying anything. They rocked, Mullet aware of her softness like she was a bird in his hand.

For long moments they stayed this way until Rae-Anne said, "Is this dinner work or pleasure?"

He stroked her hair.

"More pleasure than work."

"You're impossible," she said, looking up, waiting for his mouth to come down on hers.

46

Tommy crushed two buttons of Mandrax in a saucer using the back of a spoon. Beside him on the table was a bottleneck stuffed with one part tobacco, three parts grass. He sprinkled the white powder onto the mixture, tamped it down with his thumb. Adonis jiggered about the room, a cigarette in each hand. Like a drama queen deluxe.

"I told you, china. The man said Friday."

Adonis took a puff from the stick in his right hand, then from the one in his left.

"Till then this is the best I can do." Tommy held up the neck.

"You said . . ."

"Forget what I said." He reached for a Bic lying on the table and flicked a long flame. "The man said Friday."

"The man, the man, the man. Fuck you, darlin."

"You don't wanna tune me, china. You don't wanna feel the fire." He waved the lighter like a wand.

"No f-f-fuck you!" Adonis came at him with both cigarettes. He was sobbing. "We gotta get our money."

Tommy hit out. His blow sent the cigarettes flying, the lighter flame scorched across Adonis's arm. The guy went down on the floor, howling, curling into a foetal position.

Tommy lit the neck and took a long drag, holding it in. The white crackled, pushed a slow heaviness into his head.

"You want some?" he said, bending down to Adonis.

Adonis blubbing, "I gotta have it. I gotta have it."

Tommy jerked him upright and put the stop in his hand. "Suck it."

"Please. Please, bay-bee, please." Adonis's face was running tears, snot, mouth-drool. He took the bottleneck and sucked at the white pipe until there was nothing left. Tommy let him. He knew where Adonis was. He had the sweats and the nausea himself. No ways he was going to last till

Friday without a solid hit of smack. They had to get money. Fork Mr forking Woo.

Tommy crushed two more tabs and filled another pipe. Adonis lay on the floor, still curled, his hands stuck between his thighs. He'd stopped sobbing.

"We gonna have to do something," he said.

"You think I don't know," said Tommy.

47

Candy Liu was good. She did five Nora Jones covers straight off. Mullet reckoned if you closed your eyes you'd think you were getting the real deal.

Rae-Anne went mushy at the first note: playing footsie-footsie with him under the table using her peg leg, reaching across the top to hold his hand. Nora Jones tweaked her heartstrings. Which was fine. Mullet didn't get Nora Jones, way too crooner in his book, but if Candy Liu did it for Rae-Anne he wasn't going to come over the music connoisseur. The more Candy Liu worked on her now, the better it would be for him later.

He shifted his chair next to Rae-Anne so that he could watch the singer.

Rae-Anne said, "You getting fresh, or what?" And kissed him on the ear, no sign of the earlier tension when she'd said, "How about I move in this weekend?" and he'd said, "Saturday we're going fishing with these clients, you're invited," and she'd come back, "No, no, I'm not into stalling tactics." The heat in her voice scorching any 'but' he might have used in retaliation. "Doll, this Saturday I'm packing. If you're going fishing that's cool. On Sunday you're booked. Mullet's Removal Services." She gave him a straight no-smile, dare-you-to-do-otherwise glare.

He took a forkful of seared tuna steak but what had been succulent before wasn't melt-in-the-mouth anymore. He chewed to get it down.

"Right then."

"Right then exactly." She raised her wine glass, clinked it against his. "Come on, toast."

He filled his glass and they clinked and drank.

"You can smile about it, doll. It's not the end of the world." She leaned across and traced a finger along his jaw line to the corner of his lips.

Heck of it, Mullet thought, if you've taken the decision you've got to make the jump. He caught her hand.

"I'm good. It's just . . ."

She waited.

"You know."

Rae-Anne shook her head. "Not really."

Mullet drank some wine. "I want it to work. Us to work."

She gave him the doey eyes. "You're sweet."

And then Ricardo hit the piano and Candy Liu came out of the dark wearing a white number that Mullet found breathtaking. He'd seen her tarty. He'd seen her sporty. This was Candy Liu ravishing. Black hair. Oriental eyes. Milky tea skin. Delicate triangle tattoo with Chinese symbols on her right shoulder. The voice of an angel.

Candy Liu's set lasted about forty-five minutes then the pianist said they were taking twenty. Stick around patrons, he said, enjoy the wine, there's more of Candy to come. He made a bow so sharp his wig almost fell off.

Mullet waited until the pianist had stopped his dreadful tinkle and joined Candy Liu at a table behind the reception desk.

"What d'you say I get her autograph?" He took the promotional flyer from his shirt pocket and smoothed it open.

Rae-Anne squinted at him. "I'd say you were up to something."

He grinned back. "Maybe" – and headed for the singer.

"Excuse me," he said as he approached her table, "would you mind signing this?" He held out the flyer and a pen.

"Sure thing," said Candy Liu. "Hey, I've never had this happen before."

Mullet crouched beside her. As she was writing he said, "Can I ask you a personal question?"

"Depends how personal."

"D'you know a guy called Roger Oxford?"

She swung on him, her face alive. "Know him? He's my dad."

48

Tommy put on a clean shirt and jeans. Splashed Aramis till he smelt like forking Delmont. He had the shakes worse than flu.

Adonis lay on the floor not even looking up as Tommy stepped into the corridor and headed for number 33. An old woman lived there, walked with a Zimmer frame. Mrs Kaplan. Once or twice in the first weeks after he'd moved in he'd come down while she was collecting her post. She'd scowled at him. He'd said morning ma'am as if he were greeting the Queen of England. That got a blank face out of her.

The next time he came swinging through the foyer door she was zimmering towards the lift. He pushed the floor button, kept the doors open while she clomped in.

As they were getting out he said, "You like perlemoen, ma'am? Free from the sea."

She said, "What?"

He opened his gym bag. "Pearlies."

She picked out a shell.

"You want some, I'll clean them for you."

She dropped it back into the bag.

"You are a poacher?"

Tommy laughed. "Me!" His voice up two octaves. "Do I look like a poacher?"

Mrs Kaplan nodded. "You bring me two," she said. "Nice and clean."

He had, and she'd paid. She'd asked his name and said she liked the emeralds in his teeth. Twice since then she'd bought bags of ten each.

The second time he grinned at her. "You forking dealing."

She held up a finger. "Watch your language."

He knocked. The television was up full ball. She wasn't gonna hear a rat-a-tat above that racket. Thing was he didn't want to knock louder and draw out some nosy Yiddish from one of the other flats. He wondered, maybe he should go down and buzz her from the street. He started off, then stopped. The white pipe had blown all kinds of smoke into his brain, he couldn't think straight. He smacked at his head with the heel of his palm.

Knock, he said. Knock louder.

He gave the Beethoven da-da-da-daaah rap. His ear against the door, he caught the movement of the old woman rising from her chair. The volume of the television dropped.

"Who is it?"

The spy-hole in the door darkened.

Tommy whispered, "Your neighbour, Mrs Kaplan."

A cylinder lock clunked twice. The door opened on a security chain.

"What's it you want, Tommy?"

He glanced up and down the corridor. No one bothering, everyone focused on *Sex and the City*. He stuck his hand into the gap. "Feel my hand, auntie. I'm sick."

Much to his surprise the old woman touched the back of her hand to his.

"I need some Panado. Asprins. Disprins. Whatever you got."

She stared at him. "What's wrong with the pharmacy?"

"Please, auntie."

"Don't call me auntie."

"No, ma'am," he said.

The old lady closed the door and he thought, Fork it! Then he heard her slide out the chain. The door opened.

"I've got some Disprins. But you owe me a box, alright?"

"Yes, ma'am." He followed her into the flat, closing the door.

She disappeared into her bedroom while Tommy hovered in the lounge, his eyes flicking from the television to the family photos on the side tables. He picked up a paperweight. Solid brass with strange lettering. It fitted in the cup of his hand.

The old woman's Zimmer frame clanged against the bedroom door as she manoeuvred her way back towards him. Tommy kept hold of the brass weight. She held out the packet of painkillers.

"Here. Take it."

Tommy took the packet. "Thanks." He hesitated.

She kept her eyes on him. "What's it you really want, Tommy? Money? For drugs?"

"No, ma'am." The words a high squeak. He gripped the weight.

"How much?" She shook her head. "You think I don't know? I know."

He stared at the floor.

"I was a nurse."

"On Friday," he said. "I can pay you back. In pearlies."

"How much?"

"Five hundred."

She took her time with this. Her eyes all over his face. Then she nodded. "Alright."

Tommy let the stiffness out of his shoulders. He watched her clomp back to the bedroom. The door was open wide enough for him to see her take a bundle of notes from a drawer in the bedside table. She drew off some and put the rest back. He smacked the paperweight into his right hand.

49

All the flight back Jim Woo wondered why they'd let him go. They had to be dangling him. Hanging him out. Because they knew, they had to know. Woo closed his eyes as a chill convulsed his body.

Or . . .

Or White Paper Fan was giving the wayward brother a chance to redeem himself. Heigh ho for White Paper Fan. Because Dragon Fire would have played it by the book. Oaths ten and sixteen; swords and thunderbolts.

That they'd let him go was Dragon Fire's condescension to White Paper Fan's wishes. To White Paper Fan's position. A last patronising gesture to the old man before he heaved him aside. Because Jim Woo was the old man's protégé. If he didn't work out the disgrace would fall as much on his head as on the head of his sponsor.

What had the old man said?

"We do not maintain the spirit of fraternity. Devotion. Filial piety. We show no respect. No honour."

To hell with it! He owed them nothing. Least of all White Paper Fan. Over the years they had had their money back in interest and profits. He had taken the risks, he had built the businesses. If money was owing, it was due to him. But Woo could not convince himself for long. No matter how many whiskies he ordered the shadow crept back to darken his mind.

They knew.

He had a few days. As long as he reassured them constantly they would keep their word. He stood up to stretch, too agitated to stay sitting. About him people slept or stared at their television screens, numbed by the monotony of the flight. With his fingers he kneaded the stiffness in his neck. Four rows back he caught the eyes of a man gazing at him. Their glance slid apart and Woo felt his skin prickle. It was a man on business, he told himself. A man trying to get through a flight that offered few distractions, even in business class. At first thought the man was Dragon Fire's henchman. On second glance, with relief realised his mind was playing tricks.

Woo sat down. Everywhere people were covered by blankets but he was hot and clammy. He could do with a shower. He could do with Marina. One of her massages, starting in his scalp. He closed his eyes to get the sensation of her hands working out the tension at his temples, moving down, easing the tautness that made his shoulders hard as teak. For a quick moment he allowed himself to think of the two of them floating in an azure sea fringed by white sands, the beach house back among palm trees. The Cayman. But it was a fleeting image so as not to tempt fate.

Instead he thought of Roger Oxford, who'd suggested the Cayman Islands in the first place.

"You can't do better. Discreet. Professional. Much better weather than Switzerland."

Roger Oxford who knew where the money was, who had transferred it there, who knew all the details, all the account numbers. All fifty-four of them.

Roger Oxford who was the weak link. If the Brotherhood came looking they would find him soon enough. And within fifteen minutes of knocking on his door they would have all the information they wanted. Roger Oxford the problem. Then he snapped. They wouldn't come looking because they already knew. They had already got to Roger.

Woo buried his head in his hands. In the blackness stood Roger Oxford against his high office window with the bay beyond. What did he know of this man? That he had a big house in the leafy suburbs. That he had a good business. That he'd probably gushed when Revenue Services came calling. That if he gushed then maybe he'd long ago gushed to the

Brotherhood. Maybe they'd been onto Roger for years? Maybe he had told them everything? Maybe they had Roger in their pockets?

Woo opened his eyes.

On the screen The Bride was hacking off arms and heads.

He breathed out slowly.

Uma sprang, twirled and blood spurted.

He had to hit the ground running.

Arno was waiting for him in the arrivals hall. Woo came abreast of him and kept on walking. Arno stared at the man's back. His uncreased jacket.

Fucking Chink, he thought, then moved to catch up.

"The Brotherhood give you a hard time." He tinged the last two words with a smirk, making it more a statement than a question.

Woo ignored him. "Marina at the estate?"

"Not when I left. She's got insurance guys crawling all over her."

"Very funny. The heist went off without hitches?"

"It got tense for a bit, Marina says."

"With the surveillance?"

"With the fuckheads. Tommy wanted to whack the pretty boy at one point. Probably they were stoned. But they kissed and made up."

"I'm pleased to hear it. You get to Roger?"

Woo waited while Arno unlocked the boot, making no effort to heft his travel bag from the trolley. Arno reached for it without thinking, half-way through the move realised what he was doing. He tossed it into the boot and slammed the lid, fired at his subservience. He gave no answer to Woo's question.

On the highway Woo got back to the heist.

"Marina say anything else about the job? Like how did the half-caste make out?"

"He recognised Tommy."

"Aaah, isn't that nice."

Arno turned his head just enough to glimpse Woo's face: deadpan.

"Putting old friends in touch is so satisfying."

Woo gazed out at the shacklands spreading over the dunes. Every time he made this run there were more of them. The peasants streaming in from the rural areas like things were better in the city.

"Will they ever wise up and stop these black guys coming in?" Woo gestured at the sprawl. "Goats on the verges, cows grazing the centre island. Traffic either side at one-twenty. Very quaint."

"Doubt it," said Arno. "They're brothers." He did the heh, heh, heh, heh.

Woo relaxed back against the leather. "The place is fucked."

"Probably." Arno took the off-ramp into the winelands, the shacks replaced with vineyards on the turn.

"Not even AIDS will sort it out."

"Health minister thinks it might."

Woo let some kilometres click by. "So what are you going to do?" The when-I'm-gone part left unsaid.

"Sit in the Bushveld. I know the Afs."

"You better hope so." Woo adjusted the air-conditioner to get the draft on his face. "You plan to keep on with the safaris?"

"Sure."

"Big game only? Canned lion?"

"Most likely."

"No balls for the urban hunt, hey Arno?"

Arno shrugged. "What if I told you the street kids came to kill us."

"I'd laugh."

"Wait till you see the lead in the front door. Huge chunk outta the passage wall too."

"The kids had a gun?"

"Hadn't jammed, maybe you wouldn't have had anyone to pick you up."

Woo whistled. "You believe they were onto us? They'd actually worked out where we came from? Uh-uh. No ways. No ways in hell."

Arno shifted down for the approach to the Helderrand turn-off. "I can't see another explanation. Those kids get to know stuff. You think they're glueheads. Outta their minds. But they're sharp." He swung onto the dirt road between the vines. "First time I saw the one kid he was standing right about here. His face painted white."

"There were how many?"

"Two. I got the one only. Buried him out in the dunes. Minus his head."

"Gruesome serial killer strikes again."

"Something like that."

They both laughed.

"I don't bloody believe it."

"Believe it," said Arno.

They came out of the vineyards and into the oak avenue. Woo pressed the window-down button, took a deep breath of dust and leaf-mould releasing scents where the dew hadn't yet dried. "You know I might even think about this place from time to time. It got to me."

"When're you going?"

"Tomorrow," said Woo. "You too."

Arno kept shut-up, thinking, Fuck, but the Brotherhood musta put a cracker up Woo's pipe.

Arno parked in the shade. Woo was out and heading for the house before he'd killed the engine.

"Bloody expects me to get his bag," Arno said aloud, watching the guy in the rear-view mirror striding off. He saw Woo whip out his cellphone and start pressing numbers. Would be a pleasure to be rid of the slit-eyed fuck.

He eased out of the car and called to the domestic in the kitchen to fetch Woo's bag. "And green tea for the boss, Lena. Full English breakfasts. Chop-chop, hey."

He headed after Woo and found him crouched at the bullet hole.

"Impressive." Woo straightened up. "Almost through solid teak."

"Almost through my fucking shoulder."

"He hit you?"

"Winged, you'd call it. A scrape." Arno swung the door open. "Have a look in the passageway."

Woo went in, ran his hand over the bullet furrow in the wall.

"You find the lead?"

"Nah. Didn't look either."

Woo glanced at his cellphone, pressed connect.

"Almost finished off the Great White Hunter."

Arno grimaced.

"Taken out by a street kid. Not a good epitaph, Arno."

Marina came on the line and Woo's voice went goofy. Arno thought,

Up yours china. He moved off, the last thing he wanted to overhear was lovebird talk.

Woo crossed the stoep and went down the steps onto the lawn while Marina brought him up to speed. The early heat prickled his forehead in perspiration. He listened without comment. It was all details, meaningless stuff of benefit only to David Welsh. Assuming David got the insurance payout before the Brotherhood came calling. But that was David's problem, except he didn't know he had a problem.

Marina was telling him that Saldana and Mendes were coming up on the weekend to collect their fee.

"You're not going to be there," he said.

"I'm not?"

"Saturday we're State-side. In-transit Miami. Picking up a connection to Grand Cayman."

Marina laughed. "So soon?"

"Can't be soon enough."

He heard the intake of her breath. "They're onto you?"

"I'm assuming. My theory is they got to Oxford some time ago. So they'll know about the Cayman accounts."

"Jesus. And you don't think they'll have someone waiting? Isn't that a little naïve?"

Woo flushed at the criticism. "I don't think so."

"Come on, Jim. They're playing you."

"That's what I thought first and it's partly true. They're giving me a chance to do the honourable thing." He snorted a laugh. "As long as I do it within ten days." Woo wiped at sweat beginning to trickle down his temples. "I'll keep them sweet until we've disappeared."

He got silence from Marina.

"Marina?"

She sighed. "This is scary, Jim. Totally frightening."

"Trust me." Woo stared over the vineyards to the mountains, blue and distant in the haze. "We can do it."

She didn't respond.

"Till tomorrow morning. About ten. Here." Woo turned to face the house. Arno was standing in the doorway watching him. "I've got to go," he said. "Speak to you later."

"You want me?" he called to Arno.

Arno blew out smoke. "Tommy was on the landline whingeing for his bucks."

Woo made as if he were waving away flies. "He can wait." He climbed the steps and sat down at the table. White linen tablecloth. Good silverware. A pitcher of grape juice. A pot of green tea. Woo helped himself to tea, not offering Arno.

He thumbed to Roger Oxford's number and connected. Woo let his adviser go through the polite spiel before he said, "Come to supper."

"No can do, I'm afraid," said Oxford. "Previous engagement."

"Cancel, Roger. I'm talking priority."

"How about first thing tomorrow?"

"Six o'clock, Roger. You can enjoy the mountains turning purple."

He cut the connection before Oxford could respond.

Arno sat and crushed his cigarette into an ashtray. "The man's not happy?"

"Whenever is he?"

They sat silently while Lena served them: eggs, sausage, bacon, fried tomato, fried banana, toast.

"Make some fresh tea," said Woo, "for when we're finished."

"Yes, Master Woo," she said, dropping a half curtsy.

As she left Woo said, "I like that. She's been good."

Arno shook a dollop of HP sauce onto his plate. "A dying breed."

"I suppose," said Woo. "Another sign the place is fucked."

What Woo hated about eating with Arno was that the guy ate with his mouth open, as if it were some kind of race. The way goddamned hyenas fed, right in the food. Woo took a mouthful so that his own chewing would block out the thwack and smack of Arno absorbed. At least the guy didn't mix talking and eating.

All the same it was Woo who finished first. He pushed aside the plate and connected to Tommy on his cellphone, leaving it lying on the table. He didn't need to have him screeching in his ear.

"You got my bucks, Mr Woo?" was the way Tommy opened.

"Good morning, Tommy," said Woo.

"Howzit, Boss Woo. Welcomes back."

"You had no problems? It all went well, and the abalone is packed and delivered?"

"As we speak, it's gone. So when can I fetch my bucks? This afternoon?"

Woo dampened his thumb, picked up the crumbs on the plate. "Tomorrow afternoon, Tommy. About three."

"No, no, Mr Woo. It's too late. You don't have to give it to me personal. Just leave it in the kitchen with the maid. In a plastic bag. I'll be in and out like a shadow."

"Tomorrow afternoon at three, Tommy."

"It's too late, Mr Woo. We need it sooner to make a purchase."

Arno grinned at Woo. He leaned over the phone. "Stay off the horse, Chommy."

"Who's that? Who's that talking? Fork you, Arno."

"Friday afternoon at three, Tommy."

"Please, Mr Woo. Like I said it's too late. This's urgent for today."

"You're not listening, Tommy. I don't want to see you until three o'clock tomorrow. Got it?"

Woo disconnected, took the cellphone from the table. One more phone call to Dragon Fire and then he could relax. Take a walk among the vines. A dip in the pool. A couple of hours' sleep. Then have a talk to Roger. He watched Arno crunch into the toast, spraying crumbs over the tablecloth. The guy should feed with the pigs.

Through a mouthful Arno said, "What're you going to do about Roger?"

Woo waited while Lena put down the fresh pot of tea. "Depends," he said. "Depends on what he's got to say."

50

Mullet mused. Stared over his newspaper at Vincent. Vincent sitting at his desk using Mullet's new Nokia to snap self-portraits. Mullet mused about being taken for a complete arsehole.

The guy's goddamned daughter!

The wife sets him up to watch her husband have a late-night dinner and a Sunday afternoon chat with his own daughter! Probably made up the paedophile picture too. Then when she gets the information she wants she stops answering her phone and doesn't return calls. Families! The stuff that went on in them was freaky.

He dialled Judith Oxford for the second time that morning. Voicemail again on both phones.

Vincent looked up at Mullet's sigh. "D'you think the guy's got another one for sale? Beats an Instamatic." He shut the phone and lobbed it to Mullet.

Mullet had to send the newspaper flying to make the catch. "Are you crazy?"

Vincent grinned. "Hey! The man's alive."

Alive to what? Mullet wondered. He snapped his fingers. "What you know about tattoos?"

Vincent shrugged. "Not much."

"What's one that's got Chinese symbols on the points of a triangle?"

"Wildfire. Metal Machine. Silver Dragon."

"This cute little singer had it on her shoulder. Turns out she's probably my client's stepdaughter. You think anybody's gonna tell me what's going on here?"

Mullet rolled the newspaper into a baton, waved it at Vincent. "You done any thinking on what I said yesterday?"

"What was that?"

"The guy in the white Golf."

"Not much."

"Not anything, you mean."

Vincent leaned back, tipping his chair until he came up against the wall. "I've done some."

"And?"

"And I dunno."

"Heck, Vince."

"What I know is what I know. I watched a heist go down. One of the perps is a poacher and maybe the shit who killed my wife. Whatever you say." He shot Mullet a warning glance. "For some of the ride home the heist van is tailed by a white Golf. End of story."

"Except there are these connections. The job I'm on is connected to the job you're on."

"By a white Gholf."

"And some other bits 'n pieces."

"So whatta we do?"

"I dunno, Vince. I don't bloody know."

"What I know," said Vincent, "is I'm going back to watch the drop house."

Mullet stood up. "Uh huh. Rather you go sit your motor car in Sea Street, watch for Roger Oxford."

Vincent glared at him. "You're kidding."

Mullet shook his head. "No."

"And you're gonna be where?"

"Getting Judith Oxford to tell me what's going on." He shrugged into his orange jacket. Vincent brought his chair down, full-on hang-dog. "Two hours, Vince. Max. Then you can go 'n track down your Tommy Chommy." Mullet headed for the door, Vincent hard after him.

"You found the piece yet?"

"Jesus," said Mullet. "Let it go for a while, hey!"

Mullet pushed the intercom buzzer at the driveway gates. Roger Oxford's yes took him by surprise.

He hesitated, maybe the best was to back out of this. He hadn't expected Oxford to be home this late in the morning.

"Hello. What is it?"

Mullet's cellphone started ringing. He knew if Oxford was at the intercom in the hall he'd be watching him on the monitor. The screen on his cellphone read Ted.

He connected. "Give me a mo."

To Oxford he said, "For Mrs Oxford."

"In what connection?"

"A lost credit card."

"Really?"

"She reported it missing."

"Where are you from?"

Mullet cleared his throat. The Doberman was standing dead centre of the wrought-iron gates staring at him, snarl-mouthed. "The City Improvement District."

"Have you found it? The credit card?"

"Not yet. We need more details."

A beat. "I see. My wife is not in at the moment. Do you have her cellphone number?"

"I've already left a message."

"Perhaps you could try this afternoon."

Strange, thought Mullet. Clients like Judith Oxford wouldn't normally leave things hanging. As he reversed into the street, the Doberman went into a barking frenzy. Mullet tapped the accelerator twice to rev the engine and the dog. The dog hit berserk. Mullet pulled away and lifted his cellphone. "Speak to me."

Ted was laughing. "City Improvement District? You made a career move, Mullet?"

"Very funny."

"Hey, what you private dicks get up to!"

"Yeah, yeah."

He heard Ted flick at a lighter, the suck as he fired a cigarette. "You know what?"

"What?"

"We've got another candle."

Mullet said, "What d'you want me to say?"

"That you'll come take a look?"

"You're joking."

The whistle of Ted exhaling. "Come'n, man. We're stumped."

"This happens."

"Please, man. Same place. Just take a look for us. Won't take you long. See if something new strikes you. Naidoo's not around either."

Mullet sighed loudly enough for Ted to hear. "You don't believe what I think anyhow."

"Give us a break. You worked this kinda thing."

"So?"

"So, I'm asking a favour."

The naked corpse lay on a plastic sheet. It was drawn up in the foetal position, the head missing, the arms folded onto the chest, the hands tied together with string in the prayer position. A candle was still stuck in the kid's arse. It hadn't been lit. An older kid than previously, maybe thirteen. A scrawny street-kid body. A neat puncture wound through the upper right thigh.

Mullet let out his breath in a long whoosh. Ten metres away was a black plastic marker where the first body had been found. You drew a line from that marker to the marker for body two then this one formed the pinnacle of a triangle. Heckuva neat.

The area was taped off again and the tech guys were scouring the sand. They didn't need the tape. The only person who had been out in the dunes in ten days had been the killer. The sandboarders were going elsewhere for their kicks.

Mullet looked up at the dunes. From the top of the high one you could probably see the bay and the city. Down here you were in another world. Tall stands of clumpgrass. No human noise, only insect buzz. Might seem desert-like but probably in winter the water table rose and a pool formed at the base of the dunes. He'd known such a place as a boy. Where he'd gone shooting frogs with a bow and arrow.

He turned to Ted and André, André leaning against an unmarked double-cab 4x4.

"He was buried the same as the others."

"Arse in the air. The killer telling us, screw you. Everything styled for our delight."

"What killed him?"

"Same as before. Arrow through the heart."

Mullet walked towards them. He could smell the menthol of André's cigarette.

"The body wasn't here two days ago," said Ted. "When we last checked. Also we didn't expect another one so soon."

André stubbed his cigarette against the double-cab's front tyre. "Wasn't for my diligence I wouldn't have checked this morning either. Makes a great start to your day."

"So what d'you think?" Ted detached himself from the 4x4 and dug his hands into his pockets.

"Got an estimate on when?"

"The doc's thumbsuck: two days ago."

Mullet nodded, traced a half circle in the sand with his right foot. "You know there's a street kid sleeps on my back stoep sometimes?"

Ted snorted. "Mullet the missionary."

"Are you gonna listen?"

"Sure, sure. Tell us about your street kid."

Mullet glanced back at the body. "Yesterday Rae-Anne found a bolt under his sleeping bag. As in crossbow bolt."

"You're shitting me?"

"This your street kid?" André took off his sunglasses to eyeball Mullet.

"I dunno. Can't say without the head."

"What're you saying, Mullet?" Ted jiggled at small change in his pocket.

"Maybe nothing. The kid was on the stoep the morning we went fishing. Before that I hadn't seen him in a coupla weeks. But that's no big deal. He's probably got a wide territory and I reckon he uses my stoep when he needs time out. You know, he's feeling sick or maybe he's got to stay low. Whatever. No hassle for me." Mullet paused. "Then on Sunday he flashes Rae-Anne. Outta the blue."

"Jesus Christ! And you allow this boy on your stoep."

"We're having a braai in the backyard and Rae-Anne comes outta the kitchen and the kid springs his boner as she passes."

"Bloody hell! You kicked him out?"

"No. Rae-Anne wasn't into a scene."

"Bugger that."

"So I delayed the riot-act thing. Only next morning the kid was gone. And hasn't been back."

Ted put his hand on Mullet's shoulder. "Take another look, hey?"

They walked over to the corpse.

"We just pulled him outta the hole," said Ted. "The tech boys have gotta sift it still."

Mullet stared down at the body. Skinny-arsed, bruised. How the heck was he supposed to know if this was Bom-Bom? He shrugged. "I can't say."

"OK," said Ted. "But what d'you think?"

"Like some guy getting his jollies whacking street kids?"

"Selling their heads for muti."

"Could be."

"But you're not putting your cock on the block."

"No. For muti you've gotta take the organ alive. That's the point."

Ted turned away. Mullet considered telling them about his missing gun but decided against it. Chances were this wasn't Bom-Bom.

"What the fuck's going on here?" Ted swung back at Mullet, his face red. "Why isn't this a straightforward serial? What's your problem?"

Mullet and André exchanged glances. The technicians stopped their searching and looked across at the three men.

"A serial's gonna make it easier for you?"

"It's gonna mean we know what we're onto. Except you keep saying no." Ted kicked at the sand, sending a spray of grit over the corpse. "So what d'you say?"

"The same as I've told you before. This's someone stringing you."

"Why? For God's sake tell me why?"

"I can't," said Mullet. "It's just a feeling."

"Just a feeling. For fuck's sake, what am I supposed to do with a bloody feeling?"

51

Mullet had been sitting in Sea Street since 3 p.m., going on for two and a half hours now. This stake-out went on any longer he could open a bloody office. His back hurt. He wanted to get out and walk around. He checked Vincent's SMS again.

O arrived 12.20. Styd in 4 lunch. Im outta here now 2.10.

Oxford was in his office, he knew that having put through a test call on his new cellphone. Judith wasn't at the house or if she was, she wasn't answering either the landline or her cellphone. Vincent was heck knew where, not answering his phone either. And what he couldn't get out of his mind was that the corpse was Bom-Bom. Just a feeling. Except the sort you had to trust. The issue was: where had the kid ended up dead? And where was his gun?

Mullet popped a mint chew and looked around for street kids. Nada. Too early. They weren't going to move in until the office workers had moved out. And he couldn't go looking for them in case Oxford decided to call it a day.

Which happened ten minutes later: the Pajero nosed slowly into the street, Oxford looking left and right. Mullet eased down in his seat. He was parked behind a well-dinged sedan and probably out of sight. Oxford stopped on the ramp, scanning the street.

And now? Mullet wondered. What's this about?

The next thing the Pajero turned towards him and Mullet dived prone as the vehicle roared past. In a week's worth of stake-outs he'd never turned right out of the parking garage.

It's like he's looking for you, boykie. Mullet came upright and fired the ignition. He laid down rubber going after the man in the 4x4.

On the highway out of town he zipped in five cars back of Oxford. This wasn't the normal home run. This, Mullet schemed, was three got you five a trip to Mr Woo, with Oxford ten up on the speed limit and shifting into the fast lane as the traffic cleared past Century City.

Mullet stayed hidden in the middle lane, glad the Subaru looked like any old Ford. You flashed your eyes to the rear-view mirror, all you picked out was a white car. Only thing you couldn't do was outrun this particular white car. He let three cars overtake then hit the outside lane on the stretch across the flats to the Panorama hill where the highway opened into four lanes.

Oxford went fast up the hill flashing his lights at slower cars. Mullet thought, what's the hurry, pal, keeping hidden in the centre lane while the Pajero got farther and farther ahead. He glanced at the dashboard clock. Five forty-five.

On the brow of the hill the road curved down into the Tygerberg cutting and narrowed again to two lanes. The traffic thinned as drivers took the off-ramps to their northern suburbs cluster homes. He could see the Pajero up ahead, cresting a hill almost a kilometre away, and accelerated to close the distance. The suburbs gave into smallholdings, a glimpse of sheep behind the verge trees. Mullet eased on the speed although for long moments he lost sight of Oxford in the dips. But the exits were fewer now and he was confident of the guy's destination.

There had to be another story running here. Something else going on that he hadn't been told about, certainly hadn't been paid to investigate. It stirred his curiosity. Brought up the cop within him. But should he care? Outside the brief was outside the brief. None of his beeswax.

"Just keep your nose clean," he said aloud, slowing down as Oxford headed left onto the off-ramp.

Mullet stopped on the verge and gave the guy a half-minute lead. It was plain sailing: five kilometres to the crossroads, hang a left, two kilometres on was the gravel road to Helderrand. When Mullet reached it,

Oxford was a storm of dust between the vineyards going into the avenue of oak trees.

So much for so much, thought Mullet. A quick ride back to surprise Judith Oxford, then home for an early night alone. A last chance before Rae-Anne moved in to get well and truly stoned with Johnny Cash.

Halfway to the city his cell rang. Mullet thumbed it on without looking.

"You wanna stop by the office?" said Ted.

"Not particularly."

"When can we expect you?" The tone in Ted's voice not exactly chatty.

"Ah, come'n Ted. What's it now?"

"Serious shit."

Mullet heard Deputy Commissioner Naidoo screech in the background: "Just get him to get his bloody arse here."

"You heard."

"Thought he wasn't around."

"Stuff changes."

"What's going on?"

"I told you, serious shit."

Mullet thumped the steering wheel. "Right then! Fifteen minutes."

"And bring the crossbow bolt."

"I'm gonna have your balls, Mendes," he heard Naidoo shout before he cut the connection.

52

From the stoep, Jim Woo watched the Pajero turn in at the estate's entrance and drive too fast along the gravel road through the vineyards. He lost sight of the 4x4 when Oxford entered the avenue of oaks.

"Our man approaches," he said to Arno.

Arno sipped at his beer. "I've got ears."

"Punctuality is one of Mr Oxford's virtues."

Woo glanced down at the man he'd placed so much trust in. "You ready for this?"

Arno studied the level of the beer in his bottle. "Just one thing. What about the guy's wife?"

"Judith thinks he's having an affair. It's what I told her. Even recommended an investigation agency. Roger stays out, she's going to think he's screwing his bimbo."

"Who'd you tip: Mendes & Saldana?"

"None other."

Arno went heh, heh, heh, heh. "You tempt shit, man. Tempt it like it's never gonna bite back."

Woo smiled. "Spice of life, Arnoldus. The way I told it to Oxford's wife, it's about putting people in touch with one another." He watched Oxford drive into the courtyard. "This should be most interesting" – and walked across the stoep and down the steps to meet him.

He waited, arms folded, feet apart while Oxford pulled into one of the parking bays and cut the engine.

As he got out, Woo said. "You made it in time. The sun has yet to set. The mountains have yet to turn purple."

"It was a rush," said Oxford, reaching for his briefcase and laptop in the cab.

Woo clapped his hand on Oxford's shoulder. "Come. A drink, a cigar, there is much to discuss." He ushered his financial adviser towards the steps with a flourish of his left hand. "Please."

"I have brought all the paperwork you need to see," said Oxford. "It is best to deal with the taxman promptly."

"Yes, yes." Woo waved it aside. "We'll get round to those matters. First things first. A drink?"

"Gin," said Oxford. He put his briefcase and laptop beside a chair and lowered himself into it. "If you don't mind."

"Oh it's no bother," said Woo, lifting a bottle from the drinks trolley.

"Hullo Roger," said Arno.

"Ah, Arno," said Oxford. "I didn't see you there in the shadow."

"The Invisible Man."

Oxford forced a laugh.

"Mr Invisible wasn't so invisible that some young thug didn't attack him the other night," said Woo. He cut a slice of lime and added two ice cubes to Oxford's gin and tonic. "Right here on the stoep."

Woo handed Oxford his drink. "It may look all very peaceful," he said, gesturing at the vines stretching towards the mountains, "and it might be as its name says a beautiful hill or whatever, but there is danger in beauty." Woo moved away to pour himself a whisky. "Even here."

"You have security," said Oxford, raising his glass to take a sip. "You must do. Surely?"

Woo wagged a finger admonishing him. "Roger. We have yet to make a toast."

"Of course." Oxford lowered the glass.

"I have Arno," said Woo. "What better security can I want?"

Arno grunted and drained his beer. He wiped the back of his hand across his mouth, burped.

"Even if he insists on drinking his beer from the bottle and has uncouth manners."

Oxford tightened his grip on his drink. What he wanted was a sip, a mouthful to take away the taste of bile on his tongue. He watched Arno ease out of the lounger and lift another bottle of beer from an ice bucket on the trolley. If ever the word killer needed an embodiment here he was: thin and mean as a ginger hunting spider.

"You can't drink beer from a glass."

Oxford cleared his throat. "What happened to your attacker?"

Arno dropped back onto the lounger. He uncapped his beer with a bottle opener on his penknife. "Buried and forgotten."

"Farm justice," said Woo, offering Oxford an Havana.

"You can't . . ."

"It's a street kid, Roger. A fucking AIDS orphan. Who cares?" Arno took a swig at the beer.

"Be honest, Roger," said Woo. "They're a pest."

Oxford concentrated on snipping his cigar. "All the same."

Woo flicked a lighter. "All the same, what? We should call the police? Come on, Roger. They have enough trouble dealing with the rapists and murderers in the townships. And here" – he waved a hand at the vineyards – "we have lots of ground. Maybe in twenty or fifty years his skeleton will be found. But that happens every day. What's new?" He held the flame while Oxford lit his cigar. "In fifty years we will all be dead. In twenty years we might be dead. Or sooner. Who knows?"

Woo pulled his chair beside Oxford's. "You see, the mountains are turning purple." He exhaled a cloud of cigar smoke. "Spectacular. And now a toast." He paused, raised his glass. "To the Cayman Islands." He clinked glasses with Oxford.

"To the Cayman Islands." Oxford took a sip, controlling the urge to gulp.

"You are a financial wizard, Roger Oxford, and for that I am grateful," said Woo. "But tell me one thing . . ."

Oxford flicked a head of ash onto the stoep. His palms were clammy. Woo smiled at him.

"Tell me, when did you first meet Ge Fei? Or maybe you know him as Dragon Fire?"

53

The cop at the front desk told Mullet to take the stairs to the second floor. First room on the left going down the corridor. The Deputy Commissioner was waiting. He grinned. Mullet kept blank-faced. He walked through the metal detector but the bolt in his jacket pocket didn't set it off. The bloody thing probably wasn't working. Or the cops switched it off because too much hardware was passing back and forth it was more a nuisance than a wise idea. What'd cops need a metal detector for anyhow when they were gonna strip-search everyone they brought in on a chain? Mullet heaved a sigh, glad he was out of it.

He took the stairs two at a time. Same gloss lime-green walls as there'd been for all the years he could remember. New government, new ideas about everything except the paint jobs on public buildings. Typical. He turned left on the landing and braced himself outside the door. A grumble of low voices inside. He knocked.

Ted opened. Mullet glimpsed the uniformed Deputy Commissioner Naidoo standing at the window, André on a straight-back chair to the right, blowing menthol exhale into the room. Lying centre-piece on Naidoo's desk, a pistol: a Tokarev TT-33.

Ted said, "You put foot" – standing back to let Mullet in.

Mullet shrugged. "I was summoned."

"Goddamned right," said Naidoo. "Want to tell us about this?" – he pointed at the pistol.

"It's got your prints all over it," said Ted, closing the door.

Considering that it looked suspiciously like his missing piece Mullet wasn't surprised.

"Take a seat." Naidoo sat down himself. "Story time, Mendes. Let's hear what you're gonna cook up."

Mullet glanced at Ted. "You're sure?"

"Positive. No licence number though."

"Right then." Mullet held up his hands but kept looking at the gun. "Where'd you find it?"

"We'll get there."

"So what's the big deal?"

"No big deal. Just tell us why we've got it and you haven't. And also why you had it at all."

"Heck, man." Mullet thought in the days when he smoked about how he'd have gone through the drill, bought some time, worked out the moves. Got a sense of what was going down. Instead he said, "There a chance of some coffee?"

"Sure," said André, not making a move to get it.

"Well?"

"Well two days ago I noticed it was missing."

"From your safe, hey?" Naidoo leaned forward. "From your god-damned locked safe no doubt!"

Mullet felt his face go numb. A tingling in his hands. He took his eyes off the gun slowly raising his gaze to the Deputy Commissioner's face. They stared at one another, neither backing down until Ted reached across to jolt Mullet on the forearm.

"Let's start at the beginning."

"You wanna hear this, just keep your shit to yourself, OK?" Mullet said it quietly, evenly. He watched Naidoo frown, the anger tightening in the set of his shoulders, but the Deputy Commissioner kept his mouth zipped.

André crushed his cigarette into an overfull ashtray.

"Tell him," Naidoo said to Ted. "Tell him the serious shit he's in." He leaned back, his hands gripping the chair's armrests.

Ted lifted a cigarette from a new box of thirties and tapped it against the desk.

"The gun's been fired," he said. "If you had a full clip, then three rounds before it jammed." He made a gesture at André to toss him the lighter. "It was buried in the same hole as that kid this morning."

"Oh Christ!" Mullet wiped a hand over his hair, into the nape of his neck. "So that's Bom-Bom."

"Bom-Bom?" said Naidoo.

"The street kid who sleeps on his stoep." Ted fired the cigarette. "I told you. The one who left the crossbow bolt."

"Right." Naidoo nodded. "And this's about what? The crossbow bolt?"

Mullet stared down at the knot of his clasped hands. He heard Ted breathe out and André fidget with his pack of cigarettes. Heck knew what they were thinking. Or what he was thinking for that matter. He reached into his jacket pocket and withdrew the bolt.

"Hey, look at that," said Naidoo, "Gladwrapped like they tell you in the training schools."

Mullet dropped it onto the table next to the pistol.

Naidoo unfastened his arms and reached across for the weapon. "Jesus. A Robin Hood special."

"Off the shelf. No licence required," said André.

"OK," Naidoo pointed the bolt at Mullet, "this's my understanding. Correct me if I'm wrong. We have a crossbow bolt that you say was left by a street kid who sleeps on your stoep."

"Occasionally sleeps on my stoep."

"Occasionally sleeps on your stoep." Naidoo used the bolt to jab at the gun, knocking it so the barrel swung to point at Mullet. "We have your pistol that isn't licensed, that you say went missing some days ago, that gets fired three times, then ends up in a hole in the sand dunes with the headless body of a street kid. Where two other headless bodies of street kids have been found. All three killed by crossbow bolts through the heart." Naidoo thumped the desk. "Explain this, Mendes. Explain what the goddamned hell's happening here."

"I can't," said Mullet. "I can't tell you anything more."

"Try this. Try telling me about the street kid."

Mullet sighed.

"Humour me, Mendes. Humour me."

Mullet glanced from Ted to André. Ted was unhappy, keeping his face closed, unwilling to meet Mullet's eyes. André grimaced, looked away. Mullet caught the doubt. "You don't . . . You bloody don't . . ."

Naidoo lifted his palms from the desk and held them out, inviting a confession.

"You've gotta be bloody kidding."

"Come on, Mendes. It's your gun. You got the bolt. Your street kid's in the hole. I hear your street kid flashed your girlfriend."

Mullet stood up. "Fuck this."

"Sit down," said Ted.

"You don't actually think I've got anything to do with this . . ."

Naidoo whacked his desk again. "Why not?"

"No, to heck with it."

"He's riding you," said Ted. "Just relax. Sit down."

"What d'you mean, relax?" Mullet turned on the Deputy Commissioner. "Screw you, Naidoo. Up yours."

"No, screw you, Mendes." Naidoo was on his feet, his chair toppling over. "You're the guy jerking our wires. Everywhere I look in this thing I find one-time Captain Mendes, the cop who couldn't take the heat."

Mullet felt his stomach churn, an acrid taste sour his mouth. He swallowed, kept his eyes on Naidoo: seeing a fleck of white spittle on the DC's lower lip. Mullet wiped a hand across his own mouth and watched Naidoo mimic the gesture. The fleck disappeared.

André said, "I'll get some coffees."

"Come on, Mullet," said Ted. "Cool it."

Mullet grinned at Naidoo. "Right then." He sat down.

The Deputy Commissioner raised his finger. "Just don't fuck with me, Mendes!"

"Heck no," said Mullet. "Never."

A silence settled and dragged, then Ted asked where the gun came from.

"It's a memento," said Mullet. "From a trip I did to Czechoslovakia. Years ago, when it was still Czechoslovakia."

"Why didn't you license it?"

"It's obsolete. They went outta production in the 1950s. It's a relic."

"Still works though," said Ted.

Naidoo gave a splutter laugh. "Until it jams."

Mullet got home close to midnight. Bloody Naidoo. So much for a night with Johnny Cash and a Camberwell carrot. He took a beer from the fridge and rolled a small joint, going out on the stoep to smoke it, half expecting to see Bom-Bom curled on the piece of foam that had been the guy's mattress.

It had to be the kid. Poor bastard.

He held the smoke in to the count of ten and exhaled slowly. Took a mouthful of beer and another toke at the joint.

He could still hear Naidoo shouting down the stairwell.

"You're a fuck-up, Mendes. You were a fuck-up in the Force and you're a goddamned fuck-up out of it."

They'd been chasing the jackal for two hours when he stood up and said, "This is a waste of time." No one had disagreed. They just hadn't expected him to walk out.

Mullet smiled, remembering the astonishment on Naidoo's face, the tired grin Ted had given him, André's eyebrows raised in amusement.

Then the sight of Naidoo's moonface a floor above him as he descended the stairs. "Don't think you're in the clear, Mendes. This's serious shit you're playing with."

Mullet hit the spliff for a last time and stubbed it in the perlemoenshell ashtray. The heck of it was he'd save a few bucks not having to buy new bedding for Bom-Bom. Some saving. "Hey, guy," he said. "It's just too bad."

54

First off when he woke Mullet called Judith Oxford. Didn't matter that the time was 6.37 a.m. He reached for his cellphone, thumbed through to her name, connected. He got voicemail. He tried the landline. After seven rings it went through to an answering machine. The ringing had to have woken them. He repeated the procedure with both phones: got voicemail again.

"Enough," Mullet said aloud, clawing his way out of the tangle of sheet and the light blanket Rae-Anne called a throw.

"Woolies special, doll," she'd said. "All the rage."

And Mullet not quite sure if her tone was straight or undercut with sarcasm had said, "Really!" The thing about it with Rae-Anne you could never tell. When you thought she was playing it, she wasn't. When you took her as dinkum she was having you on.

And the next day she'd be moving in. Which was a thought that gave Mullet the stomach flutters. He switched to immediate matters: shower, dress, coffee, hit the road.

Half an hour later he was threading through the suburbs to avoid the morning rush hour, Meat Loaf doing *Bat Out of Hell* volume one on the CD.

Even this early the day was whited out with wind-swirl and dust. The south-easter had picked up in the night and pushed Devil's Peak back behind a salt haze. From False Bay a long cloud poured over the mountain chain. In the streets the wind thrashed and thrummed, schoolkids on bikes battled into the howl. A wind like this would bring in some of the shoal fish, or off the beach the blunt-nosed galjoen. It mightn't be all grit in the eyes and raw nerves.

8 a.m. when he swung into the Oxford's driveway and buzzed the security phone. Nada. No sign of any movement in the house. Mullet switched off the ignition, wondering should he scale the wall. The tops were fringed with spikes hidden in plastic foliage, nevertheless could do great damage where it was least wanted. Also there was the Doberman. You needed to get back over the wall in a hurry, the spikes could be a problem. Mullet was about to try the phones again when he noticed a grey-haired black guy ambling up the driveway, the Doberman trotting beside him, all snarl.

Mullet got out of the car but stayed behind the shield of the open door.

"Can you let me in, madala?"

The black guy stopped and looked at him.

"What you want?"

"To speak to the madam."

The guy shook his head. The Doberman had its snout through the bars of the wrought-iron gate, issuing a low growl. Mullet didn't move from behind his car door.

"You have a problem?" said the man.

"No problem," said Mullet. "Just to see Mrs Oxford."

The man stood gazing over Mullet's head, until Mullet felt he should turn round to see what had got the guy's attention. Eventually the old man said, "That is the problem."

"Yeah?"

"It is too bad. The madam she is gone."

Mullet, irritated, glanced at his watch. "Already?"

"You must talk to the master," said the man. "From Wednesday she is gone."

Mullet clenched his fist. What he wanted to do was thump the roof of his car. The old man was staring at the sky again.

"You're the gardener?" he said.

The man nodded. "I am Privilege."

"That right?" Mullet stared at him. Privileged for what? Being alive? Working for Oxford? Then he realised, it was the guy's name. "You live here, Privilege?"

"No." Privilege held up three fingers. "I am here Monday, Wednesday, Friday. Half past seven to four o'clock."

"You were here when Mrs Oxford left?"

"Yes, she called me to take her suitcase. It was too heavy for the master to manage."

Mullet dragged his left forefinger and thumb across his eyes and gripped the bridge of his nose. What was happening here? Judith Oxford went away with a suitcase while her husband stood around? An argument? An ultimatum? Mullet blinked to clear the spots. Wednesday morning she had shown him the picture of Roger getting blown. She'd been upset. Gunning for the guy. When he'd phoned her with the news about Candy Liu she hadn't answered.

"What time?" asked Mullet.

Privilege frowned. "Three o'clock. Afterwards the master said it was alright I could go. He took me to the taxi."

Not an argument then. Husband and wife acting normally in front of the gardener.

"You know where Mrs Oxford's gone?"

Privilege rasped a hand over his beard stubble. "You must speak to the master at his office. You want the number?"

"No worries," said Mullet. Halfway into the car he said, "Mr Oxford's at work?"

The man nodded.

"Right then." Mullet banged the car door and the Doberman went berserk: barking, jumping, red-eyed with the urge to tear into human flesh. Privilege watched without attempting to restrain the dog. Mullet gave a half wave as he drove off. The time had come to have an in-your-face with Roger Oxford. Find out what he was being played for!

Two minutes down the street Mullet realised he should have asked to see the maid. He pulled the car into a U-turn. Privilege was digging in a flower bed near the gate, the Doberman standing in the driveway. The way it looked the dog was there to keep Privilege from running away. Mullet shifted the gear into neutral. He leaned out the window and shouted at the gardener. "Hey, Privilege, is the maid here?"

Privilege straightened with a sigh. He turned to look at Mullet but focused again on that spot in the sky. "Nine o'clock she comes," he said.

A pity, the maid would have been good, especially on how Roger and Judith were doing. But Mullet had no thoughts of hanging around. He gave the engine a slight rev, and pushed the window-up button. Privilege went back to his digging. As he drove off Mullet caught the Doberman in the rear-view mirror: its head through the bars of the gate, slavering with rage. "Nice doggy," he said.

In Sea Street there wasn't a parking space to be had. He cruised for five minutes then stopped in a loading zone. The heck with it! Given that it wasn't much after nine it would take the meter maids at least another hour to work their way to the side streets. By then he'd long be finished with Roger.

The moment Mullet switched off there were two street kids at his side window. He recognised them: Spokes, the kid with the sharpened bicycle spoke, and his mate, the smart who'd done all the talking.

Was still doing all the talking. "I'm so hungry, Mr Gentleman," he whined, rubbing his stomach with one hand, his other palm up.

Mullet shifted his gun into his pocket without the boys seeing it and climbed out of the car. He slammed the door shut and pressed the remote lock.

"You know the boy Bom-Bom?" he said. "Doesn't talk much."

The kids gave him the blank eye, already glued up.

"Bom-Bom, hey?"

"Ja, Mr Gentleman," said Smarts.

"Where's he?"

Neither answered. Mullet dug a twenty from his pocket. Spokes made a grab for it, but Mullet was ready.

"Uh-uh. Not so fast, china. Where's Bom-Bom?"

The boys shifted their feet, eyes down.

"C'mon, help me out here. Where's Bom-Bom?"

"Dunno," said Smarts. "He did a job for Mrs W there at the Haven, then we's didn't see him again."

"But you heard something, hey?"

Spokes jabbed at his mate, "Tell him."

Smarts shrugged, hitched up his jersey that had slipped off the knob of his shoulder. The movement released an acrid smell of piss and smoke.

"What'd you hear?" Mullet waved the twenty.

The boys kept their eyes on it.

Spokes said, "He's finding the Lord."

"Naai, man, he's gone to kill the Chinaman."

Mullet laughed. What these guys came out with was amazing.

"Strue."

"Name o' the Lord, Mr Gentleman."

He handed over the money. "Right then. You hear any more about Bom-Bom you let me know." The boys took off. "Buy some bread," he shouted after them, knowing bread was the last thing on their minds.

Mullet put aside thoughts of quite how Bom-Bom might have found the Lord and headed down Sea Street and round the corner to the front entrance of the tower block where Oxford had his office. The distance was from the nineteenth century into the bustle of the modern world: delivery guys on bikes, interns hitting the Seattle for a quick latte and muffin, the suits of both sexes doing business meetings on the trot. Not a street kid visible. Not a vagrant in sight. Although Mullet knew they could be conjured from the air quicker than ghosts, all you had to do was stand still for a moment. It was movement kept off the horrors of the present and the past. That was the trick to living in the now – keep moving.

At reception Mullet signed in and was handed a security card.

"Fifteenth floor," said the uniformed guard behind the desk.

Mullet swiped his card down the slot in the turnstile and pushed through. He waited at the bank of lifts that expressed to the tenth floor. A knot of people gathered, all focused anxiously on the indicators above the doors. When a lift arrived two cops stepped out, young uniforms, as he'd been once. Mullet let the thought go no further, he stepped into the lift and took a spot at the back in the corner. People stared at their shoes, two guys discussed heading for the mountains for a weekend's paragliding. Mullet wondered about his boat, about the chances of going fishing up the West Coast.

On the fifteenth floor he paused at the board listing the offices. Oxford's Blue Sky Investments was down the left corridor and cops stood outside the large glass-panel doors. Mullet said, "Oh, yeah!" under his breath, getting a glimpse of how the place had been tossed as he approached. Papers everywhere. Manila folders scattered over the reception sofas. A woman standing in the midst of it, her face in the rigor of disbelief.

The cops stopped Mullet.

"I have an appointment with Mr Oxford," he said.

"Speak to the secretary," said one of the cops, indicating the woman.

Mullet went in. The woman glanced at him, her eyes blank.

"Excuse me," said Mullet. "I need to speak to Mr Roger Oxford."

The woman blinked. "We've had a robbery."

Mullet nodded. "It happens."

"I can't believe it. We don't keep money here. We're not a bank."

Mullet cleared his throat. "Is Mr Oxford here?"

"Whoever did this had a key. That's how they got in. With a key. It's terrible. Absolutely awful."

"It's a mess," Mullet agreed, looking about. The sort of mess spoke of a Revenue job. Or clients changing advisors.

The woman dug through the papers on her desk and uncovered a diary. "I don't know what he's going to say. Why would anyone want to do this?" She found the date and glanced up at Mullet. "You don't have an appointment."

"No." said Mullet. "No, I don't. My name's Mendes. You see Mrs Oxford lost her credit card, and I'm from the insurance company, and I need to get an authorisation signature. But Mrs Oxford is never at home so I thought I'd ask Mr Oxford to sign proxy. If you see my problem?"

"I don't know where he is." The woman stared at Mullet, the concern watering her eyes. "He's not answering his phone."

"I see," said Mullet. "Do you expect him soon? Maybe I should come back."

"He's an hour late," said the woman. "Normally Mr Oxford is very punctual."

"Maybe he forgot to tell you about some prior arrangement?"

"Never." The woman snapped the diary closed. "He tells me everything. Everything."

A policeman appeared at the door to an inner office. "Ah, miss," he said, "could we ask you to check something?"

"Yes, of course." She moved round the desk. "Perhaps you could come back on Monday?" she said to Mullet.

"I guess," he said, turning to leave. "I hope nothing serious is missing."

The woman shook her head, on the verge of tears.

Mullet waited for the lift poker-faced, teasing out a scenario that had Roger too drunk to go home from the wine estate and maybe included a dark interlude with a boy. How the burglary played, Mullet couldn't figure. It could be unrelated.

In the foyer he dropped his security card in the turnstile bin and the levers let him through. He headed for a corner and put a call through to Helderrand.

The voice that answered was the voice he'd heard before.

"I'm trying to contact a Mr Roger Oxford," Mullet said, "I believe he spent the night there."

"You've got the wrong number, pal," said the voice.

Mullet repeated the number he'd dialled. "Is that Helderrand?"

The line went dead. Mullet glanced at his watch: nine-forty.

He called Vincent.

"Where're you, boykie?"

"Hey, there's something wrong with good morning?" said Vincent.

Mullet ignored him. "Listen, do me a favour."

"I'm engaged."

"Well, guy, disengage." Mullet watched two young women signing in at the reception desk. The one had her blouse so low buttoned he could see her tits. "Heck, Vince, this's urgent." The women headed for the lifts: both had stunning legs. Even so Rae-Anne's single outdid them. "Won't you go to the Oxfords' place. See who's there for me. Talk to the maid."

"You don't think I've got better things to do?"

"Like what? Sitting waiting for Tommy Chommy. Come'n, Vince, get real."

Vincent kept quiet a beat to make his point. "So what's it you want me to talk to her about: China and globalisation?"

"Ha ha, Vince. Ha ha. I wanna know where Judith's gone. If Roger slept there last night. Do Judith and Roger get it on together."

"And the maid's gonna know this?"

"She changes the sheets I'm supposing." He rattled off the address. "You got that?"

"I'm a dickhead?"

"No offence, Vince."

"And you're doing what that's so important?"

"Taking a drive to the winelands. Maybe do some wine tasting. A nice day like this." Mullet disconnected before Vincent could respond.

55

Arno dropped the phone on its cradle. Had to be that arsehole, Mendes. "Fast work, china, but not fast enough." Thinking, what'd Mendes know? That Oxford had been here last night? Big deal. That his office had been sacked? Do me a favour! First suspect would be Revenue Services. The hotshot Scorpions doing an asset forfeiture.

He lifted his bags off the unmade bed, toted them outside and put them in the boot of the Golf. Went back indoors for his jacket and the paperwork: Woo's parting declaration of thanks, the deeds giving Arno ownership of the safari lodge, and an air ticket to the Bushveld.

"Maybe in a couple of years I'll do a safari," Woo had said as he placed the documentation in an envelope. "Shoot a couple of trophy heads myself."

"Why not?" Arno had taken the envelope, tapped it against the table-top. "You think you'll be back?"

"The way the world works, probably. The only pity of it's leaving this place." He gave an expansive gesture towards the vineyards, the mountains. "Still, this is not the only paradise from what I've seen."

Ten minutes later Jim Woo and Marina were dust going down the oak avenue.

In the kitchen Arno gave Lena a bundle of notes: ten grand that he'd got Woo to part with only after some persuasion.

Lena bawled her eyes out when he gave it to her. "Oh master. Oh master. Thank you, master."

"Yeah well," he said. "It's from Mr Woo."

He could see she didn't believe him. Didn't even ask him to thank Mr Woo.

"Nobody's gonna be here for a coupla weeks," he told her. "Just keep the place clean, hey."

Except as he stepped out of the kitchen into the courtyard there was Tommy and his pretty-boy sidekick driving in, the Beemer booming like a minibus taxi. What was it about coloureds and darkies they always had music up so loud it was liver-pounding? Arno thought it would be better to have the nine mil handy at this point but the nine mil was in the glove box of the Golf. He went down the stairs to get closer to it. Tommy shot out of the driver's side, leaving the engine running as he approached.

"Where's the larney?"

"Mr Woo to you," said Arno.

Tommy jigged from foot to foot.

"He said to come get my money."

"You're too late." Arno opened the Golf's passenger door. "Mr Woo is gone. Know what I mean. Vamoosed."

"What you mean?"

"Gone, china. Auf Wiedersehen. Leaving on a jet plane."

Tommy stared at him. Snarling a grin, his lips pulled back letting the emeralds twinkle in the morning light. He slammed his fist onto the BM's bonnet so hard it left a dent. Rounded on Arno. "He's ducked? You tuning me he's gone?" Taking a step forwards.

Arno judged the situation, reckoned matters could still be handled without the hardware. He nodded, snapped a glance at his watch. "Maybe he's not boarded yet. Phone him. Get it from the horse's mouth."

"Catching a plane?"

"You're fast," said Arno, holding out his cellphone. "Just push connect. Save yourself the charge."

Tommy took the phone and thumbed the green button.

Arno sat on the passenger seat, watching the creep in his baggy cargo pants falling off his arse grovelling.

Tommy said, "I'm here for my packet, Mr Woo."

Then: "The money for robbing your place."

Then: "No, you didn't pay us yet, Mr Woo."

Then: "You said to come Friday."

Then: "Twenty Gs, Mr Woo. Straight up."

Then Woo did a long spiel and Arno could imagine where he was directing Tommy's problems. Just for the hell of it. For a laugh.

"I'll tell him, Mr Woo," said Tommy, passing the phone to Arno. "He wants to talk to you."

"Arno," said Woo, "it's your baby. We're boarding now. You want my advice: tell him the cheque's in the mail." The last Arno heard of Woo before the connection went down was his laugh.

Arno put the phone on the dashboard. He looked up at Tommy. "He said I must tell you the cheque's in the mail."

Tommy ran his tongue over his lips, flexed his fingers. Arno reached into the cubbyhole and came out with the nine mil. He put it on Tommy.

"Best thing for you Tommy Chommy is you get back in your fancy car 'n drive away."

Tommy didn't move.

"You want to keep your sparklers, now's the time to scoot." Arno stood up and took a pace towards him. "What's it you don't understand about what I'm saying?"

Tommy stayed tight.

"Fuck's sake, Tommy, just get," said Arno. When Tommy didn't, he pulled a shot beside the guy's ear.

Tommy screamed and lashed out but Arno caught his arm, had him face down on the bonnet of the Beemer with the muzzle buried in his earhole, the metal singeing.

Tommy howled.

Arno dug the gun in deeper, bunched his fist into the collar of Tommy's shirt, and yanked the guy upright. "You're gonna get back in the car and drive outta here. No fuss, no pus. Gettit?"

Tommy clapped a hand to his ringing ear. "You forking deafened me."

"I'm gonna do more than deafen you." Arno pushed him against the driver's door.

"You . . ." Tommy stabbed a finger at him. "You's a dead man."

Arno stared back at him. The chances were Tommy had a gun but he wouldn't use it. The sort of shoot-out Tommy liked was where nobody else had guns.

He waited. The guy got in and the sound system started booming. Arno tapped on the window. The boom died, the window came down.

Arno waved the gun from Tommy to Adonis. "You swallow or spit him?"

He stood back coughing his heh, heh, heh, heh laugh as the Beemer churned dust.

"You letting him? You letting him stand there?" Adonis looked back at the guy in the courtyard. "Reverse. We can take a quick pot."

"Fork him." Tommy eased on the accelerator. "You hear that laugh? The guy's toast. Forking boer."

They drove down the oak avenue in silence, then into the stretch through the vineyards.

Adonis said, "So where's the payment?"

"You heard."

"You leaving it?"

Tommy smacked at his stinging ear. "You see what he did, white poes. I'm gonna be deaf."

"He's gotta pay us."

"Forking white poes."

"We did the job. They gotta pay."

"They's fulla shit."

"Where's Mr Woo?"

Tommy turned out of the estate onto the tar road. He pushed the speedo to one hundred and fifty.

"Where's Mr Woo?"

"Taking a holiday."

"'N he didn't tell you?"

"We gonna do him," said Tommy. "Fork Mr forking Woo. We gonna clear out his sheds. Every forking pearlie."

56

Mullet got out of Sea Street with a wheelspin, shot two lights on the orange and took the N1 at the speed limit retracing his route of the previous evening to Helderrand. On a loop through his mind was the refrain, Heck's going on here? Heck's going on? Strange stuff, boykie, strange stuff, was all he could come up with. Topping Panorama hill, his new cellphone rang, Rae-Anne's name on the screen. He slotted the phone into the hands-free bracket and turned up the volume, turned down The Band singing about a man with stage fright.

"Hey, babe, what's the jol? Wherea you?"

"Doing a bit of speed work." Mullet gave a riff on the hooter, partly for her benefit, partly to get a rust bucket out of the fast lane.

"Something bad?"

"Dunno. Something odd."

Mullet heard her bite into an apple. The beaniehead in the rust bucket wasn't switching lanes. He hooted again, knocking the gear down to fourth, the engine roaring.

"Wanna know what I'm doing?"

"Eating an apple."

She giggled. "Sorry."

And he heard her swallow. "So tell me."

"Packing. Boxes and boxes. I didn't know I had so much stuff. Maybe we're gonna have to move into a bigger house, Mul."

For-get-it, he thought, saying, "Maybe." This time at his hooting the beaniehead drifted left, causing a car coming up too fast on the inside to brake and give a blast of hooter. Mullet trod on the accelerator.

He heard Rae-Anne gasp. "You alright there, babe?"

"Sure," he said.

"Sounds like chaos."

"Par for the course." He geared up as the needle on the rev counter hit five.

"So what d'you say to a bigger house?"

"Like I said, maybe."

She laughed and he imagined the shake she'd give to her head, swirling her hair. "Cool. Somewhere on the coast."

"Don't look at me for the millions." Mullet flashed his lights to move a Merc hogging the right lane.

"Me neither."

He heard the crisp tearing of apple flesh. "You're making me drool," he said.

"Where?"

"Where?" his voice rising a pitch. "Jesus, girl. You've got a dirty mind." The Merc changed lanes and Mullet passed, giving the old suit a hostile eyeball.

"'N you love it." She made sucking noises, like she had too much juice from the apple in her mouth.

"I'll call you," said Mullet. He reckoned he had about five minutes to the off-ramp.

"Mull," she said, hesitant. "We could do a coupla loads tonight if you bring the bakkie."

"Sure," said Mullet, "I'll call you" – ringing off non-committal, thinking, coward. Then again most times it was best delaying issues with women until they couldn't be delayed any longer. Like reminding her the Isuzu was up the coast, and that he and Vince were going to fetch it while she was moving in, leaving out the bit about doing some fishing while they were at it. Mullet punched up The Band, grimaced at the thought of what an issue this was going to be.

He turned onto the Helderrand dirt road between the vines, driving slowly. Half a kilometre on, the road swung into an oak avenue with a gabled manor house at its far end. Mullet grimaced, difficult to come up unannounced on anyone who had an approach this long. Halfway down the oak stretch he had to brake hard as a string of guineafowl ran out of the vineyards behind the trees and squabbled across the road. His heart rate up a beat that the guineafowl had caught him unaware. Dust swirled about the car. He edged into the flock, sending half of them flying and continued at a crawl towards the house.

Farther on the road upgraded into cobbles and turned into a courtyard surrounded by a low white wall. Ahead were steps onto the front stoep of the manor and a double door that Mullet guessed led to a cellar. To his right another courtyard leading towards what was probably the kitchen. He switched off the engine and sat for a moment. No one came rushing to see what he was doing there. No dogs either. Which was a relief, if surprising. Seemed like the owners weren't home. Mullet cracked the door, swung his feet onto the cobbles and stood up, tucking his T-shirt into his jeans. He pushed up his sunglasses, did a one-eighty scope: lawn, lavender bushes, gravel path leading into the vineyards in front, staff cottages about two hundred metres behind in a stand of eucalyptus trees, smoke curling at a chimney, but otherwise no one visible there either. He let the car door clunk closed and headed for the steps, shrugging into his burnt-orange jacket as he walked.

The stoep was wide: some teak benches against the white wall of the house either side the grand front door. Beneath a sun umbrella a solid all-weather table, on it two champagne glasses, an empty bottle of beer. One of the champagne glasses smudged at the rim with red lipstick. This morning's breakfast. No wind out here to overturn tables. Mullet rang the push bell and heard it chime deep in the house. A National Monument plaque dated the manor to 1769. The brass plaque well-rubbed and shining: that it hadn't been ripped off yet by the scrap metal collectors said something. He glanced around for security cameras. Nothing. Or rather, nothing obvious. Pushed the bell again. Stood waiting, staring at the door. Which was when he saw the neat hole. Low down. He crouched to take a look, fingering the entry point, had to be from a bullet. The trajectory was downwards. Mullet pulled a ballpoint from his back pocket and inserted it in the hole. It stubbed up against the slug. Door like this would've stopped a nine mil. He stood and tried the handle. Unlocked. The door swung open easily. Mullet stepped into the hall. Listened.

"Hi there. Anyone home?"

No answer. He called again. At the same time noticed the bullet gouge in the plaster. No slug in this one, the bullet had ricocheted off. There was a chip high up in the wooden cornice that looked newish. Maybe, Mullet thought. But whenever the shooting had happened it had been some days back. Still, made him pleased he had the Astra in his belt.

"Hullowa," he sang out once more for good luck.

Back came the sort of no-answer Ted would've called the silence of the grave. It gave Mullet a rittle of gooseflesh.

He stood indecisive, then headed down the passage for the door at the end, the wide boards groaning beneath his weight. As he'd supposed it led to the kitchen. Empty. Clean marble surfaces. Eye-level oven. Gas hob. Breakfast dishes and cutlery for three stacked in the dishwasher. Lipstick on one of the china cups. The back door closed but unlocked. Mullet went through the other rooms: in the lounge and the dining room not an undusted surface. In two of the bedrooms the beds stripped to the mattress covers, fresh white linen laid across the obligatory ox-wagon kist at the foot of the bed, ready for remaking. In the en suite bathrooms clean towels, crisp, smelling of fabric softener. What Rae-Anne would call very country life. No clothes hanging in the cupboards, no socks and underwear in the dressers. The other bedrooms were unused, the beds scattered with cushions.

"You ask me," Mullet said to his reflection in a mirror, "I'd say definitely the people've gone fishing."

He went back into the long passage that bisected the house. Somewhere a cellphone was ringing but the tones were muffled. Mullet paused until the ringing stopped. As far as he could tell, no one had answered the phone.

Halfway along the passage was a recess, a door in it with a latch handle. He tried it. Like everything else it was unlocked. He stepped into a narrow passage that led down a flight of stairs into what he guessed was a wine cellar. He groped along the wall for a light switch and flicked it on. A fluorescent light buzzed above his head and another in the room beneath. As Mullet descended, the phone started chirping again, somewhere below. He stopped, listening for movement. After six rings the phone went quiet, unanswered. Mullet started down again into what appeared to be a winery and tasting room that ran nearly the length and breadth of the house. Racks of wine along the walls. A flagstone floor. Huge table with some bottles on it and a brass spittoon. Some evidence of bonhomie. Enough wine glasses on a tray to hold a party. A low reed ceiling spanned between thick wooden support columns made for a rustic atmosphere, although the air was cold and pungent with the reek of fermentation. The temperature had to be fifteen degrees C or so. Damp, too. He glanced at the door at the top of the stairs: this cellar was not the sort of place you wanted to be trapped in. Mullet went back up and checked the latch release. No way anyone could lock it without a padlock. Worst came to the worst he could shoot his way out.

Down in the winery, Mullet did a closer inspection of the good-time remnants. No dregs in the spittoon. Among the wine bottles with the Helderrand label, two were uncorked: a cabernet and a port. The cab full, like it'd been uncorked then put aside; the port about two-thirds gone. In the sink, a glass dirty with port sediment thick as blood. Two cigar stumps in the ashtray. Enough ash there for about twenty minutes of smoking time. Beneath the table was a wicker wastepaper basket, three beer bottles, two bottle caps in it. The way the stools were arranged, two people sat side by side with the ashtray between them for a little session of port tasting. Strange thing then was why only one port glass? Mullet reckoned the guy he'd spoken to on the phone had to be the beer drinker: Mr Brush Cut in the white Golf. You did a forensic on the cigars, one of them'd been smoked by Roger Oxford. Didn't take a private investigator to work that out.

He looked about. Wine barrels were stacked close to the door that must give onto the courtyard. At the opposite end there seemed to be a room, maybe an office, closed off from the winery. He went towards it, in the gloom crunching over glass. The cellphone started ringing. Mullet caught his breath. Six rings, then silence. But he was sure now the phone was in the office. Someone was desperate to make contact.

He scraped his shoe on the glass, bent down, ran his hand lightly over the flagstones and the shards until he found a bigger piece: it explained why there weren't two glasses in the sink. Judging by the stain across the floor, the glass had been fairly full when it shattered. He dropped the shard and straightened, listening, smelling. There was an odour beneath the damp and the fermentation that he hadn't smelt further away. Something he recognised. It was faint, so faint you would think you'd imagined it. Standing there he wouldn't swear to the whiff before a judge. Then, as if the air had moved in the cellar, it came again: the smell of human death: shit, piss, blood.

Mullet took three quiet steps to the office door, standing ajar. He pushed it and the door scraped against the flags, hardly budging. Another shove and it opened, but the dark inside was impenetrable. The stench was ripe though, acrid. He felt for a light switch along the inside wall. Nothing. For a moment Mullet hesitated, wondering whether to go back to the kitchen for matches and a candle or to move farther into the room by feel. He sniffed at the foulness and slipped through the door moving sideways to his right.

A light snapped on. Spots, triggered by a sensor, the glare blinding.

Mullet crouched and rolled, pulling the revolver from his belt, coming up on whoever walked in the door. No one did.

For tight moments Mullet listened but the house was still. He let out a long sigh of breath, turned to where the spotlights pointed: a dead man lashed to a wooden support column by a cord pulled tight under his arms. Another round his knees.

The man's shoes were fouled. His pale blue shirt purpled with blood, his suit trousers stained. His head was held upright by a crossbow bolt through the neck. A deep gash across the forehead had pooled blood in his left eye.

Mullet stood. It couldn't have been an easy death for Roger Oxford. A bolt through the neck you're probably going to drown in your own blood, your lungs filling as you bled out. Whoever whacked you this way didn't rate you high up his list of friends. Also, whoever whacked you this way didn't give a toss about the cops. Although they probably didn't expect anyone to find you for a good few days.

He pulled out his cell and thumbed through to Ted's number. Before he could connect, the elusive phone rang again. In Oxford's pocket, vibrating like a mouse burrowing through cloth. Mullet reached into the bloody pocket for the phone. His hand came out red and sticky. A book of matches dropped to the floor. He smeared the blood from the screen, reading there: Dragon Fire. The man in the photograph walking in the garden. With the phone held in his fingertips, he put it to his ear, but not close enough for skin contact.

"Roger Oxford's phone" – sounding like a goddamned secretary.

"I wish to speak with him."

The unmistakeable lisp of an Oriental.

"That's not possible right now."

International crackle.

"This is a phone call from Taipei. I must speak to Roger Oxford with extreme urgency. My name is Ge Fei."

Mullet glanced at the corpse and cleared his throat. "Are you a business associate?" He heard muffled talking that wasn't English.

The voice of Ge Fei came back on: "Where is Mr Oxford, please?"

Mullet decided to take a flyer. "You know a man called Woo? James Woo, I think it is."

Again cellphone static. "Would you confirm please, is Mr Oxford alive or deceased?"

"You had better contact his wife," said Mullet, thinking the jump from Woo to Oxford's death was interesting.

More muffled talking, then: "Would you confirm please, is Mr Oxford murdered?"

Very sharp thinking. "He is," said Mullet, the phone slippery in his fingers. "Look," he began but the voice interrupted.

"Thank you." And the line went dead.

Thank you! Mullet walked back into the winery, thumbing a search through the cell's phone book in case there was any number for Judith or Candy Liu that he didn't have. Nothing for Candy Liu, which was odd, and only the cellphone number Judith had given him. He put the phone on the tasting table. At the sink washed his hands. Into his own phone he stored the number and the name, Dragon Fire. Dragon Fire was a wine Vincent's mom sold. Product of China. Tasted worse than retsina.

He called Ted. Ted listened, told him to stay put.

Mullet sat in his car with the door open, toking on a small stop, The Band playing softly.

See the man with the stage fright . . .

He held the smoke in until he couldn't hear the music over the sound of his own blood, then exhaled. Mullet could feel the heat of the end against his fingers. He took a last hit: a short sharp intake that billowed in his lungs before he blew out a plume through the corner of his mouth.

The Band was on a loop through his mind. See the man in the spotlight. He killed the roach in the car's ashtray.

From where he sat, Mullet had a view of the kitchen door in case the domestics turned up, not that they seemed in a hurry to make the beds or take the glasses off the stoep. Could only be because everyone had gone fishing.

He thought about Judith. About why Roger Oxford didn't want to tell him where she was. Assuming she wasn't dead. What he needed was a favour at the airport, someone to check the departure lists. But he had nobody there.

He thought about Roger Oxford. The guy'd driven out here to see his client, like he'd done before. Had to be that the last thing on his mind was that maybe his client would pop him. In his diary it wasn't a high-risk call. Nobody was going to tie him to a column and aim a crossbow at him.

He thought about the crossbow bolt. Just like the one that had ended up among Bom-Bom's stuff. Unusual weapon. Twelve years back he'd worked the case of a Taiwanese found in the Black River with a bolt through his head. No leads at all. The murder put down to squabbling fishermen. Taiwan. Taipei. Dragon Fire.

He thought about Jim Woo. About the coincidence of the guy featuring in two jobs. And the street kids saying Bom-Bom had gone off to kill a Chinaman. He thought about how he'd heard China was opening up as an even bigger abalone market than the rest of the East put together. Shanghai restaurants going all out for international reputations. It brought Vincent to mind. He rang him.

"You at the Oxfords' place?"

"I was."

"Find out anything?"

"From Privilege?"

"From the maid."

"She didn't pitch."

Mullet paused. "Oxford's dead."

"Hey, what?"

"Murdered. Killed with a crossbow bolt."

"Jesus!"

"You're right, Jesus. You remember the Taiwanese guy that got done that way?"

"Ten, twelve years back?"

"Something like that. A coupla guys thought it was Triads."

"So did my mother."

"That right?" Mullet kicked at the gravel. "Look, I've gotta go. Why don't we make it at the office. Say two hours."

"You easy there?" said Vincent.

"Sure," said Mullet. "The hotshots're on their way."

Two hours later cops were all over the place. For an hour Mullet had been trying to leave.

"Anything else?" Ted kept asking, like there was something he was deliberately holding back.

"You've got it all. Everything I know. Everything I did here. My prints'll confirm it." Mullet kept quiet about Candy Liu. He didn't want the cops getting to her first.

"You're sure his wife's disappeared?"

"You find her, ask her to call me."

Ted dropped a butt and ground it into the lawn. He pointed at the house. "Nice place. True what the government says, foreigners buying up the land. Putting the prices way off the reach of locals."

Mullet started moving towards the courtyard. "Wait for the auction."

"You think there's gonna be an auction?"

"Mr Woo's not coming back."

"You ever meet this Mr Woo?"

"Vincent did."

"Talk to him at all?"

"Only his muscle. Or what might've been muscle. The guy I told you about."

Ted leaned against the driver's door of Mullet's Subaru.

"Naidoo's gonna want to see you again."

"Sure he is."

"Everywhere he goes there's Mullet Mendes. This time he's even beaten to the scene. Another crossbow scene. Maybe not even twelve hours old. That'll burn his hole." Ted shook a cigarette from his pack. "He'll wanna hear it all over again. Just to get your goat." He fired the tip and sent a plume over Mullet's head.

Mullet said, "While you're checking the flight lists can you do me a favour?" He eased between Ted and his car, got the door open.

"What'd that be?"

"Check if a Judith Oxford flew out Wednesday afternoon."

"Considering it's part of the investigation?"

"Isn't it?"

Mullet got into his car and closed the door. Ted tapped on the window, mouthing something. As the window came down, said, "Maybe a change of T-shirt would be good."

Mullet grinned. "You get queasy at the sight of blood?" About to fire the ignition when he paused. "Hey, you know anything about tattoos?"

"Like what?"

"Like a triangle with Chinese symbols at the points. Very delicate."

Ted flicked ash off his cigarette. "Maybe Triads."

"Was on the shoulder of a young woman. A stunner. Peachy boobs. Voice of an angel."

"All the rage, Chinese tattoos."

57

Jim Woo and Marina sat in the business-class lounge at Johannesburg International, the flight being called even as they finished their drinks. Woo stood. He was edgy. Had been edgy all the flight up from Cape Town.

"Relax," said Marina, "everything's fine."

"Everything's fine when the plane takes off," he said. "Everything's fine when we get to Cayman." He swirled the ice round the glass and knocked back the last of the whisky. Johnny Walker Blue Label. What was bothering him especially was the call he had to make to Dragon Fire. The call he'd been putting off all morning.

A hostess came up with a charity bucket, said any spare local currency they didn't know what to do with could be donated to a night shelter. For street children, she emphasised. Woo emptied his change pocket.

"That's very kind of you, sir," said the hostess. "I hope you enjoyed your stay."

Woo nodded, not saying a word.

Marina, on her cellphone to the half-caste private dick, Vincent, smiled at the hostess but made no move to fish out her purse. The woman turned to an American couple.

He heard Marina say, "Tomorrow will be fun. See you then" – her voice silky, coming on to the guy. She disconnected and looked at him.

Woo said, "Are you ready?" He was toying with his cellphone.

Marina nodded, gathered her handbag and her jacket. "I won't be a minute."

Woo watched her heading for the toilets: that pert behind in the smart slacks. But she'd been irritating him ever since breakfast. Insisting on a last champagne on the stoep. Flirting with Arno. Arno putting his arm round her, trying to grope her breasts. Marina not in any hurry to be away. Maybe if he'd taken her down and shown her Roger Oxford, she'd have been more skippy about heading for the airport.

And then on the flight up, suggestive as an escort girl. Standing up to get something from the overhead locker and leaning over him, rubbing against his shoulder. So close he could smell her. Her skirt riding too high on her thighs.

When she sat down she'd said, "Daytime flights are no fun."

He'd cracked the complimentary newspaper. "For God's sake."

Marina had shrugged, given him a frown. First thing she did at Johannesburg International, even before they went through passport control, was change into slacks. He didn't comment. She didn't either. She didn't need to.

Woo flipped open his phone and put the call through to Dragon Fire. They followed the formalities of politeness, Woo listening for any signals of distress. The background sounded restaurant.

Eventually he said, "Everything's done. You'll get the capital next week." He pictured the guy sitting in the emporium with White Paper Fan and the two thugs, a clutter of food on the table.

Dragon Fire said, "Of course."

The way it came across to Woo, Dragon Fire was telling him he hadn't expected anything else. Then he heard the guy say, "I am unhappy about Roger Oxford."

Woo sat still as ice, the blood thumping in his ears.

"You have killed a Brother."

A hostess was hovering, Marina walking towards him, smiling. Ever the elegant woman: a V-neck T-shirt, a linen jacket thrown over her shoulders. A Brother? He shut off the call.

Marina said, "That was abrupt."

Woo had the sweats, could feel the perspiration running under his arms. Had to swallow to get his heart back into his chest. His phone rang.

The hostess said, "Excuse me, sir, ma'am, could you board please?"

Woo picked up his cabin luggage and headed for the door.

Marina hurrying after him, saying, "Aren't you going to answer?"

58

On the highway into town Mullet keyed through the voicemails on his old cellphone.

Elizabeth: "I seem to have run out sooner than expected. If you could manage to come round over the weekend I would appreciate it. Only if you're not going fishing that is."

Vincent: "Where are you? I've been waiting an hour. Call me. I'm outta this dump."

Professor Summers: "So I'm here, Mendes. Visitors' Centre, one o'clock, as we agreed. But you've taken fright. Not the main dealer you make out to be, are you? You had better deliver to my home. I can't hang around here any longer." And then: "You're an arsehole, you know that?"

The account exec at the advertising agency: "Yo, Mullet, it's me. Help! It's the weekend and there's nothing in the tin. Pretty please." Followed by three smooches.

It brought a smile to Mullet's face. But it didn't last long. What he wasn't looking forward to was telling Candy Liu about her daddy.

He tried the Blue Dolphin first, hoping the manageress with the permanent smile wasn't in. She didn't seem to be. He asked the waitress at the reception desk where he could reach the singer Candy Liu.

"I can't give out that sort of info," she said.

"Pity," said Mullet. "Some guys from a London label want to hear her sing."

The waitress went, "Oh wow. She's on tonight."

"Sure." Mullet helped himself to a peppermint from the bowl on the counter. "May I?"

She said, "Be my guest."

"These guys're scouting. I told them she's really hot."

"She's better than Nora Jones, Joss Stone put together."

"That's what I believe." Mullet gave her the wrapper to throw away. "You see the record guys have to fly out tonight. Know what I'm saying, they're gonna be halfway up Africa by the time she starts singing."

The waitress glanced round towards a back table. Mullet followed her gaze: there was the smiler having lunch with the piano man, Ricardo.

"She didn't come in last night," the waitress whispered.

Mullet sucked at the peppermint. "She didn't?" He shrugged, thinking, oh shit!

"They can't get her on the phone either."

He crunched the peppermint. Mint chews were just so much better for your teeth. "My people are gonna be disappointed."

"I can give you her cellphone number," she said.

"That'd be a help."

She searched through a contact book and scribbled the number on her order pad, tore off the sheet.

"I didn't tell you."

"Course not. Thanks." He looked off at the manageress and the piano man, considering that Ricardo must have her address. Must have been round there to see if she was alright. With a bit of bullshit he could get the address out of him. Then again, a call to her cellphone provider would deliver the goods without the bullshit.

"I hope there's nothing wrong," said the waitress.

Mullet smiled. "I'm sure she's fine. She'll be even better when she hears about my guys."

Her address was Avalon Court, a block of flats in a street right behind the News Café. Mullet parked in Gabriel's patch. The car guard ambled over to him with a wide white smile, recognising his face but not quite placing him.

Mullet held up the phone with the picture of Desirée on the screen. Gabriel greeted him like a friend he hadn't seen in ten years.

"You ready to try her blow job?" he said.

"Maybe some other day," said Mullet, pressing the remote lock button on his key ring. "But a friend of mine's after one like this."

"You tell him I sell quality."

"I don't have to. He's seen the phone."

"He calls here tomorrow he can have one." As if the car park was a cellphone shop. "You tell him the phone is quality with a capital K."

The guy laughed and so did Mullet, thinking he wouldn't correct him because maybe that was the joke. He flipped the guy a five-rand coin. "I won't be long."

"I can get Desirée here in fifteen short," he said.

"Some other time, hey," – and Mullet crossed the road, going up the side of the café into the shaded streets. He found Avalon Court without trying. A three-storey block that maybe had been something once with its arches and columns, but about fifty years back it'd needed paint. The inner courtyard smelt of blocked drains. All that was left of the sun was a diminishing patch high up the wall. He took the stairs to Candy Liu's flat on the third floor.

He knocked. No movement inside. He knocked again. Then phoned her. No sound of a phone ringing in the flat, and after seven, eight rings it went to voicemail. Mullet didn't leave a message. Instead he knocked on the next-door flat. The pensioner there said she hadn't seen the little Chinese girlie for some days.

Mullet said thanks and made as if he were leaving. He waited in the stairwell until he heard the pensioner's door close and the chains sliding back. Gave her three minutes to settle in front of the TV.

Getting into Candy Liu's flat took him less than thirty seconds with a credit card to slide back the Yale lock. Rog should have had her put up better security. Which reminded him was something he'd promised Rae-Anne he'd do before she moved in, and still hadn't got round to.

"Mullet, the locks. You promised."

The sort of nagging that could fray his nerves.

The flat was a furnished bachelor. Wardrobe, bed, table with two metal kitchen chairs. A small television set. Hanging above the bed a framed black and white photograph of the Cape Town pier taken sometime in the 1930s to judge by the way people were dressed. Small bathroom, the bath stained, a plastic cistern over the toilet bowl, cigarette burns in the lid. In the tiny kitchen a two-plate stove, kettle, toaster and a bar fridge. Crockery and cutlery for two people.

Not the sort of place he could see Roger Oxford being happy with. You'd have thought Rog would've insisted his daughter had the best. What worried at Mullet was the feeling this spoke of temporary. Like this wasn't her real home.

He let himself out and went bothering the pensioner again. This time the old woman kept her door on the chains. Mullet said sorry to trouble her but could she tell him when Candy Liu moved in?

"Beginning of the month," said the pensioner.

Ten days back.

Mullet went into his sorry-to-trouble-you spiel, but the old woman closed the door on him, making a noise of shooting the bolts.

On his way to the Oxfords' house, Mullet thought, what the heck're you doing, boykie? What do you care what's going on here? This's got nothing to do with Mullet Mendes. You've done your client's work, forget the rest. Do some drops. Go 'n help Rae-Anne pack. Buy some new locks for the doors. Run up the coast and fetch the boat tomorrow, hang out a rod for a few hours. Heck's sake, leave the cop stuff to the cops. They're the guys getting paid.

He pulled up outside the Oxford house. Two police cars in the driveway, the wrought-iron gates closed, no sign of the Doberman. Or of Privilege. The cops probably quizzing him, getting him to talk about his employer. Mullet sat in the car, the engine running, staring at the house, glass and chrome. And Roger let his daughter stay in a dead-end dump? No way, José. He pressed the intercom buzzer.

A woman's voice answered. He told her he was looking for Judith Oxford, that he had the garden plants she'd ordered. The woman said the gardener would come and sort it out. Mullet had to keep the grin from his thank-you. He switched off the ignition.

Two minutes later, there was Privilege strolling up the driveway towards him. Mullet got out of the car.

The old man nodded at him, said, "You don't come from the nursery."

"I want to ask you something," said Mullet. He ducked into the car and came out with the Blue Dolphin flyer for Candy Liu and Ricardo. "You know her?" – passing the flyer through the bars of the wrought-iron gate.

Privilege took it. "She is Mr Oxford's daughter." He handed it back. "The police say Mr Oxford is dead."

"I've heard," said Mullet. He quartered the flyer and glanced up at Privilege. "Did she live here?"

"She went to stay in town."

"How long ago?"

Privilege had his eyes fastened on the spot in the sky which had been so fascinating earlier. "At the end of last month," he said. "Since then she has not come back."

"Why'd she go?"

"The madam she didn't like her."

Mullet gave him the thumbs up, thank you.

"What about the dog?" said Privilege.

"The cops'll look after it," Mullet said. "Don't worry, they like dogs."

The end of it, Mullet thought as he drove off. Whatever the Oxfords had been working, this was the end of it. The loose ends of it. Which was irritating but none of his business. He'd surrender, go and help Rae-Anne pack her flat.

"Babe, I didn't know you cared," she told him when he walked in with two pizza boxes, one Napolitana, one vegetarian with extra olives, and a litre bottle of Coke.

She hooked a lock of hair behind her ear and smeared the sweat from her brow with a forearm. Standing there in her shorts and tank top, flashing her belly like a teenager. Rae-Anne tapped her fibre leg on the floor. "Come 'n give us a kiss."

Mullet did, wondering if maybe he should take it further. Until she broke away.

"Hey, dollface, we've got things to do first."

While they ate Mullet told her about his day: all the weird stuff, men-tioning the stiff in passing.

"Jesus, Mull," she said, "I'm eating." But it didn't put her off lifting another wedge from the box.

One of the things he appreciated about her, her stomach for the rough 'n tumble of life.

When he'd finished with Candy Liu, she said, "You think the girl's dis-appearance is tied in?"

Mullet took a long pull at the bottle of Coke. "I don't know what to think."

Rae-Anne reached for the bottle. "She was nice. A great singer."

"I don't know and what do I care. To heck with it." He stood up. "Come on, we'd better get back on the job."

"Give me a break." But she took his outstretched hand and let him pull her upright. They went into a clinch, standing holding one another for long minutes. "You still worried about this?" she said into his chest.

He stared round at the boxes. All the boxes packed to go. So many boxes piled all over the lounge floor. Her stuff. Which was going to be unpacked in his house. Boxes of clothes, shoes, bedding, plates, pots, or-naments, rugs, posters, medicines, perfumes, women's stuff. The pyjama dog that sat on her bed. That would sit on his bed. Her CDs that would get mixed in with his.

"It'll be fine."

She looked up and they locked eyes.

"We're going to do this thing," she said.

"Heck yes. We're halfway there." He dropped his hold on her but she kept her arms round his waist.

"Mullet, I need you," she said. "I want more of you."

He nodded. His mouth was dry. He needed a swig of Coke. With a hit of brandy would be good. There was a pain starting to throb above his right eye.

"I know you. I know you like your space. So we set up boundaries. Your shelf. My shelf. My cupboard. Your cupboard. It's not rocket science, hon. Living together."

He heard her. Felt her squeeze gently, and responded by putting his arms about her shoulders. The pain tightened across his forehead.

"Think of the good things. Someone to keep the place tidy. Someone to cook, well, some of the time. And the best part, I'm low maintenance, Mull. I like my own time. You can go fishing all you want." With that she broke away, picked up the pyjama dog and buried her face in it. "It'll look cute on our bed. Don't you think?"

Mullet said, "You have any Panado handy?"

Rae-Anne laughed. "Only joking, babe. Only joking. I might have had him since forever but there comes a time . . ." She let the sentence hang. "You know." And lobbed the dog into a box. "You still want the Panado?"

Mullet rubbed at the spot above his eye. "I reckon."

She went into the bathroom and came back with two tablets. "Don't think I'm going to be doing this for you in future."

He popped the painkillers to the back of his throat and washed them down with Coke. "The thing is . . ." – he stopped. Where he wanted to go was if this doesn't work out we can always go back to separate places. Except he knew it wouldn't be like that. If things didn't work out, things didn't work out. As an item, they were finished.

Rae-Anne said, "The thing is what?"

"I dunno." He shrugged.

"The thing is Mullet Mendes, you're shit-scared of commitment." She eyeballed him. "Admit it."

It was true but he wasn't going to say so.

"Say it, Mull. The world won't fall to pieces."

He turned to the window. Heck of a view over the city to the harbour straight ahead. You could even see the cranes. Beyond, ships in the bay.

"You're scared of waking up next to me every morning. That every evening we have to come home and talk to each other. How's your day been? That we're gonna sit around like old farts watching TV." She came up next to him. "The only change, Mull, is that I'm going to be there not here. We're not gonna play housey-housey. You can lie on the floor and get stoned with Johnny Cash every bloody evening. And we don't have to switch on the TV."

It didn't reassure him. "Great view," he said.

Rae-Anne coughed a laugh. "Huh!" She glanced at him. "You mean I'm mad to swap it for a mean backyard that's mostly taken up by a boat and a van. You're right. But I think it's worth it."

Mullet nodded. "I'll miss this."

Rae-Anne swung back into the room. "Don't work me up, Mull. Here." She picked up a toolbox. "Do some man things. The dishwasher's coming. So is the washing machine."

He took the box. The dishwasher? The washing machine? She thought there was room for them? "What's wrong with laundrettes?"

"Don't start."

He did as he was told. Rae-Anne put on White Stripes to ease his headache. But it didn't. Nor did the tablets. The pain bored into his head, intense as ever.

About six Mullet said, "Wanna take a break while I make some drops?"

"You go," said Rae-Anne. "I'm almost done. Another hour 'n we can move some boxes."

Mullet grimaced. This being the moment he'd not been keen on getting to. "I haven't got the bakkie. We can do some small ones in the car."

"Where's the bakkie?" Rae-Anne snapped the locks on a suitcase.

"The plan is to fetch it tomorrow. With Vince. Up the West Coast."

"On the day I'm moving in?"

"The clients owe us, Rae. Also I want my stuff back: the Isuzu and the *Maryjane*."

"Jesus, Mullet, why didn't you tell me?"

"I thought I'd mentioned it."

"Well you didn't." Rae-Anne threw herself into a chair, glaring at him. Mullet not meeting her eyes. "No, fuck it, Mull!" She thumped the arm of the chair. "You can get the boat some other bloody day. We can all go on Sunday. But tomorrow I'm moving. And you're helping me. End of story."

Mullet didn't respond.

"Mullet? What?"

He fidgeted with his car keys.

"Commit yourself. Come on, tell me you'll help me."

From somewhere he could hear a television advertorial. Commit yourself. Come on, tell me you'll help me. He moistened his lips.

"Right then. I'll help you."

Rae-Anne turned away. "This I've gotta see."

"Jesus!" Mullet exploded. "What d'you want? I told you I'll do it."

"Don't you shout at me." Rae-Anne pivoted towards him, her face livid. They stood glaring at one another.

Mullet felt the fight draining from him. This was what Rae-Anne could do to him, bring up the weakness. "I've gotta go," he said. "I'll see you later."

"Mullet," he heard her calling after him. "You've got to face these things."

Like heck he had to, thought Mullet. The trouble with Rae-Anne was she couldn't see that sometimes stuff wasn't simple. You had a business to run, sidelines to manage. You had to take time to do it. What nagged at him was that they'd rushed into this shacking up lark. Maybe they should of just left stuff alone. Your house. My house. It had worked for eighteen months, why change it? Because that was Rae-Anne, couldn't let be a bloody thing. The pain pulsed above his eye.

You're a weak bastard, he said to himself, you let women walk all over you. They move in, they deball you, simple as that.

In the car Mullet bit into a mint chew to get the bad taste out of his mouth.

He did his first drop at the account exec which cheered him up. Got him a kiss on the cheek, too. In celebration he slotted Massive Attack's *Mezzanine* into the player for the ride to Elizabeth's. His headache was fading.

"Jeffrey! My hero," she said as he stood on her doorstep holding a brown paper bag of the finest Durban poison. "Aren't you a star."

She was in jeans and a T-shirt, bare feet and granny glasses. Her long grey hair at shoulder length. Sexy wasn't in it.

"You want to come in?" Her eyes mischievous as a little girl's. "For a puff?"

"Maybe next time."

She leaned towards him. "That's what you always say, Jeffrey Mendes." Mullet wondered if she'd maybe had a toke or two already.

"You're not going fishing? That was good fish."

"You might get lucky."

"Jeffrey, you're a godsend," she said as he backed out the garden gate.

Five minutes later he knocked on the front door of Professor Wanker Summers, the reek of cat piss all-pervasive. The professor took his time answering. Mullet reckoned the old fool stood watching him through the spy hole for almost two minutes before he opened.

"What happened to you, Mr Sugarman?"

The professor in his sleeveless cardigan and grey slacks with a cigarette burn at the knee glared at Mullet.

Mullet shrugged.

"Tell me, Sugarman, tell me what was better at one o'clock that it detained you?" The professor counted two-fifty bucks onto Mullet's palm. "So?" He took the bag of grass.

"You don't want to know," said Mullet.

"Try me."

"Right then. Husband of my client took a crossbow bolt in the neck. A headless corpse was found in a hole with my gun. How'm I doing?"

The professor shook his head. "You're a pathological liar, Mendes. You need help." He shut the door before Mullet could answer.

When Mullet got to his office the phone was ringing. He lifted the receiver as the answering machine kicked in, Ted's voice burbling below the recorded message.

"Talk to me, talk to me," Mullet shouted, scoping the room for any sign that Vincent might have been in during the afternoon. A polystyrene cup on his partner's desk was evidence of coffee from the downstairs café, but Mullet put that at a lunchtime refreshment. Same as the cold Americano on his desk, bought by Vincent for the meeting that never happened. The guy was all heart.

Ted said, "Don't you like your cellphone anymore?"

"Why?" Mullet sat down, put his feet on the desk.

"I've left four messages over the last so many hours."

"It hasn't rung." Then he remembered: "Aw heck, I'm using a new one" – trying to place where he'd left the old phone. Probably in the car out of juice or in a drawer somewhere.

"So you wanna know what we've got?" said Ted, sounding like he was the cat with the cream.

"I'm listening." Mullet heard him draw at a cigarette.

"For starters, your client skipped on a Wednesday afternoon flight for . . . wait for it . . . Atlanta, gateway to the Americas."

"No onward ticket?"

"Nope."

"Doesn't mean she hasn't got one."

"Nope again."

While Ted sucked at his cigarette, Mullet said, "You find any reservations for Jim Woo?"

The whoosh of Ted's exhale. "Not a thing. Which doesn't mean squat. But how about this, dead Roger was due out Friday heading for . . . you guessed it . . . Atlanta." Ted coughed, hacking to shift the tar off his lungs. He cleared his throat, in a strained voice said, "This coming together for you in any way?"

Mullet stared at his suede slip-ons. Some blackish goo had stained the uppers on the right shoe. He lifted his feet off the desk. "Not really."

Ted made another go at clearing his throat. "You wanna know the real dirt?"

Mullet waited.

"Well, do you?"

"Jesus, Ted."

"We found a skull at Helderrand. Small size. Early adolescent. Bright white. Tech boys reckon it must've been boiled clean."

"Where?"

"In an oil drum"

"Ha, ha. Where'd you find it?"

"Drum was beside a shed. Not exactly hidden away."

"Nice one." Mullet took a closer look at the mess on his shoe. Had to be blood.

"Doesn't mean just because you've got a body in one place and a head in another that you can say snap."

"You're doing a DNA?"

"As we speak."

"And you've said snap?"

"Wouldn't you?"

Wouldn't he just, Mullet thought after they'd hung up. Thought, even if they got a match there was no way of saying it was Bom-Bom. Unless. Heck yes. Unless there were prints on the crossbow bolt that Rae-Anne had found in Bom-Bom's bedding that matched prints on his gun, the one buried with the body. He dialled Ted.

At the end of his spiel Ted said, "So you're not just a pretty face."

Mullet told him, "Up yours."

Then he went looking for his partner: starting and ending at the Kimberley Bar.

Vincent was steaming. Standing up against the bar, thumbing through a fat catalogue of DIY equipment. The DIY salesman giving his spiel. Mullet told the salesman: "Cut him some slack, china, this man's in the poo. Know what I mean?" The salesman winked. "I've got a wife like that," he said.

Mullet steered Vincent to a table.

"How'd you know I'd be in here?" – the words slurred into one another but not quite on their backs.

"Heck, Vince, doesn't take Sherlock Holmes. When you don't answer your phone I know you're drinking. So much for the wagon, hey!"

"Jus'a drink," said Vincent.

"Right then." Mullet reached across the table and clamped a grip round Vincent's wrist so he couldn't lift the glass. "Here's what's gonna happen. You're gonna finish your drink then we're heading for your ma's. You're gonna sleep this off and tomorrow first thing take a drive up to get my boat. You get the money and my boat and you come back. The next day we'll fetch your car."

"We not go-ing fish-ing?"

"A change of plan." Mullet looked at Vincent, the guy's eyes were staring: he was well wrecked. "You want a pie to soak that up?"

Vincent said, "Yes."

Mullet ordered a steak and kidney.

"What the heck's this about, Vincent?" he said while they waited for the barman to nuke the pie in the microwave. "I thought you'd shoved the drink. We've got a partnership, remember. Mendes & Saldana."

The barman shouted that the pie was ready and Mullet fetched it.

"You want tomato sauce?" He slid the plate under Vincent's nose.

Vincent shook his head, the smell of the kidneys rising his gorge. "I'm gonna . . ." He slapped a hand to his mouth as his stomach heaved, knocked over the table in his rush for the toilet. The beer glass broke, the pie shot across the floor like a puck.

At the commotion, the barman looked over, world-weary. "Get him out won't you, pal. He's a goddamned nuisance."

"He's going," said Mullet, righting the table. "Sorry about the breakage."

"You don't wanna know how much it costs us," said the barman. He came round the counter to pick up the pie. "You want me to wrap this for him?"

"It's fine."

"Suit yourself."

Mullet settled the bill, added twenty bucks for the damage. The barman would probably sell the steak and kidney to the next taker, no eye batted. While he waited for Vincent, Mullet called the chauffeur guys, students who ran a you-drink-we-drive business.

"One to go: Kimberley Bar to the Kloof Street Hot Wok," Mullet told the voice that asked how he could be of service?

"Gimme five," said the chauffeur guy.

He made it in seven, a blond surfer-type on a pop-pop motorbike. Mullet and Vincent were outside the bar, Vincent on his haunches, leaning against the wall.

"You the gents?" said the student.

Mullet pointed to Vincent's car, jammed against the kerb right outside the Kimberley's batwing doors. "That's the one you drive" – he said, handing him the keys. The chauffeur guy folded his motorbike into the boot. "Lay on, Macduff."

"Lay what?" said Mullet

"I'll follow."

"Right then," said Mullet.

Ten minutes later, outside the Hot Wok, he counted five tens into the palm of the chauffeur guy's right hand. "That's a useful service you do."

"It pays the fees," said the student, kicking his pop-pop to life. Mullet wedged what was left of his petty cash into his pocket. In less than half an hour Vincent had pulled him down ninety bucks.

"You're costing me," he told Vincent, as he waited for the other half of Mendes & Saldana to stop barfing in the gutter. "'N it's not as if we're getting any fun outta the proceeds."

When Vincent came upright he said, "Hear me again, Vince" – holding his partner against the Subaru. Vincent's head rolled loose. Mullet shook him. "You listening, Vince. So hear what I'm saying. I'm saying you're gonna sleep this off, and tomorrow you fetch my boat. Gettit! By yourself. Sparrowfart you hit the road. They pay you, you say thank you, ma'am, and drive my boat into my backyard. Understand? Latest you get back is five. OK? Just don't stuff this up, Vince."

Vincent pulled himself free of Mullet's grip.

"You understand? Hey, you understand?"

"Lemme go," slurred Vincent.

"Here." Mullet held out Vincent's bunch of keys. "You'll need these."

"Jus leave me." Vincent grabbed the keys and turned towards the door of the Hot Wok, staggering.

Mullet shook his head. Bloody alkie. So much for playing the Good Samaritan. He got into his car and fired the engine, pulling into a lane when there was a break in the traffic. His last sight of Vincent was of the guy fumbling to find the lock.

One down, one to go, Mullet thought, pressing Rae-Anne's number into his cellphone. Her cell was on voicemail. Not a good sign. She was pissed off, but what could he do? He left a message: "I'll be another half-hour, just gonna check out if Candy Liu pitched at the Blue Dolphin."

As he'd expected, Candy Liu hadn't made it to her gig. Ricardo, the piano man with a wig, had. He was at the same table with the manageress, eating dinner.

Neither of them noticed Mullet until he pulled up a chair.

"Excuse me," said the manageress, flashing the smile, "this is a . . ."

Mullet didn't let her finish. "I know," he said. "I wanna know what's happened to Candy Liu."

"Bah!" Ricardo spat in his food.

"Who're you?" said the manageress.

"She is gone," shouted Ricardo. "Gone without a word." His arms waving about his ears.

"Gone?"

"Left. Fucked off. Vanished."

"Since when?"

The manageress tried again. "Please, Ricardo."

"After Wednesday night you didn't see her again?"

"No. Not even a fucking phone call goodbye."

Mullet said, "You ever visit when she stayed at home with daddy in the posh suburbs?"

With a fork, Ricardo moved the conglomerate through the yellow sauce to the side of the plate. "I can't eat this shit."

"Did you?"

He glanced at Mullet. "What're you talking about, man?"

Mullet gave him a card and said if she called, he'd like to know.

"What a cock-up," said the piano man, staring at his hake hollandaise.

As he moved off, Mullet heard the manageress going, "Please, Ricardo, please." From the courtesy bowl at the reception desk, Mullet took a fistful of peppermints.

"These suck," he told the waitress. "You should get chews."

He left the Waterfront and thought of stopping in at the office, but there wouldn't be anything that couldn't wait. He drove to Rae-Anne's flat. No lights on. Not a sound. Only a note pinned to the door: Mullet, I don't want to see you tonight. Just be here tomorrow at seven. And, babe, no sulks.

He tore off the note and balled it. Tried her cellphone again. "I'll be there," he said after the voicemail tone.

At home, Mullet wavered over Cash or Cohen or Springsteen. Decided it had to be *The Ghost of Tom Joad* that matched his mood. He sat at the kitchen table and rolled a spliff while the Boss went on about the fucked-upness of the lives of Charlie and Mary, Miguel, Spider and Bobby Ramirez. It made dealing with corpses and drunken partners and angry lovers seem normal. Mullet took long hits at the joint, holding the smoke till his lungs screamed, trying to keep focused on the music. To keep the stop alive he carefully knocked off the ash into a perlemoen shell, rubbing the end gently against the mother-of-pearl.

He couldn't remember a day that had been worse. Actually two days: starting with the kid's body in the dunes. That might yet be Bom-Bom if the prints matched. Two bodies in two days, hour by hour it was as bad as in the cops. Let alone all the other shite from everyone getting on his case: Rae-Anne, Vince, Naidoo, the wanker professor. For Chrissakes! He needed someone to give him a break.

Mullet took the roach down to a short end and crushed it in the shell. Stood, exhaled at a moth flicking against the centre light. He went out onto the back stoep.

"Heck, Bom-Bom," he said, his voice croaking with the hit still in his throat.

Mullet couldn't feel the grass working. He was as hyped as he'd been when he got in, pacing the stoep like a chained bear he'd seen once in the keep of a Czech castle. Up and down, up and down. What he needed was another toke. Get the bear to quieten. He went inside and sat at the table, flattening a Rizla paper on the breadboard.

The Boss sang about Sinaloa cowboys.

Thing about Bom-Bom that rode him was that it was inconclusive. Thing about the Oxfords that rode him was that it was inconclusive. Just as he'd started getting a handle on the angle, pow, it goes large, leaving residue in the person of one dead Roger nailed to a stake. And a disappeared client, and a disappeared daughter of the killed guy. Not to mention what rode him was Vincent getting pissed.

Mullet took a pinch of weed from a bankie and pestled it in his palm to separate the pips. The few he got he flicked through the open door. He sprinkled herb along the length of the paper. The Boss sang about working the line to send the Mexicans back other side of the river. He sang about lying underneath a highway bridge as the evening sky grew dark.

Mullet rolled the joint and licked the edge to glue it. He shook a Bic and flicked a flame. The smoke went into his lungs, caressing. Slowly he let it out through his nose, took another hit straight away. A1 reefer when you got it stoked. When you got it stoked the world backed off, took on a fuzzy complexion. He rocked on the chair. Times like this he missed the cat. Missed it rubbing against his legs. Maybe with Rae-Anne here he could get another one.

You get so sick of the fighting, sang Bruce about domestic unbliss.

It's just dry lightning.

"Yeah, right, Boss." Just dry lightning him and Rae-Anne, except when the brush caught fire you didn't want to be in the path of the blaze. Then you wanted to be out fishing. Somewhere Rae-Anne couldn't pock-pock after you like the guy from the pirate story.

Mullet laughed at the idea of Rae-Anne the peg-legged pirate. He sucked long at the spliff, breathing through it, holding down the sniggers. The Boss blew his harmonica, getting all mushy about some future there across the border. A truly lovely harp with backing choirs.

"Ah to heck with you all." Mullet crushed the roach. As the Boss went into the life of Le Bin Son and Billy Sutter, Mullet folded his arms on the table and rested his head on them. He didn't hear the last track play out.

59

Vincent woke up to puke. He was lying on the back seat of his car. He opened the door nearest his head and retched into the street.

Jesus, could there be any more?

He spat to clear the residue, wiped his hand across his mouth. For a while he lay on his stomach staring blind-eyed at the road surface. He heaved again, a sour bile scouring the back of his throat. It made him sit up to stop the reflux.

At first he couldn't put it together. Where he was, what had happened. Mullet. He recalled Mullet had been in it somewhere. And then it came back. Mullet going at him, telling him to get the boat. A sweat flushed his face as he heard Mullet shouting. Just don't stuff this up, Vince. You listening, Vince? Get my money, get my boat.

Vincent groaned. Jesus, Jesus, Jesus.

He looked at his watch: five-twenty-something, his vision too blurred and not focusing to be exact. He looked about. Saw the red neon sign of his mother's restaurant. A deserted Kloof Street.

What didn't return was how he'd got there. Just Mullet's voice kept at him. Don't stuff this up, Vince. Tomorrow first thing take a drive and get my boat. You get the money and my boat and you get back.

He remembered they were supposed to go up there and do a spot of fishing. He'd spoken to Marina, she'd said come for lunch. Bring your partner. Take a day out. So what was Mullet's case? Shouting at him. In his face every minute. Didn't let up. Hanna-hanna.

Vincent patted his pockets, found his car keys. He slid off the seat, taking care not to step in his vomit. He should take a shower, put on clean clothes. But he couldn't face his mother. Better to put in at the all-night garage shop for deodorant and a bottle of water. Maybe some sandwiches too. And get the hell out to Sea Farm. Prove to bloody Mullet that when he cut to the chase, Vince was a prince. Mr In-bloody-vince-able.

Up yours Mendes, my bro. He'd be at Sea Farm by breakfast, back in town by noon. Show Mullet what's what for Chrissakes.

60

Tommy drank the last of his Coke with his head tilted back, not looking at the road, the truck drifting over the centre line. Delmont, sitting middle on the bench seat, closed his eyes and squeezed his can of diet Fanta, squashing the tin, really wanting to make a grab at the steering wheel.

"Your problem, Del, is you wanna be larney. Posh. That's why the perfume. You gotta remember your roots, bro, they's in the shit. You can't get ridda that stink." Tommy threw his empty can out the window. "What I'm saying is, people tune you grief, you give grief. Some people need a smack. That guy inna shop was asking for it."

He flicked the brights: on off, on off, on off, on, coming up fast behind a farmer's fin-tailed Merc.

"Get outta the way, whitey." He pushed his hand flat against the hooter, tailgating the Merc. The Merc stayed solid. "You ever seen a car this old?"

"Jesus, Tommy," said Delmont, "you gonna bang him."

"Hey, Del, stay cool," said Tommy, giving the Merc another paarp paarp on the hooter. "Relax, china. Enjoy the ride. You don't see the country this time of the morning much."

The time was a hour after sunrise, the country they were passing through West Coast sandveld, scrub and bush, the ocean off blue to their left.

The road was a two-way with wide reserves outside the yellow lines. Tommy flicked the lights.

"Fork, whitey, move into the yellow line, for fork's sake."

"Whyn't you overtake him?" said Adonis, jammed on the other side of Delmont against the passenger door, eyes coke-bright.

Tommy swung the fridge truck to the right to overtake.

Delmont sucked in his breath at Tommy screaming "Yaaaaaaaaaa" – coaxing the truck faster on a downhill stretch.

As they levelled with the Merc, Adonis leaned out of the window to give the Merc driver the finger.

"Swizzle sister," he shrieked, and the man shook his fist back. It got Adonis laughing, coughing, licking his finger, ratcheting through his repertoire of fuck-you gestures faster than Diddy.

Delmont shouted, "There's cars coming" – bracing himself against the dashboard.

"Hey Del, this is a chicken situation" – Tommy gripped to the wheel, lips pulled back grinning over his emerald teeth. "What you say, Del? What you say?"

The oncoming car flashed its lights but Tommy kept his foot floored, screaming, "Don't you love it, darlin." Delmont beside him going, "Shit, man, shit, man, shit, man!" hardly audible above the hooter blare and the road noise drumming through the open window, the fridge truck centred on a head-to-head.

Then they were through and passed the Merc, Tommy hammering on the steering wheel with one hand, slapping Delmont's knee with the other.

"Hey Del, you see that, man? You forking see that? That guy musta shat bricks seeing us coming."

"Let me drive," said Delmont.

Tommy took his eyes off the road to stare at him. "Fork you, Delmont. Fork you, hey."

Then to Adonis. "What you say? You happy with the chauffeur?"

Adonis fluttered a hand.

"You see, Del, Cousin Tommy's staying at the wheel." He snapped his fingers, pointing at the cubbyhole. "Gimme some shit. Come'n, gimme some of that shit."

Adonis pulled a Ziploc of coke from the cubbyhole and shook it open. Tommy licked his finger. "Come on."

"Ooo bay-bee." Adonis ran a line onto the back of his hand and as he bent to snort it Tommy swerved the truck into a zig-zag, sending the powder flying, Adonis and Delmont shouting at him. Tommy whooped at the joke, rapping Jay-Z's 'Murdergram': "Niggas is dead, dead I tell you, can't be serious."

Adonis rolled his eyes. "You gonna play little-boy games again while I do this?"

"Fork you," said Tommy, sulky until Adonis took the hit. When he'd done, Delmont passed the bag to Tommy, not taking any himself.

Tommy said, "Do it, cuz Del."

Delmont shook his head.

"Do it, cuz." Tommy pumped his elbow into Delmont's ribs.

Delmont gasped. "OK, OK." He pinched powder into his palm and hoovered it. Gave the bag to Tommy.

"Hold this." Tommy let go of the steering wheel, not taking his foot off the accelerator, the truck lurched and Delmont clutched at the wheel to pull it straight, saying, "Holy shit." Tommy spilled powder on his fist and snorted it. Great stuff they'd scored with Mother Kaplan's loan. He licked his finger and dipped it in the powder, rubbing the white along his gums. The rush stormed him and he slammed his palm against the steering wheel, bobbing to the Jay-Z track. The lyrics mixed up in his head: "Three of the illest niggas together."

Adonis taking up the jive: "Can't be serious, its murda nigga, huh, its murda."

"What I hate about this truck," said Tommy, "is no forking CD."

At the Sea Farm sign, they turned off the tar onto the dirt road, the truck sliding on the gravel. Tommy eased the accelerator until the speed was under sixty.

"Howzat, Del? You gonna stop bitching now?"

"What'd I say?" said Delmont.

"It's not your words, bro. It's your attitude. You got that pissy attitude all the time."

Delmont didn't respond.

"Like your fiancée's not putting out poes." Tommy held up his hand, his fingers spread stiff as claws. "You all uptight, Del. You gotta go with the flow."

"Cock the hot pistol and pop the hot Cristal," sang Adonis.

"Hey," screamed Tommy, "that's what we gonna do."

The two of them doing the Jay-Z number all the way to the entrance to Sea Farm and then along the sand track to the house only shutting it when Tommy stopped in the cleared area beside the house but kept the truck's engine running.

"What you waiting for?" said Delmont.

"Just checking," said Tommy.

"For what? There's nobody supposed to be here."

"The big guy."

"You said . . ."

"He forking lives here, Del."

"You said the same as last time."

"More or less."

Delmont sat forward, putting his face into his hands. "Jesus, Tommy!"

"Say your prayers, Del."

Delmont came upright. "And he's not gonna want to know what we doing?"

Tommy put the truck into gear and released the clutch, heading slowly towards the sheds.

"We doing Mr Woo's business, like Mr Woo asked. The big guy can't do anything about it. He wants to phone the Chink, the Chink's not gonna be answering his phone."

He stopped outside the second shed, twenty metres on from where they'd stopped four nights previously, and switched off the ignition. Silence. Adonis cracked his door, not getting out though.

He said, "There's dogs barking."

Tommy listened, said, "Fork it" – opening his door. He reached under the bench seat for the nine mil, racked a load into the breech. "Let's go get the mothers." The gun went behind into his belt. He snatched the packet of coke off the dashboard.

The light inside the shed was dull green from the plastic roof-sheeting. Delmont flicked a switch beside the door. A generator kicked in and fluorescent bulbs buzzed and flashed over the tanks. Sixteen aluminium baths in parallel rows, baby perlemoen covering bottoms and sides up to the water level. Next to the door was a display tank with sea horses suspended among ferns, a plastic wreck, a castle with two turrets.

Adonis crouched to get a closer look. "You think those're real?"

"They sea horses," said Delmont. He stirred the surface with his hand and the creatures kicked and came to settle, all pointed in the same direction.

"They look like they just hanging there, 'cept you can't see the thread," said Adonis, tapping at the glass of the tank. The sea horses twirled their fins, galloping, but not going anywhere.

"You think this is the forking aquarium," said Tommy. He'd laid three neat lines of coke on the concrete floor. "You bitches want some of this?"

"Hell man," said Delmont. "There's sand 'n shit on the floor."

Adonis knelt down to take his hit, using a rolled ten.

"You want it? You don't want it? Fork bro, get down 'n boogie."

When Delmont didn't, Adonis put his nose to the third line before Tommy had a chance. The extra schnarf gave Adonis a bleed, globs of bloodslime dropping on his shirt and the floor.

"You wanna be a pig, that's what's gonna happen," said Tommy, shaking his head. "You a drug addict, that's what."

Delmont fetched buckets and screwdrivers from the back of the fridge truck and they took a tank each, Adonis bitching about the cold water and the blood leaking from his nose. Tommy told him forking shut up and shook his screwdriver at Delmont before the cuz could say anything. For ten minutes they worked without talking, chiselling the perlemoen off the tank floors and dropping them in the buckets. Somewhere distant dogs barked.

Then whup, the shed door banged open and the big guy stood there holding a Rottweiler and a Great Dane on a short leash, two small dogs at his feet, yapping. The Rottweiler snarled, strained at the leather.

David Welsh said, "The fuck're you doing?"

Tommy straightened, screwdriver in one hand, two perlemoen in the other. He dropped them in a bucket.

"Doing a collection for Mr Woo," he said. "Like he told us."

"Oh yeah," said David Welsh. "How about you get the hell outta here before I let the Rottie chew your face."

"Phone him," said Tommy, pissed off at this guy standing there in his swimming costume, big hairy forker with a Jesus beard. He licked his lips.

"Get," said Welsh. The Rottweiler went into a barking frenzy, spraying a white slather, but Welsh held him.

Tommy glanced from Adonis to Delmont, both watching the big man, waiting for whatever move he made. He shrugged, wiped his hands on his Diesels. "Mr Woo said . . ."

Welsh didn't let him finish. "You heard me" – playing some slack into the leash, the Rottweiler tugging, gasping at the choke hold.

Tommy reached behind his back and pulled the gun, put it on David Welsh. Four tanks separated them.

Welsh said, "You fucking little twat." He let the Rottweiler go, shouting "Sick, sick," as the dog crashed through the tanks, with the Great Dane following.

Tommy shifted his aim and whammed two body shots into the Rottie, one into the Dane. Another into a Jack Russell nipping at his ankles. The Rottweiler convulsed, jerking underneath the tanks, spraying blood. The Great Dane toppled, but the Jack Russells kept at his ankles until Tommy kicked the one that wasn't shot in an arc that had all the lift of a rugby conversion.

David Welsh rushed him. Tommy waited until the big guy was two metres out before he shot him, Welsh taking the bullet in the shoulder but coming on not even being jerked by the impact. Before Tommy could shoot again, Welsh was at him, the two of them going over into a tank.

It was underwater Tommy fired a chance shot that ripped through Welsh's stomach. Freed from the big man's stranglehold, he surfaced and stood up, gasping.

"Fork, Adonis, Delmont! You gonna leave this all to me?"

Welsh was clawing at the sides of the tank to keep his head above the surface, gasping, moaning. Blood swirled from his stomach wound.

"Ah fork you, shut up," said Tommy and pointed the pistol and pulled the trigger. It stuck.

Tommy threw down the gun. "Delmont, what sorta piece is this?" He grabbed Welsh by the hair, banged his head against the tank rim, a dull thup thup. Stared at Adonis and Delmont, "You want an invite?"

The three of them pushed Welsh under the water and for a while he thrashed and kicked but they held him there. When the twitching stopped, Adonis said, "He's dead."

"Better be," said Tommy, climbing out of the tank. The body lay face down. He bashed his fist on Welsh's head and the bobbing released a stream of bubbles.

Tommy stepped back. "You think he's breathing in there?"

"Oh God," said Delmont, "this's shit."

Adonis laughed, coming up to give Tommy a kiss on the ear. "You a mess."

"Sexy, hey?"

Delmont said, "Let's go. This is shit."

"He's dead, Del. You worried about his ghost or something?"

Delmont exploded, kicked at the metal sides of a tank. "You said no fucking problems. You said easy meat. You fucked, Tommy. You so fucked you don't even know what's the real world. Anybody tunes you grief, you wanna kill him." He lifted a bucket and poured the shells back into a tank.

"Hey, Del, what you doing?" Tommy circled towards Delmont. "Stop that, man."

They came up face to face. Tommy took the bucket, gripped Delmont's arm. "Del, you don't wanna go soft on me. We cousins. Cousin Del 'n Cousin Tommy."

Delmont shook his head. "This is all fucked up, Tommy."

Tommy nodded. "That's right, bro, all forked up." He started for the door. "Best thing is we take a smoke break."

61

Vincent pulled into the farm stall, needing KGB hangover tablets and more water. A beer would've been good. A shooter of brandy would've been better. Why he hadn't bought at least Panados at the all-night shop was a craziness. He stopped the car in the parking area, next to the sign for the toilets. What he needed desperately was to take a piss and freshen up. The toilet block was locked. He walked over to the farm stall for the key but the door there was locked too. With his hands cupped against the glass panes, he looked through the funnel they made, scoping the interior. Racks of souvenirs, bush hats, bottle openers with springbok-horn handles, home-craft bottled goods: jams, honey, green mango atjar. Standard stock. Maps, magazines, tourist guidebooks. Fridges with cool-drinks in the corner. There were lights on. He knocked on the door. Even so early, somebody had to be about. He took another look through the window, saw legs sticking out from under the counter.

Vincent thought, shit, do I need this? He went back to his car for the tyre wrench and used it to break a window.

The legs belonged to a white guy, mid-fifties, wearing khaki shorts and a blue shirt tight over a pot belly. The blue shirt blossomed with crimson, parts of the guy's face resembling raw steak. A gory gash across his forehead, a cut below his right eye: the blood had leaked into his hair and pooled on the concrete floor.

Vincent said, "Chrissakes!" He felt for the guy's wrist pulse and found it easily enough. By the look of the face wounds they were from a pistol-whipping or a knuckleduster. The story obvious. Passing thugs had done him over for the cash float. Vincent slapped at the guy's good cheek.

"Hey, china, china! Speak to me. Come back to us."

The man groaned.

Vincent stopped the slapping. "There we go, friend. Come on, let's hear your name." He brought over a bottle of mineral water and helped the guy sit up and take a swallow.

"You the owner?"

The guy nodded. "Bloody bastards."

Vincent nodded agreement.

The guy swallowed more water. Vincent let him take his time. "You'll be fine," he told him. "Except for the face gashes."

"I was fucking unconscious," said the guy, a lot of life suddenly in his voice.

"That's right. You want me to phone the cops?"

"It was two coloureds. Pulled in as I was opening. Moffie bastards. The one, wearing that baggy pants hip-hop gear, off his arse. The other guy smelt like he showered in aftershave." The farm-stall owner drank more water, said, "Jesus, my head hurts."

Vincent found him a packet of Grandpa powders and the farm-stall owner emptied two into his mouth, washing the powder down with the rest of the mineral water.

"There's a half-jack of brandy bottom of the counter," he said.

Vincent found it behind a stack of old newspapers. The level was down a couple of tots. The stall owner took two short pulls. He offered Vincent the bottle and Vincent poured brandy into the cap and drank it, gave the bottle back to the stall owner.

"I'm opening up, being conversational and baggy arse says they're going fishing, they've forgotten to buy some Cokes and what sort of pies

I've got, and cigarettes. Can't believe he's gone without his cigarettes. As I say, chatty but rough. Anyhow I tell them snoek are running up at St Helena but he'll have to pull his pants up jumping about the rocks. Next thing this bastard's got a gun in my cheek, shouting, 'You calling me a moffie?' I make a grab for my knobkerrie to bash his brains in, he whips me. Lights out, hey. Fucking wonderful country we got now. Never mind it's not supposed to be so bad anymore."

"You want me to call the cops?"

The farm-stall owner shook his head. "What's the time?"

Vincent glanced at his watch. "Quarter to eight."

"I'm talking forty-five minutes ago. I don't even know what sorta car they were driving."

"Even so. You report it at least you can claim insurance."

"Hey," the stall owner said, "that's smart."

Vincent waited while the stall owner cleaned up his face. The gash on the forehead needed stitches but the guy wasn't into taking a ride to the hospital. "It's Saturday," he said. "My best days are the weekend. I close up, I go down ten grand. That's big money in my books."

When the cops arrived an hour later, Vincent was feeling better about the day. He'd washed, eaten, taken headache tablets, and helped the stall owner kill the half-jack. Hair of the dog had even pushed back his hangover. He drove out with a basket of home-craft goodies the guy had thrust on him.

"You're a Samaritan," said the stall owner. "Bless you, friend."

Vincent accepted the presents, considering that if he needed leverage with Mullet he could pass these on to Rae-Anne and earn plenty brownie points. Hell, just pitching up with the *Maryjane* was going to make Mullet love him.

62

They sat on the sand dune behind the sheds and smoked a couple of joints. Tommy stripped down to his boxers, his clothes draped across the truck's bonnet to dry. When he crushed the second roach, Adonis reached over and touched his arm. "Got any more white?"

Tommy brushed him off. "You wanna blow me for it?"

Adonis pouted, opened his mouth in a round O. "Any time."

Tommy laughed. "What d'you say, Del?"

Delmont stood up. "We gonna to do this job or what?"

Tommy stretched out on his back. "You the one said it was up to shit."

"I'm not going in that shed," said Delmont. "No ways."

"The forker's dead. A floater."

"You want me to help you, you bring the buckets to the next one." He pointed at the third shed.

Tommy let Delmont's ordering slide. He got to his feet, dusted sand from his shorts. "You more a moffie than Adonis." The two men eyeballed for a moment until Delmont looked away. "Maybe it's you gonna have the babies, not your fiancée."

Tommy walked into the shed. The little dog he'd kicked lay against a wall, whimpering. The Great Dane growled but when it tried to stand its back leg couldn't take the weight and the dog collapsed. The Rottie was dead. The other little JR barked at him from under a tank.

Tommy went, "Pooch, pooch, pooch," trying to call the dog but it showed its bloody teeth at him, snapping at his fingers. This dog shot through with a nine still having a go at him. Tommy had to laugh. Amazing doggie to keep up so much aggro.

He collected the screwdrivers and the buckets and picked up the gun. Piece of shit. As he straightened he came face to face with the corpse of David Welsh. The body had rolled over, was staring at him. Tommy jumped.

"Fork." He squeezed the trigger automatically. The bullet thudded into Welsh's chest. The corpse did a slow rotation until it was floating face down. Tommy swore again, backing out like David Welsh had resurrected as the living dead.

Adonis was at the shed door. "What's happening?"

"Forking gun works." Tommy dropped the buckets. "Forking amazing. The guy's swimming in there."

"He's alive?"

"Unbelievable shit."

Delmont said, "Jesus, Lord."

"Forking lotta good he's gonna do."

They took the buckets and the tools to the third shed. It was identical. Same rows of tanks, same lighting, enough perlemoen to make a China-man's heart sing.

"You start," said Tommy, "I'm gonna get dry clothes from the house." He left the gun on a table beside the door, grabbed a screwdriver in case he had to force a lock.

But the house was open. Tommy went in quietly through the kitchen, thinking, why was he tiptoeing when the guy was dead? The first bedroom had a cupboard full of women's clothes, casual stuff but good quality. The second bedroom was Welsh's. The bed unmade, the curtains drawn, paperbacks on a bedside table, one butterflied open on the unused side of the double bed. The room smelt bad. Musty, rank with dog. A stack of washed clothes on a chair, dirty stuff piled in a corner on the floor. The carpets threadbare and covered in dog hair. Guys that lived with dogs were Stone Age.

Tommy tried on some jeans from the clean heap. He could get both his legs in one side. He went back to the other bedroom and found a pair of jeans that fitted and a faded green T-shirt. Adonis realised he was wearing female stuff, he'd pull his dick.

Tommy riffled through the other drawers, nothing but old perfume, old deodorant, tampons, aqueous cream.

He wandered down the passage to the living room, like entering a museum of sea shit: compasses, anchors, seal skulls, a whale harpoon, flags, pictures of sailing boats. The room stank of dog. Every chair had dog on it. Tommy thought, fork, his mother would need a week in here with a vacuum cleaner. He was about to go onto the stoep when he heard a car. And there coming along the sand road was this white Jap-crap, stopping next to the steps that led up to the stoep. The engine died, a guy got out. Fork, thought Tommy, sometimes you even scored a luck. Vincent Saldana. Whatya know?

63

Mullet woke with his phone ringing. Red digitals on the bedside radio clock told him 6.23 a.m. He was dressed, he was sleeping on the bed not in it. As he moved he caught the sourness of his body odour. It made him wince. His mouth felt as powdery as cat litter. Tasted about the same, he reckoned. The world came back to him: at least the part about helping Rae-Anne. He picked up the phone.

"I thought you'd need a wake-up call, babe," Rae-Anne said.

Mullet pinched a thumb and forefinger into the corners of his eyes. "That's good of you."

"You have a helluva night?"

"It was late."

"Poor baby."

Mullet looked at the other side of the bed. It wouldn't be empty tomorrow. Or the day after. Or the day after that. Or the day after that. What'd his ma say? You made your bed, you lay in it.

"Give me an hour," he said.

Rae-Anne laughed. "You gottit."

He was about to hang up.

"And hon, no sulks."

"I read your note."

"Cool." She paused, said, "Don't breakfast. I'll get croissants from the deli."

Mullet hung up and headed for the kitchen. He needed coffee and a dash. He found the centre light still on, the back door open.

Heck, he thought, you coulda been killed in your bed.

On his way into town, Mullet considered phoning Vincent, then decided no, he couldn't check on him every moment although the guy wasn't exactly building a record of reliability. Still 'n all the same, just to know he'd gone would be good.

Mullet detoured into Kloof Street to pass the Hot Wok; Vincent's car wasn't parked where he'd left him the previous evening, which was encouraging. But then the guy had the hots for that Marina so maybe she'd been the pull to get him there more than the money or bringing the *Maryjane* back. He sighed. You put a woman in the mix and things got out of hand.

Rae-Anne gave him a full frenchy in the open door to the flat, pinning his foot under her prosthesis.

"This is better than Christmas," she said, taking his hand, leading him into the kitchen. "Doll, you might be freaking out, but me, I'm really grooving."

"I'm not freaking out," Mullet protested, his voice up a notch. "Do I look like I'm freaking out?" He held his arms wide, appealing to her. He had on an orange tie-dyed, grandpa-necked T-shirt, jeans that could've done with a wash and bush sandals. "I'm cool."

She laughed at him. "Height of fashion, doll."

"Well then?"

"Have a croissant," she said. "I'll get coffee."

Instant for him, French roast percolated through a two-cup Bialetti for her.

They ate with Nora Jones on the boombox. The singer Candy Liu came to Mullet's mind and he shook his head. Rae-Anne caught the movement.

"You're thinking of?"

He told her. She dunked a piece of croissant in her coffee. "Odd one. Something tells me you were taken for a ride there."

Mullet nodded. "But I got paid."

"That's one way of looking at it."

"The only way of looking at it."

"Because it's the money not the principle," they said in unison, and clinked coffee mugs.

"Damn right."

The removal guys arrived half an hour later and had the boxes and the leather couch and the white goods loaded in short time.

"You go supervise the unloading," Rae-Anne told Mullet, "I'll clean up here. And say goodbye."

64

Vincent walked up the steps onto the stoep and rapped a tattoo on the front door. He gazed off at the sea: flat, glassy like the days earlier in the week he'd been there with Marina. The thought of her flushed his cheeks. That he'd made such an arse of himself. Played the macho in her car. The way he'd talked to her, like she was a bloody therapist. And then allowing her on the stake-out. It made him cringe. He knocked again.

No movement in the room. He tried the door, it opened. Called out hullo but nobody answered. Maybe she and her brother were on the beach, not expecting him this early.

He walked round the back of the house, where the *Maryjane* was hitched to the Isuzu. From there he could see a stretch of beach across to the headland. The sand was scuffed with prints along the tideline but wherever the dogs and their owners were now they were out of earshot.

Vincent considered the options. Probably they were on the beach beyond the headland. The shortest way there was past the sheds.

He glanced back at the house, wondering if Marina wasn't still asleep. The kitchen door was open, not hooked back but swinging in the breeze. Vincent walked over and looked inside. He called, "Marina! David! Hullllooo!" Stepped into the kitchen and crossed to the passage. He called their names again. The door to Marina's bedroom was open and he could see the bed neatly made up. The other room, David's, was dark. He paused, listening. Then went outside, closing the door, and headed for the sheds.

As he went down the incline he saw the fridge truck at the entrance to the second shed. Vincent stopped. He knew the truck. It was the heist truck, same goddamned registration number. A sweat broke on his palms. If that was here, Tommy Fortune was going to be here too. He backed away, thinking, what were the scenarios: David and Marina didn't know about this; David and Marina were dead. Which was why the kitchen door hadn't been fastened. Why there were no dogs. Jesus, he breathed out. And bloody Mullet wouldn't trust him with a bloody gun!

He moved round the house to his car and popped the boot for the tyre iron, the only weapon he could think of. He considered phoning Mullet but decided no, what was Mullet going to do? The drive would take him two hours even in his Subaru. He could phone the local cops, they could get a van over in maybe thirty minutes. But thirty minutes may be too late. Chances were these guys had started early, even during the night. They'd be finishing up sometime soon. Best to switch off the cellphone and go it alone.

On the last heist there'd been three guys. Fuckwit Fortune their boss boy. The other guys obedient to his nonsense. The likelihood was the same situation. What he had to do was take out Fortune and the others would be lambs. The only downside: he was going to a gunfight with a tyre iron. But what options when bloody Mullet wouldn't trust him with a bloody gun!

Vincent closed the boot and studied the house. Whatever had happened he didn't believe Marina and David were lying dead inside. Something else had gone down. What bothered him were the dogs. The dogs didn't let a person move out of their sight. The dogs should have been around. He hefted the tyre iron against the palm of his hand. There wasn't another way, he had to go back there to the sheds. OK, he whispered, this is where we put things right, and headed for the sheds, his strategy to rush in with the tyre iron flailing for maximum confusion. Overturn tanks, cause general mayhem and in the process crack the skull of Tommy Fortune in half. Then stand on his windpipe until he died. Vincent saw the play, the thought of it mainlining adrenaline to his heart.

Outside the door of the second shed he paused with his hand on the handle. Counted: one, two, three – and burst in. The sight stopped him. He saw blood. Saw the shape of the Rottweiler beneath a tank. Saw the wounded Great Dane. Saw the body of David Welsh in a tank. Took a step in, said, "Holy Jesus!" – letting his arms drop. And sensed a movement behind him.

He crouched, pivoted, raised the tyre iron, his balance wrong, the light of the doorway blinding. Heard Tommy Fortune yell, "I'm gonna fork yous." Saw a dark shape lunge at him with a screwdriver.

65

Mullet glanced at his watch: 10 a.m. Vincent should be at Sea Farm. The guy would stay for lunch, maybe leave around three. Be back in town by five-thirtyish.

"See you at home," he said to Rae-Anne, wondering the moment he'd said it what she would read into his choice of words.

She reached out and stroked his face. Which was a kind of answer.

Maybe he was trying too hard.

Mullet drove slowly so the removal van could keep up. His mind was hammering at Vincent. There was no ways he was going to wait until five-thirty to know Vincent had performed. Stopped at a traffic light, he keyed through his cellphone's menu to Vincent's number and connected. The call went straight to voicemail.

"Heck, Vince," shouted Mullet, burning rubber when he realised the light was green, the van hooting behind him. "Yeah, yeah." In the rear-view mirror he could see the guys killing themselves that they'd spooked him. Big gap-toothed laughing mouths. Not one of them had front teeth. He waved a hand, yeah, yeah.

He tried Vincent's number again and this time left a message: "Call me, Vince. Call me, pronto."

While the removal guys unloaded and filled up his house with boxes, Mullet called Vincent once more. Same response. He pocketed his phone and got into the business of supervising. Boxes stacked up in the spare room, the washing machine and the dishwasher crowded in the kitchen, more boxes in the hallway, even one in the bathroom.

When the men had gone and he was alone in the house that wasn't his house anymore, he flopped onto the leather couch, the one piece of her furniture he coveted. It looked good in the sitting room. Like it had been there for years. He slid the palm of his hand over the softness of the kudu skin. Maybe it would be alright.

He tried Vincent again, got the same response. The time now almost half after twelve. The heck was the guy's case? He thought about ringing the abalone farm, making up some pretence for the call. Then decided to try Vincent's mother.

"Vlinclent didn't sleep here last night," she told him. "I don't know where he sleeps. He is a ploblem."

"Don't worry," said Mullet, feeling there was every reason to worry.

"He doesn't get over Amber," said Mrs Saldana. "This is his ploblem."

Mullet agreed and said he'd pop by for takeaways during the week. Agitated he leapt to his feet and went onto the front stoep. He needed space to think. If Vincent hadn't slept there last night where had he been? Dossing in the office? Or back in the Kimberley until closing? He should've seen him into Mrs Saldana's flat and got her to keep him in. On a scale of one to five, Vincent was passed out in the office. Mullet rang there, got the answering machine three times: "Mendes & Saldana. Leave a message and we'll get back to you." He tried Sea Farm next. Got an answering machine there too. Heck, didn't anyone talk on their phones anymore! He left a message.

That no one answered at Sea Farm got to him the most. Lunchtime, they had to be near the phone. Cracking beers, that Marina bringing out a seafood salad with mussels, diced abalone, peeled chunks of lobster tail. Vincent with a cheque folded in his shirt pocket. The *Maryjane* hitched to the Isuzu, ready for the ride home. Except he had a cold feeling it wasn't like this at all.

When Rae-Anne came in he said, "We've gotta find Vincent."

She dumped her handbag and a carton of papers on the couch. "This is not the welcome I wanted, Mull," she said, running a hand into her hair, the latte flesh on the inside of her arm vulnerably exposed. "I was thinking more of champagne."

"Heck, Rae, something's happened."

"You mean he's pissing it up somewhere."

"Listen . . ."

"No, hang on, you listen. He's a grown man. If he wants to wash his wounds in alcohol that's his problem. You can't keep running after him." She took Mullet's hand. "He's gotta go through his own process, Mull. I had to. We all have to."

Mullet shook his head. "It's not that."

"What's it then?"

"He was pissed yesterday. I took him home. He didn't sleep there. He was supposed to fetch the money and my boat this morning. I can't get him on the phone. I can't get anyone at Sea Farm. My sense: this isn't about Vincent pissing it up."

Rae-Anne snorted. "Who're you trying to kid?" She headed for the kitchen. "If there's no champagne, I need a beer. Want one?"

He didn't answer, saying, "I've gotta find him."

"Yeah. And leave this," she shouted from the kitchen. "I don't wanna live with these boxes for six months." She came back, holding out a Black Label. Mullet took it.

"Please, Rae." His tone made her glance at him. "We can do the unpacking tomorrow."

She sighed. "Bloody hell, Mullet."

He smiled weakly, then took a long pull at the brew.

"Your instincts had better be firing on this." She held her beer bottle towards him in a toast. "Cheers. To us." They clinked. "Why'd I think it would be any different?"

They drove first to the Long Street office to check Vincent wasn't passed out on the sleeper couch. Rae-Anne shook her head at the mess.

"You need a cleaner, babe. And some freshener to get rid of the loo smell."

"It's always stunk," said Mullet, "drifts up from outside." He shifted through papers on Vincent's desk searching for directions to Sea Farm. Nothing. The guy didn't even keep a diary.

Rae-Anne held out two chipped and unwashed coffee mugs. "You don't drink out of these?"

"They're for clients," said Mullet. "Come on, let's go. This is wasting time."

"You know where you're going?"

"Sort of. The general direction, anyhow. Up the West Coast road."

"Marvellous," said Rae-Anne. "All I wanted today was a joyride."

Mullet thought, don't give me a hard time, but kept his face poker.

In the car, Rae-Anne dropped Annie Lennox in the CD, 'Walking on Broken Glass', and Mullet let it be although on this kind of mission The Doors would have been the better soundtrack. Nasal soul didn't belong to the world of here and now.

The traffic was light and Mullet drove fast until they were round the bay into the Blouberg beachfront strip and moving at a crawl with the sightseers. Great view across the ocean to Table Mountain from glitzy nouveau apartments. Fastfood joints on every corner. Given a windfall, Mullet believed there couldn't be a better place to set up camp. Get out of the railway suburbs, get a lifestyle.

"I fancy it here," he said.

"It's fun," said Rae-Anne, her head turned from him, watching the couples walking their babies and dogs.

"Mull," she said, and he wondered what was coming, "you know how old I am?"

"Thirty-five, thirty-six?" Not sure where this was going.

"Uh huh." She shifted in her seat to face him. "Thirty-five. Don't you think sometimes this is all going too fast?"

"What?"

"Sometimes I can hear the clock ticking so loud."

He concentrated on the traffic, wondering what she was bringing this up for now.

"Know what I mean?"

"Sure, babe," he said. "Sure."

And left it there with Annie singing sweetheart take me to bed, that's where all our prayers are said.

But Rae-Anne didn't leave it. She went philosophical. "You've heard that Chinese saying life is long?"

Mullet shook his head.

"Some days I get frightened about how long it is."

There was nothing he could think of to say to this so he kept quiet. Rae-Anne sighed and straightened in the seat. Out of the corner of his eye, Mullet could see her profile but her eyes were behind shades and he couldn't tell if they were closed or open. For half an hour she seemed to sleep and when the CD ended Mullet left it.

Once was a time when he'd taken comfort in driving this stretch of road with the thick scrub going down to the sea and up to the sky, the sense of space. Then the white dunes had come as a haunting change in the landscape, and he had felt free of the city, free of the acrid smell of sweat and fear, free of himself. He'd imagined he could run on that clean sand forever. But now the dunes held the horror of headless bodies and Mullet reached for the mint chews to flavour the foul taste welling up from his gut.

At the crinkle of the packet, Rae-Anne woke. She stretched. "We should've brought juice."

"Farm stall coming up," said Mullet.

He pulled in, a tourist bus and two cars in the parking area.

"I'll get it," said Rae-Anne. "What you want?"

Mullet told her a Coke and a chocolate, fruit-and-nut. While he waited he searched through the CDs and tapes scattered on the back seat for that old standby, Neil Young's *Harvest*. Also, it wouldn't draw comment from Rae-Anne.

She came back with a bag of goodies. "Helluva thing in there," she said, as Mullet eased onto the road and pushed the speed through five gears to a cruising one-forty. "The stall owner was mugged this morning. Guy laid him out with a pistol-whipping."

"Yeah," said Mullet.

"Didn't empty his till, can you believe it."

"What'd they take then?"

"Some cold drinks."

"That's all?"

"That's what he says." She sipped at her fruit juice. "The guy's a card, wearing a bandage on his forehead like a turban. Says he's claimed on his insurance for a can of Coke and a diet Fanta."

Mullet stopped at a petrol station to ask for directions to Sea Farm. Was told down the road ten clicks, left onto the dirt, left again at the sign. Twenty minutes later they pulled up next to Vincent's car. Mullet cut the engine.

"It's quiet," said Rae-Anne. "People at these sort of places have dogs."

"People at these sort of places come out when strange cars arrive," said Mullet. He took his revolver out of the door pocket. "You wanna hang on here while I take a look in the house?"

"You've gotta be kidding." Rae-Anne dug in her backpack for her Cobra. "Not a cannon but it's firepower."

Mullet opened his door. "Right then."

They went up the steps, Rae-Anne holding the handrail for support. Mullet knocked loudly on the glass of the French doors. And again.

"No one home."

"Looks that way."

"Nice view from here, hey? Probably great fishing."

"Probably," said Mullet, opening the door.

Rae-Anne whistled, said, "That's careless. Even for out here."

They went in calling their presence. Crossed the living room into the passage. Took a look in the bedrooms, went through the kitchen and outside to where the *Maryjane* was hitched to the Isuzu. Mullet thought, at least that's right.

"Pleased to see your boat?" said Rae-Anne.

"Be better pleased to see Vincent." He gave the boat a once-over, to his relief not a ding visible. Stroked the hull as he walked by.

Rae-Anne shaded her eyes to scan the surrounds. "That one bedroom was the pits. Stank worse than your office. Hey," she said, "there's sheds over there" – pointing at a decline through the dunes and at the roofs beyond.

"Right," said Mullet, "I didn't even notice."

They went down the sand track, Mullet leading. From this angle he could see the doors of two sheds were open, only the first one closed. The track was scored with tyre marks, but how recent they were he couldn't tell. At the first door he paused, listening. Tried the handle. The door opened and he let it swing wide revealing neat rows of tanks in a green light.

They moved on to the second door. Rae-Anne touched his arm and pointed at a T-shirt discarded on the dunegrass. Next to it a pair of jeans. He nodded, brought his concentration back to the door. As they approached he motioned to Rae-Anne to wait and went on alone. The Astra held in both hands, he sprang through the doorway, scoping the shed, his arms passing through a smooth arc.

Vincent was slouched against a wall, gazing at the tank of sea horses, a screwdriver handle protruding from his chest. Blood soaked his shirt and jeans. Blood dribble had leaked from his nose and mouth and dried. Blood tracks showed where he'd dragged himself across the floor.

Mullet yelled, "Vince, Vince" – and heard Rae-Anne behind him and heard her gasp. He bent down, shouted, "Get Ted! Get medics!"

At the sight of Mullet, Vincent's mouth twitched. "Tommy Fortune," he whispered, coughing up red gore.

66

"That was a bloodbath," said Ted. "Vincent alright?"

"ICU," said Mullet. "They reckon he'll make it."

Ted stubbed a butt in a shell ashtray and set down his beer on the stoep table.

Mullet got up. "Another frosty?"

Ted said ja, ta.

Rae-Anne held up her whisky glass. "Vincent was bloody lucky. One centimetre lower it would've blown his lungs. Two to the side would've gone through his heart."

"Sort of thing makes you believe in God." Ted lit a cigarette.

From the kitchen Mullet could hear Rae-Anne going over the scene: Vincent, the dogs, the corpse of David Welsh in the tank.

Into the silence at the end of her horror, Ted said, "You moved in yet?"

"In the process," said Rae-Anne, gesturing indoors. "Place is full of boxes."

"Could do with a woman's touch."

"Heck yes," said Mullet coming out with two Black Labels and Rae-Anne's whisky, the ice clinking. He sat down and stared into the dark of the backyard, could just make out the *Maryjane*. "When'll the tech guys have prints?"

"Tomorrow." Ted swigged at the beer. "You don't have an inkling who dunnit?"

Mullet shook his head.

Ted shrugged. "Run them by me again, the links."

Mullet did: the heist surveillance, the Woo connection between Sea Farm and Helderrand.

Ted took his cigarette down to the filter and stubbed it. He drummed his fingers on what had been a box of thirty. "Where d'you think the woman is? This Marina?"

"The question," said Mullet. He shifted the subject. "You found Roger Oxford's Pajero yet?"

Ted snapped his fingers. "Hey, forgot to tell you."

Mullet thought, you weren't going to, bro.

"It was in the airport parking lot. Oxford's prints and some others. No matches with Helderrand."

"And the white Golf?"

"Returned to the hire company yesterday morning. No description. Only one set of prints that match some at Helderrand."

"Brush Cut probably," said Mullet.

"Whoever."

Later, Mullet and Rae-Anne smoked a joint: sitting quietly, gazing into the blackness. They ate what was left of the farm-stall chocolates.

Eventually Rae-Anne said, "Why didn't you tell Ted?"

"About Tommy Fortune?" Mullet smiled to himself. She wouldn't let anything go. "Because I wanna get there first."

"And then?"

"I dunno. All I wanna do is have it play out." He went inside and came back with the telephone directory.

Rae-Anne looked at him incredulously. "You expect to find Tommy Fortune in there?"

"First lesson in detective school."

The list of Fortunes ran to two pages, nine Ts.

Rae-Anne eased herself off the lounger and stood up. "Before you waste your time let me make a call."

She went inside and Mullet searched through the list of Ws for Welsh. That was easier, only two Ms. He chose the one in the City Bowl and dialled from his cell. The number rang until an answering machine clicked in and the whisky voice he remembered asked him to leave a message, which he didn't.

Rae-Anne returned waving a piece of paper at him. "The address of mother Fortune. The best I can do."

"Pretty good," said Mullet.

"Care of a contact at his alma mater prison."

Mullet took the paper. An address in Lavender Hill. It could wait. Likewise Marina Welsh could wait. What he needed now was a shower and bed.

"I'm gonna wash," he said.

Rae-Anne beat him to the door. "You got the strength to soap me?"

67

Sunday 9 a.m. the tenements were quiet, only church people in the streets. Mullet and Rae-Anne stood on Mrs Fortune's doorstep asking her where they could find her son.

"He's with Satan," she said.

Mullet cleared his throat, wondering how to rephrase the question. The woman was dressed for grief: black dress, black blouse, black hat. Her feet were still in slippers. She was holding a Bible against her chest.

"I told him Jesus saves," she said, taking a tissue out of her sleeve. "Turn to the Lord, I told him."

"Right then," said Mullet. "Ah, Mrs Fortune, can we come inside?"

She shook her head, blew her nose. "It is time for church."

"Can we give you a lift there?" asked Rae-Anne.

Mrs Fortune smiled at her. "I must change my shoes first" – and she shut the door on them. While they waited, Rae-Anne said, "Let me."

Mullet shrugged, what were the chances otherwise?

In the car Mrs Fortune asked if they were cops.

"Sort of social workers," said Rae-Anne. "You know, making sure everyone's doing alright."

Mullet kept quiet and Mrs Fortune didn't ask anything more until they reached the church. She got out first and Rae-Anne joined her on the pavement.

"Can you tell me, are you in mourning?"

The two women stood looking at one another.

"For my son," said Mrs Fortune.

"You don't know where he is?"

"He has a cousin, Delmont, here in Lavender Hill" – and she gave Rae-Anne the address. She had the Bible clutched to her chest again and her eyes searched the ground. Her voice was small. "Has he done something bad?"

Rae-Anne put her hand on the woman's arm. "Yes," she said. "Very bad."

Mrs Fortune bowed her head and turned towards the church.

"Not nice," said Mullet as Rae-Anne settled into the passenger seat.

"Not nice at all," said Rae-Anne. "You want to try this one?"

The address was in a tenement three blocks down from the church. Delmont wasn't home nor was anyone else over eleven. A young boy said he hadn't seen his brother since Friday night.

"You know where his friend Tommy lives?" asked Rae-Anne.

The boy clasped the doorknob and shook his head.

Mullet ate mint chews to calm his frustration.

They went searching for Marina Welsh's house next and found it in a classy street high up the City Bowl in Oranjezicht. A cute double-storey Victorian, upstairs balcony, downstairs stoep with wicker furniture, bay windows, green glass in the front door. A slate path leading from the garden gate to the stoep. Pretty place, fresh paint. Nobody home.

Mullet peered through a window. High up against the opposite wall was an alarm scanner. Hadn't been for that he'd have considered breaking in, the door locks a Yale and a standard lever. He shrugged at Rae-Anne. As they turned to leave, a neighbour popped up at the garden wall.

"You Jehovah Witnesses, or looking for Marina?" he asked.

Mullet raised his hands. "No *Watchtowers*."

The neighbour laughed. "She's away. Gone for two weeks she said. Left on Friday."

"That right?" said Mullet. "She didn't say anything?"

"It was unexpected. A sudden business trip, I gather."

"Nothing for it then," said Rae-Anne, "but to go home and unpack boxes."

In the car she said, "When're you thinking of breaking in?"

Mullet nodded. "Just got to get her security code first."

"And you know a guy who . . ."

He half turned to her. "I might."

68

Jim Woo, relaxed in shorts and Hawaiian shirt, walked out of the condo barefoot onto the beach. As good as the postcards. Turquoise sea. Bright white sands. Palm trees. He ambled down to the water's edge and let the warmth of the sea circle about his shins. Nice place. The sort of life to get used to. Would be better still when the paperwork was done. Cash was what he wanted. Cash that could be walked out of one bank and walked into another. No paper trail. The soft soles of his slip-ons leaving no tracks across the street. Nothing for Dragon Fire to follow. Mr Jim Woo and his fortune would disappear, poof. Woo had to smile. He raised his hands above his head, locked his fingers and stretched. Tomorrow. Tomorrow he'd be away, a new man. The thing was, what to do about Marina?

"Jimbo," she called from the house.

He turned and beckoned. "Come and soak your feet." Watched her walk onto the sand and head towards him with all the swing and panache of a model. He liked that, the easy way she walked. Sashayed was the word that came to mind.

"I need breakfast," she said. "Champagne's not enough for a girl like me. I've got eggs and bacon and fried tomatoes on my mind. Fried banana too. There's got to be somewhere in town." She splashed into the shallows. "What do you say, Mr Woo?"

He drew her in with an arm around her waist, sliding his hand into her bikini.

"After breakfast," she said, trying to pull away.

"Here, now, in the water."

She looked up and down the beach. There were people a good way off lying on the sand, and closer two figures came out of a grove of palm trees and turned in their direction.

"And what about them?"

Woo glanced at the walkers. "They see what we're doing they'll turn around. It's what civilised people do." He pushed against her.

Marina laughed. "You're serious."

"Why not? We can do what we want."

"Jim Woo, aren't you ever satisfied?"

Woo thought of a young girl clasping her legs round him in the Grand Hotel. "Sure," he said. "Sometimes." He looked over Marina's head at the people striding towards them. Two women: the one slight and delicate, the other with spiky dark hair that had previously been blonde, didn't even have to blink to recognise her. He pulled his hand out of Marina's costume.

She said, "You've changed your mind?" Then she heard Woo's name being called and turned to see a woman waving, greeting him as if she expected to find him on the beach.

Woo said, "The fuck's this about?"

"You know her?" Marina frowned. "People know you're here?"

"Roger Oxford's wife."

"What's she doing here?"

"Good question," said Woo, moving through the shallows towards the women who had stopped at the waterline.

"I should kill you," said Judith, as Woo leaned forward to brush her cheek with a kiss. "But I don't have a gun, and a bullet would be too easy."

Woo drew back.

"Instead I shall let a man called Ge Fei, I believe you know him, have you cut to ribbons. He says it will be his pleasure."

Woo nodded. "Why are you here, Judith?"

Judith turned towards Marina. "I don't know who you are, but if I were you I would pack my bags and take the first plane to wherever it's going. This man's life is about to become very ugly. This is not something you want to see."

"Judith." Woo grabbed her arm. "Why are you here?"

Judith shook her arm free. "I am here on Roger's business, James. The transactions have been completed, bar a technicality, and we will be leaving tomorrow. Before then I wanted to spit in your face. Unfortunately I can't work up enough saliva." She smiled sarcastically. "But let me not forget my manners. This is Candy Liu, Roger's daughter by his first marriage. Perhaps she will be able to spit in your face."

"Get into the house." Woo stood rigid, fists clenched. "Get into the house."

Judith shook her head. "Look over my shoulder. Do you see the man at the palm trees? That's our taxi driver. He's waiting for us. We told him we'd be twenty minutes."

"Where's the money?" said Woo.

Judith smiled. "Let me put it this way. It's quite safe." She took hold of Candy Liu's arm. "You want to hit him? Kick him? Spit at him?"

Candy Liu said nothing. Her eyes hidden behind shades, tears sliding down her face.

Marina said, "What do you mean it's quite safe?"

Judith eyed her. "The mistake I made, Roger and I made, was we didn't move fast enough. It got my husband, Candy's father, killed. Don't make the same mistake."

"What?" Marina stared at Woo. "What's going on?"

Judith fastened her gaze on Woo. "The technicality I need, James, is your signature. What you need is access to the funds. I'm sure we can come to an arrangement."

Woo snorted. "You scheming bitch. You got old Roger to pull a caper." He made a gun of his right hand, aimed it at her.

"You can talk, James. The sheer nonsense you expected me to believe.

Roger getting street kids to blow him. The smutty photograph. For God's sake!" Judith pushed his hand aside. "Stop being childish."

"The photograph was genuine."

"You expect me to believe that now?"

"Suit yourself."

Judith lowered her sunglasses to glare at him over the rim. "We have business to conclude, James."

Woo met her gaze. "This was your idea wasn't it? Every step of the way. You took Roger along for the ride. The two of you were going to pitch up here and clean me out. Roger's signature would have done the deal. You pushed him, Judith."

"Now, James, I don't think we'll go there. As I said, we miscalculated. We should have moved faster. But I am not responsible for his murder. You are."

"You pushed him to steal when he hadn't got the guts."

Judith shrugged. "He had the guts to visit you when he should have run."

"He was stupid."

"He was a magician, James. And for years he worked his magic for you." She walked off a few paces. "We'll see you for a sundowner to sort out the details."

"He was Brotherhood, Judith," Woo called after her. "The Brotherhood don't let go."

69

Davenport Street was Monday-morning quiet, all the good citizens at their jobs in the city. Including Marina Welsh's nosey neighbour. Mullet had driven a slow trawl through the streets first to get the feel of the suburb, then parked some way off and walked back.

It took him about the same time to get into Marina's house without keys as it would have taken her with them. And to punch in her security code that disarmed the armed response. He smiled with relief. You couldn't have too many contacts in the right places.

Marina Welsh's sitting room was linen and scatter cushions. What

Rae-Anne would call very *Top Billing* home and decor. To every surface an ornament, every ornament exactly what it should be: mostly 1930s figurines of naked women in wafts of gossamer. A serious collection. In the dining room, a six-seater of some dark wood, a silk runner down the middle with two silver candlesticks at either end. He went through to the kitchen: marble surfaces, cherry-wood cupboards. So new it might have been fitted a week ago. The fridge was switched off, the door ajar. Inside not a stain, no desiccated carrots. That he should have a fridge this clean, Mullet thought. Maybe he could get lucky with Rae-Anne there. He opened the kitchen door onto a narrow back garden with pavers leading between bushes of lavender to a wooden table and chairs in a bower. Very chic.

Upstairs two bedrooms clean and neat. Hers with a beaded spread and big pillows on the wrought-iron and brass bed. A dressing table with lights above the mirror. He opened the curtains a chink to see a good view of Lion's Head. She could lie in bed and watch the rock climbers. In the bathroom he ran the hot tap but it stayed cold. A woman who knew to switch the geyser off. Knew where to find the switch.

The back room was her office. A bookcase of legal books, a filing cabinet that was empty except for a few folders of Sea Farm documentation, receipts, invoices, VAT returns, company papers and a clutch of personal bank statements. No signs of legal work. No trace of a practice. On top of the cabinet a photograph: Marina and some guy leaning against the bonnet of a red Z3. Vincent's great drive. Where was Vince now? Strapped up to IV bags. You just didn't know where you were driving. He put back the photograph thinking, Marina was a stunner, easy to understand why Vince had got ideas.

Mullet sat down at her desk, switched on the art deco reading lamp, and went through the drawers. In the first one found a Rolodex, flipped to W. Welsh, Milton and Associates crossed out. But not so badly he couldn't read the phone number. The receptionist told him Welsh, Milton and Associates had been dissolved ten months earlier, it was now Milton and Xaba, could they help him? They just had, he said. He paged to M. The last entry of ten was Mendes & Saldana, street address, telephone numbers for the office and his cell. Beneath that Vincent's cellphone number. He tried W again. The only other entry a restaurant, the

White Horse. Under Helderrand he found a postal address, the name of Jim Woo and a cellphone number. He dialled it but the call went directly to voicemail. He checked the Os but Oxford wasn't listed. Under Sea Farm was the landline number and two cellphones. The initials TF next to the one, and circled. Mullet ran his finger up the alphabet to F. There he found Tommy Fortune's name and address and a repeat of the TF phone number. These he punched into his cellphone directory, thinking, nice girls sometimes kept strange contacts. Why an abalone farmer would have a perlemoen poacher's telephone number wasn't obvious. He thought about taking the Rolodex to study back at the office then decided, no, he got to Tommy Fortune, he got to the answers. He wiped down the surfaces he'd touched and the handles of the drawers. Before he left, Mullet opened the narrow-blade louvre blinds to see what Marina Welsh looked at when she sat at her desk: Devil's Peak, the tower blocks near parliament and on days when there was no brown haze probably the distant mountains. He wondered where she had gone for two weeks? Or if she was lying dead somewhere courtesy of Tommy Fortune.

Half an hour later Mullet found the beachfront building where Tommy Fortune had an apartment. He couldn't believe it. Cruised past again to make sure he'd got it right and then had to drive around searching for parking. A car guard waved him into a space in a side street. The guy wanted ten bucks up front. Breathed one-hundred-per-cent-proof methylated spirits into Mullet's face. Mullet said, forget it pal, and walked off, the car guard stumbling after him. Wasn't a wonder the foreigners were easing the locals out of jobs. He hurried across the four-lane coastal boulevard onto the Sea Point lawns.

The question was, what tactics? Flushing Tommy Fortune this quickly in the game was unexpected. Then again, you had to know what game you were playing.

Mullet walked over to the promenade and leaned against the wall to get a lungful of sea smell, the sort of sea smell you got nowhere else on the Peninsula: kelp and salt and mystery. What he needed was to be out on the *Maryjane*, alone, not heading into a hot situation on a sunny day. He looked down at the black rocks and the tidal pools. Kiddies digging in the sand, two moms under an umbrella. A mist on the sea obscured Robben Island. He turned to the block of flats and singled out the one he reckoned was Tommy Fortune's. The guy was pulling serious bucks to be renting here with sea views. Only perlemoen or drugs would score him that much tom. Mullet pushed off from the wall and walked across the lawns towards the entrance to the flats.

The glass doors were locked but he pushed a number at random and said chemist delivery to the voice that answered and the voice said not for me but buzzed the unlock anyhow. Outside Tommy Fortune's door he dialled the cellphone number that he'd copied from Marina Welsh's book. It rang and rang but wherever it was ringing it wasn't inside the flat. He disconnected, and knocked. No sound of movement. He knocked again, and heard a door open down the passage, an old woman standing there in her Zimmer frame.

"Can I help you?"

Mullet said, "You know if Tommy Fortune's been around lately?" He walked towards her.

"That's his flat."

"Sure, I know. What I meant was is he around or on holiday?"

"Sometimes he's here. Sometimes he's away." She squinted at Mullet. "Are you a cop?"

Mullet laughed and shook his head. "I've got business with him."

"You look like a cop."

"The name's Jeffrey Mendes," said Mullet. "Importer exporter. Maybe you can tell him I called, Mrs . . ." He stuck out his hand but the woman made no effort to shake it.

"Kaplan," she said. "Why don't you phone him?"

"Sometimes phone calls aren't a good idea. You know what I mean?" Mullet made a show of sniffing at the aroma of cooking coming from her flat. "Smells like perlemoen."

"I wish," she said. "Mussels and crabsticks, fresh from the freezer. You want to eat our perlemoen you better fly to Shanghai."

Mullet laughed again. "You got it. You tell Tommy I called, Mrs Kaplan."

She didn't move. "You're packing," she said. "That's a gun under your jacket."

Mullet held open his jacket to reveal the revolver stuck in his belt.

"It's a wild world, Mrs Kaplan".

"Cat Stevens," she said.

70

Tommy hadn't put his key in the lock before Mrs Kaplan was calling him.

"There's cops after you," she said.

Adonis said, "Oo la la, bay-bee" – and gave a swagger of his hips going into the flat. "John Thomas has been a naughty boy."

"Fork you," said Tommy at Adonis's giggling. "Fork you, hey. One's in, all's in." He turned to the woman with the Zimmer frame. "What you say, auntie?"

"Don't call me auntie."

"Yes, ma'am," he said, grinning at the rebuke.

"You better stop grinning," she said, squinting up at him. "About three, four hours ago this big chap came looking for you."

"A uniform?"

"Doesn't have to wear a uniform for me to know he's a cop."

"What sorta guy?"

"Jeans, an orange jacket, running shoes. And this gun stuck in his belt."

"He showed you?"

"Didn't have to, I could see the bulge." She wagged her finger at him. "You're in deep shit, my boy."

Tommy forced a laugh. "Ag, ma'am. What's deep shit?"

"You and your moffie pally."

Tommy gave her a flash of emeralds. "Hey, auntie, did the boer tell you he's a cop?"

"Of course not. He said he did business with you. He called himself Jeffrey Mendes." She brought the Zimmer frame round and clomped back to her door. "You want my advice, my boy, you'd better show a clean pair of heels."

Tommy rushed round to hold her door open.

"Thanks, auntie," he said. "Is auntie enjoying the pearlies? That sorta size is nice 'n juicy."

"Tommy," she said. "Are you taking me seriously?"

"Yes man, auntie."

"Then pay attention. Number one: don't call me auntie. Number two: pack your bags and go away. This man is serious trouble." She shook her head. "Now close my door."

Tommy did and went slowly back to his flat. Mendes. Mendes was the guy Saldana worked for. Mendes wasn't a cop anymore. The cops wouldn't have got to him this quickly. The cops would come in pairs. The cops would wait.

As he closed the door, Adonis said, "You gotta talk to Delmont." Jiggling there like he wanted to pee.

"Hey what?"

"They's chasing you, oo la la. Not only this cop."

"So tune me. Cousin Del's home safe 'n sound."

Adonis flicked his fingers. "Like auntie ma'am says, you's in deep shit."

"I'm shaking. You gonna tell me?"

Adonis shook his head. "First you gotta cut us a line."

Tommy rummaged through the packages on the kitchen counter top. "You know what? You fulla shit."

Adonis giggled. "Don't you love it, darlin!"

"So tell me." Tommy spilt coke onto the marble top and used a flick knife to chop the crystals and shape two lines.

"His boetie says a man and a woman wanted you yesterday. The woman walked funny, like she's got a prostate leg. Sexy, sexy."

"Fork," said Tommy, snorting his share in a single hit. "What you saying, bro, we gotta run from a peg leg."

Adonis ruffled his hair and bent to take his line. "I'm saying, who's this?"

From another packet, Tommy pulled a Bushmills single malt. "In a box, forking class-A, what you say? You want some of this?" He poured good measures into two tumblers and dropped in cubes of ice. "The larneys drink this, they always put in ice." He swirled the cubes to set them clinking. "You wanna know who's this?"

Adonis rubbed at his nose, nodding.

"Forker's called Mendes. Used to be a cop. Got this funny motor-mac haircut, short sides, long back."

"A mullet, they call it." Adonis drained his whiskey in a single swallow. "That's him, Mad Mullet Mendes."

Adonis slid his empty glass across the counter. "So, let's party. Rage or Angels or Galaxy?"

Tommy splashed more whiskey into their glasses, stared at the pretty boy. "You so white you could of played pale male in the old days."

Adonis blew him a kiss.

Tommy smiled and took a sip of the malt. What he needed was a cigar. They should of bought some of those. He put a hand on Adonis's wrist. "Say what. Fork the clubs. Say I phone this chick 'n we go to Sun City for a few days? Blow some bucks?"

Adonis sprang into a jive. "That's a deal. Let's go, let's go." Giving him the fist to fist.

Tommy was about to tap a number into his cellphone when it rang. A number he didn't recognise. No caller ID. The voice said, "Tommy, I'm onto you. The name's Mendes." Tommy pushed disconnect.

Adonis said, "Who's that?"

Tommy said, "I'm gonna fork him."

Adonis said, "Yeah, bay-bee, yeah" – pumping his fist.

"We can sort this. We's strong. It's one alone, bro, one alone. You can't be scared of one alone. One forker against two guns."

"Who's this?"

"Poes Mendes. Saldana's forking bossman." Tommy ran another line of white and washed it back with whiskey.

"You don't want us to run, bay-bee, like we shitting our undies."

"Nobody's gonna run," said Tommy. He poured more whiskey, re-capped the bottle. "We's grabbing a Sun City super-special blackjack-'n-cocktail break. But first." He held up his glass. "First, we gonna screw Mendes one time."

Adonis went into his jive. They clinked glasses. Adonis said, "Why we waiting?"

71

Rae-Anne saw the Beemer parked right outside the gate. Ted had an old-style Beemer like that. Her shoulders sagged. One of the downsides of living with Mullet she hadn't reckoned on was his cop and fishing pals. Ted was fun but not too often. And not at the end of a hard day when she wanted to uncap a beer, unstrap her prosthesis, put her foot up and watch the soapies. If there weren't still boxes in front of the TV.

She turned into the driveway and saw the *Maryjane* and the Isuzu but not Mullet's car. Which was a relief as it meant that the Beemer wasn't Ted's and she'd have some time to herself. Maybe get in a bath before the beer and soaps. She switched off the ignition and dialled Mullet.

"Where're you, babe?" she said at his voice.

He told her going to check out Tommy Fortune's flat one last time.

"Then you're coming home?"

He said, yeah he thought maybe Fortune had done a runner. The cops were tracking him now. Ted had confirmed his prints on the handle of the screwdriver in Vince's chest. Talking of Vincent, had she visited him?

"I thought maybe we should go tonight."

Mullet said, right then, he'd thought to pop in at the hospital but now he wouldn't.

"See you soon," said Rae-Anne.

He told her about half an hour.

Rae-Anne got out of the car and collected her bags from the boot: the laptop with her drug presentation, the backpack she used as a handbag. She jiggled the door keys from her jacket pocket and went round the house to the back stoep. In all the time she'd spent there, sitting on the plastic chairs while Mullet cooked a fish braai, she'd never noticed how bare it was. Slabs of cracked concrete. A heap of tin and wood stacked against the fence. No pot plants. No greenery. Yet it could be so good, she thought, some pavers, gravel paths, beds of flowers, even a veggie garden would make it home and leisure.

She unlocked the door and went in. The stench was the first thing that hit her.

72

Tommy was peeing over the kudu skin couch. "Come'n, how long you gonna take to work down a shit? Go 'n lay a curlie on the bed."

Adonis pulled a face. "I'm a girl goes once a day."

"So come on his pillow. You always pole-dancing." Tommy did a slow spray ending up in a box of jerseys. He shook off. "You knew what this forker did you'd mess shit all over his bed. Wank a loada dhal in his socks 'n jocks." Tommy zipped, picked up a small brass Buddha, lobbed it at the television hard enough to smash the screen. "So when you done a piss we outta here. Point percy, man."

"You wanna watch me?"

Tommy lifted a jersey out of the box and held it up. "Too bad. It's all wet." He dropped it. "Maybe she's got another leg here somewhere? Like a spare." He upended a box of crockery and glasses. "Ag man, cheap stuff that it all breaks. You gonna piss or not?"

Adonis fished in his cargo pants for a joint and fired it. He took two tokes. "I was screwing her, I'd wanna feel the leg."

Tommy held out his hand, waggling his fingers. "You gonna give me some of that?" Before he took a pull, said, "I'd wanna rub her stump."

As he blew out a long plume, they heard a car turn into the driveway. Adonis said, "All aboard for Sun City."

Tommy took a look out the side window. "It's the pussy."

They watched the woman drive her car up to the Isuzu and stop and make a phone call.

Adonis tugged at Tommy's sleeve. "I gotta pee."

"So do it, man." Tommy shrugged him off and went through to the kitchen, Adonis traipsing behind him, clutching his crotch. They watched while the woman hauled her bags from the boot and started for the back door.

Tommy said, "She walks funny like Delmont said."

Adonis said, "I gotta go" – and ducked into a room.

Tommy grinned. "Hey, my bro, we just scored a luck."

73

Mullet pressed Mrs Kaplan's buzzer and imagined the granny getting out of her chair in front of the TV, clutching the Zimmer frame, clomping across to the intercom phone. Gave her forty seconds to respond.

On thirty-five her voice said, "What do you want?"

Mullet had to smile at the aggro. "Just to find out if your neighbour's been home."

After a pause she said, "I don't talk to cops."

"That's fine. I'm not one."

"You're being economical with the truth, Mr Mendes," she said.

Mullet laughed. "Cross my heart and hope to die."

"Don't hope too hard."

"So has he?"

"What?"

"Been home, Mrs Kaplan. Like I asked."

Again a silence. Mullet wondered whether she'd hung up.

"I told him to pack his bags and go away."

Mullet almost thumped the intercom board in exasperation. "And why'd you tell him that?"

"Because he's in serious trouble."

"More like deep shit, Mrs Kaplan."

"My words exactly."

"You had the cops here yet?"

"Only you."

Mullet leaned in close to the mouthpiece. "You know who your neighbour is, Mrs Kaplan?"

"I have some idea. I suspect he is a perlemoen smuggler."

"And you believe that's someone worth protecting?"

"I believe what's in the sea is for everybody, not just the big corporations."

"What if I told you he murdered a man on Saturday and almost killed another?"

"I'd say he needs a lawyer."

Mullet sighed. "Mrs Kaplan, I don't even know why I'm talking to you."

"Mr Mendes, I only hope that our justice system allows him access to a lawyer."

Mullet wanted to swear, instead he walked away while a young couple buzzed their friends. The guy called after Mullet, "Excuse me, there's a woman still talking to you."

"It's nothing I wanna hear," said Mullet. He went back to his car, wondering how far down the track Ted was in tracing Tommy and whether he should help him out. Decided, nah, at this point it would only lead to awkward questions.

74

Tommy hit the woman smack hard in the face and she collapsed. The pain of the contact shot through his arm.

"Bitch." He shook his hand, examining his fingers. "You got a donkey jaw." To Adonis he shouted, "Where you, bro? Come 'n help me, man."

"Taking a pee," Adonis called back.

Tommy grabbed the woman under her shoulders and dragged her into the bedroom. There was Adonis squatting on a fluffy rug, a yellow stream squirting behind him. Tommy dropped the woman, amazed. "You pissing like a girl now. You had it cut off or something?"

Adonis stuck his tongue out. "We all got our habits." He stood and pulled up his pants, zipped his fly.

"How d'you do that anyways? Clench it in your bum?"

The woman groaned and tried to sit up but Tommy kicked her head and she curled into a foetal position. They looked down at her: she wasn't moving, wasn't groaning anymore either.

Adonis said, "Pretty chick for a hotnot."

"What you saying?"

"You still gonna slit her?"

Tommy edged his foot between the woman's thighs. "Why the fork not? Poes is poes."

Adonis said, "I got a scheme."

Tommy glanced at him, the guy's face all leery. "You gonna tell me?"

"First you get the sweetstuff."

Tommy shook his head. "Nah, you, 'n bring the gun."

While Adonis was gone, the woman tried to sit up and Tommy kicked her again in the small of the back wishing he had on some heavy Cats rather than the soft-toed Reeboks Woo thought were so cool. Forking Chink bought Chink fakes and thought no one could tell the difference.

He put in the fake Reebok, two short strikes that made the woman moan. "You just lie there, bitch. Soon it's time for fun."

Adonis returned with the coke and the Beretta.

"Now," said Tommy, "we setting up a siege?"

Adonis posed with the gun raised in his right hand. "This is hot."

They did two lines each and Adonis crushed a couple of Mandrax tabs and sprinkled them into a joint. Tommy sucked the smoke in, thinking what was missing was the single malt and a cigar.

"So what's the scheme?"

Adonis let smoke trickle out the corner of his mouth. "We tie her on the bed 'n let this Mullet man give her the sodomise."

Tommy nodded, smiling. "Don't you love it, darlin."

75

Mullet was heading up Eastern Boulevard at speed behind a minibus taxi, the thump-thump of the taxi's sound system audible despite the traffic when his phone rang. Ted.

Mullet went straight in. "You got to anybody yet?"

"Not a fandango. You?"

"I'm working on it."

"'N you'll let us know."

Mullet laughed. "Like any good citizen." He followed the taxi into Hospital Bend, the guy accelerating down the straight towards the airport highway, the needle dancing at one-forty.

"How's your mate Vincent?"

"Hanging in there."

"But outta ICU?"

"Maybe tomorrow." Mullet stood on his brakes as a red Alfa Spider angled into the gap between him and the taxi, the driver giving him a wave. "Arsehole," he said aloud.

"What?" said Ted.

"Bloody guy in front."

"You got a moment you can spare us?" said Ted.

Mullet thought, ah, what now? Said, "I'm heading home."

Ted cleared his throat. "Naidoo's on your case again, boykie. The guy's pissed off. Mightily. You don't wanna know how browned. Everywhere he looks there's Mullet Mendes. He goes out on the dunes, there's Mullet Mendes. There's a corpse in a wine cellar, Mullet Mendes calls it in. Guy ends up dead in an abalone tub, Mendes is on the scene. Naidoo's jealous as a virgin's daddy."

"So what's he want?"

"For you to join the dots."

"He knows there's dots?"

"He's a smart guy is our Dep Com."

Mullet took the Black River off-ramp to head back to town. "Heck, you guys!"

"You're a pal," said Ted. "And I've got some stuff for you about Judith Oxford."

Mullet scrabbled for a mint chew in the bag on the passenger seat. It was almost empty. "Now you tell me. What's it? You've found her? You've found her body?"

"Hey, Mull, get here we'll tell you."

76

Rae-Anne heard voices. The one saying, "Will you forking look at those cans!" The other going, "Ooo mommy."

She hurt. Her face hurt, her head hurt, her back hurt. She tasted blood. She groaned and opened her eyes: two guys stared down at her, the one waving a machine pistol for Chrissakes, the other with a flick knife in his right hand.

The one with the flick knife stuck out his tongue like he was licking something, said, "I like your boobies, sista."

The one with the gun pouted, made kissing noises.

She recognised the knifeman from the mugshots Vincent had circulated when his wife died in the car crash, except now the guy had front teeth. Green stones in them. The other lowlife she made for a moffie, gun or no gun.

"Afternoon, darlin," said the one she recognised as Tommy Fortune.

Rae-Anne tried to ease up on her elbows, realising then that her T-shirt was slit from waist to neck, her bra sliced through.

"Fuck you," she said, trying to cover her breasts, hugging them.

Tommy Fortune flat-handed her across the cheek and she collapsed again, her lip split and blood strong in her mouth.

"You like hitting women, big boy."

Tommy hit her again. "I wanna see your tits, sista." He leaned forward to slide the knife blade from her chin down her throat into the gap between her breasts. "You don't wanna have your boobies sliced, darlin." Rae-Anne felt a hot sear as the blade opened a cut, and screamed. She kicked up, snagging Mr Beretta in the balls. He disappeared and she heard the gun clatter to the floor before Tommy whacked her straight in the nose with a hard fist. It pitched her flat on her back, pain stabbing across her face.

She felt the knife in her ear and Tommy telling her, "Be calm darlin or you gonna be deaf and disabled."

She heard the guy she'd kicked sucking air and groaning.

Tommy said, "Forking get up, Adonis. Forking get this bitch sorted."

They stripped her, rolled her face down on the bed: her hands tied with scarves behind her back, her legs spread, the good one tied to the headboard.

Adonis said, "Here we go, sista."

Tommy said, "Check that leg" – and Rae-Anne felt his hand stroke down her thigh to the prosthesis.

"Fuck you," she said, but the way her neck was stretched the words were a moan.

77

Halfway back to town Mullet decided to heck with it, who was Naidoo in his life? This guy jerking his strings like he was still in the Service. So the Deputy Commissioner was pissed off. Big bloody deal. He could stay pissed off for another twelve, fifteen hours. Heck, man, you're toying with maybe dropping a tip about Tommy and the Marina woman because they're getting nowhere fast, then they pull a we're-the-dudes number. You let the Dep Com so much as smell you'd done a B&E and he'd be all over the moves instead of shutting it and being grateful for the info. So nah, boykie, he decided, Naidoo could stay pissed.

Mullet took the Woodstock exit and pulled an about-turn at the first intersection to head right back in the direction he'd come. Heck with them. Heck with Judith Oxford. Heck with Ted for throwing out a baited hook. If it was her body they'd found it wasn't going to make him sleep any better or worse. And another night on the slab wasn't going to cause her further grief. Then again, if it was her in person they'd tracked down, well, knowing that now or tomorrow morning wouldn't bring any more joy to his world. Her world neither. So nah, boykie, he decided, Ted could keep his titbits.

At a corner café Mullet bought a bunch of daisies. Not the greatest at the end of the day, the heads drooping over the newspaper wrapping but, hey, nothing a shot of bleach and iced water couldn't straighten. And Rae-Anne would count the thought, not the flowers. You wandered in with a single rose, her eyes went soft.

Mullet turned into his street and saw a Beemer parked outside his front gate. Looked like Ted's car. But no way it could be, unless they'd reckoned all along he wouldn't pitch at the station and maybe they should go pay him a visit. The sort of line of reasoning Naidoo would take.

Mullet groaned, punched at the steering wheel. The lousy bastards!

78

Tommy's hand slid over the stocking, down the leg to the ankle. He lifted it, moved it up and down.

"It's got forking toes!"

Adonis giggled. "For footsie-footsie."

"Painted toenails. You wanna do a pedicum on the lady?" Tommy kept pumping the leg. "Forking light, you'd think it'd break the first step you took." He let the leg drop, noticing the release button on the inside of the calf. "And this?" He pressed it and the leg popped off.

Adonis got the full-on giggles, the white pipe working at the funniness. "I'm gonna piss myself."

Tommy stood in wonder. "Would you forking look at that!" He pressed the leg back up against her stump, heard the click of the pin and ratchet locking. "Forking A1 smart." He went through the routine again. Pop, snap. Pop, snap. "No straps, no buckles. Simple like a pimple. Modern science." He glanced at Adonis, crouched on the rug, pissing backwards again. Shook his head. "Fork, china!"

"I didn't finish the first time." Adonis stood up, shaking off.

"You still gotta flick out the dribbles."

Adonis pulled a face.

"You wanna see how this thing works?" said Tommy, pumping the leg.

Adonis rested an arm on Tommy's shoulder. "Show me."

Tommy shrugged him off, clicked the release button. "What I scheme is we roll down this stocking 'n the whole thing comes off. We could see the stump."

Adonis pouted. "So. You gonna have him do it on or off?"

"Who?"

"The guy. You know. The guy's gonna poke her."

Tommy looked down, running his eye from the woman's arse to her feet. He grinned. "We gonna take it off, paint the nails a new colour."

Rae-Anne groaned, her words inaudible.

"Whatya saying?" Tommy leaned forward, caressed strands of hair from her ear. He brought his lips close. "You got lovely legs, darlin. Specially the one with the stocking. But we wanna stroke your stump."

79

Mullet stopped behind Rae-Anne's Fiat Uno and let Meat Loaf's wispy choirs bring 'Lost Boys and Golden Girls' to a wooo wooo end. He'd got a look at the BM driving in and it wasn't Ted's. No way Ted would drive around with a smashed headlight. The car got a scratch Ted had a complete spray job. As he reached over to get the flowers, Mullet found a mint chew on the passenger seat that hadn't been there more than a few days, since Saturday probably. He dropped it on his tongue, the sweet gritty but he didn't spit it out. He gave the flowers a shake, brushing petals off his jeans.

So this was how it was going to be. You came home to someone waiting for you. It was an alright arrangement. He smiled. She just mustn't think she was getting flowers every night. Mullet got out and slammed the door closed. He looked towards the kitchen half expecting Rae-Anne to appear, a frosty in her hand. What he could do with right now.

The kitchen door was unlocked. Mullet frowned. Maybe the locks weren't the sharpest in the world but you kept them locked you had a fighting chance of keeping the baddies huffing and puffing.

"Hey, babe," he called out opening the door and stepping into the kitchen, "you forgotten what keys are for?"

Other side of the room was a guy pointing a Beretta machine pistol at him. The kitchen table between them.

The guy said, "My bro, the best thing is you hold the flowers with both hands."

Mullet did so, staring at the guy, especially the guy's trigger finger. The gun on automatic: three-fire bursts per pull. He shifted his gaze to the guy's face. "You're Tommy Fortune."

Tommy grinned. "Howzit Mullet." He gestured at the flowers. "You wanna give those to the lady? Step this way, bro."

"That your shit on my table?"

Tommy smirked. "Let's go."

Mullet didn't move. Tommy waved the gun at him. Mullet said, "You wanna stay alive, Tommy. Now's the time you should leave."

Tommy held up the gun in his right hand, tapped his head with the index finger of his left. "You got a screw loose, man? You know about this gun? Come. Come. Let's give the flowers to your lovely lady."

Mullet saw another guy appear behind Tommy's shoulder. The guy smearing on lipstick he recognised as Rae-Anne's.

"You've touched her, you're dead chickens," said Mullet.

Tommy got riled. "Hey, hey, hey. What you talking about, bro? You gonna come in here and give me and Adonis a little entertainment. We kept your lady all special for you. Just don't kiss her too hard. Her nose hurts."

Mullet shouted, "You OK, Rae? You OK?" He caught her moan. "You're dead. Botha yous."

"Bro." Tommy dragged out the 'oooo', raising the tone. "Get real, broooo."

"She can't talk," said Adonis. "On account of how she's lying." He giggled, holding up the prosthesis. "But she says she wants her man to give her one inna bum. Special like coloured chicks like it."

Mullet kept his hands loosely about the bouquet of flowers. The guy Adonis tossed the lipstick over his shoulder, from his back pocket took out a flick knife.

Said, "She wants you to come 'n kiss the little cut on her boobie. Make it better."

Mullet felt the room draw closer. The air go thinner. He could see white crusts on the flanges of Adonis's nose. He caught the glisten of saliva over the emeralds in Tommy's teeth. He kept his breathing easy. His gun was in his belt, on his left hip, hidden by the fall of his jacket. He watched Tommy edge round the kitchen table, getting behind him.

"Let's go, bro." The snout of the Beretta jabbed into his back. "Let's not keep the lady waiting, hey!"

Mullet walked into the bedroom, Tommy and Adonis coming in close behind him. He saw Rae-Anne naked on the bed, trying to drag herself into a crouching position, her hands tied behind her back, her stump leg drawn up beneath her. She turned to look at him: her nose mixed with blood and snot, her lip split, tears starting.

Mullet swung, lashing backwards at Tommy, grabbing the Beretta, the two of them wrenching at it. Somewhere in his head, Rae-Anne screamed. From the corner of his eye Adonis came at him with the knife.

Mullet ducked out of the light into the dark.

Out of the light in a village clearing into the dark of a hut.

He howled as he had howled.

Grabbed the hands holding the Beretta as he had grabbed the hands holding the Kalashnikov.

Screamed above the automatic fire while the man danced with the bullets, as Adonis danced with the bullets going off tuk-tuk-tuk in three-fire bursts until the clip was empty and the dead man lay on the dung floor of the hut, and Adonis lay in the bedroom doorway.

"What you do that for?" said Tommy in the after quiet.

Mullet remembered the AK in his hands, going outside the hut to puke. He pulled his Astra. Put a load through Tommy Fortune's skull.

80

After, Mullet sat with Ted and André on the back stoep staring into the dark.

Ted said, "You gonna sleep here tonight?"

"I wouldn't," said André, draining his Coke.

Mullet emptied the last of the whisky bottle into his and Ted's glasses. He shook his head. "The bloody day she moves in. The bloody day."

"One thing I never realised," said Ted, lifting a cigarette from the box on the table, tapping it against his knee, "was what a thirty-eight can do up close." He fitted the cigarette into his lips and leaned towards the lighter André held out. "The guy's head exploded like a burst melon." He inhaled and blew out a plume. "You seen that before?"

"Wasn't a thirty-eight," Mullet said.

"No!" Ted exhaled.

"A thirty-eight would have done it." André dug a menthol from the packet in his shirt pocket. "It has that effect."

"It's calibrated for something else?" said Ted.

".357 Magnum."

Ted flicked ash into the perlemoen-shell ashtray. "That's handy."

"I need another joint," said Mullet.

Ted said, "Don't mind us."

Mullet fetched a bankie from the kitchen and rolled a spliff.

"She's never gonna want to come here again," he said. "That's over. We're gonna have to move all her stuff back to the flat." André handed him the lighter. Mullet inhaled deeply and held the smoke. He took another hit then offered it around. Ted shook his head. André held up his cigarette.

Mullet said, "I had this weird thing happen. I could smell fire. Like grass on fire. Burning thatch. Like I wasn't here at all. It was weird. I was in this village. There was this guy with an AK. Him and me fighting. Me trying to get the gun from him."

"Border shit," said Ted.

"Ja," said André, "what they call post-something or other."

"Post-traumatic stress."

André nodded. "That's it."

Mullet took another deep lungful. "I was back there. Fully. Something that happened, I dunno, twenty-one, twenty-two years ago. I was back there."

They sat without speaking, smoking, drinking the last of the whisky. Ted drained his glass first and stood up. "You wanna sleep at my place?"

Mullet crushed the roach in the shell. "Nah, I'm gonna go to the clinic. Sleep in a chair beside Rae-Anne."

André let out a whistle. "She was lucky. One fucking lucky lady."

Mullet squinted at him through the smoke but said nothing.

"I mean, shit what could've happened."

Ted said, "André."

André said, "What?"

"Let it go, hey."

André shrugged. "You know what I mean."

Ted put his hand on Mullet's shoulder. "Go 'n lock up."

Mullet wandered through the house, checked the front door. Closed a window in the sitting room. Went into the bedroom to get a change of clothes. Blood and brains still everywhere for the tech guys in the morning. Rae-Anne wasn't the only one didn't want to live here anymore. You just got your life together, then it all went to hell and cherries.

He locked the kitchen door and joined Ted and André waiting at his car.

Ted said, "You gonna be OK?"

"Sure." Mullet beeped off the car's alarm.

"Here." Ted offered him a pistol. "We've got yours, you take mine."

Mullet stuck it in his belt.

"Oh yeah, a small thing," said Ted. "You ever heard of a guy called Arno Loots? Apparently he worked for Woo."

Mullet thought about it and shook his head. "Don't know the name."

"Seems he was maybe Woo's muscle."

"You making him for the Oxford murder?"

"Murders." Ted held up two fingers. "Mrs got done in a Cayman hotel. Found your lady with her throat slit on Sunday morning. That's what I was gonna tell you. Judith Oxford is dead."

Rae-Anne was asleep, her nose bandaged, her hair tied back. Mullet pulled a chair closer to the bed and sat down. He sipped at the sugared tea he'd got from the nurses, watched her, watched her measured breathing and wondered if this was the end of them as an item. It'd happened with him before. He'd seen it with others. You got bitten. The fangs sank into your flesh and shot their poison. Nothing you could do about it after that.

You could pray to any god you wanted, that poison was going to turn things bad. Mullet sighed and finished the tea in a single swallow.

He leaned back, getting the sounds of the hospital: low voices, air-conditioning, the flush of a toilet. Closed his eyes, and heard Rae-Anne say, "Mull, what're you doing here?"

He couldn't figure if he was asleep or awake, even when he opened his eyes.

She was reaching for the glass of water on the side table.

He smiled.

"I can't smile," she said, "it hurts" – her lips spreading in a smile anyhow.

"You managing?" he said.

"Spaced out. Not feeling a thing if I don't smile."

He reached for her hand and felt the pressure of her fingers around his.

"I've been beaten worse," she said.

He didn't respond and they went quiet, Mullet convinced she'd gone under again.

"Know what?" she said eventually.

"What?"

"You couldn't have done a better thing."

81

Mullet sat at his desk, nursing a coffee. He wondered if he shouldn't maybe clean the office. Like in preparation for Vincent's return one day.

"I'll be back," Vincent had told him that morning. Two days out of ICU and dragging his IV kit around the room in search of someone to talk to.

Some terminator, Mullet had thought, leaving him to drool over pics of Tommy Fortune minus his brain.

The thing about cleaning an office was that probably it was better to go fishing. Phone Rae-Anne, maybe try and get her to park off on the back of the ocean. You didn't get better healing than sun and sea.

Mullet swept his arm across the desktop, gathering unopened letters, notepads, flyers, newspapers, and herded the clutter towards an open drawer. He paused. Lying in the drawer was his old cellphone, the one Ted had been ringing. He switched it on. Four voicemails from Ted, one from a buyer but he'd already sorted the order. Also an SMS from Judith Oxford. Or at least from Judith Oxford's phone. From the previous Saturday evening, almost five days back. The day before she was found dead. Mullet opened it. The message was a website: www.jimwoo.com.

The heck was that supposed to mean? Time was coming, he realised, he would have to get connectivity. Easier than trotting up Long Street to the internet café underneath the Traveller's Inn. On the other hand, useful to have a kid guide him through the moves.

He paid for half an hour. A black kid with short-knot dreads sat him down, tapped at the keyboard and clicked him through to the site.

"Basic site," said the kid. "Not much happening here." The screen was black: two icons, the one said Headhunters, the other Oath Ten. "Cool," said the kid. "Just click on the icons, see where you go." He slid the mouse under Mullet's right hand. "You want some help, shout."

Mullet clicked on Headhunters. A video clip opened without sound: city street scene at night, the image unsteady but Mullet reckoned it could be Long Street. No one about, no traffic, the strip being filmed through the windscreen. The vehicle stopped, the focus tightened on a bunch of street kids asleep in a doorway, then cut to the interior of the vehicle, probably a ten-seater minibus. Three men dressed in black, pulling down balaclavas. A match flared and lit the fuse of a cracker, the camera swung in a blur of lights back to the doorway where the kids were sleeping. A flash. The cracker exploding among them. The kids woke, two jumped up and started running. The second kid fell, lay writhing on the ground. Another blur as the camera picked up on the men, the nearest crouched on one knee aiming a crossbow. He shot. The kid was hobbling away, bent over, staggering into parked cars. A shop window behind the kid shattered. The scene changed to the stoep at Helderrand, a group of well-dressed men and women standing around in the sun drinking champagne. The men waving at the camera.

The clip ended and linked back to the home page.

Mullet said "Shooo" – wiped a hand over his jowls. His palm as sweaty as his face. The second kid found in the sand dunes was gut shot. This had to be the kill. As he moved the mouse onto the Oath Ten icon he wondered how Judith Oxford had got hold of the clip.

He left-clicked.

Here was Candy Liu in shorts and a blue halter top walking along a beach, smiling at the camera. Time of day late afternoon.

Here was Judith Oxford also in shorts, a white linen blouse smartly tucked in. Her hair no longer blonde but so dark it might have been black. Eyes hidden by sunglasses.

Same background for both scenes: a beach house with coconut palms. Stepmother and stepdaughter together. No obvious animosity. Mullet said, "Ummm," softly.

Now Judith pushing at the door of the beach house, hesitating, turning, looking straight at the camera with a quizzical expression. Saying something, pushing at the door, the door swinging open, the camera trying to look over Judith's shoulder. Judith mouthing what could be, "Candy, slowly!" Judith standing in the middle of the sitting room, the camera panning around the room taking in the cane furniture, pictures of yachts, wall hangings of bright patterns. Moving to the open-plan kitchen: remains of a meal, dirty plates, empty wine bottle, smudged wine glasses. Now going upstairs, Judith occasionally looking back at the camera, unsure, worried.

The camera now inside a room focused on the door. The door opens slowly, in comes Judith. Her face goes rigid with shock. Her mouth open but Mullet believed she wouldn't be screaming. Her hand coming up to cover her face. The camera panning away from Judith's right to a woman lying on the bed, her throat slit, going in over the blood for a tight framing of the woman's face. Mullet recognised the woman he'd met in his office: Marina Welsh. Whoever had cut her throat knew what they were doing.

The camera back on Judith, Judith stunned, turned to her left. Candy Liu moving the camera in the same direction: there was a naked guy tied to a heavy wooden chair, his arms strapped to the arms of the chair, his ankles tied to the chair legs. He'd been slashed. Slashed until there was no skin left, no muscle intact and his guts spilled out. The camera held a long steady take on the torso, then moved slowly up to the face. Gash marks on each cheek but otherwise untouched. A Chinese guy with his eyes wide open. His mouth too. Had to be Jim Woo.

The clip went black, linked back to the home page. Mullet glanced at his watch, he hadn't been there ten minutes. He thought, it was her. Whatever was going on here, it was her. Ted hadn't mentioned anything about another woman called Candy Liu. She'd sent this to him, not Judith Oxford. She'd found the headhunting clip. He clicked the Oath Ten icon again. He'd have to find out what it meant. The second time you looked, the smile on Candy Liu's face as she walked on the beach was something else: knowing, cunning even. She knew. She bloody knew. The camera work so deliberate, so staged. Jesus, Mullet thought. She'd done it. Done Judith, too.

When the clip ended he called over the kid who'd helped him.

"I close this down, I'm not gonna lose it?" Mullet asked.

The kid shook his head. Took hold of the mouse and closed it down there and then. Mullet stiffened. Another click the kid had it back up again.

"Anyone can get to it?" said Mullet.

"Anyone," said the kid, "as long as they got the address."

Mullet stepped out into the buzz of Long Street. He paused considering his options. Whatever Judith Oxford had been up to she was outta her league. Swimming with the sharks. As for the little Candy Liu, well . . . He shook his head. Nothing he could do about any of it. Naidoo was going to be the heck pissed when he phoned in the website to Ted.

Behind him the kid standing in the door of the internet café said, "Nice day. Better to be surfing waves than surfing the net."

"Or fishing," said Mullet. Except there was cloud forming on the mountain, meant the wind was getting up over False Bay. Which put fishing out of the question. Which left the office clean-up. Mullet shrugged, nah there had to be something else. Maybe phone Rae-Anne, see if he could coax her out of the flat. Persuade her to a lunch in the Gardens. His watch said twelve.

The noon gun fired on Signal Hill and Mullet jumped.

The kid said, "Goes off every day. Always comes as a surprise."

Mullet grunted. "That's the heck of it."

Sam Cole is the pseudonym for writers Mike Nicol and Joanne Hichens.

A full-time writer, Mike Nicol was born in Cape Town. *Cape Greed* is his fifth novel to be published in the United States. His previous novels, *The Powers That Be*, *This Day and Age*, *Horseman*, and *The Ibis Tapestry*, have been published by Knopf to high acclaim and translated into several languages.

An author of young-adult literature, Joanne Hichens has honor degrees in fine art and psychology and a master's degree in creative writing. She lives in Cape Town, where she is hard at work on the sequel to *Cape Greed*.